NEW WRITING 12

Diran Adebayo is the author of two acclaimed novels: *Some Kind of Black*, which won the Saga Prize, a Betty Trask Award, the Authors' Club's Best First Novel Award and the Writers' Guild's New Writer of the Year Award for 1996, and *My Once Upon a Time*. He has also written stories for radio and television, and is a frequent cultural commentator in the British press. His third novel, *The Ballad of Dizzy and Miss P*, comes out in 2004.

Blake Morrison was born in Yorkshire. He has worked for various newspapers. Blake's non-fiction books include *And When Did You Last See Your Father?* (1993), which won the J. R. Ackerley Prize and the Waterstone's Non-Fiction Book Award, and *As If* (1997). He has also published novels, critical works, poetry and plays. His latest memoir, *Things My Mother Never Told Me*, was published in 2002. He lives in London.

Jane Rogers's novels include *Mr Wroe's Virgins*, *Promised Lands* (Writers' Guild Award, 1996) and *Island*. She has dramatized fiction for radio and TV, and edited the *Good Fiction Guide* for OUP. She teaches on the writing MA course at Sheffield Hallam. Her new novel, *The Voyage Home*, will be published in 2004.

Also available from Picador

New Writing 10

New Writing 11

New Writing 12

edited by **Diran Adebayo**, **Blake Morrison** and **Jane Rogers**

PICADOR
In association with

First published 2003 by Picador
an imprint of Pan Macmillan Ltd
Pan Macmillan, 20 New Wharf Road, London N1 9RR
Basingstoke and Oxford
Associated companies throughout the world
www.panmacmillan.com

Published in association with the British Council and Arts Council England

ISBN 0 330 48598 9

Collection copyright © The British Council 2003
Introduction copyright © Diran Adebayo, Blake Morrison and Jane Rogers 2003

Edited by Diran Adebayo, Blake Morrison and Jane Rogers.
For copyright of contributors see pages 331–2.

Every effort has been made to trace all copyright holders, but if any has been inadvertently overlooked the author and publishers will be pleased to make the necessary arrangements at the first opportunity

The right of the editors and contributors to be identified as the authors of this work has been asserted by them in accordance with the Copyright, Designs and Patents Act 1988.

All rights reserved. No part of this publication may be reproduced, stored in or introduced into a retrieval system, or transmitted, in any form, or by any means (electronic, mechanical, photocopying, recording or otherwise) without the prior written permission of the publisher. Any person who does any unauthorized act in relation to this publication may be liable to criminal prosecution and civil claims for damages.

9 8 7 6 5 4 3 2 1

A CIP catalogue record for this book is available from the British Library.

Typeset by Intype London Ltd
Printed and bound in Great Britain by
Mackays of Chatham plc, Chatham, Kent

This book is sold subject to the condition that it shall not, by way of trade or otherwise, be lent, re-sold, hired out, or otherwise circulated without the publisher's prior consent in any form of binding or cover other than that in which it is published and without a similar condition including this condition being imposed on the subsequent purchaser.

Contents

ix   Introduction

1   **Glenn Patterson** That Which Was *novel extract*

12   **Vicki Feaver** *poems*
     The Gun
     The Borrowed Dog
     Gorilla

18   **Nick Barlay** Talking About Love: Three Monologues *stories*

30   **Julian Gough** The Great Hargeisa Goat Bubble
     novel extract

41   **Patience Agbabi** *poems*
     Seeing Red
     Celtic
     Man and Boy

46   **Ian Sansom** Where Do We Live? *non-fiction*

54   **Diran Adebayo** 'Come back, we'll do some calculus'
     novel extract

62   **Adèle Geras** the square *poem*

65   **Hilda Bernstein** Room 226 *non-fiction*

73   **Gerard Woodward** Milk *story*

90   **David Morley** *poems*
     Ludus Coventriae
     Patrin

95   **Maggie O'Farrell** The Distance Between Us *novel extracts*

102	**Sophie Woolley** Epic Slinky	*story*
109	**Alan Jenkins** *poems* The Wait Tidal Wildlife	
114	**Alex Clark** Only	*non-fiction*
120	**Binyavanga Wainaina** According to Mwangi	*story*
129	**Julia Brosnan** Give Him My Love	*novel extract*
141	**Tim Liardet** *poems* Madame Sasoo Goes Bathing Chickens in Chinatown	
144	**Gideon Haigh** C.L.R. James	*non-fiction*
157	**Alice Oswald** *poems* The Stone Skimmer River Psalm Time Poem	
160	**Rajeev Balasubramanyam** A Man of Soul	*story*
168	**Barbara Trapido** Letters	*novel extract*
175	**Jane Stevenson** Hunger	*non-fiction*
185	**Fred D'Aguiar** *poems* 19 Victoria Street, Shrewsbury Jump Rope	
190	**Lesley Glaister** As Far as You Can Go	*novel extract*
200	**Bill Broady** In a Mist	*story*
209	**Tamar Yoseloff** *poems* Weekend Christmas in London	
211	**Wayne Burrows** *poems* The Archway Altarpiece A Game of Pool Underground	

217	**Matthew Davey** Waving at Trains	*story*
223	**Amanda Smyth** Look at You	*story*
237	**Helon Habila** Harmattan	*novel extract*
249	**Matthew Sweeney** Hair	*poem*
250	**Emma Brockes** Visiting Time	*story*
256	**Nicolette Hardee** Wordperfect	*story*
264	**Sasha Dugdale** *poems* The Film Director Explains His Concept Faking It	
267	**Jill Dawson** Flat Earth	*story*
277	**Royston Swarbrooke** The Last Dodo	*novel extract*
284	**Patrick Neate** Good TV	*story*
295	**Sarah Maguire** The Foot Tunnel	*poem*
296	**Maria McCann** Minimal	*story*
311	**Sukhdev Sandhu** 'One-ah, Two-ah'	*non-fiction*
323	Biographical Notes	
331	Copyright information	

Introduction

What makes us fall in love with someone? It might be the way that he or she smiles, or speaks, or walks, or eats, or holds a glass, or sees the world. Whatever it is, we'll find it hard to put into words. And it won't be something we go looking for, but something that catches us by surprise – unexpected, inimitable, unique.

As with love, so with literature. When we began to edit this year's *New Writing* anthology, we didn't know what it was we were after. But as we discovered it – as each of us came across pieces which made us say YES! – so an understanding of what we all liked became possible. In particular, we found ourselves responding to voices: imagined voices, authentic (seemingly tape-recorded) voices, voices which come at us from unfamilar places, voices which shock and move. If there is any common thread to this volume, beyond that of exciting, good, new writing, it is to do with the skilful use and exploration of voice. From the interior monologues musings in Nick Barlay's virtuoso modern love triptych, to the crazed, milk-obsessed world of Gerard Woodward's narrator, to the brittle and frighteningly empty voices of Sophie Woolley's 'Slinky', and to Binyavanga Wainaina's glorious spoof on authentic voices in Kenyan 'litterachuwa', here are tales which aren't just told but are told in a powerfully original way.

When we emailed each other with our enthusiasms, we usually abbreviated the name of this anthology to *NW12*, which sounds like a London postcode. And traditionally the *New Writing* anthologies have showcased poetry, fiction and essays by British writers, many of them based in London or its surrounds. But this time we wanted to spread the net wider, not out of some vague notion of inclusiveness, but because we knew much of the best writing in English today comes from outside the UK. So we travel, in *NW12*, from Belfast to South America, from Hoxton to Nigeria, and from Ilkley to – in Julian Gough's wickedly twisted skit on market economics – Somalia.

We also wanted to feature new work by older as well as younger writers, believing that – contrary to the mores of much contemporary publishing – many authors improve with age and experience. The current prejudice against older writers is so insidious that we're fearful of putting a name to our less youthful contributors; suffice it to say that one is an octogenarian and a number of others are the wrong side of fifty. Their work was selected for its energy, insight and skill, and for the excitement it generated in us – in the same way as the work by younger writers excited us. This year the UK has seen the promotion of twenty novelists under forty, in Granta's *Best of Young British Novelists* anthology. We're happy to have had a broader brief: to highlight new writing in English by writers of all ages and nationalities.

It was no great surprise to discover, when we arrived at our final selection, that half the best pieces were written by women. Since gender in no way influenced selection, it's almost embarrassing to mention this. But in a literary world where shortlists for literary prizes regularly feature twice as many men as women, and where poetry anthologies including half a dozen women out of fifty contributors aren't yet a distant memory, this selection is glowing evidence of the equal talents of today's female and male writers.

There are a number of pieces of non-fiction in the anthology. But with the exception of Gideon Haigh's reappraisal of C. L. R. James and Jane Stevenson's 'Hunger', these aren't what one would think of as 'essays' – and even those two are so passionately argued that they resist the label. Witty, incisive autobiographical writing is now part of the cultural landscape, as is shown here by Alex Clark's meditation on being an only child, or Sukhdev Sandhu's revisiting of 1970s England from a provincial British Asian perspective. Other pieces occupy the dangerous territory between fiction and non-fiction – the vengeful anguish of Emma Brockes's bereaved father is frighteningly authentic.

We're also pleased there's a lot of humour in this collection. The graver the subject matter, the livelier the jokes. Glenn Patterson's only-too-real Belfast; Julia Brosnan's grief-stricken account of a brother's death; Royston Swarbrooke's sepulchral south London; the poems of Vicki Feaver, Tim Liardet and Sasha Dugdale: all are proof that solemn subject matter need not preclude (indeed often demands) lightness and irony.

Several of the voices in this anthology are new. But the concerns are perennial. Love, loss, sex, hunger, laughter, justice, a sense of place: the seven great themes – and the Seven Ages – are all here. We hope you enjoy reading it as much as we've enjoyed putting it together.

Diran Adebayo
Blake Morrison
Jane Rogers

Glenn Patterson

That Which Was

[novel extract]

The *East Belfast Community News* (verified free delivery to 31,094 households) is, by definition, a paper that recognizes its own limits. This is not to say that the paper wants for hard news. Alongside the pictures of councillors squeezed into chicken suits for charity, of local comedians holding basketballs above the reach of leaping schoolchildren; alongside the ads for carpet clear-outs, for genuine reductions in genuine pine and genuine leather, and stories of disrepair and disputed access, which – beyond 31,094 households – most people would consider free too high a price to pay to read about, there are, week in and week out, reports of the sort of violence familiar to anyone who has lived in what once could fairly have been called the industrial inner city and of the sort peculiar to a place where for three decades everything from an ideological difference, through an upsurge in car theft to plain looking at someone funny, has been regarded as a cause for paramilitary intervention.

Not even the summer months are slow for the *East Belfast Community News*. Summertime is marching time, the time of bonfires planned and improvised and of nightly confrontations along (a popular summer term) the sectarian interfaces. It is no news then, though it takes up column after column, that there does not exist a single East Belfast community.

For all that, the paper is not without its own silly-season moments. Among the sillier in the midsummer of 2000 was the feature on the Presbyterian minister who had once been a junior manager with a leading Northern Irish bank, though he had left banking in the earlier Nineties and at the time of the feature had been minister to his church, a mile and a half east of the city centre, for close on eighteen months.

Under the predictable heading 'From Savings Accounts to Saving Souls', the Reverend Ken Avery (34) jooks out from behind a stack of collection plates, smiling the smile of those coaxed into such poses by community newspapers the world over – uncertain, but keen to oblige – wearing his clerical collar attached to a light-coloured short-sleeved shirt. It's a light-coloured, short-sleeved sort of piece all round. The minister admits he has yet to get used to being the Reverend as opposed to plain Ken Avery – to his friends he has always been even plainer *Avery* – and later confides (eyes, says the paper, twinkling) that he has never been a great one for quoting chunks of the Bible by heart, beyond the obvious, of course – Genesis 1, verse 1, John 3:16.

It was this last comment which prompted a call the following Monday to Radio Ulster's lunchtime phone-in programme by an adherent to a variant – he would have claimed purer – form of Presbyterianism.

What kind of a man, the caller wanted to know, so badly he could nearly not get the question out, what kind of a *minister* is it makes jokes about not remembering the Scriptures, the word of God as handed down? Did Christ himself not say in Matthew 13 and 22 . . .

And that was the start of it. For the next hour and a half every second caller wanted to address the subject of the Reverend Ken Avery. The presenter lamented, as he was often moved to do.

Folks, there are wars on out there. There are natural disasters, matters of great po-li-ti-cal moment. Is this really what you want to be talking about?

Still, the next day he phoned the Reverend Ken Avery live on air.

So, what's all this about you not knowing the Bible?

The minister said what he might have been expected to say – that his remarks were being taken out of context.

Never been a great one, the presenter read from the article, for quoting chunks of the Bible, beyond the obvious. That seems pretty clear. Has your congregation not a right to expect a bit more knowledge than the *obvious* from you?

The Reverend Ken Avery had apparently not heard the previous day's programme and might not until that moment have grasped how seriously this was being taken. Knowledge and memory were not the same, he countered. (Those who had seen the photo in the *East Belfast Community News* but had never heard him speak, might have been surprised by the sudden flintiness in his voice.) Just because his wasn't a mind that retained things verbatim didn't mean he didn't know where to go looking in the Scriptures for what he needed.

The talk-show presenter, who was rumoured to have been head of Belfast's drug squad in a former life and who sounded as though he was already searching through the papers on his desk for the next topic, switched from bad cop to not-so-bad cop and asked the minister, before he went, if he didn't have one – I won't believe you if you tell me there isn't *one* – favourite verse off by heart.

Well, not a complete verse, the minister said, a line, from Paul's letter to the Romans, chapter 14 and verse 5: Let every man be fully persuaded in his own mind.

A good Presbyterian one, said the presenter. He had evidently found what he was looking for and was able to be attentive, and conciliatory, in signing off.

The Reverend Ken Avery, realizing maybe that he would be addressing more people in these next few seconds than he would address again in his entire ministerial life, said it was how he tried to approach all major decisions and dilemmas. If you couldn't be sure of your own mind, where were you?

Indeed, indeed, the presenter said. There you have it, folks. And if you want to give us a piece of your minds, on the Reverend Ken Avery or anything else, you can ring us on all the usual numbers.

By the next day the topic had been well and truly exhausted, the day after that the new edition of the *East Belfast Community News* was delivered to its 31,094 households and three days after that the Reverend Ken Avery climbed into his pulpit a mile and a half east of the city centre to deliver his seventieth Sunday morning service.

*

We begin our worship this morning by singing together psalm number 23, The Lord's my shepherd I'll not want, Avery intoned, then switched off his microphone as the organ repeated the line and gave the congregation, rising to their feet, their note to begin.

The congregation's feet this first Sunday in August numbered ninety-five. Michael Simpson arrived and left in a wheelchair, but insisted on standing at every opportunity in between, one hand gripping the hymnal, one hand gripping the pew in front, in defiance of the cowards who had attached a booby trap to the underside of his car a dozen years ago, robbing him of a leg and an RUC colleague of his life.

Forty-eight people in a church built to seat four hundred and fifty-two more couldn't help but look and sound thin. At this stage of the summer, though, you were grateful for what you got, in general the extremely devout, the extremely elderly, and young couples clocking up the worship hours necessary for their September weddings. Seasonal visitors weren't entirely unknown, though since this part of east Belfast had neither the attractions nor the accommodation for out-and-out tourists, these tended to be individuals back from abroad to see their families.

Into this category, Avery decided, his gaze flitting from face to face as he sang, fell the man standing alone right side of the aisle half a dozen rows from the back, eyes turned towards the ceiling as though on the watch for the oil with which the Lord his head would at any moment anoint.

Avery blinked. Forgive me, he said inwardly. The organ hit the last verse fortissimo and he raised his own eyes to the ceiling, letting the words goodness and mercy shape his mouth and his thoughts.

A– the congregation sang then dropped an octave –men.

Avery turned on the microphone. Let us pray, he said, and raised his hands at right angles to his shoulders.

A motorbike passed on the main road, trailing its noise into the distant silence.

The congregation sat, stood again, sang, sat, put money in the collection plate and listened to Avery preach from Paul's first letter to the Corinthians, chapter 13: Though I speak with the tongues of men and of angels and have not charity, I am become as sounding brass.

It was a minute after midday when he spoke the benediction over them. A moment before the sun had burned through the morning haze to shine directly on the stained-glass window and cast a bright purple puddle on the aisle's royal blue carpet. Through this puddle Avery, descending from his pulpit, walked, a nod now to this side now to that, to Michael Simpson, swaying as mildly, as necessarily, as a skyscraper in a hurricane; to Dorothy Moore; to the visitor from out of town, who looked for a second as though he was about to speak (thanks were not unheard of) if Avery's relentless, nodding momentum hadn't already carried him a pace too far – yet another pace while he wondered should he have stopped – and then, prevented by the traffic that was building at his back from turning, out onto the front step.

Across the road a boy in a black baseball cap was pulling the push door of the Co-op mini-market. A girl arranging the display outside the neighbouring florist's called to him to push. The boy went on pulling, said he wasn't effing thick.

The freezers are on the blink, Avery heard someone shout from inside the shop. We're not open.

The boy – he couldn't have been more than eleven or twelve – swore again and aimed a kick first at the door, then for no apparent reason at a parked Ford Orion, setting off the alarm. The boy stood a moment, mesmerized, before fleeing up a side street. The owner of the Orion ran out from the florist's, stems of red gladioli dropping from the sheet of patterned paper unravelling behind him.

He went up that street there, shouted one of Avery's congregation.

He can't have got far, shouted a second, though the Orion owner seemed more interested in the damage to his bodywork than in pursuit.

Three faces now looked out – scared, bashful, indifferent – from behind the Co-op's locked push door.

The girl from the florist's gathered in the gladioli. She placed her feet toe to heel when she bent, balancing as though on a ledge, as though the world beyond her shadow was all traps and pitfalls.

Frances Avery arrived at that point by her husband's side. By her side, covering her ears with the heels of her hands, was the couple's soon-to-be-five-year-old daughter, Ruth. On Frances's inside their second child, gender as yet unknown, was fifteen weeks away from birth, God willing.

What have I missed? Frances asked.

Yahoo, Dorothy Moore said, though not in reply and absently taking Avery's hand. Dorothy Moore was more elderly than devout, the imbalance left her a touch crabbed. I recognize the wee fella. Know his father. Yahoo too.

The car alarm was deactivated. Somewhere leafier a hedge trimmer hummed.

Cautiously Ruth uncovered her ears and watched over her shoulder as Michael Simpson was steered backwards down the wheelchair ramp. Every minute was filled with wonder when you were soon-to-be five.

Avery shook another hand then another, then there were no more hands to shake.

I've the oven and all set, Frances said. Will we see you back at the house?

No, hang on, said Avery, I'll not be a minute.

*

He walked back through the church and was halfway along the L-shaped corridor to his room when he met Pat Broudie.

There's a man wanting to talk to you, Minister, said Pat, in a whisper so low Avery had to ask him to come again. Pat increased the volume the barest degree. A man wanting to talk to you.

Pat's whisper, like his insistence on referring to Avery as Minister, was the legacy of a life of civil service in the rather grander corridors of the parliament buildings at Stormont. Though he had retired years before to the shores of Strangford Lough, he still made the thirty-mile round trip for every service – every meeting of Kirk Session, management committee, quarterly magazine editorial board – in the church he had attended since he was a boy. Avery had been assured that a look of pained disappointment was habitual to him.

I told him, Pat said, the minister didn't normally see people after morning service.

Avery sensed that he was being told this too and while he didn't see people normally there was no rule said he couldn't.

That's all right, he said. Pat shrugged, his duty discharged, his advice (not for the first time, his expression said) spurned.

Round the corner, standing before the door of the office, hands clasped behind his back, looking at the bare wall on the other side of the corridor, was the stranger Avery had noticed during the service. Middle forties, medium height, hair midway between fair and grey. Avery lengthened his stride.

Very sorry to have kept you waiting.

The man turned. There was, Avery thought despondently, effort in the smile.

No worries, he said. Good of you to see me at all.

The accent was more assertively Belfast than Avery had imagined, though there was definitely somewhere else, somewhere Scottish, mixed in. A hand came round from behind his back and he seemed to be about to offer it, but slipped it instead into his trouser pocket.

His movements were deliberate to the point of sluggishness and as Avery held the door for him to pass through he involuntarily breathed in a little deeper, though he detected nothing with certainty.

Avery's room was not large. A B&Q cupboard, a desk, two chairs. In the cupboard hung his suit jacket and the tan boiler suit he wore when helping Ronnie, the caretaker, with odd jobs about the church. On the desk were a phone-fax combo and a leather-bound bible; in its single, deep, locked drawer a laptop and a portable printer. The page-a-day calendar on the mint-painted wall was by Gary Larsen and was three days in arrears.

Please... Avery said, leaving room for a name – Larry, the man said – Larry. He pulled the second chair out from the wall. Take a seat.

Larry did, awkwardly, and remained sitting in silence, his smile growing weaker by the second, so that at the end of half a minute it was hard to imagine he had ever had the strength to muster it. Something about his appearance – how would you put it? He seemed a little crushed, from the inside out. He passed a hand across his forehead and Avery had to frown to banish the thought of oil dripping from the ceiling of the sanctuary.

Was there something you wanted to talk about?

Larry looked up at him, looked down, looked up again and sighed. This time Avery caught the unmistakable smell of night-old alcohol: jammy, tainted. So that's what this was about. Morning-after guilt and self-loathing. Where did it all go wrong, Reverend? In his last – and first – church in Holywood, along the north Down Gold Coast, most of the crises Avery dealt with were more spirituous than spiritual in origin.

We can't offer you the full all-singing all-dancing confession, of course – he chanced a smile that wasn't returned; sometimes one approach worked, sometimes another – but if you're in need of a little heart to heart . . .

Larry's gaze drifted off Avery's face.

Is that there OK? he asked.

Avery looked over his shoulder. The bible was completely obscured by his own back. All he could see was the telephone and fax machine.

This?

He pointed. Larry nodded.

You mean the two things together? Do they work all right?

I mean can anybody hear us.

Avery laughed, nonplussed, picked up the handset.

Not unless we ring them first, he said, and when this got no response he tapped the earpiece against his palm. It's just an ordinary phone.

This was a hangover of a wholly different order he was thinking at the same moment as Larry sighed again and said, I think I've got blood on my hands.

Avery glanced from the hands to the door. He weighed the telephone handset in his palm a second or two longer before replacing it lightly on the cradle. The insides of his mouth felt shrunken.

Last night? he asked.

What?

The blood.

For the briefest of moments the corners of Larry's mouth twitched.

When the Troubles were on, he said.

Ah! Avery was almost relieved. Now he had him. I see.

For the past two years the prisons of Northern Ireland had been emptying of paramilitary prisoners. Any day now the most famous prison of them all, the Maze – Long Kesh – would close its gates for good. For the past two years Avery, like most members of the clergy, had been attending conferences on issues arising from this early-release scheme. Many of the prisoners had found the Lord while inside, some had even become pastors and in a few cases established their own congregations.

It was expected, though, that for the vast majority the enormity of their deeds would only become apparent once they were on the outside again away from their comrades, having to cope on their own.

Avery replayed Larry's words. I *think* I have blood on my hands. Classic reluctance to accept responsibility.

He leaned forward, elbows on his knees, hands loosely joined.

Do you want to tell me about it?

I'm dying to, Larry said and sounded it.

Avery waited, a full minute.

So?

Larry was massaging his forehead.

I don't remember.

Don't remember what happened? Avery started to say, but Larry cut in.

Don't remember what, don't remember where, don't remember when.

It crossed Avery's mind to ask him was he sure about the if, but Larry looked scared. His fingers now held his forehead in a tight grip.

It's OK, Avery said. It's OK.

It's not OK. Larry's voice was rising. It's doing my head in.

There was a moment's silence in the room, broken by a knock without.

Avery?

It was Frances. Avery heard Ruth asking what daddy was doing, when they were having lunch.

It's all right. You go on ahead, he called. He wanted his daughter well away from this. I'll catch you up.

Larry hadn't moved. Avery sat back in his chair, feeling on the desk for the bible. He brought it round on to his lap, opened it where it was bookmarked – 1 Peter, chapters 2–4 – trying to buy himself a few more seconds' thinking time. *Christ the corner stone*, ran the caption and, facing that, *Rules of Conduct*.

I keep getting these flashes, Larry said without warning. Like waking nightmares. People's faces looking at me like they know they're about to die, like I'm the one's going to kill them.

Avery closed the bible.

Only somebody doesn't want me to remember. They've been tampering with my brain.

His fingertips had left white marks on his forehead. Avery watched them fill with colour, which was when he noticed the scarring a fraction below the scalp at Larry's right temple. An inch, two inches long. He peered. No, longer, faded to a faint sheen for another inch, but still unbroken.

Oh, no.

His heart closed in on itself, leaving his chest hollow and chill. The scarring – the *scar* – ran almost the entire length of Larry's hairline.

Larry was looking directly at him

Would you like to say a prayer with me? Avery said, grateful for the opportunity to close his eyes.

Heavenly Father, he began, who sees and knows the least of our thoughts and deeds, we ask today that you might be with your servant, Larry, in this time of great trouble and confusion.

There was the sound of movement in the room, the door opened and closed, Avery prayed on.

And grant us all, O Lord, when we are sure in our minds of the right thing to do the strength and courage to carry it through.

*

Frances asked him at lunch what was on his mind.
　Nothing, he said. Why?
　Because I had to ask you three times before you heard me.

Vicki Feaver

The Gun

Bringing a gun into a house
changes it.

You lay it on the kitchen table,
stretched out like something dead
itself: the grainy polished wood stock
jutting over the edge,
the long metal barrel
casting a grey shadow
on the green-checked cloth.

At first it's just practice:
perforating tins
dangling on orange string
from trees in the garden.
Then a rabbit shot
clean through the head.

Soon the fridge fills with creatures
that have run and flown.
Your hands reek of gun oil
and entrails. You trample fur
and feathers. There's a spring
in your step; your eyes gleam
like when sex was fresh.

Killing brings a house alive.

I join in the cooking:
jointing and slicing, stirring
and tasting – excited
as if the King of Death

had arrived to feast, stalking
out of winter woods,
his black mouth
sprouting golden crocuses

The Borrowed Dog

Her name was Blaze, for a diamond
of white hair on her chest.
But I called her Goya
after the dog in his painting
with its tawny head appearing
over the edge of a sand hill.

That was Blaze: always nose first
at the edge of a territory
on the lookout for anything
breaking into a run. 'Blaze! Blaze!'
I'd shout, stupidly, because she didn't stop
for Blaze, or Goya, but streaked
over the fields like a fox: plunging
into a spate river; disappearing
among reeds in a marsh; returning
when I thought she was lost
to shake herself at my feet,
shower me with muddy drops.

She got to think I was a dog: peeing
on the grass where I peed;
pulling my knickers
out of the laundry basket
and chewing the crotch.

And I got not to mind the stink
of her breath; her tongue licking
my ears and nose and chin;
even to love her yelps

when I came back to the house;
her knocking me to the ground
and gripping my arm in teeth
that could rip to the bone.

Gorilla

He was my first love.
Why else would I cycle, every Saturday,
to the museum in the park?

It wasn't the working model
of a coal mine; or specimen jars
of seasonal wild flowers;

or the families of striped snails
and black and white plaster mice
demonstrating the Laws of Mendel.

I headed straight past the jigsaw-
coated giraffe (its head peering over
the balcony) to a case

stuck away in a gloomy corner;
but not so dark I couldn't see
the glossy pouch of his penis and balls.

He was posed against a backdrop of jungle,
one arm grasping a vine,
standing on two legs like a man.

The boys at the dancing class
(I always got the spotty or fat ones)
gripped me with clammy paws.

His hands were like padded gloves
stitched from smooth black leather.
He could swing me off the floor.

I looked up at his lolling tongue;
at his jaw of ferocious teeth.
I gazed into his yellow eyes:

and he gazed back, as if to say,
if you loved me enough
you could bring me back to life.

Nick Barlay

Talking About Love:
Three Monologues

1. Dear Ella

Does one stand at the exploded window following the lines of jagged shards with a knowing eye, with sixteenth-floor gusts flapping the curtains and driving dust and loose papers towards the back wall; does one stand there scraping clots off the sill, along with ancient pigeon shit, and say: this is where it happened? Or does one crouch over a cracked skull on the pavement, in among the murmuring crowd, and say instead: no, it must have happened down here actually?

Well, the bruises have come up. Submerged, they appear as purple anemones decorating a strange fish, too large in the bath to move meaningfully. The sudsy efflux from an apricot bath bombe clings to the contours of my breasts. The water is long cold. I thought they'd be here by now. I thought they'd have made it long before the water got cold. Someone should have put two and two together, glanced up, seen the broken pane, counted the floors, made the necessary arrangements or exclaimed, simply: look.

And they would have been up in a jiffy, well within their response parameters. But every second after it happened, whether it happened up here or down there, is an infinity too late. They'll still come, of course. I suppose they just got held up in traffic. Because they'll get here. And head after head will poke through the hole to imagine a body spreading its wings in semblance of flight. For a second they'll wonder about the aerodynamics, the defying of gravity, before turning to the facts. *Now then, Miss.* And I would tell them what? Say what? He's dead? My God. No.

I can't believe it. It cannot be true. Yes, yes, I thought I heard something. But then again one hears lots of things. And the bath was running.

Or did I run it later, after finishing my replies? I was deep in thought. Too deep to hear a thing, quite frankly. I get so wrapped up. Don't hear the phone sometimes. Friends say I'm a bit mad. Goes with the territory, I tell them. But all this doesn't help to unravel it, does it, Officer?

Shit. I crumpled the letter. I can see it through the open bathroom door lying under the Himalayan wind chime on the £17.99 per square yard basket-weave matting recommended to me at a party by a psycho-spiritual counsellor. *Stimulates healthy blood-flow from feet to scalp*, she said. *Invigorates your sex life*, she said, *not that you need it. You're so amazingly sorted out.* Friends say I'm a bit mad, actually, I said.

I crumpled the last of the letters. That was silly. Thoughtless. Not very sorted out of me. Not really what you'd call skilful life management. Could end up as evidence. Of sorts. But of what? It's odd the way both the guilty and the innocent have to cover inconvenient tracks, one to hide the truth, the other to prove it. That letter should have remained in its pile, read, thumbed, even blurry as if cried on, but uncrumpled, ready for the publication file complete with my reply. Only I have yet to write it. The other half dozen might as well have been on a loop with just the initials altered for authenticity. Mrs D. K. Ms L. T. Mrs F. F. *Dear Ella, I've got an eating disorder.* I love it when they self-diagnose. Eating disorder? I should be so lucky, I write. So many problems but eating's never been one of them. It's the throwing up . . .

Dear Ella, I just can't seem to shake my cellulite. Well, then, you're a sad loser. *Dear Ella, all my friends died in a horrendous fireball.* Bathe in aromatic oils; treat yourself to a facial. *Dear Ella, I think my husband is abusing our teenage daughter.* Has he tried a loofah?

Of course they'll look around, wonder why the water's cold. Sergeant Plook'll scratch a pimple: *You say you were in the bath when it happened?* When *it* happened, Officer? When what happened? When he masturbated himself to sleep last week? No,

I wasn't in the bath then. I was in the bed right next to him. Asleep, supposedly.

Dear Ella, thank you so much for your advice. I feel so much better now. Bitch. Yes, well, where was I? He often goes to the window, Officer. He was probably trying to save a spider. They hang from the ceiling sometimes. Abseil down to the incense sticks. Right there in front of the window. He'd save them all right. He was like that. He'd do that. He drank his tea like a pint and saved spiders. That's the sort he was. I'm shocked. Devastated. Didn't hear a thing. The bruises, you say? Mysterious, aren't they? No, of course we didn't argue. We don't. Do you know who I am?

Do I know? My toes are like prunes; my nipples like potato roots. Two cupboards full of herbal remedies, balms, cream cleansers, sauna packs and a couple of loofahs. But nothing beats a cold bath, Officer. *Dear Ella, what's the best way to hide a love bite?* Hide it? Ella says, rejoice you moron. He bit me all right, but it was never love, so goes the joke. And now the only tell-tale marks are clots on a sill and oedemal bits on a shard, separated finally from relentless happening, from urgent problems naively posted first class to a *monthly*.

Dear Ella, he burps. Dear Ella, he farts. Dear Ella, he snores. Yes, it's a rich tapestry. Ella says try hypno-regression to discover the horrors that make you unique. At least it'll put all his percolating airs into perspective. Worked for me. Alternatively, a three-month stint in the eating disorders unit. Hell, yes. Bit of bulimic company makes you love him more. Worked for me, Officer. Until, that is, I remembered he came from a pre-clitoral age in which there was no mystery about bruising. You didn't have to make excuses back then.

Would I really say all that? Could I? The water's freezing. But I've become quite attached to my alibi, necessary or not. By the time they get here I'll be cryogenically suspended. *No, ladies and gentlemen, it's not what you think, it's not at all a Siberian behemoth. Here we have an example of* fin de siècle *female, frozen in time, perfectly preserved . . . bung a coin in the slot and it lights up.* Sergeant Plook'll just have to piss on me to save my life. So what's new?

Do I hear them? I can almost see them checking their partings in the mirrored lift. I've left the front door open to save them breaking it down. But I should do something about the letter. Which is worse: to mean to do but not do or not to mean but do, inadvertently, as it were? *Dear Ella, I accidentally poisoned, bludgeoned, scalded him. Dear Ella, the stab wounds in his back were unintentional. Dear Ella, I fired a warning shot into his head* ...

My nerves went, I admit. Briefly. On occasion. Once. Twice, perhaps. Friends say I'm a bit, well, mad. But at least I woke up. I remember my first time. *Dear Ella, what was it like?* The first time I felt revulsion during sex? Wonderful. I knew I'd woken up. *Je suis femme.* I thought. From then on, I could hate him with abandon. That was a happening. Not like my mother spilling cocoa in bed most of her life and never noticing. Just got cold, I suppose, like a bath. Just got cold and the bruises came up.

There: a definite shudder in the lift shaft, I believe. A ripple in the water touches skin that is warmer. You can feel that, Officer, you see, feel it in your bones because it sort of creeps up on you, moment after moment. Not sudden. It wasn't that I could smell the cat's fanny perfume of some mutant whore. God no. Nothing like that. It wasn't that I came to despise his sock–shoe combo. Although some might say he should have been put down on humanitarian grounds for that alone.

But no, seriously. I could tell you stories, Officer. I could write a book. Or a collection: Ella's Top Selection. Sometimes I don't even hear a knock at the door. Or a window shattering. Or a scream or a storm. If such there was.

Footsteps? A shuffle, yes. Almost certainly something. A grunt, a fart: the boys are on the case. Snooping about. Rubber-shoeing. It's one big adventure playground. One whirly merry-go-round of clues. Ah, the spotting of the exploded window, the defining of the defining moment, then the exchanging of looks as they spy *Woman in Bath*. Dead? No, she's bloody waving.

All right, miss? they'd surely ask. Why shouldn't I be? What's the meaning of this . . . this invasion? Hm? Why now, right when I'm taking a soak? How dare— Do you know who—

But things move on, happening even as thinking. Sergeant

Plook searches, absently scratches his crotch, hoists his pantaloons by the belt: *Ah, now then, what's this here crumpled piece of paper doing on the floor beneath the Himalayan wind chime?* It was an accident. That's all. I shouldn't have crumpled it, I know. I mean I wouldn't, not usually. We all make mistakes, even me. But why make excuses? Do you know who I am? Sometimes it's just nice to say shit to the world and take a bath. Crazy aren't I?

But of course we're leading ourselves down the same path, the boys and me. Putting it all together we are, the bits, reconstructing the chronology, the route from A to B and back, from Above to Below but not back. Pondering deeply we are, whether it was not down there, after all, where it happened, but here, right up here, in the bloodless corridor, beneath the wind chime. Conjecture is sublime. Peps you right up. Better than Zesty Zing herbal infusion. Better than Happy Pill. Better than my best advice. Yes, let the imagination take to the air. Don't hold back for a second. Delay the diet; throw your weight. And take a sodding good run at it, says Ella. Worked for me.

Would you like a woman officer? Christ, no. *May I?* says the top of Plook's head, his body already half bent. Already reaching, picking, fingering, uncrumpling. For at last, sure as landing follows flight, there is the painstaking unravelling of the evidence. Plook, reading: *Dear Ella, what would you do if your man . . .?*

God, I know what I'd do. Says Ella.

2. Three Is More

god wha'm I like – I can't believe I just said that – go on say something – stop laughing – no no wait I know what you're gonna say but truth be told me myself I'm not like that – people just think I am – they can say anything they want but they'll never know the proper truth unless I proper – no no listen – cos even if I do proper tell them they can believe what they like cos believing and knowing is different things even though in a way they're – no no listen – they're the same because at the end of the day what's it – no listen – matter what people believe or know?

anyway I know me myself I'm not like that I'm not and I wasn't like that when it started – when he tore his maligament and got himself out of the whatever army or police – I can't remember what he said now – he could have been a traffic warden – probably was – god wha'm I like is that terrible of me I'm not usually like that well whatever he was a man in uniform – not that I saw him in uniform but after he told me he was in the army or the police – I'm sure it was the army – you start imagining you know all those buttons and everything – I'm suggestive – I am that's what my best friend kylie said – she's a receptionist in a fitness centre

so I'm imagining all those buttons and everything and course one button led to another – it was round my friend kirsty – dave her boyfriend was there and me and him had well already you know – they met through me put it like that – but I'm not jealous or anything – I don't mind cos she's my friend and he's more her type well that's how it started with mark cos he was dave's friend and he turned up that night and well once there's something going on in a room – like there was between kirsty and dave – and I'm in that room I get all you know like my nan's dog – and I just have to you know have it – god wha'm I like but it's true – it's true – so when mark turns up I'm thinking I won't be such a gooseberry – not that I mind being one – I mean just watching can be a right laugh – as long as there's something to drink and I like the people

but no I mean mark I'd met before and nothing happened or anything but I knew he fancied me in that top – you know the one I was wearing when I met you – god sorry wha'm I like – why am I saying sorry? you understand – I mean when a top works it works – but thing is mark he was with carly at that time and she was pregnant – not from mark from dave – not that dave he's a pud-puller – I shouldn't say that should I – but it's true – I meant the other one – you know who used to be with lana – lana who you used to fancy I know you did cos she told me you'd had a snog or two in the wellington – that was a mental night and I know you didn't end up with lana – you don't have to end up with someone just cos you snog them – although there's snogs and there's snogs like the first snog we had wasn't a snog snog just a snog and I never thought it was gonna god wha'm I like – anyway who were we – carly? well carly she was you know pregnant about a month and you can't expect a bloke to stay with you while you're baking someone else's – I mean that would be love – wha'm I like but it's true – it is – love's expensive and who's gonna spend love money for a snog? in any case you didn't end up with her lana I mean because it wasn't a snog snog for you either – it better not have been – no no wait I know what you're gonna say but it's ok cos lana's my friend and I don't get jealous – not proper jealous – just don't snog snog her while you're with me – it's not the aids thing I mind cos snogging's a toilet seat – wha'm I like but it's true – snogging's the toilet seat of sex cos you can't get aids off of it – unless you lick the blood off of it – that's what dave said he is so gross I – hate it when men talk like that – it's like me quack quack quacking about my favourite vibrator or something – but anyway he stopped being gross after he met kirsty – I just wish he'd stopped being gross after he met me cos he's toned down so much now I'd share him with anyone – god wha'm I like but it's true

Cos you can fancy someone then stop fancying them and then after a while you refancy them again cos even if your brain's saying catch a bus your body remembers why you fancied them in the first place – or maybe you refancy them cos you see them like you've never seen them before or just wearing a new shirt or something and it's like my nan's dog all over again – only my nan's dog can fancy anyone more or less – for ever and then some – and what my nan's dog fancies you wouldn't wish on your worst and for def you wouldn't refancy them – not that there's a rule against refancying but it leads to situations and the worst situation is when you refancy an ex while you're fancying the one who's one day gonna be your ex – god wha'm I like but it's true – fancying the new ex while refancying the ex ex puts you in a right one – not like putting all your mobiles in a bucket at the end of a night out – cos I mean that's just lucky dip – do you mind me talking about past relationships? me myself I don't usually talk about past relationships but that was before I fancied and refancied at the same time – it's like having a split personality with one bed

so I couldn't help thinking about dave and kirsty and you and lana and kirsty and you and I thought why hedge my bets when I can have it both ways? and if I'm honest who will mind and who will know? unless I proper tell them or you do and if you or me tell anyone it'll be for a laugh cos nobody's a gooseberry and even if – so we can double up and still be friends my new ex and my ex ex and me myself – it's not like we're kids and even if – cos who's to say what love is or was? and truth be told if there was love with any of us the first time round or during the action replay wha'm I like but it's true – if there was love then or in the meantime do you think me myself I'd be here now with the pair of you?

I mean at the end of the day they say two is company but what do they know? cos me myself I swear on my nan's dog three is so much more – god wha'm I like but it's true – no listen – stop laughing – go on say something

3. Real Thing

Control, listen, listen to what I am sayin. I am tryin to . . . It happen . . . It happen like this . . . She get in loose an dangerous with ha chest all slippin an slidin an ha big twisty hair like a Saturday Night Loretta.

Oi Fola, stop fuckin broadcastin. It's a busy circuit.

Control, just listen. Please listen. They warn me before about ha. They warn me she come quick an disappear like a flash into tha night. They say: *Fola Bulubayo, maybe you are SuperFly to all tha chicks but you will end your days in your radio control cab with a knife in tha back an your big mouth still talkin boosh.*

My sister Rosie she said she look in ha cup an that is what she saw. An of course ha number one Cherry she always say what Rosie say an do what she do.

Fola, for fuck's sake get off of the airwave.

But what do they know? They wah sittin pickin over chicken bone an watchin Eddie Murphy video like Queen Tikkitakki an

Princess Pullipulli. Both of them wah drinkin gin an smokin king-size an smellin like tha downtown fruit market. They wah readin tea leaves an signs that don't make no sense an sayin: *No money no honey: Fola Bulubayo: this is the story of your life.*

Then they wah rollin an laughin with their gold mouths bright like headlights. An their laughin soundin like windscreen wipers on high speed. So I say to them: look if I go die some day it will surely be at tha wheel of my cab. But I will have gin drippin from my fozzy chin an boosh comin from my big mouth because I am Fola Freedom Lifetime SuperFly an I will be livin large on tha power of my natural high. They laugh at me more an more an more. An then Cherry she say: *A big mouth lead to tha grave sure as a cab take you to tha railway station. An in future don't talk when Eddie is talkin.*

God but tha rain fall hard this night. Of course Saturday Night Loretta is lookin for Saturday night action. I am drivin AD, which mean as directed. This—

AD? I told you point to point, you silly muff. I got cash jobs stackin up. Fol—

This is OK by me. So Loretta she is directin me this way an that through tha steamin dark. Tha wipers are on with red-blue rain washin over my face. My life is flashin at me from tha pavement an yellin with a thousan voice. People –

People are fightin to get into tha clubs an restaurants an tha panic is settin in. Like everyone must find their place in tha world before tha end of tha night. Which is not easy because of tha parkin restriction.

But Loretta she don't look like she care. She tell me she is not early not late just right on time. She say to me she say it is just good to be out of tha rain an off tha street an that is that. Loretta ha voice sing to me an fill tha whole cab.

But me I tell Loretta I don't mind if she stay a while goin nowhere. Tha day has gone an I am not inspire to skank more fare like Driver SlickDick from Paradise Car across tha High Street.

Loretta she begin to like my attitude very much. My eyes an ha eyes they meet in tha mirror as yellow shadow fall on tha back seat. If ha voice sing then ha black eyes dance. I must say Fola SuperSmooth resist charms from anyone, especially on Saturday night. But Fola Bulubayo he is fallin in love, that is sure, an soon Loretta she has tha exact same feelin back. That is what Rosie should be readin in ha teacup. Outside some dirty place they are fightin like there will be no tomorrow. Already blood mess tha pavement an still they go on an on. Two gangster boys are scrappin an fightin an everyone is climbin over each other to get through tha blood.

But nothin move backward or forward at all. Tha traffic was slow tonight. More slower than ever.

The traffic's slow he says. I'm givin yours to Jimbo. I'm warnin you . . .

Rosie she warn me I know. She an ha number one Cherry wah entertainin two fly-by-night men: Casual Johnson an his number one Polycarp. They wah wearin silk shirt an gold watch an crocodile shoes that require no sock.

Rosie say they are importin tha goods from all over tha world. All of them they wah drinkin whiskey cola an watchin tha latest Eddie Murphy video. When they see me Rosie she say: *Look, Mommaboy Bulubayo is home.*

Casual Johnson he laugh an he say: *No, it is Eddie's idiot love child.* Polycarp he laugh an he say: *Ahar har.* Rosie she also laugh an she say: *Ahee hee.* An Cherry point an she say: *No money no honey.*

Soon they are all foolin an applaudin theirself. An as I am drivin I am still hearin their laughin. Even Loretta's voice is like nothin compare to their laughin. But I see ha in tha mirror, ha big lips sayin somethin I cannot hear but I know she is tellin tha story of ha life. Then Loretta she is pointin with ha long gentle finger at four persons on a street corner. First I think she want to introduce ha friends. It is important to meet the friends of your lover. But tha four persons they are comin straight at tha—

Fola, you been told. You understand?

They are comin straight at tha car wild from angry drinkin. Loretta she roll down tha window an show tha fourface night a toothbrush razor. A beer bottle strike on tha roof. That is when Fola Freedom push tha pedal to tha metal an drive away FormulaOneStyle.

Loretta she say she only do what she do to save me an that she do not normally act this way from windows. Maybe she do not say it in words but from ha honey smile Fola SuperFly can tell. Now it is just me an ha.

Loretta she say to keep drivin nowhere. Sometime we cannot drive because tha lights will not change. She could be late for the last airplane. But she do not mind. Cash jobs are stackin up. But I do not mind. We do not mind just driftin drivin together. Or just stoppin still. Love is like that. An it prove our love for each other not mindin tha very same thing. Rosie she warn me. Control he warn me. They all warn me before. She an ha number one Cherry an Casual Johnson an his number one Polycarp wah eatin special rice behind my back. I break shift one time an find them stuffin their face lookin bigeye at each other like it wah all secret from me. Casual Johnson he say: *Maybe it is a secret us eatin tha special rice. But what secret are you keepin from us?*

They laugh more harder than before. Then even more harder than ever. An when I tell them my true secret eight eyes are lookin at me like snakes are comin out from my ears. *YOU ARE IN LOVE?*

That is what they ask with one voice. I reply: yes, it is tha real thing. Casual Johnson he shake his head an he hold up two finger: *Only two real thing: Coca-cola ... an 'moi' ...*

Rosie an Cherry scream with laughin: *Prove it to us SuperFly Bulubayo. Prove your real thing. Give us ha name. We want ha name. Tell us ha name ...*

Tha rain fall hard tonight. So hard. Then even harder than ever as tha night begin to fade. Loretta an me we are stop at tha light. We are dreamin tha same dream. That is tha proof of everythin, the proof of our love to dream tha same dream. After a whole traffic light silence I say to Rosie an ha number one Cherry an to Casual Johnson an his number one Polycarp, I say: Loretta ... Loretta is ha name. *Liar*: they say. *Liar ...*

My head begin to feel heavy. Like I am rememberin so many—

Fola, for the last time: where the fuck are you?

... so many things sudden as rain. I am rememberin all tha things I have said to Loretta. All tha things they have warn me. All tha Eddie Murphy movie I have ever seen. An now with cash jobs stackin up on a busy circuit tha back door is open, tha back door is open wide an Loretta is gone an I am sittin still as tha death, control, listen, still as the death I am sittin at tha red. I am holdin my face. I am sittin an bleedin. Control listen, listen to me. I am bleedin an I am wonderin how to take a hold on my love or how to take a hold on any love when all love slip away so fast, so so fast, more faster than tha night, more faster than the fastest traffic, more faster even than—

Oi, Fola, you know what? You're fuckin history.

Julian Gough

The Great Hargeisa Goat Bubble

[novel extract]

The snow had stopped. The world lay paralysed beneath it. We would be here for some time.

'Ibrahim Bihi,' he said, extending his right hand. 'Dr Ibrahim Bihi. I am Somali. Oh, it is a long story.'

'Jude O'Reilly,' I said, extending mine. We shook. 'Please, tell the story. I like stories.'

'Very well, if you are sure...'

He cleared his throat and began.

'I eked a meagre living, exploiting a fundamental structural discrepancy in the price of goats.' He looked me in the eye.

I nodded. 'You've lost me,' I said.

'I must apologize,' he said. 'My degree is in economics and it has had an unfortunate effect on my conversational English. Allow me to begin again...' He composed himself. 'My story is a sorry tale, of the dismal science, in the heart of the Dark Continent...'

'Lost me,' I said, nodding.

'A story. Of economics. In Africa.'

'Ah, grand. I have you now,' I said, entirely gratified by this excellent clarification. I'd known he had it in him, if he only made the effort. 'Now we're sucking diesel! Sound man. On you go.'

He recomposed himself and, after a pause, continued.

'After the final collapse of the Somali state, the confiscation of my property, the destruction of my possessions and my repeated relocation due to the to-ing and fro-ing of multiple overlapping civil wars, I eventually found myself in Hargeisa, owning only a goat.'

'What was she called?'

'Who?'

'The goat.'

'She was a goat. She didn't have a name.'

'I find it hard to follow a story without a name,' I said. 'It is a weakness in me.'

'Call her anything you like.'

'Can I call her Ethel?' I said, for I had a fondness for the name, it being the name of the unmarried sister of the orphanage cook. Ethel gave us all a bag of Emerald sweets to share every Christmas. Thus, every third year I got one and, by rationing my consumption of it to a judicious lick at bedtime, could usually make it last till the taking down of the decorations on 6 January, or a little later. The sweet wrapper itself, stored under my pillow, often maintained a trace of coconutty, chocolatey fragrance till March.

'Feel free to think of the goat as Ethel.'

'Thank you.' I closed my eyes. Ethel the goat shimmered and came into hard focus, replacing the faint, nebulous, nameless goat Ibrahim Bihi had originally introduced. Ethel chewed meditatively and tilted her head to one side, looking at me unblinking.

Opening my eyes again, I urged him to continue.

He continued. 'The forced sale of a goat in wartime is unlikely to realize the full value of the goat.'

I mentally substituted the word 'Ethel' for the terms 'a goat' and 'the goat', and the meaning became entirely clear. I closed my eyes and smiled fondly at Ethel, as he continued.

'Alternatively, the slaughter and personal consumption of the goat, while keeping one alive in the short term, would lead in the medium term to having no goat and no money. In the long term, with neither assets nor capital nor cash flow, death would inevitably ensue. Luckily, my PhD thesis had been devoted to aspects of arbitrage; the exploitation of price discrepancies in imperfect markets. I thus resolved to apply my knowledge of temporary market inefficiencies to my goat.'

He thus resolved to apply his knowledge of temporary market inefficiencies to Ethel, I said under my breath.

'This final, or ultimate, goat, on which all my hopes rested, had only three legs, due to shrapnel from a mine stepped on some weeks previously by my second-last, or penultimate, goat, on the trek to Hargeisa.'

Hastily naming the penultimate goat Charles, I exploded it immediately before I could bond with it, and removed Ethel's rear left leg.

'Thus the surviving goat's movements were slow, and my search for arbitrage opportunities was limited to the immediate vicinity of Hargeisa Airport, where I was sleeping at the side of the runway, for the UN presence at the airport made it a safer place for the homeless, friendless wanderer than in the lawless town proper.'

I remembered seeing a postcard of Knock Airport sent to Brother Patrocles by Monsignor James Horan to congratulate the orphanage on winning the Harty Cup. I imagined Knock Airport, removed the drizzle, clouds and fog, drained the bog, covered it in sand, and increased the temperature by twenty degrees. As an afterthought, I mentally located, just over the horizon, all the stories I had heard the older orphans tell of Limerick City, including the one about the lad getting stabbed in the head with a screwdriver, the one about the ten-year-old in the bus station toilets, and how Aengus McMahon smuggled the bar stool out of Driscoll's after the Microdisney gig.

'I thought long,' he continued, 'I thought hard. I ate the final remnants of my penultimate goat, which I had cured in salt and carried on the tottering back of my ultimate goat to Hargeisa. I came up with a plan. The next day I ate the mutilated fourth leg of my ultimate goat as I refined the plan. I wiped my mouth as I finished and drew a deep breath. It was now or never. I had neither friend, nor relative, nor roof, nor occupation: I had, in all this world, one solitary three-legged goat. This poor goat, which I had come to love: its hazel eyes: its trim beard: its dry dugs: this poor beast comprised all the Surplus Value I possessed. It was the Rock of Capital on which I stood, raised above the perilous sea in which so many of my countrymen around me desperately swam or, ceasing their struggles, drowned.'

In life, in front of me, Dr Ibrahim Bihi closed his eyes and drew a deep breath, perhaps in unconscious echo or memory. His voice began again, filled with a strengthening passion.

'That poor goat was my stepping stone to a safer world, a better world, some greater island raised higher above the perilous waves of Life. My first stepping stone to the Capitals of Capital: to London, Tokyo, New York, thrusting so far above the sea of subsistence that the people there think the world dry land, so that their inhabitants till recently flew from great Island to great Island far above the sea of suffering, never looking down. Some glanced perhaps out the windows of their planes: but if they saw us they must have thought us waving, not drowning, for they did not come to save us. They did not come. I believe some troops arrived in Mogadishu. Eighteen died: they went home. A million of us not worth eighteen of them. A million not worth eighteen. America, which built her wealth upon the surplus labour of twenty million African slaves. There was no Marshall Plan for Africa.'

'What happened to Ethel the goat?' I said, somewhat appalled that he appeared to have forgotten her plight. In my mind's eye, she teetered bravely on her three legs, yet still stood proudly erect, the hint of a tear in her hazel eye.

'Hmm? Oh.' Dr Bihi opened his eyes. 'I waited until the daily UN food plane was committed to its final approach: as its wheels touched down at the far end of the dusty runway and I saw the puffs of dust, I drove my goat out of the long grass and into the middle of the runway and, leaving her standing bewildered and blindfold where the tyre tracks were thickest, I ran back into the long grass. The plane was laden, the suspension heavy, the engines slung low: the propeller took her head off and the headless corpse went under the wheels.'

'Oh no,' I said, wishing now that I had not visualized Ethel in quite so much detail.

'Oh yes,' he said. 'I went straight to the control tower and demanded to see the airport manager. In Somalia it is the custom to pay a man double the market price if you accidentally kill his beast. I had the price of two goats in my hand before the plane had finished taxiing back to the terminal.'

'What luck!' I cried. 'What did you do with the money?'

'I went to the market, of course, and bought two goats.'

'They could be friends to each other,' I said, pleased.

'The next day I drove the two goats into the path of a Gulfstream jet from Riyadh.'

'Ah!' First upon my fingers and then in the quiet caverns of my mind I extrapolated from one to two: from two to four: from four to eight: and so on for some time. 'And thus,' I said after a while, 'you quickly became infinitely wealthy.'

'Sadly, no,' he sighed. 'It is the tragedy of arbitrage opportunities: they are killed by those who love them. The market abhors a price discrepancy... But oh, it is beautiful to watch the market corrected by the invisible hand! The success of my scheme was noted by others: by the third day rivals were driving goats onto the runway ahead of me. Our competition in the market that afternoon drove up the price of goats. Thus, the market price of two goats, paid to us that morning at the airport for each one of our slaughtered goats, was by that afternoon unable to buy us two goats in the market. Goat hyperinflation had set in, for at the airport the next morning we demanded double the new market price for the goats we drove into the path of an old Aeroflot Tu-144. The airport manager agreed the new rate of compensation. Thus, the compensation now being indexed to the market price of the goat, where the price of the goat is n and the compensation is 2n, capital was in effect free: no matter how high the goat price soared, the fresh capital for the next round of goat finance soared along with it. The tap was held artificially open and a speculative bubble made inevitable.

'However, soon the doubled and redoubled prices paid out by the airport manager had reached such giddy heights that the merchant class grew greedy and joined in. No other asset could offer so high a rate of return as the goat, so capital was now diverted into goats and out of every other asset class, and all but the goat traders were starved of investment. Men sold their very houses to raise the price of a single goat.

'Word had spread, and men drove goats in any condition to Hargeisa from all over Somaliland, and even the other statelets of the fragmented Somalia: from Puntland, from Middle Shabelle and Lower Jubba in the chaotic southern rump state, even from

Ethiopia. The market was soon flooded with goats, many of them sick or lame. However this did not matter, for the demand for goats had become infinite. The runway, being entirely unprotected around its perimeter on either side, was the Platonic ideal of a free market: there were no barriers to entry.

'However, planes were by now reluctant to land in Hargeisa.'

Wishing to pull my weight in the conversation, I ventured, 'Too many goats on the runway?'

Ibrahim Bihi shook his head. 'The goats were not the problem. Certain economic firebrands, frozen out of the goat market, had attempted to introduce the cow as an element of trade at the airport's morning meetings.'

'Ah,' I said.

'The goat cartel fought this fiercely, as it endangered their near monopoly and threatened an uncontrolled, overnight devaluation of the goat, which could badly shake confidence in the market. Also, the pilots were very unhappy. More importantly, the UN, as issuers of fresh capital and guarantors of the liquidity of the market, opposed the introduction of the cow. Any decent-sized aircraft could plough through almost unlimited numbers of the lightweight native Somali goat without risking much more than a puncture from a shattered pelvis or horn, but a couple of cows could take the undercarriage off a passenger plane. The replacement cost of an aircraft dwarfed even the inflated cost of the goats, and the UN made an informal deal that if we kept the cows off the runway, they would continue to pay out for the goats.'

'That was good?' I ventured.

Dr Ibrahim Bihi nodded. 'Of course, some fiscal conservatives within the UN wished unilaterally to halt the goat payments entirely. It was, however, too late to do this, as an enormous reallocation of capital had already occurred, and the personal wealth of the entire Hargeisa middle class, and indeed that of many enterprising UN employees and most of the pilots and crews flying the route, was by now tied up in goats. To abolish the payments would have led to a collapse in market confidence, the panicked sale of goats, a flooded goat market and subsequent price collapses that would have ruined most.

'As you can see, we had entered a classic momentum market, where the price of the goat had decoupled from the fundamental value of the goat: the cost of a goat now vastly exceeded the capital returns which were possible over its lifetime from sale of milk, cheese, and, ultimately, meat and skin. However, vast fortunes can still be made in strong momentum markets, regardless of fundamental values, as long as you are not the one left holding the goat when the reversion to fundamental value occurs. And so I stayed in the market, fully invested in goats.

'By this time the goat craze had become a mania. A severe shortage of goats, and infinite demand, led to excesses. The price of goats became ludicrous, and many animals were led to the town market which were loudly proclaimed to be goats, but which on closer inspection proved to be dogs, dressed up. They were purchased anyway, the frightful animals, at grotesque prices.

'The sheer length of the boom was now leading to increased confidence. There was a loosening in credit. It seemed madness not to lend to a man who could pay you back handsomely the next day. And, as a creditor, once you'd borrowed and repaid with interest a couple of times, the banks began to persuade you to borrow more.

'Soon the shortage of actual goats led to a booming market in goat futures, goat options and increasingly arcane goat-derivative products. This trade in young, unborn, and even theoretical goats allowed yet more money into a market whose only bottleneck or brake up to this time had been the physical shortage of actual goats.

'So crucial to the economy were goats now, and so fatal to our people any collapse in the goat market, that the UN appointed a UNICEF Official with Special Responsibility for Goats. Around him swiftly sprung up a bureaucracy. A thoughtful man, his attempts to stabilize the goat market were well-intentioned. However, this intervention by the authorities was, as ever, late and ineffectual, indeed, counterproductive. Reassured that the UN wouldn't let the market collapse, prices soared higher. It had become a one-way bet.

'The airport manager had by now begun to fly in goats, to sell at market for nearly twice what he was paying out, thus financing further imports. This meant both more goats and more planes arriving to run them over. Now that everybody was benefiting there seemed no need for the boom ever to end. True, the UNICEF budget for Somalia was paying out increasingly large compensation fees to the owners of dead goats, but one of the first moves by the UNICEF Official with Special Responsibility for Goats was to make the goat-compensation fund self-funding by hedging much of it in goat futures. Now, every time UNICEF pushed up the price of goats by paying out double the market price, it regained the money fourfold as its goat futures contracts soared in value.

'The only drawback was that the slaughter on the runways each day was by now so great that it was becoming a hazard to land, and it could take till nightfall to execute the day's quota of goats, with planes forced to slaughter animals all the way down the runway, then often all the way back again, to hit the ones they'd missed and to finish off the wounded, and then again all along the taxi route back to the terminal. Take-offs were being delayed while the bodies were removed from the runways, which lowered the number of flights and thus the potential revenues generated for all. This was solved by bringing in an electronic Goat Accident and Compensatory System to replace the cumbersome physical system. Now, instead of herding your one, then two, then four, then eight, then sixteen goats onto the runway each afternoon, each of which then needed to go through the labourious process of being hit by a landing aircraft's undercarriage, wingtip or propeller, you simply input your goat numbers into the GACS. The airport manager input all the flights due in that day, each flight was allocated its goats, and the compensation due to each trader came up on the big screen.

'The numbers we dealt in were by now so vast that the few remaining physical goats were a financial irrelevance of purely historical interest and, indeed, a source of slight embarassment to the newly wealthy traders of goat derivatives. The vast new electronic Goat Exchange replaced the old, dung-stinking Central Goat Market, from which the last surviving obsolete goats were released to wander where they would.

'Some missed the blood-soaked runway of the old system, the

shouts of the traders, the roar of the engines and the shriek of the goats, but all acknowledged the increased efficiency of the new system. Often two full trade cycles could be executed in a day, doubling turnover. By the end of the year Hargeisa contained fourteen thousand millionaires and UNICEF were running a paper profit of over a trillion dollars.' He sighed.

'Then what happened?' I said.

A curious sorrow seemed to fill him. 'Now that we were trading virtual goats, a peculiar lassitude began to sweep through the trading classes. Oh, certainly, paupers were becoming millionaires, and millionaires were soon billionaires merely by getting out of bed and showing their faces at the beautiful new Goat Exchange, but the heady joy of the early days had gone. The millionaires envied the billionaires: while the trillionaires feared the millionaires. Trade became vicious yet meaningless. Everyone was growing richer, yet somehow more anxious. Without a solid goat to give value to the figure, one's wealth only had meaning in relation to another's wealth, and was thus never enough. Someone, somewhere, always had another zero. On the day I became a billionaire, I felt poorer than when I had owned but a single goat. What could you do but trade more, trade harder? The social anxiety and sense of failure felt by the millionaires and billionaires in a city of trillionaires caused despair, self-harm, even suicide.

'Trade went on all night now: men hardly slept, or saw their wives and families. They spoke of nothing but goats, yet had soon forgotten what the word goat had once referred to: many younger traders had never seen a goat.

'Yet the new wealth was meritocratic: old money, in property or cocoa or oil, was easily overtaken by that of young, brash goat traders who better understood these new rules.

'Confused by all I had wrought, and by now so rich that there was no word in common use that could describe my wealth, I returned one day to the old Hargeisa airport runway, the site of my glorious notion. It was disused now, of course, for our wealthy nation had outgrown the source of its wealth. The transport of goats was no longer necessary, and we no longer needed aid.

Our luxury goods arrived through the new, modern airport and electronic Goat Exchange on the far side of Hargeisa.

'The long grass had spread from both edges to reclaim the old runway. And there I found, munching quietly, disregarded in the long grass of the abandoned airfield, two goats.'

Nell and Mick, I thought to myself, and saw them clear as day before me. Though grumpy (I thought), they love each other. Mick nuzzled Nell. Nell kicked him.

'And what happened then?' I asked, as Mick mounted Nell in my mind.

Dr Ibrahim Bihi sighed. 'While I stared at the two goats, I received a frantic call from my office: the arse had fallen out of it, and we had all lost everything. But who could have predicted that?'

'Who, indeed?' I said.

'The dream had ended, and it all went away. The luxuries, the money, the gleaming towers of steel and glass. The people lost faith in the system: good companies followed bad into ruin, for it turned out that those not trading goats had yet been corrupted by them. Envious of our billions, they had fiddled the figures and diddled the books. Now all that had seemed sane behaviour in the long dream of the bubble looked criminal madness in the cold light of day. Heroes of the goat market were fired, divorced, jailed for the very ambition and creativity that had made them heroes. All fell apart. The delicate fabric of society unravelled. Somaliland lay again in ruins. I again had nothing. It was as though it had never been . . . I cut a stout stick from the bushes, and slept at the edge of the runway to escape my hostile creditors, investigators, prosecutors.'

'What did you do then?' I asked. 'Poor, alone and friendless, again, in poor Somaliland?'

'I had learned my lesson. I had heard that the US were conducting tank exercises across the border in Djibouti. In Djibouti,' said Dr Ibrahim Bihi, 'it is the custom to pay a man triple the market price if you accidentally kill his beast. I raised my stout stick and drove my two goats north, before me, through the minefields. But that is another story.'

Unregarded, it had begun to snow.

'Please,' I said. 'Tell me the story. I like stories.'

In my mind, Mick got off Nell. Yes, in spring, there would be a baby goat. A kid.

'Very well,' said Dr Ibrahim Bihi, and cleared his throat.

I closed my eyes as the first flakes fell. Yes. I would call her Ethel.

Patience Agbabi

Seeing Red

Black mum parts my continent of head,
with glazed black cotton begins to wind
each division so fiercely my mind
bleeds black. I can't close my eyes in bed.

White mum uses fading navy thread,
the tension less cruel, more kind
but the vision colour-blind
so I see red.

I read the instructions for shocking-red dye
(freedom has given me the green light)
yet bury the evidence under a head-tie

like the insight
that I see the world through a red eye
where blood and heart mean more than black and white.

Celtic

She was brought up to lie
back and think of England

which rule she disobeyed
nightly, crossing the border

to Wales to make music with Tom
or Scotland where she would reveal

each state secret to Sean
until she was so far away from home

so lost, the only word she could remember
in English at that crucial moment was

a guttural roar, more sound than sense
a disyllabic quivering sigh,

delivered with a trembling upper lip,
her husband's name: Edward.

Man and Boy

Open the blind, son. Wide. I'm not dead yet.
Did you hear the hail? Like it was deep frying.
Your mother says forked and sheet lightning
at the same time spells trouble. I know she is.
What's it like, the sky? Blue-grey? Grey-blue?
I wish I could see it too. Like surround
sound with the ghost of a picture.
What's the use? I'm dying. Give me your hand.
Hairy from day one, you were. Born old.
We knew your mother was expecting twins,
expected one of each. Your brother Jacob
followed, gripping your heel, a born tackler.
He takes after your mother. Never trust
a woman. He intends to run the business,
but you were first. There's something I must
    tell you . . .
I've so few pleasures left. Will you prepare it?
It's OK. Use the Volvo. I'm not going
anywhere, am I? Son, I know you do.

Who is it? Son, is that you? Back so soon?
Come off it. Do you take me for senile?
I've taken leave of one of my senses
not five. Come a bit closer. I don't bite.
You smell, feel, like my eldest son yet sound
like Jacob. Is this some kind of a joke?
Forgive me, son. Must be the side effects.
It isn't age that kills you, it's the drugs.
You know there's too much pepper in this soup.
OK. I've kept it buried long enough.

Do something for me first, though. Lock the door
and if your brother knocks, don't answer it.

No one knows this. Not even your mother.
I wish you'd known your grandfather. We're all
cut from the same plain cloth. Identical.
I was an only child for years. We did
everything together, man and boy.
I'd just turned twelve. My father woke me early,
We're going for a drive. There were two men
I didn't know, the one on the back seat
beside me had black hair, a nervous twitch.
The car smelt of sweat and burning leather.
The journey took for ever. No one spoke.
The next thing I remember is the office.
A huge black director's chair, a table,
a telephone, the decor was old-fashioned
but classy. Me, my father, no one else.
Sit down, son. I've never felt so small.
And then he did the thing that shocked me more
than anything that happened since. He tied me.
Tied me to the chair. No. I didn't.
He was my father and his word was law.
He pressed a gun hard up against my head,
my inner eye. Twelve years flashed in a second.
Then the explosion of the phone ringing.
He let it ring eight times then answered it.
He didn't speak. Just put down the receiver
and fired the gun towards the candelabra.
We never talked about it. In the car
on the way home, I noticed his grey hairs
for the first time. I never blamed him for it,
I understood. He always kept his word.
He would have fired that shot. He knew I knew.

Bless you, son, I'm fine. I need to sleep.
Wake me in three hours' time. I'll drink to that.

Who is it? Who? I'm far too old for this.
If you are who you say you are, then who
the hell sat on my bed, shared my secret?
I've lived too long. He should have pulled the trigger.
Where are my tablets? I'm a dead man.
I have two sons... forked and sheet lightning...
first come, first served. The sins of the father...
Forgive me, son. He let it ring eight times.
I'm sorry, I'm too weak now. Ask your brother.
There's too much salt, I have no appetite.
He went grey overnight. Where are my tablets?
What time is it? Where am I? Who are you?
I only have one son, never had two.

Ian Sansom

Where Do We Live?

A couple of years ago, on 2 December in the year 2000, from three o'clock in the afternoon onwards – to accommodate all the children – my wife and I had a party in London. We hired the upstairs room of a pub, laid on sandwiches and put a few pounds behind the bar – to celebrate, to tell our family and friends that we were moving to Ireland.

There is general agreement at the party that this is a very good thing – a sweet idea, something to be admired. Backs are generously slapped, hands warmly shaken, and there is the all-round raising of glasses of Guinness, and of stoups of Bailey's by the ladies. It's a good party. We are in high spirits.

Our friends say they will miss us, but they promise to visit.

'I've always wanted to visit Ireland,' says one friend, 'before I die.'

This friend is a sensible and kind and intelligent person and not someone suffering, as far as we know, from an immediately life-threatening illness.

But to visit Ireland before she dies ... It is a noble ambition.

It's almost as if Ireland were Mecca, or Jerusalem, a place of pilgrimage, to which true believers are required to make hajj once in a lifetime, to get right with God, and to experience for themselves the craic and the thicker Guinness, and the unmetalled roads, and the lack of exotic fruit and vegetables in outlying areas. Only the very lucky or the very devout actually get to live there, in such a sacred place. In deciding to move to Ireland, therefore, it's as if we have become holy. It is a brave decision and to be respected.

And it'll be nice for the children, like a trip to Disneyland.

You see, Ireland in the English imagination remains a place of refuge and fantasy, and good old-fashioned family values, one of those places – like the south of France before Peter Mayle, and Tuscany before champagne socialists – which, it is imagined, remain unspoilt by the American chain coffee shops and the malls and the ring roads that have ruined Arnoldian England.

Our image of Ireland – an image cherished and clutched as tightly to English chests as pints of real ale – allows us to imagine, in the darkness and warmth of that London pub, that our new lives in Ireland will no longer consist merely of mundane and tiresome work, of the endless domestic tasks of the English suburbs, but of the day-and-night drinking of Guinness, the attending of the hilarious and richly sentimental weddings and funerals of eccentric relatives, and the wandering of sandy beaches, whilst all the time being able to enjoy the benefits of a growing European economy and the sound of the curlew's song.

But then, even before our friends' glasses are set back down to stain the bar, we have to go and spoil everything.

For the Ireland *we* are moving to happens to be Northern Ireland.

There is a stunned silence. Time seems to stop. We are no longer holy. And we are no longer wise. The only sound to be heard is the ripping up of cut-price Ryanair tickets.

It's as if we have played a cruel trick on our nearest and dearest, like the mischievous uncle who points out a beautiful bird high in the sky, and then slaps you around the head as you look up: the oldest trick in the book.

The question that goes unvoiced in the silence is as clear and as insistent as it is disbelieving. 'Why?'

Well, I thought I might tell two stories that might help to explain. The first story is a story about departures and arrivals, and about my mum's mince pies, and the second is about Britain's Strongest Man.

*

The last you see of England as you leave Liverpool docks is a chemical works – you smell bitumen and the sea, and cooked dinners from the boat's kitchen. And as you sail on by there's a huge sign, each letter about the size of a man – the last words you read leaving England. The sign says HAZARDOUS AREA.

Maybe these signs are up all around the coast of England – I don't know, I haven't travelled enough. Maybe they are unique to Liverpool.

I'm on the night crossing, and in the darkness the water lathers up around the boat like purple chocolate. The boat is juddering, and my celebratory pint of Guinness in the bar seems to have obliterated my perspective completely and after the six-hour drive, having left my pregnant wife behind with the children at my parents – they're coming over later on the plane – I begin to feel a little shaky, and the waves and the currents and eddies down below look like the veins in a vast slab of meat. (In fact, I am uncomfortably reminded of the fatty beef in gravy which constituted the main course of the four-course dinner – included in the price of the ticket for the crossing on the ferry – and which I have just enjoyed down below in the company of my fellow passengers).

We seem to spend an eternity at the lock gates, waiting to leave England, waiting for the levels to equalize, and for my Guinness and stomach to settle, and then finally we're into open sea. I wave goodbye to no one in particular and make my way down to the cabin, where I can't get to sleep and I lie awake, listening to the rushing of blood in my head and the throbbing of the engines.

A man knocks on the door at four-thirty a.m. and tells me to get up, which is not necessary, I'm still in my clothes. We're in Belfast. We've arrived. I can't face the cooked breakfast – which lacks the crispness that one usually requires from bacon or from toast – and instead I have one of the remaining mince pies and a slice of Christmas cake left over from my mum's in England. I eat them staring up at the big yellow Harland & Wolff cranes – my father-in-law used to work here in the shipyard, so the place already feels like home. I'm not a welder myself, but Belfast in the morning light looks so small and so malleable and it glows so red – and I'm feeling so invincible, fortified by the mince pie – it's as though I could scoop it all up in the palm of my gloved hand and beat the place into shape.

Then it's down to the car to disembark, and when I start up the engine it stalls. This is never a happy sound – the sound of a machine asserting its right to disagree, to act unreasonably – but it is particularly unwelcome when you have a couple of hundred Ulstermen riding in white vans queuing up behind you and honking their horns. Suddenly I'm no longer feeling invincible. Suddenly I'm feeling like a little Englishman stuck at the top of a ramp unable to enter a country where I don't belong. But, there's no going back now, I have no other home to go to, so I keep turning the engine over, and eventually the car starts up and I'm off through the docks, looking for a road out of Belfast, around the coast, and on into County Down. I retune the radio. The Talks are in crisis.

*

I've arranged to pick up the keys from the estate agent at nine-thirty.

'I'm just over on the boat from England,' I tell them.

'Is that right?' they say.

I stop off at my in-laws for a quick cup of coffee, and then it's down to the new house. The keys are heavy in my pocket.

I don't know if you live in a house, but I haven't lived in a house since I was about eighteen; it's been flats ever since then for me, and mostly rented accommodation, so I've never really had to give a second thought to things like plumbing and roofs and wiring. I own no fuse wire and no buckets – we don't even possess a broom, actually, or a mop, or a cafetière, and these are all things I'm going to need over the next few weeks, along with my chequebook and a large roll of cash when the central heating packs up, and the pipes start leaking, and the drains block, and there is raw sewage running down the side of the house, and then the starter motor goes on the car, and the exhaust falls off and a joiner turns up and takes our money for materials and never returns.

But on that first morning I don't know about any of that – that's all to come. For the moment I'm happy just to find the kettle from a box in the car, and make my first cup of tea at home in Ireland. I treat myself to two sugars, and the last of my mum's mince pies from England and as I brush away the crumbs I catch my reflection in the glass of the front door – our first, our very own front door – and what's really amazing is that it's me standing there, and I'm still recognizable, even to myself. My wife and children will be arriving in the afternoon. All I have to do now is wait and maybe unpack a few boxes.

*

The town where we live in Ireland is just outside Belfast, in County Down. It's a typical decayed seaside town, a place that once boasted piers and dance halls, and bathing booths, and which now has its own small ring road, a Tesco, a Heritage Centre, and mostly charity shops on the two main streets – Main Street and High Street. There are plans, they say, for another multi-storey car park, to help regenerate the town centre.

It's a place that is good of its kind, but that no one would want to visit and that sensitive teenagers long to leave, or at least to write graffiti on. The kind of place you might like to start from or end up in, but where you wouldn't necessarily imagine yourself spending the years in between. It's like Bedford, say, or Batley, or Basildon in Essex. It is everywhere and nowhere. It is perfectly anonymous.

Except, that is, if you have small children, and boys in particular – and even if you don't, if you have girls, or even no children at all, but for some reason you've ever found yourself watching teatime television. If any of these apply, you may have heard of us – in fact, you may know our most famous son, for you may have seen a teatime television programme called *Britain's Strongest Man*.

If you haven't, let me explain. *Britain's Strongest Man* is a programme in which men who look as though they've swallowed other men go around and pick up big heavy things, and pull trains and lift cars in competition for the title of 'Britain's Strongest Man'. The final event in this mighty competition, readers of Freud may wish to note, is the lifting of giant concrete balls: the man with the most balls and the biggest balls is the winner.

It is brilliant television, better than the *South Bank Show*, or *ER*, yet in many ways not dissimilar. It's like watching gods, or monsters. At the end of every show you feel exhausted, perspiring, almost as though you were lifting those concrete balls yourself.

Anyway, if you've ever seen the programme, you may remember one of the contestants from Northern Ireland, a man called Glenn Ross. And it just so happens that Glenn Ross comes from the small town that no one's heard of where I live. He's a local celebrity.

Actually, he is *the* local celebrity. He's often in the local newspaper, and you see him around town, shaking hands and waving to his many fans. When he walks by, when he walks down Main Street – which is not often because it's steep, and I guess he might not be able to walk back up to the top again unassisted – people honk their horns.

At the top of Main Street, round the corner from where I live, there's a restaurant, although if you live in a city – if you live in London, say, or Glasgow, or Manchester – you probably wouldn't call it a restaurant. It's more like a cafe. It's unlicensed, and it's the sort of place that changes hands about every six months or so. There's a sign outside that reads, 'Our Food Is Good, So Try It'. This is what you might call typical Ulster advertising – more a threat than an invitation.

And, anyway, at lunchtimes two or three times a week Glenn Ross sits in the window of the restaurant eating big mounds of food. Steaks. And pork, and chicken, all served with chips or mashed potatoes. And, of course, pavlova.

You don't tend to see pavlova any more on menus in big cities, but here where I live it's pretty much a staple. You can buy pavlova bases in petrol stations, alongside triangular-pack sandwiches and bags of barbecue coals. No meal here is complete without pavlova. In fact, to be honest, you can hardly have a cup of tea here without someone forcing pavlova upon you.

Pavlova is really the national dish of Australia – the *pav*, I believe they call it – invented, apparently, in 1935 by an Australian chef named Herbert Sachse and named after Anna Pavlova, the Russian ballerina.

Denied the originating and naming of the pavlova, Northern Ireland's own unique contribution to world cuisine may in fact be the tray-bake – a term which covers any cake baked in a tray.

There's a baker just a stone's throw, or just a stagger, from Glenn Ross's restaurant, which offers a wide choice of tray-bakes.

They make these great little cakes which they call 'church windows', for example, which you don't find in England and which I had never come across before. Basically they're those chocolate Rice Krispie things that children make at school, except with pink and white marshmallows thrown in and few little bits of glacé cherry for good measure, and the whole thing covered in chocolate. Really, *really* wonderful. A meal in itself.

They also do 'fifteens', another surprise to me, and a pleasant surprise – they're a tray-bake in the raw, an uncooked mess of digestive biscuits and golden syrup and any other good thing you can find in the kitchen, fifteen spoonfuls or cups or pieces of each, fifteen *quantities*, all folded in together, and shaken out to a buttered pan and left to stand at room temperature for at least one hour. Delicious – food that of course may lead to the early onset of diabetes and heart disease, but whose immediate effect is to soothe and to comfort, and perhaps to count as a small sin in an otherwise blameless life.

So Glenn Ross sits there eating pavlova and tray-bakes in the restaurant round the corner from my home, and people go by, and he raises his big hand and waves, and nods his little head, and it's beautiful to watch him, a man in his prime, sitting there eating for the amusement of others, advertising all that good Northern Irish food which is available inside in the restaurant.

*

I watch *Britain's Strongest Man* with my children in our new house. We see Glenn Ross win his heat, despite a disastrous train-pull – he just can't seem to get the hang of the thing, can't get it started – but despite the train-pull he goes on to the final, which is to be broadcast later in the week.

The programmes have obviously been pre-recorded, because we happen to see Glenn Ross himself in the park opposite our house, between the heat and the final, carrying his young son on the palm of his hand – and my own youngest son shouts out to him, 'Glenn Ross! Glenn Ross! Glenn Ross!' And Glenn Ross, as befits his stature, just nods his head. It feels like a god acknowledging our presence.

On the night of the final I get the children into their pyjamas early and make pizzas, so that we can eat whilst watching the TV – we even dispense with plates so that there's no washing up afterwards, nothing that might cast a shadow upon our enjoyment.

The tension is palpable: Glenn Ross has won the title of Britain's Strongest Man for two years consecutively, and it would be a record if he won it now for the third. Can the big man from County Down pull it off? (All the men in the final are big men – big, *big* men – with faces like bulldogs and bodies like pit ponies, or bags stuffed with puppies.)

Glenn Ross does not start well. The contest is not going his way.

Our pizzas grow cold on our laps. We are staring, all of us, at defeat.

But the big fella manages to pick up some points in the later rounds so that finally he's neck and neck – and that's a lot of neck – with another big strong man with tattoos and a shaven head and in the end, as it should, everything comes down to the lifting of the big concrete balls.

Now, Glenn Ross is a man with thighs the size of my chest who can dead-lift a Citroën van and hold it for nearly two minutes. He is almost as wide as he is tall. His catch phrase is 'Who's the Daddy?!'

And he can lift more concrete balls than anyone else in Britain! He is the winner! For the third consecutive year! He is Britain's Strongest Man! You can hear shouts from the houses all around where we live. We jump up and down, and chant together, 'Glenn Ross! Glenn Ross!' And we talk and talk about it for weeks afterwards.

When I tuck my eldest son up in bed that night, after the victory, he says to me, in a voice which is just beginning to pick up the edges of an Ulster accent, 'Glenn Ross lives where we live, doesn't he, Daddy?' Indeed he does, I say.

Where do we live?

Why?

We live somewhere.

Diran Adebayo

'Come back, we'll do some calculus'

[novel extract]

At a wedding I saw him. Late, I think during the disco, and then after when Marie, my mate Sam's best girl, made this little speech. We're all scattered around by now at different tables and he's a few people down on mine. I'd been glancing over 'cos his head had been slumping inch by inch, really slowly, since she started and it was quite absorbing watching it, the way the lips go and everything. Marie was saying about what unsung heroes Sam and Lou, her man – they're nurses – were; about how they did great unheralded things that wouldn't win them any Pulitzer prizes or something, and I remember his head suddenly tilting up, twists squiggling, alive again. His eye keened at her, then met mine, and he smiled, a real one. He looked totally fucked. You could see him trying to stay together, to keep his head up, but it surely sunk back down.

He hates that I saw him first that way. Doesn't do not to hold it down in public. Big shame. But we laugh that it happened in Devon. He's so not a Devon boy.

The time we met proper was a couple of months later in the SOAS bar off Russell Square. My college was Birkbeck, down the road, but I'd been going to the SOAS one if anything for a little while. At Birkbeck there'd be people you knew who wanted to talk. Sometimes you just wanna chill out and you'd go crazy chilling out in your room all the time.

They had a pool table too. I like pool and the pool crowd quickly saw I was just into playing and didn't want to get involved beyond that. Where the pool section was was around the corner, in this alcove it shared with the drugs people. Various dealer types would pass through or take a pew along the wall benches and there'd be a lot of hands meeting and slipping in and out of pockets. By nine or so the smoke would be wafting quite thick and you could feel a little pleasantly different just sitting there. A lot of the students didn't like to come down that side, plus the puffers were generally a mellow bunch. They'd just build and chat a bit and watch the pool. They weren't all in your face and everyone has to know about it, like the drinkers. So, despite all the general, you could be quite unhassled there most of the time.

I had my Walkman headphones on and I was reading, when this guy stops by me. I didn't look up. That's the good thing about the headphones. You don't have to. Only he stoops and starts peering, close, right up me. I mean, if I had a skirt on, that's a slap. I had jeans on though – most always those days. Plus the book, between us.

'Good?' he asked, head emerging above the cover and 'Can I have a look?' already towards easing it from my grasp.

The book was *A Beautiful Mind* – about this American mathematician, who made a lot of brilliant, youthful discoveries in his field, but was funny with people, then went mad.

He flipped through it vigorously.

'What's the Field Medal?' he wanted to know. I thought about it a space, whether or not, then told him. How it was our big prize, like the Nobel. They don't award Nobels for maths.

I recognized him from the weed contingent by his hat. Floppy, green-hooped, little goatee and a gold zip-up top. A bit older, trendy in a settled not a student way. I guess I guessed him for a dealer. So it was a little, erm, surprising, these questions. OK surprising. So when he eventually asked a usual thing, could he get me a drink, I allowed it. I took my headphones off.

He had all these queries about maths. Simultaneous, quadratic equations, 'What are they for?' I explained how you used simultaneous ones in things like hydraulics, or as an architect, deciding the support needed for buildings, and quads were for financial management, say you had a business. 'Ri-ight!' he nodded, as if long anxiety had been settled. 'No one tells you this shit. If they had told me, I coulda pictured it!'

He was most impressed that a 'black' girl was doing a proper subject at a proper, old, university. 'God-damn! Maths at Birkbeck!' he kept on smiling at me, kinda proudly. 'God-damn!'

He said his old man had taught him and his brother differential calculus when he was eight and, whenever he left the house, they'd use the maths books for table-tennis bats and a net across the table. I didn't really believe him then, the first bit, but it was nice, his little science stories. Most arty types think they're so superior, that their stuff is so much more interesting, it gets on my tits. It's just 'cos everybody can have some deep view on a play or society or whatever, whereas with science it's like, to be able to talk about it interestingly, convey all the mind-blowing stuff that's going on, you probably have to have been studying it ten years, and then probably only to somebody who's studied it some. That's why people think what they think, but it doesn't mean it's not interesting.

He mentioned quite a bit of black stuff as well. It didn't surprise me – up here, I'd noticed, blacks talk about black stuff a lot. Normally... well, normally it's dreary but he was quite funny with it. Quite extreme. Kinda naughty. Like this rant, after another 'God-damn!', about how most black students weren't studying anything serious. If anything it was all these Mickey Mouse mixy-mixy modular courses: 'media an' this' and 'crap an' communication studies', and we were being fooled again, no probably not fooled 'cos we were eating it up gladly, with crazy amounts on this glamour, presenter tip, but presenters were two a penny and they'd be out on their arses soon enough and they'd never get the truly powerful media gigs – those were going to the same old cunts doing the same old subjects at the same old universities, they'd never write the leaders or any of the top shit. I remember 'cos I didn't know what he meant – leaders.

And I remember priming myself then not to say 'half-caste' or 'coloured', words that have got me into moments up here. So I must have quite liked him already.

' "Ethnics, man! Bere kendoes an' negroes," ' he grinned, looking around. 'Must make a change from Birkbeck. Is that why you come here?'

I thought about it. I told him I hadn't much thought about it.

'So where are you from?'

I knew what he meant, of course, though I did have more of an accent then.

'Malvern,' I replied.

He screwed his face. He'd heard of the water anyway. 'But your family. Where's your family from?'

'It's a long story. Another time.'

'You got Naija in you, right?'

'What?'

'You're Nigerian. Ibo. I can tell by the cheeks.' He puffed his out. 'Very distinctive. Cheeks, forehead – underneath your other stuff, man, pure Ibo boat. You wanna do a Master's, for God's sake, you must be Nigerian.'

It made me smile, how sure he was, the reasons he gave. He told me his dad was Nigerian.

'I'm really feeling I've seen you somewhere before, you know. Seriously. Some Young Ibos' jamboree? No?' He took off his hat. 'No?'

It was dense, a tended forest up there, and I was trying to figure out this style, new to me, when he pulled up a tuft saying, 'Normally I wear them out,' and I saw that they were twists, pressed down intricately all around his head. That rang the bell and, framing his face again, we got there in the end. We had a good laugh about that, him at the wedding, and it definitely relaxed me some notches, finding out. I felt safer, I guess. Connected, however vaguely.

How it happened was typical Dizzy. He's on this retreat thing, down by where Sam's parents' live, and he wanders into this pub where Sam and his stags, drinking the end of his bachelor days, get talking with him. One lock-in later they're going on bosom and they've invited him down to the wedding party there the day after. 'Too bad! I was just finished. I don't know what it was. I was a bit nervy, actually; who are these people and what am I doing here and why didn't I leave the good night at that? Musta overcompensated. Tch! I'm never like that.' He shook his head, furrowed, and was far away some seconds.

It was hard to imagine him nervous. He was very ... easy in the world. Expansive – jokey-play with the girl who tried to take some glasses away, a touch and a tale for various people he knew, passing through, introducing me to someone from Birkbeck. A purring world machine. It was quite fresh for me. I'd never known that type much. Not been interested especially. Nor they.

I did wonder what he was doing, still with me. Pool was the official reason, He'd put some money down. He'd seen me play before and we were agreed I'd lost to someone I shouldn't and he wanted me to play the guy again ('Revenge. Honour. It's good.') But we were never gonna get on, the place shut early and there were that many in front of us, and he barely glanced tablewards anyway. So... so presumably he fancies me, I thought. Hunh.

The hair didn't fit the hands. His fingernails were really mashed, bitten to the quick, and his goatee was a bit manky too, asymmetrical, when you checked it. Then his drinks! – he had all these glasses on the go, three or four at any one time, a cider, a brandy, a Baileys', and some tea, and he'd go from one to the other, cold then hot then cold again, sip, slurp. And none of them ever finished.

I was glad for these little things. I think otherwise he might have been too much, too slick for me. But these made him better, softer. You're soft when you're not fizzing, throwing heat. Soft-toned baby's dimples, eyes like almonds. Soft when you're sorry. Soft, I was thinking. Quite a sweetboy.

Come closing he retrieved his change, downed every last quarter drink and we stood there awkwardly, official reasons over. I didn't want it to be over just yet; him, this flattered feeling.

'I'm just a bus away,' he said when we made outside. 'Brixton. Come back – we'll do some calculus.'

Chuckle. 'I'm just around the corner.' I said.

'All right. I'll walk you back.'

I remember feeling self-conscious, walking through the halls and past other students and up to my poky room, about how he was a big person, and, you know, how this was all probably extremely uncool. And, not frightened exactly but a bit second-thinking myself, what I was allowing. But it was OK. I had a bit of whisky and we had Irish coffee and it was OK because soon he was quite the same: head out the window, picking and flicking, something about my handwriting. 'Jesus!' he went, springing to lower the volume on the stereo he had started. 'Classical music is crazy, man! You forget – how it goes up and down.'

He built a spliff, this properly manicured slip between tatty fingertips, then up again to enact some student memory and I took a few puffs and wondered, if he were an element, what he would be. One that fizzed at room temperature.

He says that I barely gave anything, that all I did was stare. Well, I don't know. It's not everyone can be frank like him first thing. Most nobody. Anyone's gonna seem a bit cards close against him so extra. Sure, I don't like small talk either, but that's different from spilling your A to Zee. Why? I might never see him again.

I don't know. People say I can be like that.

After a bit it was enough anyway just to listen to him. I was quite zonked, after the puffs, and you don't mind hearing someone else's A to Zee, if it's interesting, He'd been a lot of places, arting and stuff before. He'd just been somewhere showing that *Last Suppers* picture, I remember. He said there'd been stuff about it in the papers. Looked a bit disappointed that I hadn't heard of it.

Part of me was relaxed, near to drifting to his voice, now he'd stopped whirring, the other bit alert, waiting for a boy thing. Wondering what I'd do when he did it. I looked at his lips and saw if I could welcome them kissing mine. I could.

I guess I would have offered him the floor pretty shortly when he said something that erm . . . huh!, just threw things off. He began talking about his exes and I pricked, supposing this was the prelude, only it quickly became this story of how this ex had caught PID, pelvic inflammatory disease, off of him. I'd never heard of it. It didn't sound nice. She knew he'd given it her 'cos it's only sexually transmitted and she'd been a virgin before him. He said he was pretty sure he hadn't given it, that there must have been some confusion, but anyway she'd kinda got her revenge now 'cos he'd been having this bad burning pain at the tip of his dick recently. It hurt when he came, he said. It was odd, d'you know what I mean? Weird. I mean, why, who would tell a sleazy story to someone they presumably want and want to want them? Maybe I did stare at him hard then because shortly after he said he should go. And I was glad about it. I wanted space to digest, you know, especially the last bit.

At the door I didn't notice he had my CD in his hand till he tapped it.

'Let me check out Monsieur Chopin. I heard good things I think, once upon a time.' He grinned. 'Your music. It's er, it's interesting. Unorthodox.'

'I don't really lend out my things,' I said.

Tut: 'Come on—'

'I've just met you.'

'But you can see you're gonna like me, right? You know you're gonna like me quite a bit. So let's just skip till later and you lend me this CD.'

I stayed firm so he handed it back, grin undimmed, but a bit different.

'See you,' he said.

I guess it was about two.

I lingered a bit by my little music shelf. He had separated out the ones he was interested in when he'd been flicking before: this Prokofiev, other 'classical', Bjork, a couple of folkie things, and this irritating dance compilation I hardly ever listened to. A Christmas present from this aunt who doesn't know me. He'd pulled out the blank sleeve from this *Deep Soul Heartbreakers* I'd taped off a friend. 'Why don't folk write down the names?' he'd pencil-scribbled inside.

Not very black. Not very cool. Not very much.

In bed, after, I decided that he could only have told me his dick story because he was keener to make an impression than to get off with me. I don't think I had quite seen someone do that – rather make a noise than do what they came for, not in something like this. If that's what's he came for. I'd already seen he was frank, but this was more, irrational. Properly odd. Made him a curious boy. I couldn't quite decide if it was, you know, should be a cautionary sign, but my gut said it was.

It's funny: looking back, I feel I got him more right that first night than he me. He thought I came to the School of Oriental and African Studies for the colours and that I liked the music

I liked so much I had to have it on. Didn't know my Walkman was tapeless and that I came for the pool.

I don't know though. Sitting in bars an' that, I guess, deep down, I might have been waiting, hoping, for something.

I jotted down his name, whilst I still remembered, and for how to pronounce it, in case he called. I'd given him my number.

Ayinla. I thought it was a nice name.

'Ayinla (*Eye-In-La*)', I wrote. Must remember, must remember...

Adèle Geras

the square

so theres this square   and us sitting
tourists round a table   everything youd expect
youve got it in your head   the picture
isnt that right   parasol with beer-bright letters
singing brandnames into the sun and me
with coffee even though chocolate
would melt if any bugger was stupid enough
to put a praline on a cobblestone   here we are

and the first thing is the silence   whys it quiet
decor   props   characters arranged for summer
but no talk   no trannietunes   no birdsong
from the mobile phones   nothing
we are talking   and at every other table
theyre staring across silver lakes
of tabletop   at whoever they came in with
women in white gloves and pillbox hats

then a man with a dog comes striding
round the outside   whats it called
perimeter   leatherjacket shades
headshaved combattrousers leatherface
but we cant take our eyes off the dog
dragging him round the   whats it
the perimeter of the square   and someone says
thats a wolf   thats not a dog

wolf is right   so all the silent people
white gloves quivering look away from
the yellow eyes   and paws that arent

dog paws but something from forests
green long before the square   before there was
even a house here   and the wolf has the man
at the end of a chain   metal links fat and glittering
like weaponry   they disappear into the far corner

and here comes the witch with a black dress on
and a pointy fancydress witchs hat   her skirt
sticks out stiff from her wooden body   shes got a
    tray
dangling from her neck like someone selling
icecream to the tourists   its so hot today
something is moving on the tray   we see the
    movement
but not what it is till she gets close
and its ferrets wriggling at the end of ribbons tied

to the tray somehow   two of them   shes bonethin
and belongs in the clock tower behind her
how did we miss that tower   its the kind
you have bad dreams about   she could be
a figure that comes out to tell the time
when bad days roll around   maybe a jollsome bloke
in leather shorts pops out for happiness
hes not in the square today though   nowhere

and everyones quiet and we drink our drinks
and ive seen a woman with a wounded leg
walking along in a summer dress with blood and pus
and congealed stuff crusting the rim of the wound
that takes up scarlet space along her shin   weeping
and im not saying a word about that in case
its a figment or something worse   which
it very easily could be here

and we go back tomorrow
down to the station   onto the shining train
that will remove us from this place

where forest trees sprout in the clean hotels
and towers out of books that are better closed
mark every boundary   we will travel back
on railway tracks that should have all been lifted
torn from the earth they lay on   lifted and burned

Hilda Bernstein

Room 226*

When I had become, not adjusted, but resigned to living for the time being in Johannesburg because I had married a South African and started to establish a family, I found myself, like other white South Africans and quite a number of non-whites too, employing a domestic servant.

My antagonism to things South African extended to the idea of telling someone else to do work that I had been accustomed to doing myself. And in any case I simply did not know how to give orders. It embarrassed me. However, the practical convenience of having the servant outweighed any theoretical dislike of the idea. It meant I was released to do other, more interesting things. The pity of it, of course, is that the majority of white housewives, released from the repetitive drudgery of washing, cooking, cleaning and the rest, don't make more use of this freedom, but spend it gathering in groups over bridge or tea tables to discuss the never-exhausted topic – the servant problem. And I suspect that the minority of women who have used their lives to do something worthwhile, in whatever sphere, would have found ways of doing the same even with the millstone handicap of having to do all their own housework. But it would have been harder.

The person who made it easier for me to plunge into public activity in the 1950s and 1960s, to become a city councillor, and to spend days and weeks and months running around Johannesburg and its townships, was a woman who I will always think of as 'my most unforgettable character'. (The *Reader's Digest* used to run a series under that name, usually about American

---

* This essay was written in the days of apartheid, long before its abolition in 1994.

eccentrics whose qualities of kindness or generosity or disregard for the material things of life made them stand out from their compatriots.) Bessie had three children of her own. But when her eldest daughter was about twelve and her third child four she left them with her parents in the country and came to look after my children. Her husband had died some years before, and in the country town – Newcastle – from which she had come the top wage Bessie could earn as a domestic servant was about £2.10 a month. As her parents were now too old to work and she had to support them as well as her three children, she had no alternative but to come to Johannesburg where wages were higher.

She started work at about six-thirty every morning and the working day was long. Two afternoons a week, Thursdays and Sundays, she was 'off'. As if the hours she worked were not long enough, many times when I was ill, or in a nursing home having a baby, or otherwise in need of assistance, she would relinquish her free time and continue working. This I never asked for, and sometimes tried to persuade her not to do. But she did not listen.

She rarely complained; the strongest expression she used was not for herself but for her people. When one of her numerous relatives was caught in the net of the pass or other laws she would say, 'It's too heavy, too heavy.' It was the weight of the load carried by all Africans, by all poor people, that was too heavy. Life itself became too heavy for her in the end.

She was the one in a large family who always bore the burden of the family's responsibilities. One of her brothers worked as an unpaid squatter on a white man's farm: six months' work for the farmer, and in return a small piece of land and six months' work for himself. He fell ill, became too weak to work and finally returned to his parents' home in Newcastle. As he lay ill and dying the white farmer came and took away his wife and two young daughters, because he had not yet finished the six months' work that was his due to the farmer. He died alone while they were still labouring in serfdom. Bessie had to go to bury her brother and to help his family.

All through the years Bessie sent money to her parents and paid what rent and rates were due on their small piece of ground. Her father often told her that when he died the land would be hers. But when he did die he left only the intention, not a written will, and by native law the land became the property of a second son. This one was a ne'er-do-well, never in work, often drunk, often beating his womenfolk. The fact that it was Bessie who paid for everything – funeral, transfer deeds, whatever was needed – did not count; nor could lawyers do anything to help her, save take more money to confirm that the land was not hers.

After she had lived with us in Johannesburg for some years, Bessie had another baby, the father a Zulu flat-worker. She returned to Newcastle for the birth and came back to me with the baby when he was only two or three months old. But Bessie's mother wanted the child and demanded that she should leave him with her. This Bessie, as a good daughter, could not refuse, so she took her baby back to Newcastle.

There he fell ill. Once more Bessie needed money for the train fare to fetch her baby. It was a shock to see him, he had grown so thin and weak. He recovered and, when he was once again fat and healthy, Bessie said she would take him back to her mother.

'Let him stay here,' we urged her. 'Your mother can't feed him properly. He needs you.'

Bessie sighed and shrugged. 'She's too old to care for the baby,' she said.

'Then why take him back?'

'She has asked for him,' she replied. Her sense of filial duty was very strong, and she had been brought up in the strict rules of obedience to the parents' wishes that were part of her semi-tribal background.

Once again the baby became ill. She was informed by a letter written by a relative. We thought then that he had recovered, but one afternoon a telegram arrived. Bessie stared at it in horror, for she knew that any telegram could only convey bad news.

'Read it to me.'

I read: 'Come at once. The baby is dead.'

She let out a desperate cry and flinging her apron over her head she ran to her room. But a short time later she returned to the house and, seizing a duster, started polishing a table with fierce intensity while asking me to find out about train fares and when would be the best time to get a Newcastle train. All afternoon she worked and polished and could not be persuaded to stop for a moment.

Bessie's eldest daughter, Nancy, came to Johannesburg as soon as she was old enough and worked as a domestic servant.

Her second child was a boy called Sampson, who stayed in Newcastle until he had finished school, and when he was about seventeen came to Johannesburg to work. He found a job in a hotel, but he couldn't get a pass; because he was not born in Johannesburg he had no right to work there, even though his mother lived there. After a few weeks his employer informed him that he could not keep him on without a pass.

Sampson then found another job in a different type of hotel – a Bantu eating house. The proprietor was an African who found a most convenient way of obtaining workers without having to pay them at all. He employed young boys who had come from the country to find work and who had been unable to obtain passes. He promised them a certain wage, but when the time came to pay them he constantly put them off with one excuse after another. These lads would eventually become wise to the fact that he had no intention of paying them (he provided them with meals and accommodation – wasn't that enough?) and they would leave. But they had no way of claiming their wages because they had been living and working in Johannesburg illegally. To go to the authorities would have been to get themselves kicked out of town.

Sampson, too, would have had to relinquish his wages, except that Bessie told us what had happened; and, in this case, the threats of a white person wrung out the wages due to him. But it was a small victory, for he was still unable to get a pass, and after many fruitless attempts he was forced to return to Newcastle, there to work for a while in a very low-paid job, far from the protective eye of his mother.

There now took place a series of events that have happened thousands of times over. After saving some money Sampson came back to Johannesburg and found a job. He then returned to Newcastle with a letter from his employer requesting that he should be given a pass and permit to work in Johannesburg. The

Native Commissioner in Newcastle gave him the permit, but it was conditional. The pass had been endorsed permitting him to 'reside and work in the proclaimed areas of Johannesburg' only for that one employer.

He worked there for a while, but then was offered a better job, which he took. The change of employment had to be registered at the pass office. When he handed his pass to the official with a note from his prospective employer, his pass was stamped 'Endorsed out'. This meant that he had to return to Newcastle – permanently – by the date stated, never again to live or work in Johannesburg.

By that time Bessie's father had died, the land had reverted to her brother, and Bessie had brought her mother and her youngest child to Johannesburg, where she had invested her life savings in a little house in the township of Dube. Even this had only been made possible through the hours we spent patiently arguing with officials and persuading them to allow her, a woman, to buy a house because houses were sold only to men. Sampson therefore no longer had a home in Newcastle. His uncle had sold the land. All his family were now in Johannesburg. Being 'endorsed out' meant that he must go and work on a farm for slave wages. He was, at that time, not more than about nineteen years old.

I phoned the municipality and after much difficulty obtained the information from a senior official that Sampson had the right to appeal against the endorsement of his pass. 'Come to room 226,' I was told.

Before Sampson and I had even entered the huge building of the Municipal Non-European Affairs Department in Albert Street, we were told that our quest was useless. This information was conveyed by the uniformed African whose job it was to keep non-Europeans from entering the department by the main entrance. When I asked the way to Room 226 he took Sampson's pass, looked at it, shook his head, returned it to me and indicated that I was wasting my time.

However, I was not prepared to be put off by such an insignificant employee so I walked up the steps. Sampson had to go round to the side entrance and meet me in the corridor inside, because 'nons' were not allowed in at the white entrance.

Inside, there were queues of people, coveys of clerks sifting, sorting, directing, demanding fees, tax receipts, labour certifications, endorsing in, endorsing out ... what a lot of people would be out of work if the department closed down.

I approached a clerk and asked the way to Room 226. He asked me what I wanted. I displayed Sampson's pass and explained. He examined it, shook his head and said I was wasting my time. 'They can't do anything for you there,' he said. When I persisted he directed me up the stairs to Room 226, but said that the native boy (Sampson) would have to go round the back way. I explained to Sampson that he must go out of the side entrance to the back entrance, up the stairs, and meet me again outside Room 226.

After keeping us waiting long enough to impress us with their busyness and importance, two clerks in Room 226 allowed me to come in and tell Sampson's story while he – 'the boy' – waited outside. The clerk merely glanced at the pass. 'Can't do anything here,' he said. 'You could try Room 51.'

Off we went to Room 51, I going down one flight by the front stairs, Sampson having to go by the back. There we met, waited, repeated our story, handed the pass to the clerk. He simply shook his head and said, 'You are wasting your time.'

Slowly and loudly, as if speaking to a thick-headed foreigner who refused to understand plain English, I explained again. 'His mother lives in Dube. He is contributing towards the rent of the house. He hasn't any relatives or anywhere to live in Newcastle.'

'It's nothing to do with us,' the clerk said. 'His pass had been endorsed by the government. They're the only ones who can change that. You can try Mr Ferreira if you like, Room 21, Government Pass Offices, Market Street.'

We went to the other end of town, to the old, sad buildings with their endless, sad queues; and we found Mr Ferreira. He listened to the story, took the pass, shook his head. 'This boy was born in Newcastle. He must return there.'

I had now spent several hours shuttling from one office to another and waiting outside doors. 'Look,' I said, with that damp feeling that I get in the nose and throat in such situations, 'I've just explained. His mother now has a house in Johannesburg.

She needs his contribution toward the rent. All his family live in Johannesburg, He hasn't anywhere to go in Newcastle, no home, no family, no job. He has a job here and a house here.'

Mr Ferreira said 'That's got nothing to do with it. He was born in Newcastle. He had no right to come to Johannesburg in the first place. His mother had no right to come here. They shouldn't have let her have the house. His pass can't be changed.'

Words deserted me. I wanted to ask Mr Ferreira how he would feel if it were his son who was being told he had no right to live with his own family but must leave and go to a distant town where he had nothing to do and nowhere to stay. Instead, I simply sat and looked at him, fighting with my overwhelming frustration and misery.

After a few minutes' silence he said, surprisingly, 'I know what you are thinking. It doesn't make any difference. I can't do anything about it. The boy must return to Newcastle.'

The next day, when I had calmed down and was once more in a fighting mood, I phoned the Non-European Affairs Department and asked to speak to a senior official. I told him Sampson's story and asked him if it was true that Sampson had the right to have his case reconsidered.

He was very polite. The higher up the official the politer they are. He assured me that Sampson had the right to appeal. 'Bring him to the Non-European Affairs Department,' he said. 'Room 226.'

*

For a while Sampson worked in his new job, while his former employer continued to sign his pass to overcome the difficulty of not being allowed to change his job without being endorsed out. Then he tried, like thousands of other (many succeeded), to buy a pass. He did not get one. He had to leave his job when the police began to make enquiries at his former place of work. He joined up with other young lads of his own age, passless and usually jobless, adept at dodging the pick-up vans, even at recognizing the ghost squad (police who dressed in shabby civilian clothes to intercept and catch pass offenders).

Years later, when Bessie was in hospital and dying, Sampson

had become a true son of the slums, a tsotsi boy, familiar with the jails, familiar with the art of living on the fringes of existence. Bessie longed to see him, but he did not even bother to visit her, and only came once when we had sent, by devious ways, a message threatening him with retribution if he did not go.

There are tens of thousands, hundreds of thousands, of Bessies in South Africa. They live in such homes as my Bessie had – a small room in the backyard of their white employers' houses. These Bessies work for little reward. All Johannesburg's fine homes, its beautiful northern suburbs with their tree-lined streets, the bougainvilleas and jacarandas, the magnificent gardens; its southern suburbs; Hillbrow with block upon block of luxury flats: all those places, with gleaming polished floors and well-pressed linen, represent the years of sacrifice of these women. They needed so little to make them happy. All Bessie wanted was a small home – even a couple of rooms – where she could have her children *with* her. It was like reaching for the moon.

'Tula, tula,' she would whisper softly as she soothed a troublesome child to sleep. In return she had nothing; a baby who died of malnutrition, a daughter worn out with child-bearing and poverty, a son who joined the tsotsis. I can never forget her.

Gerard Woodward

Milk

1

This could be the start of something big.

I am perfectly situated on the corner of Milwain Road and Cotton Street, the bus station on one side and the market on the other, with all the human traffic in between. Every few minutes, at peak times, a double-decker will swing into one of the yellow bays, unfold its doors and produce a random selection of humanity. From there, weary and thirsty, they will pass my transparent frontage.

I've done a count. A thousand people an hour at peak times. Inevitably they will be tempted. Who wouldn't be? I've a hundred glasses clean and sparkling, a hundred fluted goblets, Corinthian-lipped, of viridian-tinted Venetian glass waiting. My interior is the last word in up-market cafe design – walnut veneer cut-out all-in-one chairs hitched to chrome-steel frames, round tables of tortoiseshell pink Formica, each one decorated with a smoked glass vase containing a sprig of subtly unrealistic buttercups. The floors are violet lino, the walls mint-green ceramic tiling intaglioed with cows. At three and a half feet the tiling gives way, via a black dado, to pink plaster, on which hang a series of Lichtensteinesque dotty pop-art canvas paintings of cows, grass, fruit, igloos, bees and pint bottles of milk. At the back is my servery – steel and glass with pink fittings, a spotlit display of cold bain-maries brimming with sliced fresh fruit, slender cylindrical jars of chocolate shavings, carafes of runny honey, cinnamon shakers, censers of allspice, jugs of cream. The centrepiece, however, is my Schweinfurth-Burmeister mkIII LactoMixa – glass silos of milk, chrome jugs like fairground mirrors, and the triple-headed, five-speed, carbon-spindled loops of my power whisks.

As I look at it now, an hour before my grand opening, I feel I am witnessing the last moments of its virginity. Those unstressed chairs. That spotless floor. It will never look like this again. Not quite. Over the coming months and years these pristine surfaces will slowly accumulate the traces of use, the marks, scratches and stains that are left even by the purest and cleanest of customers. But it will never look dirty, tacky, threadbare or rundown. It will never look old.

It will be the mother of replicas in neighbouring towns. In two years I will have a branch in Manchester, then Liverpool, Leeds. I will spread across the north of England like a sweet epidemic. And then I will move south. As I said, this could be the start of something big. An empire.

Business empires are always all built around a single, usually very simple idea. Mine is this – quality milkshakes. Milkshakes for the milkshake connoisseur, for those discerning milkshake drinkers who are disgusted by the pink gunk of the seaside promenades, the purée'd bubblegum of the burger bar, or the syrup-based strawberry froth of the greasy spoon. My milkshakes are a rethinking of the milkshake. They are made from the best-quality milk (full, half or fat-free), real fruit pieces (strawberry, raspberry, banana, blackcurrant, kiwi, melon, mango as well as other seasonal soft fruits), sweetened with heather honey, seasoned with spices, thickened with cream, garnished with any of a wide range of toppings (mocha, aniseed, crushed cloves, white chocolate leaves, fresh mint, lemon balm, chopped pistachios). Each milkshake is individually tailored to a customer's wishes. Each milkshake is a gourmet experience, a celebration, a festival in a glass. I have reinvented the milkshake.

So that is my idea. Such a simple idea. So simple it barely merits being called an idea. To be honest it wasn't even my idea. Nor was it Mary's idea. Mary is my ex-wife. She left me the day I put the idea to her.

2

'You're what?' she said, her voice dangerously quiet, her nose shrunken with disgust. She was holding Theodore at the time. He was gently pounding the side of her head with a corduroy frog. I repeated what I'd said.

'I'm reinventing the milkshake, like I said. I'm going to totally rethink this unsophisticated beverage and I'm going to transform it into the designer drink of the Nineties. It's never been done before; quality, specialist, haute-cuisine milkshakes. Milkshakes for grown-ups . . .'

Mary snatched Theodore's frog and threw it at me. I let it hit me.

'How could you?' she hissed. Only Theodore's presence was preventing her from screaming. 'Milkshakes. How could you?'

'What are you talking about? I'm doing this for us. You'll be able to give up work . . .'

'This was her idea, wasn't it?'

'Whose?'

'Janet. That cow.'

'No . . .'

Theodore blew a raspberry. Mary wiped spit from her reddened cheek. Our marriage was over in that instant. I had overlooked one essential fact when laying the foundations for my business empire – Mary my wife, my sweet ex-wife, detested, loathed, was repulsed by and feared more than almost anything that simple, white, nearly odourless substance – milk. Where most people see a harmless, innocent liquid, Mary sees phantoms, disease, decay. No one can really explain this, least of all Mary. We've always assumed she'd had an unpleasant experience involving milk as a child, although she couldn't recall one. And she was right about Janet. It was her idea. *Janet, that cow.* I wonder if Mary was, in the last few seconds of our marriage, making a joke there. Janet, you see, lives in a cowshed.

3

Mary and I first met at art school. I discovered her lactophobia the very first time I invited her back to my hall-of-residence hovel and offered her a mug of hot, sweet, milky, flesh-coloured tea. She peered into the mug as if into a hot abyss and withdrew sharply as the steam hit her face.

'Could I have one without milk?' she said, her voice taut with self-control. She went on to describe the horror she felt at the very idea of milk. She'd never tasted it. To be in the same room as milk was only barely tolerable. The thought of drinking it induced nausea. Even the thought of touching it was horrific. Once, a clumsy tea drinker had squirted a jigger of UHT over her, and she'd had to rush home and shower. I laughed, thinking her to be trendily neurotic, endearingly eccentric, original in her phobias as in her art.

Later that same sultry north London afternoon she unfastened the fish-shaped mother-of-pearl buttons on her white silk blouse to reveal the twin treasure of firmly ovoid breasts with salmon-pink nipples at which I was to suck drily for the next twelve years.

In those days she still had the legginess, the spidery clumsiness that was the last trace of the child in her body. After an awkwardly bumpy session of love-making I made the first of thousands of cups of black tea.

It quickly became routine. Two teas – milk for me, none for Mary. Ordering coffees in cafes it became automatic to say, 'Two coffees – one black.' Perhaps once a year her milk attitude became the subject of a brief, playfully teasing conversation along the lines of

– How can you not like milk, it's got no taste?
– It's disgusting.
– How can it be disgusting? It doesn't smell.
– It smells like blood.
– Was your mother frightened by a cow?
– I've never asked her.
– A milkman?
– I don't think so.

– But you like cheese, yoghurt, butter . . .
– But I hate cream, blancmange, rice pudding . . .
– But you like ice cream . . .
– It doesn't matter if it's derived from milk, what matters is if it's milky, if it has that horrible, milky, yukky quality . . .

And she would perform a series of theatrical retchings, extending her tongue and hawking up invisible vomit.

We'd laugh.

4

But I turned into something of a disappointment in Mary's eyes. When we finished art school I became suddenly and briefly famous – the New Contemporaries, the Whitechapel Open, the John Moore's, and then I was taken up by a Cork Street gallery. Colour photo-spreads of my work appeared in the glossies. I was profiled in the Sundays. My paintings began selling for four, then five, figures.

I'd developed a reputation as the artist who paints sewage farms. Water treatment works. Purification plants. To me they were charming little clearly bordered territories filled with ellipses, parallelograms, cubes and pyramids. I was fascinated by their boundedness. I painted sewage farms in fauvist reds and greens, sewage farms populated by zebras and giraffes, I painted sewage farms as sites of carnal bliss, abstract sewage farms, sewage farms floating in the sky. My public lapped up my sewage farms. My reviews were rapturous:

> he sees the sewage farm as a site of elemental renewal, of bodily resurrection, as a place that processes dead matter to produce rivers of life . . .

ran one, under the title 'Fra Filippo of the Filter Beds'.

I wasn't surprised by my success. I felt an arrogant sense of entitlement, of expectations fulfilled, of satisfaction. I had the swagger of an innocent youth who's jaywalked the boundaries of the art establishment and pitched a shabby tent there. To have shown surprise or delight at my own achievement would have been to admit that my gift was not embroidered into my very chromosomes. That I was not a natural.

It all went wrong at my first major one-man show which, set as it was for touring to New York, LA and Berlin, should have sent my fame into uncharted heights. But as the show approached I felt a need to change direction. I'd been painting nothing but sewage farms for nearly five years. I'd painted all I could paint about them. I felt it both prudent and daring to change my subject. I painted racecourses.

Chester, Fontwell, Derby. To me they were a logical development. I painted racecourses in fauvist mauves and oranges, racecourses on which zebras and giraffes endlessly competed, racecourses whose green furlongs provided lush sites for exotic love-making. But above all, as with my water-treatment works, it was their boundedness that attracted me. These fenced-in, measured spaces.

The show flopped.

> having abandoned the richly fertile ground of the sewage farm for the sterile and pointless looped turf of the horse-racing circuit, he could be said to have pulled up at the first fence ...

or some such ran one cheaply punning review. My reputation evaporated. Did they expect me to paint sewage farms for the rest of my life? Some collectors of my work even tried selling my sewage farms back to me, seeing them shed layer after layer of investment value.

I could no longer support Mary and myself. We agreed that she should take a teaching job in Leeds while I put my career back on track. We both saw the sense of it. It wouldn't be long before my work was selling again, and Mary could leave teaching and concentrate on her own painting.

We settled in the gritstone isolation of Ravendale, the Pennine mill town Mary had grown up in, and I rented a studio in a disused woollen mill. Traces of fleece, little tufts and wisps, could still be found in its crevices.

The hills around us were dotted with reservoirs, some of them were great, elevated seas, others little more than ponds. Every fold and hollow of those wet mountains, it seemed, had been dammed and allowed to fill, the water piped to the towns and cities below. These quiet, sequestered, liquid harvestings became my new subject. I painted reservoirs in constructivist greys and browns, reservoirs like glass menageries, liquid beds (the site of aquatic love-making), reservoirs sailing in the sky tethered by spindly streams to the ground.

My early success didn't return. A decade had skipped by. People who were still in nappies when I was entering art school were now being hailed as the future of art. Painting was proclaimed dead. Landscape irrelevant. I tried to laugh it off as the transience of fashion, but my laughter had an echo in it. It came back to me. It bounced off the white walls of my studio. The empty walls.

And then Mary had a baby.

5

Little Theodore showed me a path out of the white fortress my painting career had become. I slowly forgot about making paintings and became instead a house husband.

I'd watched Mary's skin slowly burnish itself with fine and lush hair, her dome become drum-tight and hard as marble, and I'd watched her breasts stock themselves with milk.

Mary was not troubled by the prospect of the bodily cataclysms of pregnancy. Her only fear was that of becoming a milk-bearing creature. I pitied her and tried to imagine the horror she must have felt as her body became not only a repository but a manufactory of the substance she considered more toxic than cyanide. She believed she was becoming a depot of vileness and feared she would develop a need to suppress her own milk production, to escape her own body, to sever her own breasts.

But when it came, sealed up and present only as a weight in those antenatal weeks, she felt at first an indifference and later a pride in the new, pert stance her breasts were taking. And when the miraculous puppet, more bird than person, of our baby appeared, and the engine of her milk was, after several false starts, started, she felt no horror or repulsion as she filled the intestinal loops of Theodore's tiny gut with her pure white thread.

For a while we wondered if her lactation might erase the horror she felt for cows' milk, and that we might enjoy a future of shared milkiness, of creamy desserts, rice puddings, blancmanges, milkshakes. But her feelings for cows' milk didn't change, and she could still feel a repugnance, though mild, if her own milk found its way back to her, if it leaked and dripped onto her skin, or if Theodore brought up a posset of her partly digested self, or more vigorously vomited, bearding himself like a curdy Father Christmas. But she could cope with it.

I continued making black coffees and black teas. I once tried whitening mine with Mary's milk, but it rose to the surface in oily droplets. I suckled at her once only. It was like drinking sweetened olive oil, carpeting my mouth wall to wall, floor to ceiling, with fatty deposits.

And this is where Janet comes in.

6

We'd been in Ravendale for three years and I had made no friends. Mary saw chums from her childhood and had an adequate social life around the Leeds college where she continued to teach. I had spent my time in the white cube of my studio watching my canvases shrink and fade to nothing. There were other artists in Ravendale, a surprisingly large number in fact (there was even an area of back-to-backs and converted engineering workshops that called itself the Bohemian Quarter), but they were mostly young and I found their ambition and optimism relentlessly depressing. I felt a need to meet people unconnected with me or with painting and so, from the meagre list of social activities pinned to the notice boards of Ravendale Library (UFOs, Feng Shui, Tap Dancing), I chose to join the Ravendale Archaeological Society, which met fortnightly.

At first the membership didn't look promising as a source of future companionship. Aged ladies with grey hair set in stiff, meringue-like waves, post-adolescents whose faces were pinned and ringed with silverwork like out-of-use noticeboards, self-consciously anachronistic gents with mutton-chops and tweedy, damp-smelling clothes. Janet presented a dazzling contrast to this motley assembly as we listened to a guest speaker discourse at length on Greek revivalism in the mill chimneys of Ravendale Valley and surrounding areas.

Janet had a freshness, a newness, about her. What, I wondered, was something so colourful and alive doing at a meeting of antiquaries, whose interest in dust and rot I was already finding dull. Neither did she look like the farmer's wife she claimed to be, not in her zebra-skin leggings and leather jacket, with her bobbed blonde hair and lunulate earrings. As we milled about with cups of tea after the lecture she shimmered towards me, a beacon casting its light on a lost ship. I was expecting welcoming pleasantries from her – *nice to see a new face*, or *how long have you been interested in archaeology?* Instead I got

'Were you breastfed as a child?'

'I think so,' I replied, although I had no idea. 'Why do you ask?'

'You have a glow about you.' She moved her hands – palms out, fingers fanned, in contrary directions around the surface of my personal space, as if warming them there. 'Only breastfed children have this glow. It lasts them all their lives.'

I had not thought of myself as a glowing person before. People had often commented that Mary glowed during her pregnancy, but I was never thought of, in any way, as luminous. If anything, I thought of myself as something shined upon, and therefore a producer of shadows.

As Janet's hands lifted, completing their loop of my radiant aura, her leather jacket opened to reveal her tightly T-shirted torso, the low neckline of which half-disclosed her lifted breasts. They were not young breasts. Her body had aged in a way that her face had not. I found this slippage of synchronicity between her body and her face strangely exciting.

Surrounded by the sluggish chatter of physical historians she told me everything about herself. How she was married to Jack Tilley, who managed a herd of twenty-three Friesians on the pastures between the precipices of the valley and the heather of the moorlands. How she'd provided him with two children, twin boys, both of whom had gone into dentistry. How Jack had failed, over twenty-seven years of their marriage, to see any real difference between his wife and his cows.

'I was just another of his herd. I happened to walk on two legs, live indoors, make interesting food and produce human children. When I left him his way of tempting me back was to convert an old cement yard at the back of the farmhouse into a lawn. He seemed to think that I'd always wanted a lawn. I just laughed at him and he became very, very angry.'

She'd left him only to a distance of three hundred feet. She'd moved into an old cowshed, built of gritstone and roofed with Jurassic rock, which they'd previously converted into a cosy holiday cottage for letting out to tourists. She let it out to herself, permanently.

Jack never fully understood why she left. He took to pounding on her stout oak door all through the night, posting scrawled messages on torn paper through her letterbox (*The herd's not right since you left, their milk smells of onions. You trying to ruin me? You got to come back, love*). He was not a violent man and never threatened her physically. He whimpered that he couldn't manage the kitchen. Eventually he turned sour, claimed he hadn't wanted to marry her in the first place, said he was happy alone at the farmhouse. They lived totally separate lives on the same farm. She only ever saw him as a tiny figure in the distance, fetching his cows, sweeping slush, making silage, filling his quotas. Occasional bouts of loneliness caused him to knock at her door and beg for her return. She always stood firm, but was not cruel and tried to comfort him when she could.

She took me to her cottage that evening after the lecture in her battered orange 2CV. We climbed the steep, dark lanes past the derelict church of St Simon, followed the Möbius strip of the lane that led to her farm, chased the beams of her headlights into the farmyard. On the journey we talked about archaeology. She'd become interested in it when a team came to excavate some tumuli on her land. They found a skeleton, an Iron Age chieftain's wife (no sign of her husband), with a horse buried alongside.

'It fascinated me to watch them uncover her, but it made me

wonder – is it right for us to dig these things up? To disturb what was once a sacred site? I wept when they began lifting her, bone by bone, out of the dust. It was her right, surely, to be there for ever. We're always in a dilemma between knowledge and preservation. We can't know anything without damaging it, no matter how careful we are. But I can see you have a special, historical sensitivity . . .'

Her voice was melodious, soft, grassy.

The interior of her cottage was an odd conjunction of the rustic and the Bohemian, as was Janet, I suppose. Above the lovingly restored black range hung a stuffed zebra's head. Over the nested teak tables in one corner the face of James Dean was outlined in blue neon. The varnished flagstones of the floor were adorned with zodiacal rugs.

We made love for an exquisite hour in her bedroom. The cows, in their modern shed, thirty feet away under a roof of corrugated iron, coughed and shuffled.

At midnight I returned to Mary, already asleep in our bed. I sensed her flinch unconsciously as I entered, as though she could already smell my contamination.

7

Our affair developed slowly after that first night. Our meetings were brief. By day I spent my time filling Theodore with milk Mary had expressed, bottled and stored in the fridge. I would supplement this with formula milk, sterilizing the bottles in a plastic tank, scooping the sulphur-coloured powder into a measuring spoon, levelling it off with a knife. I'd rock Theodore to sleep and then phone Janet. We'd talk about history, animal husbandry, the mysteries of human relationships. She told me how Jack had taken to baking complicated iced cakes which he offered to her as sweet, pointless gifts. She told me that he'd started having singing lessons.

I saw him from Janet's window, sometimes, in the brief and occasional evenings I spent at her cottage. He represented for me a figure of complete isolation, a tiny little man in blue overalls, so small I could cover him with the nail of my little finger, a blue dot in the green pastures. Once, wellingtoned, he clumped right past the cottage and I was suddenly shocked by his near-presence, the magnification of his body, as he swaggered beneath me.

Sometimes, as Janet and I lay in a post-coital stupor on her bed, the cows would be grazing in the near field at the back of her cottage. The only sound would be the tearing of grass, the relentless pulling and ripping up of young shoots. I felt an odd sense of envy. I envied the cows their hunger.

I entered into infidelity with an ease that shocked me. I looked upon the deceit as a form of invention. Of creativity. The lying was a species of fiction-making. It didn't seem difficult. And if I felt guilt it was at not feeling any. I wondered why I didn't feel bad about what I was doing. I began to think of myself as a rather skilful adulterer. Until Mary said to me one day:

'Are you having an affair with Janet Tilley?'

Mary had known Janet since childhood and had never liked her.

'Who? Janet? No. Janet who? Oh, that Janet. No.'

I wondered how that clumsiness had found its way into my denial. Something in me wanted to tell her. When I noticed a shadow of disappointment cross her face I couldn't tell if it was because she believed me or disbelieved me. I went for belief. Mary needed a reason to get rid of me. I was nothing but a burden to her, a morose failure lugging around the sack of his missed opportunities. I felt I'd been given coded permission to continue and develop my affair with Janet.

8

And then my mother died.

You don't need to know anything about her. All I will say is that she admired Mussolini for his multi-lingualism and violin playing, but wouldn't comment on his politics. She bought a house with my father (now ten years dead) in 1949 for next to nothing that was now worth a bomb. My share of it came to sixty thousand pounds.

'We need to think very carefully,' said Mary, after reading the solicitor's letter over breakfast (two teas – one black, one white, three bowls of cornflakes – two wet, one dry). 'This might be a way out.'

'Of what?'

'This mess.'

'Yes,' I said thoughtfully, adding, 'which mess do you mean?'

'I mean the mess of us having no life. Me working all the time and never seeing Theodore, you with Theodore all the time and never working. Which mess did you think I meant?'

'That one. You're right. I was thinking – I could set myself up in business. I could find some way of supporting both of us.'

'Business? You?' she said, without intending any insult.

'Why not? Something on the arty side I mean. An art shop with gallery upstairs, picture framing...'

'I don't want you to take this the wrong way,' said Mary with the quiet authority she'd developed over her years as a teacher and which I found rather frightening, 'but you will tell me, won't you, before you spend all this money on some half-baked scheme? It's not that I don't trust you, but I'm beginning to think you have a fear of success. Every time something you want is within reach you kick it further away. Don't feel frightened of this money, don't feel you need to rid yourself of it...'

Theodore, in the midst of some wild game, thumped his cereal bowl and flipped it upside down, showering us with cornflakes.

9

I mentioned my inheritance to Janet. We were in one of Ravendale's coffee bars spooning cappuccino froth into our mouths. We were surrounded by goatee'd young men and angular, attenuated young women sitting in stern silence with their espressos.

As if developing an idea that was latent in the beige and black decor of the bar she poured forth the whole concept of a milkshake parlour for Ravendale. In a few minutes she had detailed everything from the recipes for the shakes to the dairy-and-fruit themed design of the interior. She convinced me that there were enough writers, artists and media evacuees in Ravendale to support it. There would, she pointed out, be an interest in it for her. She could supply the honey. I'd seen the little cluster of hives in the field behind her house, like a row of clapboard cottages wherein the heather of the moorlands was refined and processed into the sweetest honey of the Pennines.

I began experimenting that afternoon. I bought four litres of milk in plastic bottles and filled Mary's Moulinex with milk, chopped fruit, honey, cinnamon and anything else I could think of. I hacked my way through strawberries, bananas, kiwis, pineapples and melons and tipped them into the graduated beaker, pressed the button and watched with great pleasure the pink and yellow vortices, those torrents, tornadoes, maelstroms of milk and fruit trapped within. All that afternoon I spun milk and fruit while Theodore watched from the high chair, laughing, although the frantic engine of the mixer frightened him at first.

I poured out the inflated liquid, upholstered a glass goblet with it and drank. It felt as though I was drinking liquidized tropical gardens, fluid flowerbeds, flowing blossoms. My drinks were the concentrated essence of sheer beauty. I knew then that I'd discovered a beverage that couldn't fail. A drink that would change the world.

It was when Mary returned from work that evening to find the kitchen a yoghurty mess of fruit peelings and splashed milk that I broke the news of my milk-shake parlour and she reacted so badly. Her whispered rage soon gave way to shrill anger. Theodore put his small hands over his ears.

'Why are you doing this?' she shouted. Her voice was so strange. It was almost as if she was singing. I felt scared. She seemed on the point of losing control. Theodore was trying to climb down from her. For a moment, in her crimson, swaying anger, I thought she might throw him. I moved towards her, my arms extended, to catch any hurled baby, to contain any explosion that might come. She drew back, her nose as wrinkled as a walnut.

'Get away from me, don't come near me, ever!' Her 'ever' was said with such force it was as though she'd vomited the word out.

I haven't touched her since then. I tried everything I could think of, including the abandonment of anything to do with milkshakes, the confession and renunciation of my affair with Janet, the promise of exemplary dad- and husband-hood, to make Mary stay. But she was gone that evening with Theodore, first to her mother's at the other end of the valley, then to a female colleague's in Leeds.

10

So now I am fifteen minutes away from my grand opening. In my fridge are two pergals of milk and a further two quart bottles from the Co-op dairy in Huddersfield. They sit there in the dark – marmoreal, cold, unchanging. I've fruit, spices, honey. The honey is from Safeway. It is not Janet's honey.

Although she helped me, comforted me, encouraged me as I set up my milk parlour, something had changed in our relationship. I wanted to move in with her, but she said her cottage was too small, too 'hers'. I asked her to move in with me, but my house was too big, too 'mine'. But she helped me find this property, the old wool shop on the corner of Milwain Road and Cotton Street, perfectly situated. She helped me with all the admin – sorting out the rental agreement, business rates, insurance. We worked together on the design, carefully thinking through every last detail. We scoured the glass catalogues of the world for just the right tumbler, which we found in Iceland (Norglass Inc). But a week before opening I went to her cottage and she wasn't there.

Puzzled, I hung around the filthy, splattered farmyard, wondering at the silence. It wasn't just the silence of her cottage, my knuckles echoing on her stout oak door, but the silence of the farm itself. There was something missing. Then I realized it was the cows. They'd gone. It was their clumsy footsteps, their coughing and snorting, their nervous shuffling that was missing. Nor were they in the fields. The sound of tearing grass had stopped.

Just then, from round the corner of the steel byre, came the clumping weight of Jack Tilley; blue overalled, wellingtoned. His head was down and he was walking purposefully towards me. Unaware of my presence I thought he might walk right through me, but he stopped when he was just six feet away and looked at me without any surprise in his face. He didn't say anything. Neither did I. We looked hard at each other's faces for perhaps fifteen seconds, both of us curious to take in every detail of what we'd only seen distantly before. I noticed the stiff, coarse texture of his skin, flecked with broken capillaries, the blond wickerwork of his eyebrows, the moistness of his eyes. As I looked into his face I knew that she was back with him. Jack Tilley walked past me.

I got a letter a couple of days later in which she tried to explain. Jack's herd had fallen to the disease that was yet to become famous. The disease that grew in their brains like rot, that caused them to stumble like drunks, that poisoned their flesh. Jack's herd had gone to the abattoir, the carcasses piled and fired, the first Pennine cows to be culled in an effort to halt the spread of the disease.

'*Jack's ruined . . .*' her letter read, '*he's lost everything. I can't abandon him now, not when he needs me so much. I hope you understand . . . our cows. I keep thinking of the smoke. The black clouds our cows made . . .*'

*

My family have become people I visit occasionally in a city the other side of some mountains. Theodore fills the loo with paper when I arrive. Mary is busy, but she says she'll try and come over for my opening if she can. Imagine that – Mary in a milk parlour. I'm sure if she actually saw what I've managed to put together here . . .

The floor needs one more clean. You look at it, think it's spotless, a minute later it's thick with dust. It's the same with the windows. I've cleaned them twice this morning, but they still look filthy. That's the trouble with glass. It shows up the dirt so easily. I remember my mother saying that about the windows at home. Even though no one ever touched the windows, they needed regular cleaning, so where did all the dirt come from? I asked her once. She said the dirt was just made by people living, people breathing and sweating, stirring up dust. She said a man could stand stock-still in a room doing nothing but breathing, and the windows would still get dirty.

I'd better give them just one more go.

David Morley

Ludus Coventriae

i

Their world, and that of the Catesbys on Cook Street,
differed, like
the egg-shell hue of the wren and linnet.

ii

'Aslepe as Coventree this faire morning'
(the sycamores drip from pressure prior to the eclipse)

whose farms lie smack against canal basins,
whose long-faced beasts yawn and bask in their midge clouds.

iii

So sleep as Coventry sleeps this morning
with low sky catching alight from street lamps.
The sweeping bus views from house to town,
Herod the king, in his raging.

iv

Glossy stare and red squirrel
oblivious in eave or dray
are mass and matter
by close of day.

v

Out of desert, from the hard stone
three air-raid wardens run, three kings
late up with pick, spade, lantern,

tracing the star of each explosion and making there.

vi

For most stay put,
squat among their own brick and bone
or worse, stray underground
beneath the burning stairs or buried cellar.

vii

With low sky catching alight from street lamps
there Billy is, workshying, dribbling a football to the shopfloor.
Inside, the cleaners sluice the floors of its blue dye.
In the yard, rain rinses – 'that's where the foreman Dan
chucked up' – clots of eel flesh, peas, fried potato.

viii

Out of danger shall us release.
Out of whose dangers? The sword
Or sharpened cross? The cross-wires
of bombers or radio signallers
that drag those planes across?
Red, the town is taken; alight,
a light; and all its fired temples.

ix

With low sky catching alight from street lamps,
enough light to register from one thousand feet above
nettle-tree architecture of church and spire –
its foreshortened spear, gimlet-eyed cockerel –
sufficient to land on almost, for a horsefly
or a linnet, or firebombs too.

x

The spire writhes in high pressure prior to the eclipse.
Fire-rods brim the blackening moon-circle.

Billy forgets. *This is not the morning after,
it is the morning before.*

Godiva pouts in state from his locker door.

xi

Billy, head down like a hod of stones after long carrying:
gently and gentled into balance on his pillow; and the day
unloaded stone by stone as though ready for slow walling;
is when he feels the tilt, and the grip goes sliding.

Moleskin gloves and polypropylene;   head of a mallard;
   pashed dishevelled nest;   cloudburst of
   milestones;
of frosted manure;
   of buckram coaches flouncing up from the exploding
   museum;
pink snow of records (adminstrative, personal);   axe of a
pub sign;

arrows,   apparently human bones;
   flung gravel: horse teeth or stun-stones;
stethoscopes in showers, and syringes;   splatter of
Coventry
   Blue dye;   cartoon dancing brickwall;   razed bowling
greens;
strutting graveslabs;   hail of stained glass;
   a child's kaleidoscope: a hatchet;
a bus hovering in house-high air;
   turbine bouncing off five walls and still crawling towards
Nuneaton.

xiii

Park Street, and behind that, Pilate
rinsing his mitts as the crowd thins out.
We shall show that as we can

the dog-watch on Trinity and St Michael's
breaking to wash brick muck from the corpses.

xiv

For their world, and that of the Catesbys on Cook Street, differed, like
the egg-shell hue of the wren and linnet.

Patrin

or *pateran*,
pyaytrin, or *sikaimasko*.
The marker used by Roma
that tell others of their direction,
often grids of branches or leaf-twists or
bark-binds. Used for passing on news
using prearranged forms, patterns
or permutations of these. Yet
it also means a leaf or,
simply, a page.

> Simply, a page
> yet it also means a leaf
> or permutations of these
> using prearranged forms, patterns.
> Bark-binds used for passing on news,
> often grids of branches or leaf-twists
> that tell others of their direction.
> The marker used by Roma
> *pyaytrin*, or *sikaimasko*
> or *pateran*.

Maggie O'Farrell

The Distance Between Us

[novel extracts]

Francesca is planting bulbs, her knees pressing dents into the damp lawn edge. The soil in the new garden is thick and dark. It has rained and rained for weeks, and the ground is sodden between her fingers. Each of her nails crescented with black. She presses a dense root tangle into the hole, then packs earth on top of it. She has to do this quickly. Her mother will be here in half an hour and if she sees her bending over in the garden she'll shriek about the baby.

The tight drum curve of Francesca's belly rests on her thighs, the feet of the child pressed up against her lungs. This baby is different from the first, confusing, unpredictable. It can go for hours in utter, almost eerie stillness without moving a hand or a limb. Then something will wake it – a noise, a peristaltic gurgle, the rumbling echo of a cough, Francesca never knows – and it will flip into manic, vehement action, somersaulting, flailing, as if grappling with an invisible assailant. With her first baby, Francesca felt all along that she knew her, that she almost recognized her when she was handed to her, bloodied and dripping and compressed, but with this one she has no idea what she's getting. It could be anyone.

Somewhere behind her is Nina. Francesca can hear her panting, the shuffle of her small unformed feet through the grass. A hot hand grips Francesca's shoulder and a strand of her hair, and Nina appears, flushed and purposeful, a doll dangled by its foot in her hand.

'Hello,' Francesca circles her daughter with her arm and presses a kiss into the creases of her neck. Nina staggers backwards in surprise, thrown off-balance by this sudden rush of affection. 'What are you up to?'

Nina frowns. 'Messy,' she admonishes, pointing at Francesca's hands, stained with the garden.

'It's only mud,' she says, 'look, it feels nice,' and tries to press Nina's fingers to her own. She doesn't want her to grow up fastidious, fussy.

Nina snatches her hand away. 'No-no-no-no-no,' she wails, 'messy.'

'OK, OK. I'm sorry.' The sight of her daughter's affronted, indignant face makes her want to laugh, but she bites her lip. 'Sorry,' she says again more seriously.

Nina is surveying her, assessing, critical, her wide green eyes travelling over Francesca's face, hair, shoulders and neck, coming to rest on the swelling beneath her shirt. Francesca doesn't breathe, but waits, tense and ready. She hasn't mentioned the pregnancy to Nina yet – a child-psychologist friend of Archie's told her to wait until Nina asks. Is she going to ask? Is she? Oh, please ask.

Nina's eyes flick to her mother's face then back again. 'What's that?' Nina enquires in her high, reedy voice.

Francesca's spine straightens and lengthens towards the spring sky above them, as if an invisible thread is pulling her upright. She's had this rehearsed for six months and is now so excited the words are tumbling around her mouth like bubbles in champagne. She breathes in through her nose and out through her mouth, like they teach her in antenatal classes.

'It's a baby,' she says, beginning the first words of the speech she has down pat, because she wants these sisters to be happy, to love each other, more than anything she has ever wanted in her whole life. 'For Nina,' she adds.

Nina frowns and leans closer, her fist gripping the collar of Francesca's shirt. Francesca feels the baby shudder and flex, arching its back as if waking from a long sleep.

'For Nina?' Nina repeats.

'Yes,' Francesca swallows, nervous. She presses the back of her hand to her cheek. Pregnancy makes her feel hot and full. 'For you. It's going to be your sister. When she's born she's going to be very small, like this,' Francesca holds her hands apart like a fisherman measuring a fantasy catch. She speaks slowly, watching Nina's face. 'And we're going to have to look after her, you and me, because she's not going to know how to do anything. She won't know how to feed herself, or dress herself or—'

'A sister.' Nina says and Francesca realizes she's never said that word before. 'For Nina.'

Francesca nods. And takes Nina's hand in hers and presses it to the hard, dense dome of her stomach. 'Let's see if we can feel her moving.'

They wait. A lawnmower roars and belches in the garden over the wall. The tune of an ice-cream van unwinds somewhere in the distance. Nina looks unconvinced. Come on, Francesca wills the baby, just this once. She pictures it as she saw it first in the grey, soupy fuzz of the scanning machine, floating upside-down, a trapeze artist in freefall. Then there is a flash of movement, a twist, like a snake shrugging off a skin.

Nina's face is stretched, disbelieving, like a traveller who's been told that the earth is flat after all.

*

The ceiling above her is a patchy, grey-white. Nina knows off by heart the pattern of frail cracks that run through it like rivers through mountains, seen from a plane.

Nina's never been in an aeroplane. But this ceiling is how she imagines it might be. She would look down and see the puckered earth passing far beneath her and the flickering shadow of the plane, printed there by the sun.

She moves her eyes inside their sockets. It seems to take a great deal of effort, as if they are weighted or as if a machine inside her is slowly cranking down.

The room is dark, the blinds lowered. From where Nina is lying she can see the black slits of night reaching into the room. She is puzzled. Weren't her parents here just a minute ago? Or was that a long time before? She can't remember. She has a slight recollection of Stella. With their grandmother in the corridor, looking in at her. But maybe that never happened. She can't remember when she last saw her sister.

She lifts her eyes to the clock on the wall opposite the bed. She can see the second hand jerk and stop, jerk and stop. To her right, she is surprised to see, is a nurse. Sitting in a chair beside her. Eyes bright as mercury through the gloom. Nina doesn't know why the nurse is there, watching her.

Nina looks away, looks down the length of her body, draped in the hospital blanket. It's odd. She could have sworn that her arms were folded over her, fingers tucked into the elbows of the opposite arm. But now she sees that they have been placed by her sides. At the end of her body, her feet fall away from each other in a symmetrical v, the blanket peaked over them.

Beyond the room, beyond the grimacing faces of cartoon characters daubed on the windows, is a noise. Someone running, feet cracking against the lino. Nina knows that lino. She remembers its dark red, pocked surface, the slightly grainy, uneven feel of it under her soles. On the last day that she'd been able to walk, she'd moved along it. All by herself. All the way to the bathroom. She wouldn't let them carry her, no she would not. She'd shaken and tipped sideways and had to cling to the wall and it had taken her a long time and it had hurt. But she'd done it.

A small figure whizzes past. A boy from the ward down the corridor. Nina's seen him before. He's running, pulling a drip stand behind him like a train on a string. His laughter is torn off as he passes her open door.

Then she hears something else. Feet coming after him. Heavy feet with a broad sound. Adult feet. A nurse.

'Come back,' the nurse calls. 'I mean it.'

'You can't catch me!' the boy cries and his voice sounds distant as if he's turned a corner. Nina thinks that there is a corner that way, turning off into a larger hallway. She used to see it when she used to leave the room. Then. Before.

Then the nurse outside is hissing in a low voice. 'Be quiet.' Nina will hear it again later in her head. 'There's a little girl dying in there.'

For a split second Nina feels sorry for the little girl and is wondering how old she might be, what age you'd need to be to die, and whether the little girl is frightened and Nina is turning her eyes on the nurse beside the bed to see if she is sorry too. But the nurse is looking cross and strangely ashamed. She is darting up out of the chair and slamming the door and making sure it's shut firm.

When she comes back to sit down again she won't look Nina in the eye. Nina stares at her, stares and stares. But she won't look up. And then Nina understands.

*

An old jazz song was playing, a woman who later died a tragic death crooning about there being no sun up in the sky, the pulse of her voice stretching at the carpeted walls of the tiny studio. When this building had been built, someone told Stella once, the architects had been anxious about the noise of traffic being heard on air, so all the studios were buried deep in the centre of the building, like the tiniest figure in a set of Russian dolls.

James was leaning back in his chair, one foot on the table, his headphones slipped down around his neck, chatting to the weather girl. Stella leant over the mike that connected her to the studio. 'Two minutes twenty-five, James.'

Through the glass she saw him sit up and reach for his mike. 'OK. We're ready.'

'Weather first and then we've got some calls lined up for you. One minute fifty.'

She turned back to the mixing desk. The door swung open and a man from the production team leant in. 'There's a call for you, Stella.'

Stella jerked her head round to look at him. 'I can't. Not now.'

'It's urgent, apparently.'

'Who is it?'

'I don't know.'

She yanked her chair towards the phone and pressed the flashing line. 'Stella Gilmore speaking.'

'Stel, it's me.'

Stella raised her eyes to the ceiling. 'Jesus, Nina. I'm right in the middle of a programme.'

'I know. I heard you.'

'Then why—'

'Listen. I've left Richard.'

Stella sighed, tapping the end of her pen on the desk.

'Neen, is there any way—'

'Can I come and stay?'

'Er . . .'

'I'm at the airport,' Nina said threateningly. 'I'm—'

'Look, can you call back later? I'm . . . I've got plans for tonight.' Rob had promised to pick Stella up from work, drive her home, and then ravish her. Which Stella had been rather looking forward to.

'If you don't want me,' Nina burst out, 'then maybe I'll just have to—'

Above her head, Stella saw the green On Air light come on. 'Of course I want you,' she said, distracted. In the studio, the weather girl was reading from a script. Stella glanced at the levels and nudged one up with her knuckle. 'Of course you can come.'

Nina sniffed, slightly mollified. 'OK. I'll see you later. There's a flight that gets in at about quarter past midnight. So I'll get to you about one.'

'Great.'

'I got a late one because I knew you were working.'

'Thanks.'

There was a pattern to Nina's occasional marital crises. Richard committed some misdemeanour (usually obscure and often incredibly minor), they rowed, Nina flounced out, not to return for several days, during which time she threw herself heart and soul into various types of outlandish behaviour – sometimes buying lots of expensive clothes, sometimes sleeping with someone else, or sometimes disappearing to distant places. Richard either always forgave her or perhaps never knew the full truth, Stella could never tell which. Nina's freak-outs seemed to be part of the fabric of their marriage, somehow.

Stella finished the show, ignoring James's on-air digs about his producer always chatting on the phone, called Rob to cancel, rushed out just in time to catch the last bus, stopped in at a 24-hour shop to buy supplies because Nina would be hungry after her flight.

In her flat, a tiny first-floor studio, her answerphone was

glowing with a message: 'Stel, it's Nina, just wanted to...' a crackling interlude while there was some static and then some giggling, '... calling on Richard's mobile. I called him after I spoke to you and he came to the station to get me. So everything's OK. We're in the car just now...' more giggling and rustling and the rumble of Richard's voice in the background, '... not to see you. Bye.'

Stella picked up a glass – one of the tall, thick-based ones stolen from a pub for her by the first man she'd ever loved – and hurled it at the wall.

Sophie Woolley

Epic Slinky

Canning Town

I was in her mouth. She was beautiful, although I didn't notice at the time. She had a Product 250 T-shirt on with the sleeves hacked off. She had borrowed it from the last boy she picked up. He wasn't getting it back. After I had her, the T-shirt was torn slightly at the front. She covered the tear with some gaffer tape. She was very stylish.

King's Cross

I was beautiful. I was slinky. In high, high Jimmy Choo boots. I had a ponytail and everything. It was Saturday. I went to the disco.

The promoter said hello to me and we climbed the stairs. He was my friend. He was a kind man.

My heels clopped up the winding stone staircase and my hamstrings tugged.

I was slinky. My thighs were glistening trunks, my knees were snow-capped volcanoes, my smooth shins encased in spike boot heels, poised step by step as if to puncture chests, and my dusty soles to crush faces.

The promoter was out of breath. 'I'm going to die on these stairs one of these days.'

'That's a good idea,' I said.

'Thanks' he said and meant it. He liked good ideas.

I met my friend at the bar. She hated her boyfriend. He was in the toilets. He was a DJ, but she wished he was in a band. The promoter bought us drinks and we got drunk.

When there was a lapse in conversation, I did a series of somersaults across the room, showing off. It was quite busy in the bar, but after you turn the first somersault a path always clears for you. I'd done it before a few times. I was good at it. I cut my hand on a piece of glass this time, but it wasn't too deep and I was past caring.

There was a band on downstairs. They were girls. They were called Emergency Girls. They were dressed in fake Gucci jewellery and charity shop clothes circa 1985. The promoter managed them. The singer was called Police, the guitarist was called Nurse, bass was Fire and the drummer – who was so drunk she wet herself during the second song – was called AA. The song was raw, but sort of catchy. Police introduced it saying:

'This one's for all the accidental fathers in the house. You can run, but you can't hide. The CSA will find you, and I will be waiting, for the weekend.' And then she screamed. And sang the song.

> 'Young dad, young dad
> Don't you make your baby sad
> Young daddy, young daddy
> All laddy so laddy
> Fit young dad in Mothercare
> He's got previous in his hair
> He's got access
> To Practice
> To get it right the second time around
> His bareback prick is bound for market
> Morten Harket
> Aha, aha
> You fucked up, you cocked up
> Now put your prick up me and see what comes out
> (*Heavy panting*)
> Baby baby baby
> Baby baby baby
> Baby baby baby
> Baby baby baby
> A young daddy, young daddy
> Young daddy with no money

> I could be so good for you
> Love you like you want me to
> Young daddy, young daddy
> Young dad, young dad
> Don't you make your baby sad.'

The promoter looked happy. 'They're mental,' he said proudly.

Later on my friend decided to try and annoy her boyfriend by getting off with Police. The three of us left together, teetering across Pentonville Road to try and talk our way into the Turkish club. The doormen weren't going to let us in because we weren't Turkish. But Police insisted that we had been invited by someone called Don Juan. I don't think that's a Turkish name, but they let us in all the same. Inside we drank more. My friend started getting off with Police at the bar. Like a switch had been flicked, the atmosphere in the bar changed. All the men dimmed their conversation and looked over. A big man with a moustache slid along the bar and grabbed my arm. 'My sister says you look lonely, she wants you.' He pointed. I looked along the bar, and saw another big man. His whole face wobbled like jelly when he laughed.

I persuaded my neo-lesbian friends it was time to get a taxi. We left the Turkish men to their coffee and staggered towards King's Cross station. The Sunday papers were on sale. Sunday was here already. Police lifted a copy of the *Observer*, ditched the supplements and rolled it up into a fat baton. She launched an assault on a blamless, trampy-looking old man who was sat on the pavement outside W.H. Smith's. She thwacked him about the head. We managed to pull her off the tramp and bundled her towards the front of the long, long taxi queue. People complained. My friend pushed Police into a taxi and climbed in. 'Get in,' she told me.

'No,' I said.

I went back to the disco. Climbing the stairs was a bigger job this time. The boots hurt.

The karaoke was in full swing when I got back to the top bar. A celebrity and her non-celebrity friend were singing 'All of me'. They were quite good.

I spoke to the celebrity and her friend. They wanted more drink, but the bar had closed. I spoke to the promoter, who rustled up a bottle of vodka. We drank more. I curled up in a toilet cubicle for a while, with my arms around the bowl. Everything flashed red and white. The noise outside was getting quieter. After a long time I pulled myself up and staggered out of the toilets. Nearly everyone had gone. I gathered myself at the top of the stairs and began to fall.

I was proper slinky now.

I managed to land on my hands and flip over and nearly made it onto my feet again, but my balance was shot, I skidded down a few more steps on my knees, then clutched at the wall. I fell spinning and tangled up for a flight and managed just one more somersault before I stood, walked a couple of steps and then my legs gave way. I reached the bottom of the stairs in a heap of legs and arms. I stood up in front of a bouncer.

'I fell,' I told him.

'Don't worry, love,' he said, 'you fell like a star.'

Like the model Michelle de Swarte from Streatham, in Gucci in Milan? Like Naomi in Vivienne Westwood? Falling gets you places.

I slunk out of the door towards the celebrity and her friend. They were getting into a car. 'I fell,' I told them. They stared at my knees. Blood had erupted and was flowing into and over my boots. Perhaps my leg was broken. But I was past caring.

'Come with us,' said the celebrity. She was very kind.

We went to her house in Primrose Hill. It was nice. There was a small waterfall in her fireplace. And a Damien Hirst above the mantelpiece. I slumped down into an expansive red-leather settee. She put *Girl on a Motorbike* on her widescreen TV with the sound down and brought up a bottle of absinthe. We danced to Michael Jackson. Then I don't remember anything for a bit.

Primrose Hill

I drove the three girls to the celebrity's house. They sat in the back clacking away to someone on the celebrity's mobile phone.

I looked over my shoulder at her friend. Her friend winked at me and opened her legs, then laughed and shut them again. I had only kissed her once, after the celebrity had finished talking to me at the club. She was a crazy. When we got out of the car the celebrity and the girl with bleeding knees went into the house. The celebrity's friend grabbed my hair and we stood kissing in the middle of the road. It was beginning to get light. The friend pulled away and took all her clothes off. She squatted naked in the middle of the road and pissed. A black taxi slowed down as he passed her. Her knickers lolled on the tarmac getting dirty. I picked up her dress, grabbed her arm and led her inside.

We danced and drank for about an hour. Everyone was out of their minds on green stuff. The girl with the bloody knees passed out on the sofa. I went downstairs to the toilet. When I came back, the celebrity and her friend had gone to bed. The party was over, but I couldn't sleep.

The scabby-kneed, Product 250 T-eed girl was still lying there on the sofa, like she was dead. I knelt on a white tiger rug and stroked her legs. I touched her arm, trying to wake her up. She didn't move. I pulled at her arm and she stirred and tried to push me off. I kissed her face. I managed to pull her up and lean her against me. She put her arms around my shoulders and snorted a bit. I got her to the top of the stairs and tried to get her to walk down. She had her arms stretched out and stepped forward like a sleepwalker. I got in front of her and held her waist, and she slumped over my shoulder, all floppy legged. The top half of her was heavy, but the legs flobbed out behind her, light and easy. Plong, kerplong, kerplong. When the weight got too much for me I held her back and took two steps down and then dragged her, she plonged down easier that way. It was like dancing with a corpse. I propped her up against the banister and kicked open the bathroom door. She unwound and fell at the bottom of the stairs in a heap.

*

I started to be awake again. I was bent over. He was up me. I thought it was someone else, in a dream, someone good. He stopped for a moment. 'Come on, come on,' I muttered. He just held me and kissed my neck. Everything was wet. I pulled down my skirt and looked in the mirror. My make-up was still spot on. Then he started again and did it in my mouth. It felt sick so I got up and clung to the wall, up the stairs. Something was burning inside. I lay back on the settee and listened to the waterfall in the fireplace. It was lovely and soothing. He started kissing all up my legs. He put his head up my skirt.

The celebrity's friend appeared at the end of the sofa. The kissing stopped. I sat up and looked at the man and the woman. I didn't know who the man was. The woman was shaking. She seemed angry. My mouth was open.

'YOU ARE EVIL,' she shouted.

I didn't say anything.

'I HATE YOU,' she screamed and ran down the stairs. I followed her. This needed sorting out. In the kitchen, she got a knife and held it to my neck.

'EVIL WHORE, I HATE YOU.'

Time was moving slowly. I was evil. I must have done something very, very wrong. I racked my brains.

'Sorry.' I hoped that would cover it.

The man pulled me away and out of the house. 'Thanks for having me,' I called back. 'See you soon.'

Canning Town

I was in the car with the man. He drove to Canning Town. It was light now.

I stood with the man by the Thames. I could see the Millennium Dome. Some big warehouses and a rusty barge. The man looked at me. His skin was deathly pale and his hair was matted with dry sweat.

'What's wrong with you?' he asked.

I am slinky. I flip, I fall.

He took me to a room in an empty warehouse.

'This is my studio,' he said. The studio was filled with electronic music equipment and computers. There was a mattress in the corner. It was cold. He gave me a beer. 'You don't even know my name,' he said, shaking his head. I felt guilty. We swapped names.

He put some music on.

'Do you like this?' he said.

Perhaps it was a test.

'It's OK.'

'I've got to go in a bit, got to see my little girl.'

He showed me a photo of a little girl.

My T-shirt was torn. It wasn't mine. I picked up some gaffer tape and ripped off a length to cover the tear.

He held me down on the mattress in the corner.

'You're very beautiful,' he whispered.

My mobile had run out. I looked at the cracked ceiling. A leak dripped onto my face.

We went outside again. A security guard wandered over. He looked just like a security guard. Tubby with a grey moustache. He said hello to the man and gave me an odd look. It might have been pity.

'Kept you here all weekend, has he?'

'No.' I smiled. Everything was good.

The security guard wandered back to his Portakabin.

I gave the man my number and then walked to Canning Town station.

There's a party next week, in Hoxton. I might go if I feel like it.

Alan Jenkins

The Wait

'There's a feeling of disaster in the air, which I now
know I have felt for a long time.'

– Ian Hamilton, May 2001

Our usual place, and everything in it
Exactly as we had learned to expect:
Most tables empty, the 'interfered-with air'
Heavy with the stink of recooked fat
That got into the clothes, into the hair
Along with cigarettes smoked at such a rate
It was like a race, and you had to win it;

The 'maître d'', a supercilious queer
Who knew we had too much class to be there
(These nights, I have to keep going back
To meet you, though it's still only me there) ...
Breathless from the cold, my coat unchecked,
I found our usual table, where I sat;
'Some wine, *sir*?' 'No thanks,' I said, 'I'll wait.'

And wait I did, my *Standard* open at
The horoscopes (Predictions for New Year!
Your Stars, That Break, and You! – as if),
My mind snagged on Failure of Drug Czar,
My eye swivelling from page to watch
And back again, and then to some
Embarrassing artwork above the bar ...

Once or twice, I'd known you to be late
But there'd never been a time you hadn't come,
Grim-faced, apologizing. So I sat on,
Through the looks of waitresses who guessed
I'd been stood up, who wondered what had gone
So wrong for me I'd choose this place for a date;
Through the 'chef's' indifference, the whiff

Of something raw, the turning spit. It was a test,
A trial of sorts. And since what we are
Takes the piss out of what we wish we were
And nothing we can do helps shake off 'the dread
That how we live measures our own nature'
(How many times had you quoted *that*?),
I ordered, first a scotch, and then another scotch.

The room forgot me. I didn't have to stir.
Any moment you'd come in, take off the hat
You wore to hide the fluff of white hair growing back
Now you were 'in remission' – from the drugs –
And sit down, drink and smoke. (You never ate;
Just pushed things round and round your plate
Till you could decently light up again.)

A couple slouched in, a few single men
And glancing round each time I heard the door
I logged a face or two, flushed from the street,
For when you turned up, as you would any minute;
Would you 'just have to go and make a call'?
Or, patting pockets for reserves of ten
And feigning interest in the menu, greet

Our waitress with a show of blinks and shrugs? –
Such gentle flirting... Christ, that was months ago.
No jokes, now, about the new kid on the 'scene',
Your last advance, or what you had to do before
You could be let off, the slate wiped clean...
As if. Were you trying to get through?
Or slumped in a cab – another scare?

I dialled your number, spoke to your machine;
Then sat again. Did I *want* anything at all?' –
No thanks, I said, and went on with the wait, not
    knowing
(And how like you, somehow, that I should not know)
What strange new circumstance prevented you
From joining me, from getting up and going,
To the phone, out to the tall night, anywhere.

Tidal

These winding streets are *liable to sudden flooding*
and now I glimpse the river through leaves of oak and beech
and horse chestnut, my eyes are liable to sudden flooding
as I think of how he courted her along this green suburban
 reach
in the leaf-rich summers, in the bonfire-scented autumns
on the Surrey side, in the suburbs of his pleasure
before he was allotted (and he knew this was his portion)
other men's allotments, squares of laurel and horse chestnut,
avenues of limes; flotsam-scattered cobbled slipways,
houseboats, boathouses, the smell of mud on slipways
when the tide has flooded them, towpaths shaded by horse
 chestnut
where they walked together, a sense of due proportion
in all things, in their pain as in their pleasure,
in the river-borne summers of their life, and the smoky autumns.

Wildlife

She loved the mountain ash that flowered above the garden,
outside my bedroom window – the tiny four-square garden
that they weeded, tended, watered through my childhood
after lunch on Sundays, trimming privet, planting wallflowers;
then one year I came home and the patch of garden
had grown smaller, meaner, it had shrunk like childhood,
the fence and privet hedge were gone, and there instead
was a little low wall behind which the wallflowers
and mountain ash looked foolish . . . The bright seed packs of
   childhood
are gone now, there are brochures for old people's homes,
the mountain ash has gone too, the stump is dead
and 'Next spring I'll see about the garden,' I say mildly
to the old woman who lives here, a widow, and the fox that
   roams
through waist-high grasses as she watches from the window,
   staring wildly.

Alex Clark

Only

I'm not the only Sixties-vintage English child to have grown up with the Waltons, but I might be the one who became most transfixed by their bedtime rituals. At the end of each episode, as night fell in Jefferson County and the mist curled around Walton Mountain, the family settled itself down for a decent rest before the lumber mill jerked into action once more. But, before sleep could come, there was the business of the goodnights. Goodnight Mary Ellen, goodnight Jim-Bob. Silence. Goodnight Mama. Goodnight Erin, goodnight Jason.

In suburban Essex, where there was no equivalent to the Blue Ridge Mountains, where seven children, their parents and grandparents didn't gather round a vast trestle table for a chatter-filled evening meal, and where every day didn't seethe with incidents and dilemmas conveniently resolved by the outgoing theme music, there were also goodnights. In self-conscious imitation of the family's favourite TV show, they took much the same form, the punchline coming with that annoying little game of waiting until silence fell, and then chirping up again. The only thing was, it was a game we had to try very hard to prolong. Where there were endless permutations of Walton communication, here there were only two adults and a child. It wasn't something that could be pulled off without a certain amount of repetition.

By rights, our nightly envois should have been more like those of Corabeth and Ike Godsey's, the Waltons's neighbours and bit-part foils, who had only their adopted daughter, Aimee, to wish sweet dreams – not that we were witness to them doing so. But my family was always perversely cheerful about its diminutive size and not to be deterred from joining in with the happy-go-lucky noise and banter of units far larger and more complicated. Committed to not missing out on a shred of communal entertainment, we too played Monopoly, mounted garden hunts for Easter eggs and sang songs in the round on long car journeys.

Decades later, when I came to try and write about the particular and peculiar experience of being an only child, I found myself wondering if there really was any poignancy in that bedtime ritual, or whether I was retrospectively introducing it, the better to explain my sense of being not quite equal to the world's chatter, of not having quite enough solid ground to stand on. There were a few things that I could remember that had the ring of truth, that seemed as if they might have been true: the mixture of fear and fascination with which I contemplated outsized families (in other words, those that totalled more than three members, adults included), who never seemed to need anyone outside their immediate circle to kickstart things into happening, or to make experiences real; a recollection of my mother in the supermarket, complaining that chicken breasts and pork chops always came in packs of two or four, and never three; and an addiction to those very intricate melodramas in which a long-lost son or daughter would suddenly appear out of nowhere, both usurper and saviour. I still wonder if the knock at the door might come; if somewhere out there is someone in need of a game of charades at Christmas.

But most of my feelings are more nebulous, much harder to locate in specific anecdotage, or to tie to discrete memories. It's just a sense, which always seems to have been there, of being somehow provisional, lacking in the real rootedness that comes from being part of a dynasty – or that I imagine does. Maybe it's partly because I was the only child of two only children, because not only were there no brothers and sisters, but nor were there uncles and aunts, cousins, nephews or nieces. The widespread and slightly bogus practice of family friends becoming "aunties" and "uncles" took on an extra, vaguely desperate feel; second cousins were promoted to the inner circle even when we didn't like them very much. Not liking people very much – and talking about it in endlessly detailed and nuanced ways – was a pastime my family excelled at, which might be why I've grown up thinking that virtually everyone outside the trinity is extremely weird. But you can't think that other people are weird without that inner whisper suggesting to you that you might be weird yourself.

My tiny family often felt curiously random, out on a limb at the edge of by normal life, verging on being beyond the pale; and for me, well, I was there only by chance. In one way it was true, and in another the complete opposite of the truth. The family mythology played heavily on chance, on the accident of my mother, veering anxiously towards her thirties, exiled in her home town after an unfortunate and unsuccessful first marriage, sleeping on her aunt's pullout couch and working in the department store in which she had had her very first job, aged fourteen, suddenly glimpsing an advert for staff on a cruise liner. On my father, a silver-service waiter in the ship's grand dining room, going into the arcade my mother managed on the first day out of harbour, and asking her to put a tube of toothpaste and a packet of razors on his slate. 'No credit for crew,' rapped out my mother. My father was a spindly, pale 28-year-old, and when my mother's assistant remarked later in the voyage that she thought he was keen, my mother retorted, 'Keen? He doesn't look as if he'll see Christmas.'

Why had two only children ended up on a boat? Did they talk about their lack of siblings with one another, and find comfort in their joint solitude? I've never asked, but something obviously clicked. In the end, they took their chances with each other, and just when my 38-year-old mother had given up on the hope of ever having children, I arrived. One of her favourite stories is that the hospital doctor who came to see her before I was born repeatedly asked her to verify her age; the figure on her notes, he felt, must be wrong. In those days, first children at thirty-eight edged on indecency.

Writing about your parents feels like grand larceny, something to which morally you never fully adjust. If you are an only child, bonded since birth into an eternal triangle that seems to imprint its shape on your consciousness, to filter quietly into your every thought and movement, it feels even more crucial, as if you're flirting with burning the only bridge across the river. Having no thought of betrayal, I felt simply a deep anxiety at striking out on my own, at speaking about the experiences of an entity whose default position was privacy, secrecy. I felt like a mason about to reveal the secrets of the lodge to the gutter press. But there was, I thought, a story to be told, and not one merely about me or my life.

A magazine and website dedicated to only children – American, incidentally, although you might have been able to guess – seemed to agree. Luckily for them, only children are a growth market – too many women putting it off, too many marriages crumbling after the first birth, although they would recoil angrily at such a negative interpretation, and probably call it self-hatred (more unresolved issues, more big business) – and one that is currently under-resourced. Equally fortuitously, you can work up some extremely favourable spin on the subject. More only children equal fewer demands on the state, on the environment, on housing, on parking spaces. I was intrigued by the idea of family-dictated motoring problems. Are children from larger families more likely to drive those enormous jeeps, and are only children more likely to be the ones plastering 'Fuck off back to the range' stickers on them? I do, in fact, drive a very small car: is it because I feel I don't have the right to take over more than my fair share of the road? (Or am I just canny about my road tax?) When I get jockeyed out of my proper position at the head of the bus queue, is it some crazed middle child, the competition for space hardwired into their muscle memory, doing the shoving? (Or am I just too polite?) Either way, I liked the idea of a shadowy organization helping me to stick up for myself. Having never been able to locate myself within any particular visible minority, it seemed that the world of support groups and pride marches might be within my grasp.

A self-help guide I stumbled on made slightly less comforting reading. Its currency was the case study, endless tales of obsessionally serious, sensible, punctual, non-confrontational, well-organized and driven children growing up unable to form meaningful relationships, caught between the misery of isolated introversion and the claustrophobia of interactions they had no training for. Something you never escape from, they said; an illness for which there is no cure. The moderators of this massive piece of printed group therapy were sympathetic and helpful, but only up to a point: was it sensitive, I wondered, to remind their charges (somewhat gleefully) that Hitler and Stalin were both only children?

A newspaper report recently told the story of a man who had made a fortune by auctioning off his collection of Dinky toys, which he had amassed over many years and which had reached a staggering 16,000. One of his tactics, it said, had been to approach men on trains and, striking up conversation, to ask if they were only sons. If they were, they were likely to be hoarders; more importantly, their mothers were likely to have kept their childhood toys. Speaking of his £250,000 windfall, the man, himself an only child, remarked that his motivation was to provide a nest egg for his family. Hideously sentimental it may be, but I can't contemplate those carefully preserved maternal shrines without a pang. Were they still on display, carefully dusted along with the cat chasing the mouse into a smoked brandy glass, or neatly wrapped away in shoeboxes with polaroids taped to them?

An only son of my acquaintance recalls that when he left home to go to university, his mother took her mind off it by buying a pet tortoise. Revealing, maybe, because he happens to have a slightly craning neck and to be rather short-sighted.

Only children are hypochondriacs. They fret that every cough is pneumonia and every bruise a subdural haematoma, perhaps because their mothers did, or perhaps because they fear – correctly – that they are irreplaceable, without acknowledging that everybody else is irreplaceable too. Is this true? I'm a hypochondriac, certainly, and so is my tortoise friend, but so are lots of people I know. Youngest children, mainly.

Only children are over-sensitive and have problems in expressing anger. They are oldest child and youngest, firstborn and baby. In the only child, a battle is fought between introversion, because you need to be able to amuse yourself, to turn your thoughts into company, and extroversion, because you struggle to make yourself heard when you do get out into the world. Only children hang around on the fringes of large groups, but when they finally infiltrate them they make everyone do exactly what they want. Somebody, somewhere, has called this ambiversion, which I quite like. I am an ambivert, I tell myself proudly. Ambiverts anonymous. Ambiverts unite. Bumper sticker: ambiverts do it on their own – but not always!

They are terrible at relationships. They're frightened of being left, but they want it all their own way. They shy away from arguments, but they can't bear being thwarted. They occasionally want to be completely alone, but they get very cross if you leave them for too long. They do not share their last Rolo. They brook no opposition. They are passive-aggressive, and manipulative, and needy. This is wonderful fodder for the partner of an only child. Arguments in my household end with another – a sibling, of course – chanting, 'Only child! Only child!' while I stomp off to ring my mother.

Are any of these character judgements true and could an only child – the walking, self-reporting statistic – tell you if they were? Personally, I suspect that the responsibility for all this propaganda lies with a band of brothers and sisters, eager to justify their own strange, cult-like upbringings, all of them backing each other up and calling each other by pet names and remembering some peculiar game that their family invented on holiday in Cornwall and no one else can play. No matter. The proficient ambivert can always take solace in being unique. We know the truth.

Binyavanga Wainaina

According to Mwangi

Once upon a time there was a man called Mwananchi. Now this guy had one talent. As a youngster, he would stand on a street corner of Booroo housing estate and tell stories. Booroo estate was the newest and largest estate in Nairobi, built to house the new generation of forward-moving Kenyans.

Kids from phase one to four of the housing estate would pass by his 'joint' when sent to the shops by their parents. His joint was an abandoned old car, which sat next to a certain lampshade he had decorated himself in Manchester United football team's colours. He told his stories sometimes in *Sheng*, the version of Swahili that all the cool people spoke, or sometimes in that hip Nairobi English teachers laughed at.

Parents hated him. They wanted him to be exiled to some small village somewhere: whatever it took to get him away from their children, who would come home with all sorts of crazy ideas, funny new slang. Some tried to get hold of his parents to complain about him, but his parents seemed elusive – promising to come for meetings and never showing up, or sometimes simply not picking up the telephone.

What made his stories special is how they managed to capture the place the kids lived in. Their parents, still with one foot in their home villages, still with colonial hangovers, busy building the nation, had no real idea how their world worked. This was the first generation of kids in independent Kenya, the first generation to be born in a city. There were no books about them, films about them. They didn't even see themselves on television.

There were many kids in Booroo who were funny, or witty, or who came up with better slang, but Mwananchi was democratic – he didn't slag off one group of people to entertain the rest. He saved all his venom for adults, those alien people who did things differently from what they said at home. There are few secrets amongst kids, and fewer secrets amongst kids in Booroo. He had the tact, though, not to name names.

Mwananchi would weave a story out of Big Ben and Leonard Mambo and James Bond and Kivunja Mbavu and the Flintstones and Kelly Brown and Mama Milka, who sold vegetables from door to door.

He could turn a *mandazi* into a character – John Mandazi the goalie who thought the goal was a frying pan, and was always jumping about, and who would swell up when the ball came near him. One day, before the finals, some kids were on their way to the match, when they met their parents, who asked them, 'What are you doing dragging that giant Mandazi around?'

And the kids said, 'Aiee! Mammee! But he's our goalie – we can't miss the match without him!' The parents looked at each other and dragged off John Mandazi and fed him to the *Chuba na Ndebe* guy, who was always hungry.

Then there was John Mandazi's brother, Canaan Banana Mandazi, who was a fat city council official with brown teeth and four wives...

Once Mwananchi told a story about a mean old schoolteacher called 'Pingiling' who used to make his children bend to his will – and would beat them up until they did. Pingiling was a widower. In the end, Pingiling found that his family had grown tough, like Muhammad Ali. Untouched and worshipped, he had frozen into glass. So one time he whipped his daughter with the stick from a caterpillar tree and she screamed and struck back, and his eyes opened wide as he felt himself starting to shake, and his last words were 'Pingiling!'

Then they swept him into the dustbin.

One girl, Sheena Patel, started to cry when she heard that story. Years later, she refused to come back home from England when she had done her A levels. Her father had arranged a marriage for her. He died alone a few years later.

Pingiling.

Achieng was in love with Mwananchi. She was one of the youngest of his regulars. She would follow him around everywhere – thumb in her mouth, dragging a skipping rope behind her and staring at him without blinking.

Years later some would recall that they first learnt about sex from his famous story: *Muguu Wazi* and the Bouncing Baby. For weeks kids in Booroo would say in one of Mwananchi's falsettos, 'It's a bouncing baby booy!' Then they would crack up laughing. That night, after they heard the story, they released themselves and started to talk about sticky dreams, and pimples as loud as police sirens, laughing all the time. Some discovered that day that they weren't suffering from a strange illness.

Booroo is situated on the edge of the Athi plains; and on a clear night stars jump at you. Shooting stars, blinking stars, stars that are planets; stars that turn out to be somebody's headlights. The day after the first *Star Wars* film was shown at a Nairobi cinema, the kids gathered at the lamp post. Mwananchi was ignored, and the kids all stared at the sky, and talked about Obi and Princess Leia, and laughed at the Aliens who were speaking Kikuyu. Why would Aliens speak in Kikuyu?

Mwananchi was angry that day. It was the first time he had been ignored in The Joint. It was also clear to everybody that he hadn't seen the film. He sat listening to them for a while, then left angrily, saying, 'That all dead *maneno*. Dead. A story is *now*, bwana – now. I make a story, and watch you, and change it as I watch you, and you add some of your own taste, and that's a story, *bwana*. How can it be given to you, eh? Now, how is that your story bwana . . . argh.'

He left, and they paused for a minute before exploding into chatter about the film. They all got home really late that night and a few of them got beatings.

The next day Mwananchi bounced back. He told them about the rocket launch at Patel Brotherhood Hall in Nairobi, the rocket that was being powered by curry powder and *njahi* bean farts. This didn't capture their interest at first. Then he drew the characters. The Space Ahoi, he called them. Who are Ahoi, he was asked? Ai! Don't you know – the warriors of the new frontier: Matatu touts, the Mau Mau, Rastas. All those hungry, angry people. They are being taken by the Patel Brotherhood to farm tomatoes on a new planet called M'babylon. Ahoi!

Ahoi!

They all laughed.

Mwananchi made them lie down on the asphalt, and look up at the stars. Then he told them about the interstellar football matches that God plays with his angels. Against the red devils. His God had dreadlocks, and listened to Bob Marley music. Some of the kids looked at each other. One or two slipped away after hearing this blasphemy.

The red devils liked Jim Reeves and Skeeter Davis. He told them how the crew of the curry-powder-powered ship had seen this football match. One of them, Sarit Patel, drew the lines from star to star, following some hidden message in his mind – and the football match lit up for the whole ship. Mwananchi imitated Leonard Mambo Mbotela's football commentary

'Star people! *Na mpria*, Star Defender – *anachenga*, star striker, staar ... GOOOOOOAAAAL!'

Then people went off to boarding school and started thinking about sex and Michael Jackson, and keeping their curls wet, and those streetlamp sessions became uncool. Everybody migrated to the Saturday holiday fashion show by the supermarket, where boys stood at one corner pretending not to see the girls, and girls walked in giggling groups pretending to buy sugar. Sometimes they bumped into Mwananchi at his joint – talking to younger kids, but after a while he disappeared.

He was remembered in odd ways, though, over the years.

Maillu, one regular but shy member of his audience, found that the flavour of Mwananchi's wit had touched him; and sitting in the student's bar at the University, years later, he only needed to think of those carefree nights by the lamppost to lose his stutter and make people around him laugh. Some forgot Mwananchi, but the magic stayed in them in nameless ways.

Two people remembered him in literary ways. One, Njoki, in a great haste to submit oral literature stories for her sixth-form project, wrote five of his stories from memory, in *sheng*, translated them into 'posh English' and submitted them. Her teacher tore them up in horror and threw them into the bin, where cigarette butts, chewing gum and dirty magazines went.

'Dat is not oral litera-chuwa. Read Okot P'Bitek! Oh where

are ta rappits and ta hyenas, and ta grandmatter's knee? Eh! Did you go and listen to your grantmatter in ta village? When I was in Makerere University . . .'

She went to Kenyatta University library, copied stories from oral liter-chuwa books, changed them a little and got an A in litera-chuwa. She now lectures in literary criticism. Her paper, 'The Role of the Rabbit in African Mythology', was a hit at the Bonn Symposium.

Mwangi was a man desperate to be interesting, but the place in his mind where charm resides was full of cotton wool. Mwangi burned with passion for Mwananchi's words. He started his literary career listening to Mwananchi's stories, then read storybooks, and novels – not so much finding laid-back pleasure, or empathy, or validation even. He looked for ways to break them down, to understand.

Why? – Why does this work, and that doesn't? After many years, he got his PhD in litera-chuwa somewhere really prestigious in the UK. Then he wrote his novel, a beautiful thing, like stained glass: shining with prose so stark it seemed naked; some characters were gritty, some were magical, but real; some deconstructed; some stood in existentialist angst – others spoke in decolonized English. Oh! The publishers went bananas, a Kenyan voice at last! Many bought the book, which sat next to the set of *Encyclopedia Britannica*, a trophy. Students of literature around the world pounced upon it, and libraries groaned with the weight of literary papers. The plot coiled and struck like a snake in places; then balmed like a mother's kiss; then built coils in the stomach – then uncoiled them – all this by page ten. From page eleven, to prove he wasn't just after giving mindless entertainment, the plot deconstructed, and the next fifty pages were one vast and profound interior monologue.

And the prizes! Li-terah-ry this, and Li-te-rah-chuwa that! Writah's this! Ai! It was all so exciting that nobody asked if anybody's belly caught fire when they read the book. Or if anybody read it and cried in themselves, saying, 'Oh, but that's me, he's just spoken my soul!'

His grammar! Oooh! Irritated by contradicting rules and defunct spellings and neo-colonial biases, Mwangi re-invented grammar, made it efficient, polished it, and it stood like clean bones in the bundu: a new set book for the world. Some schools in Scotland and Ireland, looking for an English they could make theirs, chose his grammar as their standard. The African Union unanimously passed the proposal to set up a committee to investigate the committee they had set up in London to investigate the subcommittee charged with decolonization of Language. Twelve EU committees met around the same subject and declared that, for purposes of harmonious paperwork, they would adopt Mwangics as the new English.

The Mwangics campaign had adverts running around the world saying, 'We have had enaff!'

The euphoria faded after a while. Mwangi took off to promote his book in America. Kenyans abroad stood straighter with their African compatriots. 'Have you read Mwangi?' they would ask some Nigerian or Zimbabwean. In Kenya, people with guests from abroad finally stopped giving their foreign guests Karen Blixen to read. Our Voice, they would think, as the guests would unwrap the gift and smiled with pleasure and said, awed, 'He's Kenyan? I thought he was from South Africa!'

For years, it was:

Mwangi says.

According to Mwangi.

In Mwangi's opinion.

By this time, maybe about twenty-five people around the world had read Mwangi. The rest feasted on the many guidebooks there were, memorizing the synopses. In fact, some of the guidebooks became set books.

Only one person was brave enough to say something against Mwangi, a well-known journalist, famous for his boozy ways and unapologetic opinions. He said, 'Arh! They say Kenyans don't read! Well, I say Kenyans don't read because all the great stories are not in books. Great stories sit in bars and burp and come out after a few brown ones. Mwangi will sell books because big books fill bookshelves, but who wants to take it out? The bookshelf will collapse if you take that book out.

He suggested that the English Kenyans spoke in bars become the standard. *Mwang – hics*, he called it.

The year 2000 was a wistful year for many in Kenya. Things were bad: roads falling apart; no money; retrenchments – AIDS everywhere, beer expensive, school fees consuming everybody's entire salary. Being born again started to be flashy, churches demanding this and that – they called them 'lurve gifts'. So many people sat at home, and held their children close, and reminisced. They started to phone friends they hadn't seen in years, seeking validation, wanting a connection to freer days. And so the question was being asked, 'But what happened to Mwananchi?'

– Oh he went to Bulgaria, he is a doctor . . .

– Ai! Didn't you hear! AIDS!

– Apana! Can you believe – he is a receptionist at the *Weekend* newspaper. He failed form four – got a third class coz he failed English.

– Nooo – he is married in Ukambani. Was he a Kamba?

– Ai? What tribe was he?

The rumours failed to endure. People were surprised to find that he had vanished without trace.

People who knew him started to ask in bars and churches and at the many funerals. It became clear that nobody really knew where he lived, or who his parents were, or even his surname. Some now started to think, 'Ai! Was he ever there?'

Maillu came closest to Mwananchi's legacy. When he was promoted, he became the director of school sports in his province. Travelling to sports events around the country, he started to hear this song all the schoolkids sang while cheering their team: 'Mama Milka'. It would always leave him in tears, and he remembered how Mwananchi came up with that song one day, and how people would add rhyming couplets to it. He remembered how they would always celebrate the beginning of school holidays with new additions to the song. It was a song with a bit of everything, a bit of every language the kids spoke, a bit of what films they watched, what comics they read, what new football slang had arrived from the surburb of Eastlands – the place where all slang came from. Then, a few years later, listening to this new Nairobi FM station, he heard a group of strange young youths, Warufagaa, singing the latest hit: 'Mama Milka'. It was the first time a Kenyan song was ahead of the American crooners in the Kenyan charts.

Some of the old gang, frustrated that Mwananchi had left no memory of himself, wished they had kept his corduroy jacket; or taped him, just to hear that voice. Some said, 'Argh! Why didn't he write the stories?'

Some wondered whether his stories would be as magical now, but found they couldn't remember a single story, just odd words like *Pingiling*, followed by a happy warm feeling in their stomachs.

Achieng met Njoki at a wedding one day and asked her, 'Do you remember that day, after watching *Star Wars*, when Mwananchi told us about those curry-powder spaceships.'

Njoki looked at her in surprise, 'Are you still thinking about that clown? Ai! But you! There was nowhere he was going, you know. His was so gender-biased and he was always affirming Eurocentric values! What happened to African culture?'

It was at this wedding that I met and fell in love with Achieng.

And it seemed that, as Mwananchi faded, things in many people's memories began to lose reality too. They started to ask themselves those questions that libraries don't have answers for; those questions that seem meaningless and whose answers are simply a validation that they lived, and that it mattered.

– But did the old Big G chewing gum really taste like that?

– Do you remember that ka-time so-and-so's parents came back from Shags early? He! The party!

– And the rocket that was fuelled by curry powder?

– Was there really a tree full of caterpillars at Jane Rono's house?

– What did we taste like?

Some resigned themselves and bought small plots of land in their parents' home villages. Like their parents, they started to pretend to be farmers; like their parents, they pretended confusion about things national and retreated to a tribal space. Every weekend they would head off to the village to pretend to enjoy themselves, while their children met at lamp posts and listened to 'Mama Milka' on Kiss FM.

So one day, in Westlands, Mwangi bumped into an old Booroo

neighbour as he was heading for his weekly interview with the BBC *Mwangics* show. Achieng was in a terrible mood for no particular reason, just feeling rudderless, and she asked him brashly, 'Have you ever wondered what things would have been like if Mwananchi had written down his stories and sent them to a publisher?'

Mwangi laughed and laughed and laughed, 'Ai! Are you crazy? He couldn't put together a sentence in English that guy! They would have just stamped it "sub-standard". Publishers are looking for litera-chuwa you know. Such a book would never be on any reading list that matters!'

Achieng snapped back at him, 'How is it, that among those of us who knew him, he matters so much more than you do?'

At that very moment, a waiter at a nearby cafe tripped, and his entire tray dropped on the floor. *Pingiling*!

Achieng laughed.

Glossary

Chuba Na Ndebe – tin and bottle man who used to wander around housing estates buying up tins and bottles. Parents used to scare children by saying that they would become a *chuba na ndebe* if they didn't work hard in school

Kivunja Mbavu – popular Kenyan television comedy in the Seventies

Mandazi – a deep-fried cake popular all over Kenya

Maneno – literally means 'words', used figuratively to mean 'make noise'

Muguu Wazi – open legs

Mwananchi – child of the nation, citizen

Sheng – a Nairobi version of Swahili that changes very often, picking up phrases from English and other Kenyan languages

Julia Brosnan

Give Him My Love

[novel extract]

I am in intensive care. It is a fish tank. White slithers of uniform bob and swish through the murky half light. They dart and glide past me, batting their tails between beds, bringing their faces up to mine, eyes and noses magnified to underwater strength.

It is silent apart from the hum of the monitors and universal intake of breath. All of us here are attuned to the massive hoovering up of oxygen and then the long, slow exhalations of the life-support machine.

Half-past midnight. The nurse brings me another sweet milky tea. I'm so glad I pretended to take sugar, I need that bite, that hot metallic rush, to stop me flagging. Later on I feel I've drunk so much it's risen to my head. It swishes around behind my nose, soon to lap against the backs of my eye sockets, obscuring my vision. *My vision*. Must keep awake and on the lookout, eyes peeled and skinned – for I am now on duty.

Underwater. Plucked from normal life and planted into this deep night, you feel the change. Dim pools of light and dimmer, deeper pools of black vibrate in waves in tune with the machine – that drone, that oceanic echo – it is the pulse of this damp world. *Amphibious*. You soon adapt. Here on the edge of life the night is of a different order, no daily comforts, not even any life supports for we who sit and wait.

Sick. The stench of dying skin cemented deep into these walls, lined as they are with wizened bodies, bald and rasping, flat and sucked, lost and eaten out by the mad beetle of their disease. *Sick*. Big sister at her brother's bedside. Looking out for him, just like I used to. Now here we are again, the two of us, waiting here for mother.

Will he make it? Or will he be a naughty boy and sneak away before she comes? No one knows. And as my sibling (unmoved and unmoving, unspoken and unspeakable) is pumped and flushed beside me, the only thing that I can do is sit and watch. Do my duty, keep this deathwatch, be his sister on this night.

*

'Doesn't he look well?'

She realizes as soon as it's out – not the most fitting thing to say about someone who hasn't moved since it happened, all wired up and nowhere to go. Her face is apologetic, but I don't mind. After a night shivering in the chill waters of this place I'm just so pleased to see her. Cousin Pauline got here bright and early and she's right – those rosy cheeks, these plumped-out limbs, that hearty thumping chest. Why, my brother Joe looks better than he has for years.

'I think it's the machine,' I whisper, 'it's filling him with extra oxygen and – ' I look doubtfully at the various tubes coming out of his limbs and stomach – 'maybe blood or something.' I've had so much medical information thrown at me in the past twelve hours I've lost track.

'Of course,' she says. 'Sorry, sweetheart. I just remember how he was.' An injection of silence as we contemplate that memory. It tips us off into another stretch of blushed embarrassment.

'Come on.' Briskly she resumes herself. She has come to keep us upright, even in this uncharted place. 'Let's get you some air.'

*

Outside the hospital, back on dry land, it's not the same. Sunshine usually lifts me up, but this morning's brilliant rays serve only to highlight a world which is bigger and louder than it should be. It comes at me fast and hard – flashing and scaring, honking and shoving. Granted it's the middle of London, but I've never known it like this before, not this circus of unhinged assault.

Walking past a small supermarket unloading crates of food, we are met by a wall of dough. Risen yeast, newborn bread, that warmly ovened breakfast smell enfolds me like a blanket. Then *whoosh*! it's up my nose, through my head and *bang*! it kicks down a private door inside my brain – and *dearie me* – it unleashes the most terrible thought: my brother Joe may never smell a morning roll again. That freshly baked aroma has told me more than all the underwater medics at my ear: he may not wake, he may not rise again. How it hits me. Out here amongst the cakes and loaves – a pressure round the head, a tightening in the throat, a loss within the knees and now – a tugging at my arm.

'Laurie, love, are you OK?' It's Pauline. She's got my hand.

Staring straight ahead, I nod. Something tells me that this is but the first. For years to come: a tube, a lift, alone at night – it visits me again – that this is it. It's gone for good. All gone.

My cousin leads me. Although we're on dry land, I find it hard to balance.

At a pavement cafe we get some coffee. Quite civilized – the two of us in the centre of town, nice day. We could be friends meeting for a chat before work.

'You're right about the way he looks.' My voice comes from too far inside my head. 'It's sick.' The couple at the next table look over.

Oh dear. I seem to have spoilt the friendly exchange.

'It's like you said, Laurie – the machine doing its work.'

'It makes him look OK, but we don't know how he really is. And I . . . I would. I'd rather know.'

I look into my cup, try and focus on the rim. These are the first tears since I got the news. It must be Pauline, she's so kind she's loosened the knot I tied round myself, the one designed to keep it all together. And hey – what's all this about the truth? *I'd rather know.* Do me a favour. No I wouldn't, of course not.

'Laurie, sweetheart, what've they told you?'

Later I realize she doesn't ask in order to get information, she's already had a long chat with the doctor. She's checking to see how much I've taken in.

'Well, the main thing today is the tests, on the brain and heart and that – to see how he's functioning.'

She nods. Then I remember she did A level biology, which is considerably more than me, who until recently thought you could examine your lungs by looking down your throat. I didn't like to ask the medical staff, but something's been troubling me.

'Pauline – is Joe, is he – in a coma?'

I look over and a magnificent explosion of sun sparkles behind her head. It lights up a fine brush of facial hair above her lip and over her cheeks, giving her a vulnerability, a kind of gleaming innocence, which is so acutely endearing that it catches me like a thin spear in the chest. Here is Pauline, my wise older cousin: she sorted out her children and job to travel across town at the crack of dawn, to be here when we need her most, to freely give of herself even as the sun spotlights her downy moustache, even as she guides me through this day. As the spear twists a little deeper, I see she's heard my question, taken it in. Pained concern streaks across her face, she gathers it back in an instant.

'Yes, darling, he is.'

'Oh, right.' More welling up into my coffee cup. 'I mean I thought he was, you know, but no one actually said the word so . . .'

'Look, I've got to go home for an hour or two. Why don't you come with me till your mum gets here? Have a rest and a bath. You've been up all night, you're exhausted.'

'Oh no, I can't leave.' I stand too fast, knock back my chair. The couple look round again, they shift slightly. 'I can't leave him, not now.'

Of course not. Why, even at this minute he may be calling for us, sitting up and asking for a cup of tea – or, knowing Joe – a fag. And me out here in the sun, whatever was I thinking of?

Quick. Back to the bedside. This time it's me who leads.

*

My mum. I'd rather not think about it, but Pauline's right. She's coming here today, to this hospital, by this bed. The call came yesterday afternoon. It was Bridie, a neighbour. Naturally I thought it was about my mum – seventy years old with a bad leg, already had one stroke . . . *blah blah blah* goes Bridie, yakking ten to the dozen. When she's off like that her accent is so thick I can barely understand a word . . . *that intensive ward* . . . she says . . . *clean collapsed in a park*.

'In a park?' Sounds a bit unlikely.

'Yes, lovie, yes yes. Out there with some friends they say, even playing football.'

'My mum was playing football?'

'Not your mam, lovie. Your brother, your brother Joe.'

I got a weird kind of thumping at the back of my head when I thought it was my mum, now it's my brother it's started up in the front as well. What with the noise and Bridie's accent, I can hardly hear a thing.

'Can I speak to her?' I shout.

'No, lovie, not now. She's in bed. The doctor's after giving her something. When she got the news you see, she clean passed out as well.'

Bang bang bang. It's coming at me from all sides now, but I've got to keep upright. If I collapse that'll be the whole family gone.

Pauline heard first. Joe was due to stay with her in London and the ambulance crew found her number in his pocket. She phoned my mum, then me, but I was out. At a park strangely enough, but I was OK. I came back.

It was Sunday and transport was bad. I was in Manchester and had an hour to catch the last train. But there's nothing from my mum's place in Ireland, no flights, not even if she could manage to get out of bed and to the airport. She came round from the sedative at about eight in the evening. I called her when the train was at Stoke.

'How is he?' She sounds very tiny, very far away.

'I'm not there yet, Mum. But he was still unconscious when— He hasn't woken up.'

'Give him my love.'

It goes on like this. I get to the hospital at ten-thirty. I call her at eleven.

'How is he?'

'I'm afraid he's still unconscious. He's on a life-support machine.'

'Tell him I'll be there tomorrow. I'm getting the first flight out. Give him my love.'

In the morning, just before Pauline comes, I phone again.

'How does he seem to you?'

'It's hard to say, Mum, he's still on the machine.'

'Tell him I'm bringing clean jeans and that CD thing he straps on his head.' Once more she tells me to give him her love.

*

Today. Today is the day after the night before, the Monday after the Sunday. Yesterday he took it, today we get the results. A bit like an exam, especially with mother coming for the ceremony.

As the morning progresses it becomes clear – Dr this and Mr that will visit the bed. By their plugs and clamps they will be known and by their wires and lights they will know: whether the machine stays on or off. No long-drawn-out dramas, this case can be wrapped up in a single day. *Four o'clock.* The time of the last test. That's when the cousins (all five of them came back with Pauline) crowd into the tiny consulting room with me for the verdict. The final test, for brain-stem activity, is the most important. I can tell that Pauline, she of the crucial A level, understands. Why, even I cotton on – because frankly, when it comes to the brain stem, if you haven't got any you may as well forget it.

It's fitting that he's the tallest, the bloke who does the final bit. After all, he's the most important, speaks the plummiest, carries the shiniest case and has the most letters after his name. A specialist, a man of significance, a man of some extent. *Four o'clock.* Today everything until that time is temporary – kind words from nurses, a moment in the loo to clean my teeth, even tight hugs from the cousins – all fleeting, a distraction, the merest puff of a dandelion until this point. This awful tunnel of today, which leads to this.

And yet. There's more. *My mum.* She got an early flight from her small town to Dublin and now she's at the airport waiting for a standby. She sits by the check-in desk, fearful, paralysed and steadfast until she gets a place. Today, amongst strangers, my mother is alone.

Six-thirty. Her ETA as Joe would say, Estimated Time of Arrival. He loves that stuff, mad abbreviations, even makes them up, along with the character Mr Abbreviate (Mr Abbreve), like something out of *Viz*.

Joe. I haven't taken it in myself yet. It's not even twenty-four hours and that's nothing for unconsciousness. It's only one day, which is like two nights, which is really just a long sleep. But six-thirty. *My mum.* An awful churning in my stomach tells me we are spinning further, more uncharted still. No guides, no safety barriers with her. No boundary lines, nothing to hold on to in that place.

*

'Do you talk to him?'

Still morning, we're back from the cafe, back at the bedside. Pauline has her hand on his.

'Oh yes,' I say firmly. 'Of course.'

She stays an hour then whispers, 'I'm off now, Laurie. Back at lunchtime.' Then she's at his ear:

'Bye-bye, Joe darling. See you later, sweetheart.'

And we're alone again.

Simple. Talking to people in a coma is simple. Even before I knew it was a coma (which tells me *I* must be simple. There he was, out for the count and barely functioning. How could that not be a coma? But when no one says the word it's easy not to hear) it was simple. Everybody's seen it – in films, TV dramas, soap operas – all you do is talk. But I didn't. I had nothing to say.

Then again I had plenty. I had hours, weeks and years of it. For instance: why have you done this, how could you, what are you doing and why – *why are you doing this to me?* Much later, when the fog of panic comes to me again within my lonely room, I curse him, the curse bestowed on all dead siblings some day or another. The legacy they leave us – we poor bastards stranded here on earth – we now have a duty to stick around and sweat it out. They who go first have stolen our escape route. How can any of us die now? Imagine the accusations (*how could she do this to her mother?*), imagine the scandal (*two in one family!*). Why, we'd never live it down.

Last night alone with him – it was ergonomic. That's how it started. The nurse sits me by the bed and when she leaves I find I can't reach. The bed seems cranked up, much too high; to get anywhere near his head I'd have to arch up and stretch over like a gymnast or crawl onto the bed and crouch like a cat. His ear's too far away for private conversation, I'll have to make a public speech. To get me in the mood I try to take hold – but his hands are guarded by the clips and lights strapped to his fingers; his arms are protected by the needles and bags sewn into his skin; his stomach and head are a forest of bottles, syringes and large pink curlers. *Surrounded.* I try and move my chair nearer, but something flashes and I'm frightened of pulling a wire out of the board beside me. He's plugged into what looks like an old-fashioned telephone exchange – but it doesn't work. *I can't get through.* Another trick from another machine. *I don't know your number.* Lies again, all lies.

I am ashamed.

No words come. Nothing like TV. No contact, nothing natural, not like Pauline's loving touch and whisper. At some point early in the afternoon she's back to do another check. She's very careful with me. 'Have you prepared yourself, Laurie? You know what the news might be – that we might, you might ... lose him?'

It could be the first time anyone's said it as directly as that, after all it's a bit early. Only two o'clock – still a couple of hours of tests to go. I mean *hang on*, Pauline, two hours, anything could happen. An hour and a half and he could be playing football again. I mean *hang on*. Look at him, great blooming lad, he's only thirty.

But. Yes, I am prepared and suddenly I feel very old and wise, wiser than even her. 'It's OK, Pauline, it's not the first time. We lost him years ago.'

Five years, to be exact. That Easter when I got the call, my dad this time, sounding like a policeman. *We've identified the problem* (Joe's blanking off and nodding out, money missing, jobs lost and all those unaccounted visits to the park): *apparently it's drugs.*

'What drugs?' It can't be much, not little Joey, not my baby brother.

He clears his throat, a pause. 'Heroin,' he says.

Bizarre and out of sync on my father's lips, as if he'd uttered some freakish sexual demand. *Heroin.* But that's the fact. No other way to say it apart from speak the word. And even worse: *injecting.* Skewering himself open and pouring it in. Years later, on that long night of waiting, the nurse offered to show me. *Tsk tsk*, she goes as she changes some bottle or other, *all over his groin.* The only veins left apparently, he'd knackered all the others. *A right pincushion*, she says. *Punctured like an old balloon. Look here.* But I decline.

Of course later – maybe two years after my dad told me, when Joe and I are in a phone box at King's Cross, just thrown out of his flat by the police, trying to persuade one of the few treatment centres he hasn't been through to take him on – I discover heroin isn't the half of it. My brother? He could've been a pharmacist, could've had a great career if he'd channelled his chemical fascination into a course of study rather than his own bloodstream. In this phone box, when asked what he'd been taking, the list was incredible – all Latin names, all precise dosages, all fifty-six of them. I was almost impressed.

So many calls like that – more visits from the police, rehab appointments made, rehab appointments missed, pleas, lies, arguments, emergency trips, tears, more lies, falling out with my mum and dad, them falling out with each other, then he's clean, then he's not, then my dad dies – never understanding, nothing sorted out. Joe called himself a junkie and those five years were classic junkie territory. I thought us knowing would make a difference, but he simply welcomed us aboard and together we lurched from one spectacularly inane yet potentially terrifying event to another, all sucked into the whirlpool of his need. Of course, people do come off and get clean, but there was something in Joe, the way that he just took it all, and more. At the funeral my auntie cried: *Oh if we could've done this or that, he'd still be here.* But I said the opposite. I said, *It's amazing that boy lasted so long. He should've been dead years ago.*

That was when I was bereaved. I didn't recognize it at the time, but I experienced all the main symptoms: saw him walking towards me in the street (he lived two hundred miles away); dreamed he was dead; dreamed he was alive – the bright young kid he used to be with tennis racket and football kit; heard his voice call my name; saw his face on TV. Strange, because occasionally he did actually walk towards me and call my name. He liked a joke, liked his music, liked that pop group Half Man Half Biscuit. And in those years he turned – Half Dead Half Not. Hard to tell which half because often it seemed like he was wrapped in a duvet – some sort of covering, a protection, deadened by a thick layer of polyester togs. Not so different from being in a coma, all wired up in intensive care.

One day not long after my dad's call I went to Joe's flat and (this was when I still had the power) made a speech. Sentimental perhaps, but my heart welled up to help him. It wasn't easy: a painful recollection of key childhood events and a humble acceptance of personal blame rounded off with a steadfast declaration of love and support. When it was over I turned – eyes shining, hands trembling – to embrace my refound soul-sibling, and there he was: eyes closed and mouth open, drifted off ('nodded out' is the technical term) into his private junkie fog. He hadn't heard a word.

It's hard to have a relationship with someone who always has a prior engagement with a drug, and in those five years he stretched my love so far it left me speechless. Those years wiped the memories of how he used to be – sunny, funny, smooth and sporty. That last night beside his bed I couldn't conjure up anything more than how he grew – bitter, crying, trying, falling, needing – not us, but the fortress of his duvet. A grey, unwieldy, leaking boy. Pauline was right. That life-support machine did wonders for his appearance, somebody somewhere could make a fortune. *A necromantics of cosmetics*. A final ghastly makeover.

*

Four o'clock. We hold hands in the tiny room. Not the specialist of course, not that extended gent, just us – the cousins. Holding each other as we hear the news.

*

When my mother comes she looks wild. Rushes up the stairs, doesn't use her stick for support, but waves and points it, abstract rowing through the air. *Make way*. An oar to move her faster.

Her hair racked with wind, her eyes splashing oceans, her soul stoked with fire – my elemental mother crashes into this dead ward so full of anguish, so seeped in waiting. She whom I cannot bear to see.

'Where is he then? Where is my boy?'

I usher her into the tiny room (*Ouch! Don't take her arm, she won't be pulled, not touched like that by me*), thinking it'd be best if we talk with the long man first. He speaks. Pauline and I on either side of her, she with a drink, I with tissues. He speaks. The mother asks, 'So – can I see him now?'

He lies, his rosy cheeks, his beating chest. It lies. This machine is working overtime. *We left it on*, a mermaid tells me. *So mum can say goodbye.* Off she glides, that angel fish, and down we splash, my mum and me. Inside the tank once more, the night has crept up fast today. Beside this underwater bed we try to breathe.

'What time?' she asks. So vague, so lost. And yet. She manages to hold his hand, to kiss his head, to brush his cheek, to touch and whisper all that I could not.

'Four.' I feel the waters close above us. 'Four o'clock.'

'Oh no.' She turns, now sharp and clear. 'My plane got in at five, it can't be four at all.'

'I thought you meant what time – when they pronounced him dead.'

All that training. You'd think they might let them in on a few key words, just plain and simple, cut the fancy membrane this and cerebral that. 'Coma' would've been a start. And 'dead' – that would've saved all this. Why in that tiny room today the only way I knew was when a voice yelled: Is he dead or what? And round they turned, all eyes on me. It seems the voice was mine.

Ironic. He was clean for months, the longest yet. So clean it only took a tiny dose to stop his heart. A lie. How we pretend that he was playing football in that park. More lies: that Great Machine of Grace. Joe could've been (says Mr Abbreve) a case of DOA. A lump of metal, nothing more, that source of life. All gone you see. A shell, all dead. Dead on Arrival.

She blinks. There is a moment when she looks at me and I

can see – she had not heard. Not on the phone, not the specialist and his results, not gathered from the signs and clues, not until I speak it (but then – when no one says the word it's so very easy not to hear). *She blinks.* There is a stretching free fall, horror moment. It's me. I broke the news, I am the messenger.

She wails. A dangerous electric cry and we've arrived: that lawless, boundless place is here. Unfettered anguish, the keening of a thousand mothers howls inside this murky tank. The news has whipped her heart. So private even I'm intruding; so close that even I'm outside. *No! Don't take her arm, don't go too near, she won't be touched like that by me.*

Within that cry I hear the awful years of nights to come. I hear the panic we both come to feel (choking on the Underground, trapped inside a lift or our own heads. It suffocates, the ache of his demise), and I know – the lines are drawn. Our geometry has shifted to create a new equation: just me and her, forever bound by this. But listen. What all of us with dead siblings understand – you cannot hear your mother keen like this and fail to know the deathwatch truth – how long before she says it, finds the voice I lacked to ask: Why him, not you?

*

When they finally switched my brother off he crumpled like a paper bag. His breath, his blood, his heat, his heart all gone. Began to wither into dust and so confirmed the tidal wave of his mum's grief.

Joe. My brother Joe, the junkie. He liked his music and he liked a joke. And here he lies: Half Man Half Bag. He had become a biscuit of himself, a crumb.

Tim Liardet

Madame Sasoo Goes Bathing

Madame Sasoo, sombre, but determined
to overcome her nibbling inhibitions
and have the warm Indian Ocean lick
at will about her body, does not undress, but
    dresses up

from ankle to neck in brightly figured rayon
and wears her manly shoes to wade
from shore of drums into the tilt of water
with elbows aloft, all her attention below:

she is not young, but bears herself
with subtle dignity, though her costume clings,
    grows fat,
as the weight of water starts to rock
against her, and bullies her from left

to right, so she is like a high-wire walker
riding out the admonishments
of the deluge, with grim composure,
holding that perfect damask mark

in the middle of her forehead level
over the waves. At which stage, her doubts
regroup and call her back to the shore
where her towels, and Seiko, are safe

but every article of her nakedness
she wished the water could explore
and taste like expert tongues has been
stolen long before she dared to wade.

Chickens in Chinatown

Are free to range
the square inch apiece they have got
of the cage's slave-hold in which to crouch
half in sleep, half in wakefulness,
stuffed in to take the press of wire and be baked
closer and closer to suffocation
by the overhead sun of Port Louis.

Until the smoking street-seller hoicks
out four and hands them over
tied together at the feet
like a bundle of old bags
stretched out of shape by a few pounds of breast
    meat,
weighted by heads
which knock together like pool balls in a sock
though organic, sparse of feather;
a nosegay, swung from the fist:
an udder no longer producing milk.
At which stage their eyes
are wide open enough – upside down –
to hold a vision of Chinatown in the wide-angle lens:

all those loiterers balancing there,
the smoke from their mouths trickling downwards,
    not up.

The burnt-out casino, whose giant dice
punctured with holes show straight through
to the other side of luck,
a machine with nothing inside it.

The spilt paint, on the pavement,
shortly to dry as it was slewed:

from it – red footprints walking forwards,
red footprints walking backwards.

Gideon Haigh

C.L.R. James

In Ian Buruma's 1991 novel *Playing the Game*, the narrator makes a pilgrimage to a distinguished nonagenarian critic cum cricket writer from Trinidad. K. C. Lewis, now almost blind in his south London retreat, is nonetheless surrounded by books: European history, Third World politics, Renaissance art, English literature. The collected Marx makes up one pile; a yellow column of *Wisden Cricketers' Almanack* makes up another. In Lewis's intellectual panorama, delineated in 'the cultivated accent of an English gentleman', Marx, Lenin, Shakespeare, Milton and W. G. Grace are effortlessly elided. 'Do you know as a young man I read *Vanity Fair* at least twenty times?' he asks. 'Cricket, history and literature were part of the same thing to me.'

The dramatis personae of V. S. Naipaul's *A Way in the World*, published two years later, features the West Indian Lebrun – an 'impresario of revolution', who becomes the toast of literary and political salons. 'It was rhetoric, of course,' observes the narrator. 'And of course, it was loaded in his favour. He couldn't be interrupted, like royalty, he raised all the topics, and he would have been a master of all the topics he raised.' Lebrun is, it emerges, a figure of division in the Caribbean: highly influential, utterly untrusted, with 'no popular following', but capable of manipulating the mighty with 'big technical-sounding words'. A politician, discovering Lebrun's seditious streak, remarks ruefully, 'The man want to take you over.'

It will come as no surprise that both Lewis and Lebrun are thinly veiled representations of real people – they are almost too vivid to be otherwise. But the trick of Buruma's Trinidadian Tiresias and Naipaul's Caribbean Cassius is that they share common ancestry: both were based on the West Indian, C. L. R. James. His is a unique reputation. Cricket lovers who celebrate his masterpiece *Beyond a Boundary* – which Warren Susman has called 'the most important sports book of our time' – usually have little sense of the protean political ponderings of which James's work is largely composed. Marxists and black studies scholars saluting him as an anti-colonialist avatar – Edward Said has honoured James as 'the father of West Indian writing' – have generally found *Beyond a Boundary* obscure, even unintelligible. In my well-thumbed 1983 edition, published in New York, four prefatory pages purport to describe cricket for Americans; they evoke C. P. Snow's remark that, compared with explaining cricket to a foreigner, Chomsky's generational grammar is a snap. Few other thinkers can have cultivated such discrete constituencies; it is as though F. A. Hayek also wrote the definitive masterpiece about fly-fishing.

Because it is such a personal book, tracing the ideation of *Beyond a Boundary* requires some conversance with the details of James's life, in particular his education as a scholarship boy at Port-of-Spain's Queen's Royal College between 1910 and 1918. QRC drew on the English public school tradition embodied in Thomas Arnold's Rugby, whose ur-text is Thomas Hughes's *Tom Brown's Schooldays*. It was soaked in the ethos of fair play, restraint, perseverance, responsibility and 'the old school tie'. Oxbridge-educated masters taught classics and history in English and European traditions. This educational and ethical conditioning 'never left me', James said, fostering abiding loves of cricket and literature. W. G. Grace's statistics and Shakespeare's sonnets did not compete for his attention; both were learned like passages of scripture. To everything he did, James brought a bookish intensity. According to biographer Paul Buhle, sixteen-year-old James responded to losing his virginity by reading all six volumes of Havelock Ellis's *The Psychology of Sex*.

In a letter to Felice Bauer, his confidante and correspondent, Kafka once disavowed 'literary interest', describing himself instead as 'made of literature'. The phrase also suits James. The first signs he exhibited of political conscience are the short stories of his mid-twenties, examples of the Caribbean literary sub-genre called 'barrackyard fiction' (essentially, stories featuring working-class or ghetto characters). The inspiration was, however, anything but indigenous. James's characters could just as easily have been the drifters and lowlifers populating the stories of O. Henry, and his influences were the likes of Kipling and de Maupassant. Political causes attracted him; James gradually became enamoured of the Trinidad Workingmen's Association, a group of militant returned servicemen making their presence felt in island politics, and impressed by their charismatic nationalist leader Captain Arthur Cipriani, who sought inter alia a minimum wage and an end to child labour. But it was his literary ambitions rather than his political consciousness that motivated James's pilgrimage to London in March 1932.

James arrived with three objectives: to publish his first novel; to ghostwrite the autobiography of the great West Indian cricketer, Learie Constantine, an old friend then playing league cricket in the Lancashire textile town of Nelson; and to complete an admiring study of Cipriani. The last and least likely actually came first: Constantine generously underwrote a small printing of *The Life of Captain Cipriani* in September 1932, which led to an English edition, *The Case for West Indian Self-Government*, in April 1933. And the relationship between Constantine and James was unusual. It was actually not the intellectual wakening the athlete to issues of race; rather it was James, who, at least at first, often found Constantine 'unduly coloured by national and racial considerations'. Nor was it James who brought radical politics to Nelson; rather was it Nelson, a stronghold of the socialist Independent Labour Party, which first exposed James to shafts of Marxist thought. Recently disaffiliated from the Labour Party, the ILP was in the vanguard of strike action by weavers in Nelson in August and September 1932, which James watched with dawning appreciation: in the dawn of the United Front, the Left Book Club, *The Road to Wigan Pier*, the Worker's Party of Marxist Unification (POUM) and the International Brigades, to be of the left was sheer heaven. Inspired, James veered into Trotskyism. The exiled Trotsky was then a pin-up of the liberal intelligentsia – his unsuccessful application for asylum in Britain had been supported by George Bernard Shaw, J. M. Keynes and H. G. Wells – and James devoured Trotsky's *History of the Russian Revolution* long before troubling to delve into Marx, relying in political debates on what his biographer Farrukh Dhondy calls 'intelligent bluff'. In retrospect, in fact, one sometimes wonders how deep James's political convictions *were*, at least initially, and whether their adoption was not actually part of his acculturation, an act of intellectual mimicry, like his assimilation of the ethos of fair play. Publisher Fredric Warburg observed in his autobiography, *An Occupation for Gentlemen*, that, far from affecting Orwell-like austerity, James 'enjoyed the fleshpots of capitalism, fine cooking, fine clothes, furniture, and beautiful women, without a trace of the guilty remorse to be expected from a seasoned warrior of the class war'. Like St Augustine, perhaps, James sought chastity and continence – but not yet.

All the same, James prospered between March 1932 and November 1938, the breadth of his output being as impressive as its volume. His original ambitions were all fulfilled. James's rendering of *Cricket and I* by Learie Constantine, though basic in its intent and sometimes breezy in its inaccuracy, was something of a landmark; as James commented, it represented 'the first book ever published in England by a world-famous West Indian writing as a West Indian about events in the West Indies'. *Minty Alley* then became the first novel by a West Indian published in the UK, and *Toussaint L'Ouverture* the first play by a West Indian to reach an English audience. But it was the historical events that inspired the latter which precipitated James's most original work: *The Black Jacobins*, a history of the slave revolt in the French colony of San Domingo, which began in August 1791, and the twelve-year struggle to establish the state of Haiti, which James perceived as the hinge event in West Indian history.

Linking the slaves of San Domingo with the *sans-culottes* of Paris, James began a longer-term project to align the struggles of black and colonial peoples with European revolutionary traditions – with varying degrees of success. But in seeing European events as impinging on Haitian life, rather than vice versa, it is a genuinely pathfinding work of anti-colonialist historiography. It relates a stirring story ('One of the great epics of revolutionary struggle and achievement') and locates it firmly in the Caribbean as an outcome of sugar and slave economics ('It is an original pattern, not European, not African, not part of the American main, not native in any conceivable sense of that word, but West Indian sui generis with no parallel anywhere else'). At the same time, it didn't elude James that *The Black Jacobins* would chime with the times, composed as it was not only as Italy warred in Abyssinia, but with 'the booming of Franco's heavy artillery, the rattle of Stalin's firing squads and the fierce shrill turmoil of the revolutionary movement striving for clarity and influence'.

James's successes were not as a political seer. His survey of the Third International, *World Revolution*, is possessed of fierce conviction and touching naivety: 'The huge fabrication of lies and slander against Trotsky and Trotskyism in Russia will tumble to the ground, and Stalin and Stalinism will face the masses inside and outside Russia naked.' And as a fomenter of revolution himself, James was also a failure. During fifteen years in the United States, where he moved in November 1938 seeking further fusion between the racial and revolutionary trends in his thought, he churned out agitprop with the best of them. But the American left of the time was hopelessly fissured and ineffectual, a veritable People's Front of Judea, and James's most significant work at this time wasn't at all what he considered the 'serious' stuff – books of the numbing obscurity of *Notes on Dialectics* (1948) and *State Capitalism and World Revolution* (1950). As he would admit, he was 'increasingly aware of large areas of human existence that my history and my politics did not seem to cover'.

Like Freud, James did not so much hate the United States as regret it. Trying to understand why American workers remained deaf to his dogma, James immersed himself in their popular culture, especially the cinema, but also detective thrillers, radio plays and comics. Eight long essays published posthumously in *American Civilisation* (1993) suggest an energetic engagement with plebeian taste as well as a frustration with it. 'I remember that for years I pertinaciously read comic strips unable to see what Americans saw in them,' he recalled. 'I persisted until at last today I am walking blocks to get my comics. In Europe and when I first came here I went to see movies of international reputation. Now I am a neighbourhood man and I prefer to see B gangster pictures than the latest examples of cinema art.'

James's interest in the politics of popular cultural forms also inspired *Mariners, Castaways and Renegades* – a reading of *Moby Dick* as an allegory of capitalism, exalting Melville as the only 'representative writer of industrial civilisation', written as chance would have it while James was on Ellis Island awaiting deportation as an illegal overstayer.

In sport, James found a culture even more truly demotic. His final quarrel with Trotskyism arose ostensibly because the movement was indifferent to race, and cleaved to the idea of a vanguard party. But James was vexed almost as much by Trotsky's dismissal of sport as a distraction from the class struggle. Observing American mores, meanwhile, had encouraged James to reconsider his own: 'I thought constantly of cricket because I could not see it. I was constantly thinking about cricket in this foreign environment. It gave cricket an existence of its own with the elements of a beginning, middle and an end. Whence this volume.' That is, *Beyond a Boundary*. Its composition began when James returned to England in July 1953, and James was sending chapters to political allies in the United States by March 1957, which he challenged them to read 'without at a certain stage being moved to tears'.

What is *Beyond a Boundary*? Like cricket itself, its kaleidoscope of history, philosophy, literature and memoir can be difficult to describe. It embarks from a poignant image: the junior James gazing wistfully through the window of his home on the cricketers at the nearby recreation ground. From here, he recalls, he could also 'stretch a groping hand for the books on top of the wardrobe', and 'thus the early pattern of my life was set'. Books provided intellectual sustenance, sport an ethical education: 'I never cheated. I never appealed for a decision unless I thought a batsman was out, I never argued with the umpire... From the eight years of school life this code became the moral framework of my existence. It never left me.'

A lengthy reconsideration of the author's youth ensues, with vivid depictions of famous cricketers such as Constantine and George Headley, alongside lesser lights like Wilton St Hill and George John, seasoned by the realization that 'cricket plunged me into politics long before I was aware of it'. A key decision, for example, concerned which of two local cricket clubs to join, Maple or Shannon. Maple was a bourgeois, brown-skinned outfit; the people whom as an educated man he would 'meet in life'. Shannon, though noted for the 'spirit and relentlessness' of its play, was palpably of 'the black lower-middle-class'. James's choice of the former he regarded in *Beyond a Boundary* with anguished hindsight: 'So it was that I became one of those dark men whose surest sign of ... having arrived is the fact that he keeps company with people lighter in complexion than himself ... Faced with the fundamental divisions in the island, I had gone to the right and, by cutting myself off from the popular side, delayed my political development for years.'

At first glance, an affinity for radical politics sits uneasily with an abiding love of cricket. Henry Hyndman may have turned to Karl Marx because his omission from the 1864 Cambridge University XI rankled so deeply, but cricket's strong senses of tradition and hierarchy seem more likely to inculcate respect for established forms than desire to topple them. But just as James had sensed in *Moby Dick* the tensions inherent in capitalism, so in cricket he had located a metaphor for colonialism, especially in the symbolism that West Indian cricket teams were led always by members of the local white autarchy. Which made cricket a citadel worth storming – precisely because West Indian cricket teams taking the field under white leadership mirrored the exploitation of those who supported them, James sensed that a West Indian team with a black captain would be a powerful symbol of emancipation.

The second half of James's book considers cricket as history and art. James sees the great English cricketer W. G. Grace in Hegelian terms, as 'one of those men in whom the characteristics of life as lived by many generations seemed to meet for the last, in a complete and perfectly blended whole'. The term 'Eminent Victorian' applies to Grace, James feels, without Stracheyian irony: 'No other age I know of would have been able to give him the opportunities the Victorian Age gave him. No other age would have been able to profit so much by him.' James proclaims, above all, that the temper of the times expresses itself through sport, and that sport can only be seen in terms of those times. Paraphrasing

Kipling, he issues his timeless admonition: 'What do they know of cricket who only cricket know? To answer involves ideas as well as facts.'

James thus accepts at face value what is often called the Golden Age of cricket – that period from 1894 to the First World War in which the values of amateurism are usually perceived as at their zenith, underpinned by both imperial confidence and a kind of prelapsarian innocence. The 'fall', as it were, is the so-called 'Bodyline' series of 1932–3, in which the English captain Douglas Jardine successfully undermined an upstart Australian team including its star batsman Donald Bradman through a policy of short-pitched fast bowling. James parallels the Jardinian cosh with the fascist jackboot: 'Bodyline was not an incident, it was not an accident, it was not a temporary aberration. It was the violence and ferocity of our age expressing itself in cricket.' Bradman, 'in his own way as tough as Jardine', subsequently presided over 'the age which can be called the age of J. M. Keynes'. This influence, characterized by 'the systematic refusal to take risks', still haunted the spiritless, passionless cricket of 1957, permeated as it was with 'the welfare state of mind'.

This, then, is James's historical schema. And, had he published in 1957, *Beyond a Boundary* would have finished on a note of deep despondency. But another six years would elapse before its completion. In April 1958, after twenty-six years abroad, James was lured back to Port-of-Spain by a former QRC pupil, Dr Eric Williams, leader of the People's National Movement and destined to lead Trinidad to independence. Enlisted to edit the party newspaper *The Nation*, and reunited with family, home and window, he began campaigning for the appointment of black Barbadian Frank Worrell to lead the West Indies. Incumbent Gerry Alexander, a wicketkeeper and a Cambridge blue, was the latest in a long line of competent but unremarkable white cricketers to hold the captaincy; Worrell, with 3000 Test runs at an average of 53, was the Caribbean game's outstanding personality by far.

Like the character in George Moore, James had travelled the world in search of what he needed, then returned home in order to find it. How profoundly *The Nation* influenced the deliberations of the West Indian selectors is debatable: a sceptic might submit that Worrell, boy scout, university graduate and freemason, had the inside running all along. But, at the least, *The Nation*'s role in the conduct of the controversy entitled James to a share in the successes that followed. Under Worrell, the West Indies participated in perhaps the most celebrated cricket series of the post-war period in Australia in 1960–1, won at the last gasp by the hosts, but in which the visitors obtained idolatrous support, culminating in a spontaneous parade down the streets of Melbourne. 'Clearing their way with bat and ball,' announced James, 'West Indians at that moment had made a public entry into the comity of nations.'

Evaluating James's importance in the rise of Worrell shouldn't obscure Worrell's importance in the rise of James. Not only did the summer of 1960–1 provide James with a logical and triumphal climax for his narrative, in which the West Indies were seen as sponsoring a sporting *risorgimento*, but it abetted his search for an English publisher. Hutchinson accepted *Beyond a Boundary* in June 1961, and published it in April 1963, on the eve of another West Indian triumph: a dramatic 3–1 victory over England on English soil. As the publication of *The Black Jacobins* had resonated with political upheaval at its release, so the launch of *Beyond a Boundary* seemed to echo the overthrow of sporting order. Here was West Indian cricket: united, uniting, irresistible. Here was James, *deus ex machina*, to explain it. Reviewers rhapsodized. John Arlott, the distinguished BBC broadcaster, proclaimed that 'in the intellectual sense, it is quite the "biggest book" about cricket or, probably, any other game, ever written'. It has existed in an echo chamber of endorsement ever since: even Christopher Hitchens knows it as 'the best book ever published on the history and ethics of cricket'. E. P. Thompson proclaimed it the key to James's whole oeuvre: 'I am afraid that American theorists will not understand this, but the clue to everything [in James's work] lies in his proper appreciation of cricket.'

In its epigrammatic style and epical scope, *Beyond a Boundary* is assuredly remarkable. There had been nothing like it and, frankly, there has been nothing like it since. But it clicked with cricket and Caribbean readerships for reasons other than intrinsic merit. James flattered cricket's sense of its own importance with his view that 'aestheticians have scorned to take notice of popular sports and games' ('Good to see the eggheads waking up at last, eh?'), while his radical reputation cohered with cricket's sense of itself as a broad church ('That James feller's a Commie, dontcha know! Mind you, he knows his cricket').

James, meanwhile, offered his newly emancipated countrymen – for Trinidad achieved independence in August 1962 – access to a readymade culture. Another famous expatriate whom Williams enticed back to Trinidad in this period was V. S. Naipaul, who unceremoniously bit the hand that fed him with *The Middle Passage*: 'I knew Trinidad to be unimportant, uncreative, cynical . . . We lived in a society that denied itself heroes. History is built around achievement and creation. And nothing was created in the West Indies.' James elegantly demurred: 'What Vidia said about the West Indies was very true and very important. But what he left out was twice as true and four times as important.' At a Test match, James saw straightforward cultural substitution. Where the English had 'Drake and mighty Nelson, Shakespeare, Waterloo, the few who did so much for so many', the West Indies 'fill a huge gap in their consciousness and their needs' with the deeds of great cricketers.

Was it as simple as that? Probably not. James made a huge impact with the idea that sport had to be 'seen in its social context' – in sports history, to paraphrase Richard Nixon, we're all Jamesians now. What James meant us to do, of course, was see West Indian cricket in *his* social context – the ethos of fair play that he imbibed at QRC. For the work of such a radical intellect, *Beyond a Boundary* is conservative to the point of prudery. The *weltanschauung* of *The Black Jacobins* placing the colonial periphery at the centre of the narrative is nowhere evident. The understanding that the game is English remains unchallenged. Caribbean cricketers are inheritors of ancient English traditions which the English have grown too decadent to maintain – 'Thomas Arnold, Thomas Hughes and the Old Master himself would have recognised Frank Worrell as their boy' – rather than makers of new traditions. By depicting white West Indians as the forces of reaction, meantime, direct confrontation with the ideals of the colonizing culture is avoided.

It is difficult to approach this without misgivings. The sense of incomplete and inherently uncompletable emancipation has left others deeply ambivalent about cricket's place in the Caribbean. 'Cricket is the game we love for it is the only game we play well, the only activity which gives us some international prestige,' wrote the novelist Orlando Patterson in his 1969 essay, 'The Ritual of Cricket'. 'But it is the game, deep down, which we must hate – the game of the master. Hence it becomes on the symbolic level the English culture we have been forced to love, for it is the only real one we have, but the culture we must despise for what it has done to us, for what it has made of the hopeless cultural shambles, the incoherent social patchwork, that we have called Afro-Jamaican culture.'

James's historical analysis, meanwhile, is often tendentious. It is decidedly odd, for example, that with so lofty a conception of cricket he should invest so deeply in the eristic Grace. In *W. G. Grace: A Life*, Simon Rae points out that the great all-rounder 'had no truck with the emerging pieties associated with the phrase "it's not cricket"'. Grace 'never walked, never recalled a batsman even when he knew he should not have been given out, appealed with authoritative conviction from any part of the field, and whatever the game threw up would try to turn to his advantage'. What's especially curious about James's campaign to make an exemplar of Grace is that he knows this. He acknowledges, grudgingly, that 'it would be idle to discount the reputation he gained for trying to diddle umpires', then seeks to distinguish between what Grace went in for and *real* cheating: 'Everyone knows such men, whom you would trust with your life, your fortune and your sacred honour, but will peep at your cards when playing bridge at a penny a hundred.'

'Does everyone in fact know such men?' responded the historian Sir Derek Birley in *The Willow Wand*. 'And are they regularly entrusted with other people's fortunes?' The questions are fair. Grace certainly stands for something – just not what James would like him to. This seems an instance where James could not, as Chesterton said of Tennyson, 'think up to the height of his own towering style'.

It is in the nature of Golden Ages that they are always in

the past, and always irrecoverable. Cricket's Golden Age is no exception. In fact, it is something of a Potemkin Village in cricket history: aspects of it were as gross and greedy as the mores of our own era. James misses it all: indeed, he wilfully looks the other way. His decision to define the period by its amateur ornaments, such as C. B. Fry and Archie MacLaren, is decidedly curious for a representative of both the left and of the imperial periphery. Where are the professionals? Where are the Australians? Where are the South Africans, the Americans, the Indian Parsees and, for that matter, the West Indians, all of whom toured England in the first decade of the twentieth century? Victor Trumper and Ranjitsinhji attracted thirty mentions in *Beyond a Boundary* without their origins, in Sydney and in Jamnagar, being mentioned, or what this might mean. As for James's dismissal of the false prosperity of the Twenties and the desiccated rationalism of the Thirties as entailing 'the decline of the west', it suffices to observe that Gerald Howat, not only a very credible cricket historian but a biographer of Learie Constantine, has encompassed the same period in a book called *Cricket's Second Golden Age*.

The most serious strain on James's world view, though, is exerted by professionalism. Where *The Black Jacobins* is shaped by economics, *Beyond a Boundary* never mentions it. In particular, James ignores the paltry rewards earned historically by West Indian cricketers, up to and including Worrell's era; their need to play almost uninterruptedly in English leagues and for English counties in order to earn more than a subsistence wages; the paradox that, in participating in the emancipation of West Indian cricket, team members had to condone their own continued economic exploitation.

In imagining his next world historical figure, too, James never foresaw an Australian whose *métier* was not playing ability but paying ability. West Indian players flocked to Kerry Packer, when plans were revealed for his breakaway World Series Cricket in May 1977: they had no sense of the 'old school tie'. They evolved during those seasons a way of winning matches with unsparing speed and reliable batting: they drew, in other words, on the decadent 'age of Keynes', not on their gilded Caribbean antecedents, on the example of Bradman, not of Worrell. And James knew it. He was altogether nonplussed by the West Indies' twenty-year reign as the world's leading Test team; his only article about Clive Lloyd's all-conquering XI, in *Race Today* in October/November 1984, merely dismissed as 'nonsense' their claims to be regarded as great, managing in the process to sound like a blimpish colonel from Surrey.

James could be forgiven disillusionment. By the time *Beyond a Boundary* came out, he had actually returned to London, having fallen out bitterly with Williams over the presence of the US military at Chaguaramas, and the mooted West Indies Federation. James had strongly taken up the federal cause, becoming secretary of the West Indian Federal Labor Party. But, as Jan Morris observed, the region's islands were 'far less homogeneous than they looked on the map and far more ambitious to be their own prime ministers', and the hostility of his reception when James attempted to re-enter Trinidad as cricket correspondent for the *Observer* in 1965 spelt the end of his political ambitions there. Henceforward, James's energies would be directed primarily to those regimes which sought his intellectual imprimatur, and he received political pilgrims with charm, grace and a sense of mild surprise, rather like his one-time hero Trotsky, who thought old age the most unexpected of all the things that happen to a man. These, it must be said, make up a rather melancholy list, ranging from Kwame Nkumrah's corrupt Convention People's Party of Ghana to Maurice Bishop's ragtag New Jewel Movement in Grenada – hence Naipaul's 'impresario of revolution' tag for 'Lebrun'.

'K. C. Lewis', as it were, has done rather better than 'Lebrun'. *Beyond a Boundary*'s reputation endures. It remains, withal, a work of arresting and sometimes disconcerting paradoxes – in particular, that such a passionate apostle of upheaval should have so failed to factor its possibility into his favourite game.

Alice Oswald

The Stone Skimmer

Sleepless swifts, their mobile minds held steady by longing,
swing around on the ropes of summer.
Their world so fast and perfunctory, all moistening filling forms
brimming flowering dimming diminishing.
Under the swifts and the flying silk of the wind,
he's walking   every grain of his mind,
like a current frisking through a wire,
will have changed place before he gets there.

Going down through the two small fields,
disturbing the small-seeing flies   he sees
the restless thistles, their dried skins hooked to their bones
brimming flowering dimming diminishing.
Among the thistles and the whisking pools of the wind
he's walking   he can almost feel
the spent fur of his flesh, a seed-ghost on a gust
condemned to float in endless widening circles.

Eyeless stones, their silence swells and breathes easily in water,
barely move in the wombs of rivers.
His mind so rushed and slovenly, full of forms
brimming flowering dimming diminishing:
into the five-inch space between heaven and heaven
he's skimming a stone   it's just the smack of it
contacting water, the amazing length
of light keeps lifting up his slid-down strength

River Psalm

evening river that scarcely are
                and us four in a plywood canoe

semi-resilient softness whose flatness is a floor for the barefoot steps of branches

were there not several windows where the water was clearly unfinished, I remember the unpaid stones looking up o black slat river, similar in size and scale to the strings of a cello

may your turn-ti-ti-tum bear our canoe into its vision at the misty

o geometrical straightness among billowings,
make good our partial emergence,

may we stay out long enough to lay our oars on our knees and still slide on in the rush with which clouds are swished together

may we come to the exact place and say so instantly, among a flash of flowers and the green shell song trees etcetera

o larval heaven, o finite quantity of freedom

in this marbled predicament, brought on by constantly alternating between stickles and pools you whose beauty is only approximately its long and wishing reach,

may we come to know that the length of water is not quite the same as the passing of time,

may we make do with one glimpse each,
one eye one arm one bone
in our plywood canoe

Time Poem

now the sound of the trees is worldwide

                     and I'm still here
staring when I should be bathing children.

it's late, the bike's asleep on its feet.

the fields hang to the sun by slackened lines ...

when the grass breathes, things fall. I saw
the luminous underneath of a moth. and a blackbird
mouth to the glow of the hour in hieroglyphics.

who left the light on the step?
pause

what is the pace of a glance?

the man at the wheel signs his speed on the ringroad

right here in my reach, time is as thick as stone
and as thin as a flying strand

it's night and somebody's
pushing his mower home
            to the moon

Rajeev Balasubramanyam

A Man of Soul

'Ajay, we're having a baby.'

That's all she said. So I kissed her and hugged her and thought, 'What the fuck do I do now?'

I had lost my job the previous evening. I was going to break the news that morning, but morning comes and she tells me this. So instead I smiled the fakest smile I had, which, in her equally demented state, she didn't pick, and I went upstairs and put on my uniform. Pizza Pot had my motorbike, but I made a big show of wearing my helmet and rattling my keys. They had my wage packet too. Dismissed for theft. I certainly wasn't going to tell her that. The truth is I didn't do it, but that doesn't matter now.

We kissed again at the door. There were tears in her eyes, terror in mine. I thought about seeing a movie, but I had twelve pounds, no job and a baby on the way, so I just wandered around Mile End. When the sun grew colder I bought a travelcard and rode the Tube to Ealing Broadway. I didn't get off. Just waited for it to go back. It took an hour and a half. I thought about them firing me, about how unfair it was, but most of all I thought about how I was going to be a father. I was angry, and desperate, and alone with a bunch of men in pinstripe suits with nannies and country homes and nothing to worry about but which restaurant to go to that night. I hated Pizza Pot and I hated them.

On the way back I saw a discarded *Evening Standard* and began to flick through it.

One article in particular caught my eye. A man, a black man, had been arrested on two charges. First, destruction of public property. He beat up a security camera. Took a bat to it. Smashed the shit out of it. They captured him on film, so he couldn't complain, it's the second charge that's the sick part. Get this . . .

racially aggravated crime... How could it be racial? It was a fucking camera, for Christ's sake.

Their logic... he was black; he was angry; he was guilty; it was racial. Fucking idiots. They had to drop the charge, of course. A camera doesn't have an ethnic origin.

So I look around me and we're in the city now and there are only suits on the Tube and occasionally we make eye-contact and I can see them laughing. They know I'm desperate, and they know I'm a pizza boy, and they know I'm a paki, and they think it's funny. So I think about the man in the paper. I tell myself, Ajay, whatever you do, make it count. If you're going to break the law then use your head, don't just smash up a fucking camera.

And here's what I came up with.

I would get off at Liverpool Street and I would go to a bar and wait in the toilet until one of them was all by himself and I would pretend I had a knife, make my meanest face, and take all the cash he had.

That was Plan A.

I didn't know there would be a B, C and D. Not then.

*

So I'm in the toilets and the place is crawling with suits and I know Plan A isn't going to work. There's too many of them, and they're bigger than me, and harder than me, and I'm the last person in the world they'd be afraid of.

So I went back upstairs and I ordered a drink. A martini. It cost seven pounds, tasted vile, looked expensive.

I found an empty sofa by the window and lay at full stretch. There was a couple sharing an armchair to my right, spilling white wine. Their conversation made me sick. Four-wheel drives and conservatories. It struck me that a female suit might be an easier target, but I banished the thought. I am a man of morals, if nothing else.

Two men approached my sofa and I lifted my legs to make room. They sat with their legs apart, taking far more than their legitimate two-thirds sofa space. I felt like throwing up. There I was, all bunched up in the corner, practically thanking them for letting me exist. Everyone in the bar was bigger now, bigger than before. They had grown. To make matters worse, I was drunk, or beginning to be; I've never been good with alcohol.

And then it happened... Plan B fell on the floor, right in front of me. That's right... a suit had dropped his wallet... and not one of them had noticed. I stood, shivered, and drained my glass. The liquor helped.

Silent as a cat, I padded my way across the floor, dropped my keys, fell to my knees, and took the keys in my left hand and the wallet in my right, slipping them both into my trouser pockets. Operation accomplished, I headed for the bar, reluctant to change direction. My plan was to hang around, look at my watch, then bolt, go home, see what I had landed.

That never happened. Plan C was waiting for me, leaning against the wall. The suit whose wallet I held captive in my trousers was attacking his body like a monkey in a zoo.

He starts shouting in this squeaky voice.

'My fackin wallet's gone. I've lost my fackin wallet.'

His mates try to calm him down, but he doesn't want to calm down, though no one offers to buy him a drink.

'Some fackin wanka'll have it, as well. You just know it. It'll be some fackin wanka.'

How, I tell myself, am I supposed not to hate these fuckers? They hate each other. They hate themselves. So far as they're concerned, the next man is always a fackin wanka. Makes sense.

So his mates tell him to look for it, but he isn't having any of it. It doesn't occur to him that it could still be on the floor, where he's left it. He gets himself so worked up that he leaves, just like that.

I leave too. Plan C.

I will follow him home and knock on his door. I'll say, 'Mate, I saw you drop your wallet and your address was inside (hope you don't mind me looking) and here you are.' And he will say, 'Good Lord, you are indeed a prince among men. You people put us to shame. You make savages of us, you really do. Do come in, my friend, teach me how to live.' And I would go in and drip regal splendour all over the motherfucker, and when I leave... he will feel like shit, and I...?

I would go home and tell Preethi. I would tell her that whatever happened we would walk this earth like children of god. Our child would be proud and tall, a warrior, a lover, a saint. And she would know that I was still the man who had so disarmed her all those years ago. Mighty, righteous, above all that material shit. A man of manners. A man of morals. A man of soul.

*

So I follow the cunt. It's easy enough. I was afraid he would jump in a cab, but he doesn't. He walks fast, cursing the fackin wanka who's got the only thing he's ever cared about.

His place is near Spitalfields, fast becoming another yuppie den, and his building is the sort of place where princes should live, but don't.

When he goes inside I slip in after him. I half-expect a doorman to put his hand through my chest, but all I see is a row of mailboxes, neatly numbered and full of letters. He's about to take his mail, but he changes his mind – he's too pissed off – and he bounces upstairs like a petulant child. I follow like there's rose petals under my feet.

I hear the door click shut and I wait a few minutes before I knock. He looks seriously pissed off. Before I can open my mouth he tells me he didn't order any fucking pizza. That's what he said, fucking pizza. I hold my temper and give him the wallet. But the words don't come out right. I rush it and mumble, which I do when I'm nervous. His eyes light up as he takes his wallet and . . . I'm waiting for it . . . but it never happens. I can fuck off as far as he's concerned. He's got what he wanted.

I'm his boy, his delivery boy. Today it's wallets, tomorrow it'll be anchovies with extra cheese. A pizza boy . . . a colonial wallet wallah.

I follow him in. He looks surprised, but what can he do? He can't turf me out after I've given him the happiest moment of his putrid little life.

And you know what he does? He pours himself a beer and doesn't so much as look at me. Doesn't offer me shit. Not even water. I'm standing there shaking with the humiliation of it all and he doesn't even notice. He's turned on the telly and he's drinking his beer and he's waiting for me to leave. So I sit down.

The phone rings and up he gets and he starts telling Jeremy, or whoever the fuck it is, about the stock market, so I stand and go to the kitchen and get myself a fucking beer. And then I think: While I'm here, I may as well have a look around. I've never been in a place like this.

So I wander about the apartment, and yeah, it stinks of money, and I wind up in the bedroom and I'm looking at this painting of a naked woman with this sword raised above her head when my eyes run over the dressing table and I stop. Plan D. Jack... fucking... pot.

*

There is a gold bracelet lying on the dresser. It is studded with diamonds. They are very big. The man (he hasn't told me his name) is still talking on the phone. I think: Don't think. Do it. And I pick up the bracelet, give it a kiss, and put it in my pocket.

I am sweating. I check to see if the outline is visible in my trousers. It isn't. And I go back to the living room. He is off the phone now, and when I say I'm going he looks happy. The smug bastard.

But just when I'm going to leave, the door opens and his wife walks in. And get this... she's Asian. She's fucking Asian. And she's, you know, fit, princess-style, long hair, enormous eyes, good body too (not that I cared; I wouldn't do that to Preethi) and she introduces herself, and I tell her what happened, and she says, 'Will you have some tea?'

I'm struggling, fumbling, mumbling like a fool, and she offers coffee, beer, food, and at last I ask for tea. She looks at him and he, the wanker, goes off to make the tea, cursing under his breath. Glad to see she wears the trousers, at least, but I mean, why did this stunning creature have to marry this, this...? It makes me sick. I could see the look on his face. 'Look at me. I'm an ugly fucker with nothing going for me but my prospects and I'm with this gorgeous paki bird and there's nothing you can do about it.'

I'm bristling. I can feel the anger in my blood, but this girl's so lovely, so gentle, that I find myself enjoying her company. We talk about films, and parents, and a little about food, and my tea comes and I glare at him and he fucks off into the bathroom. 'Ajay,' I tell myself, 'this girl is deprived. She needs a man who'll understand her, and she's gotta come home to this bastard.'

I don't feel resentment. I just feel sad. This girl is one of me and I want her to be happy, but she's miserable and I can feel it. But at least I can relate. At least someone understands. I suggest she comes round sometime to meet Preethi (telling her, with my eyes, 'Don't bring that fucker if you can help it'). And then I remember.

I've got this poor girl's bracelet in my pocket. And I know, I know. Her mother gave it to her. It's all she's got. It means the world to her and there's no way I can do it. No way on earth.

So now I have to get the bracelet out of my pocket and back to her. This won't be easy. She's staring at me, chatting away with this childlike voice and each word is like a drop of dew, floating through the air until it hits my heart and turns to acid. I'm writhing in pain and it's no surprise when, a few minutes later, she asks if I'm all right and can she get me anything. I say no, then realize, too late, I should have said yes. I'd do anything to get her out of the room so I can dump this damn bracelet some place where she'll find it.

I'm sweating like a camel now. My eyes are wide open. I know I look insane, but there's nothing I can do about that. I try to listen to what she's saying, but it's all words now, words, words, words. Each one makes me worse.

At last, I succeed in easing the thing out of my pocket, holding it in my fingers. She's still talking, and I'm smiling and nodding, but I begin to push it under the sofa cushion. But my fingers are running with sweat and, as if trapped inside a dream, I watch it fall to the floor, roll across the carpet, and stop by her feet.

It's lying there, right by her foot, grinning at me. But she doesn't notice. I stare. It feels like hours. When I come to my senses I say, 'Could I have a glass of water, please?' She smiles and says, 'Yes, you don't look well.' And I say something about the flu, and she goes to the kitchen.

I throw myself on top of that bracelet, then stand in the middle of the room, wondering where to put it. I find myself turning, round and around, until I see a flower vase on the sideboard. I walk over to it, then think, 'What if it's months till she finds it?'

The poor girl will drive herself sick with worry. So I consider going back to the bedroom, and I'm turning the bracelet round and around in my hand, when, before I know it, she's back in the room, with my water.

I rub some over my face and gulp the rest down without stopping for breath. She's looking at me with tremendous concern, and I'm ready to cry now. The whole world hates me. No, it's worse. I hate myself. And for good reason. But then I have an idea, and I say, 'You know what, I've got to go. But can I use the toilet first?' And I think, I'll just leave it on the sink. Easy. Easy as pizza.

But you know what? The fat fucker's still in the bath. And she asks him how long he'll be and he says, like the irritable twat he is, 'Don't know. I just got in, didn't I?' And I smile. And say, 'Oh well, never mind. I'll go in the pub round the corner,' and she looks really apologetic, and we hug, we actually hug, and for one horrible minute I think I'll never let her go. I hold her tighter and tighter and tears fill my eyes, but when I feel her growing tense I let her go, wipe my eyes, and leave.

The door closes behind me. I shut my eyes and lean against the wall before climbing down the stairs. When I get to the bottom, I see Plan E.

*

The mailboxes. Why didn't I think of it before? One for each flat. All open. Just trays really. I see theirs at once and I thank God for saving me an eternity of self-loathing. I'm reluctant to drop the bracelet in there, though, just like that. As that fucker in the bathtub would have said, 'Some wanka'll nick it.' So I pick up an envelope, tear it open with my index finger and drop the bracelet in, when I see a word on the letter inside that makes me take it out and read it. It is from the landlord.

'Owing to the recent spate of mailbox thefts I have installed a closed-circuit television camera above the main door. Apologies for the inconvenience.'

I turn, and look. There it is, hard and cynical, white and clinical, staring at me with its shiny eye. I stare back, hating the world, hating the fucker who'll watch that tape and think I'm a thief. I clench my fists, shut my eyes, and when I open them the world is red, as if drenched in blood.

There's a fire extinguisher in the corner, by the door. I walk over to it, lift it above my head, and smash it into the camera's side, four, maybe five times. The camera falls, wrenched from the wall. It watches me with its broken eye, sneering. I raise my boot and crush its ugly head, stamping again and again until nothing remains but dust.

*

Bowing to an invisible audience, I opened the door and left the building.

Barbara Trapido

Letters

Two things happen to Hermione on the day she gets the letter. One is that she gets the letter. The other is that, because Herman is away yet again, she's fallen asleep with the radio on. So she's come to consciousness at daybreak, hearing an angel. A tenor angel with his own string quartet is singing to her on the radio. Then there's a pause and there are three angels. A soprano and a bass angel have joined the tenor angel. But now maybe they've stopped being angels. Or perhaps they never were? There are strange, seductive dance rhythms in there and discords and rasping trombones. There's a woodwind instrument that has come along to join them. Just the one. Something slowed up and stretched out and sexy is happening to the angel's music. It's gone all plucked and druggy and gliding. She can tell that the music is old and yet it sounds so modern. And how cleverly all the angels are avoiding the obvious notes. This is making the music sound subversive. It's hinting at something wild and dangerous. The angels are singing in Italian, which is a language Hermione doesn't know. Not beyond the tourist level. *A che ora arrivera il treno?* So the only word she keeps picking out sounds a bit like 'screw-gender'. And then – of course – when the music stops and the announcer's come on, her mind is drifting again so she catches only one word. Stravinsky. So now she can't even go out and buy the music on CD. Irritation jolts her awake. She gets up and pulls on a bathrobe. She gulps some water at the bathroom tap. Stravinsky. She tries humming the tune, but it's left her. Gone the way a dream will erase itself within minutes of one's waking up. Stravinsky.

Now that she's properly awake, the mention of Stravinsky has made her think of Josh. Josh Silver, her friend from way back. Twenty-five years back. Long time. No see. Josh, who could routinely lift her spirits as they met up on campus between their lectures. And then, on that particular day, he'd come along with the Stravinsky story, though really it was more a story about his mother. At supper the previous night Josh had placed the book he was reading on the table beside his plate; a short musical autobiography by Stravinsky with a photograph of the composer on the front of the dust jacket. Josh is clutching the book next morning when he meets up with Hermione. At supper, Josh tells her, his mother has announced that Stravinsky is 'obviously Jewish' and she won't be shaken from this belief. This is because Mrs Silver has a gut conviction that anyone worth claiming, especially in the arts and sciences, has to be Jewish. In the daytime Josh's mother is a trade union negotiator with her head screwed on pretty well. She operates in a man's world, taking on the city's bully-boy racist bosses at various factories. But then, once she's home, she turns into this person who grates raw potatoes for latkes and makes her own sauerkraut. Plus she likes to make her own cottage cheese as well. This is why there's always a nasty, oozy little muslin bag of milk curds hanging over one of the taps at Josh's mother's kitchen sink. Then she still finds the energy to argue with her family at the supper table. Hermione loves the things that Josh's family argue about, because in her family all anyone ever argues about is whose turn it is to feed the dog.

*

Josh and Hermione are on their way to the student canteen for coffee – a daily ritual during which they always share one of those Chelsea buns that Josh likes to unwind. Once there, Josh again places the book on the table where Hermione can see Stravinsky's photograph for herself.

'Well, his glasses look quite Jewish,' she says. 'In fact, they're exactly like your glasses.' Josh isn't really Jewish at all. He was adopted. His parents took him in, aged six, just after he'd started school. Josh was got by an Irish peddlar upon a down-at-heel Lebanese Catholic in Boksburg. He can't remember Boksburg. All he can remember is those fragments of his life after his birth mother and he had drifted into Johannesburg. Hermione has never been to Boksburg. She only knows it from a joke about a man who keeps on missing the train to it.

Josh seems pleased about the glasses. 'So what do you think?' he says. He's pushing the book towards her. 'Does he look sexy then, or what?'

'Um,' Hermione says. 'Urm. Well his glasses are sexy, aren't they?'

*

And now, twenty-five years on, Hermione, who has just taken down her *Oxford Companion to Music*, has looked up the composer and has found that the selfsame photograph is reproduced within the book. Stravinsky. Does he look sexy then, or what? Yes he does. But most of all, he looks exactly like Papa Mouse in *Mouse Tales* by Arnold Lobel. Papa Mouse is obviously Jewish. Hermione once wrote a fan letter to Arnold Lobel, but he died before she posted it. *Mouse Tales* is a book that she still knows by heart because she used to read it umpteen times in a day. It was her youngest daughter Cat's number one favourite. Especially the story about the mouse who bought himself a pair of new feet. All that was a decade ago, when Cat was six. She tries not to think about Cat too much these days, so she's concentrating hard on Stravinsky. The swept-back hair, the large nose, the almost receding chin, the glasses. In fact she's staring so hard at the book that she doesn't notice, as she enters the kitchen, that Cat herself is already in there, dressed and ready for school.

'*Wotcha doon, Maw?*' Cat says, in her single-volume shout voice, which always hits the ear like an assault. Cat's consonants are fuzzy and she's dribbling breakfast cereal from her mouth as she speaks. Hermione can tell at once that it's the horrible chocolate-flavoured stuff because brown milk is leaking down Cat's chin. Cat is sixteen, but she still has an infant's sweet tooth. Cat will add extra sugar to Cocoa Puffs. Plus she'll add sugar to those already cloyingly sweet pink yogurts. Cat talks with her mouth full these days, which is a pretty hard thing to take. She does it because, while she munches and stuffs, she seldom swallows anything, so her mouth is always full. Hermione would rather that Cat didn't pretend to be eating, but Cat clearly likes the taste of food too much not to want to put it in her mouth. So for the past two years she has pursued a policy of shovelling successive spoonloads into her mouth without pausing to swallow. She stores the spoonloads, hamster-wise, in the pouches of her cheeks. That's until congestion causes bits to start falling out of her mouth. Then Cat will do one of three things. The first is to feign a choking fit and spew the chewed pile onto her plate. She'll follow this with some bogus accusation, usually directed at her mother.

'I nearly *choked* because of you!' she'll shriek. 'There are *bones* in this! There are *peppercorns* in this! What are these *disgusting* leaf things?' The second thing she does is to dash periodically for the bathroom, where Hermione is pretty certain that Cat is disgorging the hoard into the lavatory bowl because she hears the loo flush once; twice. Thirdly – just occasionally – Cat will actually swallow. When she swallows, most of the hoard will go down in one huge gulp. She'll jerk her head like a turkey. Then there'll be a bobbing in her throat and her eyes will start to water. Sometimes a coughing fit will ensue. Yet Cat is still a big girl. Big and crosspatch. And Herman, of course, just keeps on denying that there's anything amiss with Cat.

'Just because you're such a titch,' he says. 'Just calm down, Snooks. She's OK.' Hermione has recently begun to find it offensive the way he still calls her 'Snooks'.

'*Wotcha doon, Maw?*' Cat squawks again.

'I heard this music on the radio,' Hermione says, 'so I thought I'd look it up. Just to see if—'

'So what?' Cat says, cutting her short. 'Who cares what you heard on the radio?' Then suddenly Hermione finds that she knows where the music comes from. Because either her earlier, half-asleep brain has taken in more than she's given it credit for, or a word from the *Oxford Companion* has just skirted the corner of her eye.

'*Pulcinella*,' she says. 'Well, of course.' She's even danced a bit of it once, for an exam, but not the angel bit. Not the bit she's just heard.

'Pulchi-*what*? Cat says. Then, because she sees that her mother has her eyes on the book, she makes a high-risk dash for the pedal bin, where she relieves herself of the hamster hoard before swiftly resuming her pose of breakfasting normality, spoon once more in hand.

'*Pulcinella*,' Hermione says. 'It's a ballet. With songs. It's danced in masks.'

'So what?' Cat says again, but Hermione lets it ride.

'Hey, masks, Cat,' she says. 'That 3D project you have to do. What about doing it on masks? You know. African masks.'

Cat makes an irritable noise with her tongue. 'I mean, for *Godssakes*! I mean, what *next*? I mean, *mawsks*? I mean, how *schoopid* can you get? I mean, what have *mawsks* got to do with anything?'

*

Twelve years ago Hermione went to Venice with Cat for a treat, having left the two older children with Herman and with Gertrude, the live-in maid. Gertrude, who wasn't there when she got back. But let's not think of Gertrude, because that way madness lies. Hermione had gone to England to visit her two girl cousins. And then, after that, she'd gone to Venice. A four-day indulgence for herself and her little blonde daughter. Cat was a big hit in Venice, where the waiters kept saying '*Che bella*' whenever they saw her.

'But I'm not Kay and I'm not Bella,' Cat would explain to them repeatedly. 'I'm Cat.' By coincidence, her two best friends back home in the pre-school playgroup were called Kay and Bella. Cat, who was three at the time of the visit, can't remember Venice and now denies having been there. But Hermione can't forget Cat's enchanted little face pressed up against the windows of the shops with the carnival masks. Bird-like plague masks. Harlequin masks with knobbly foreheads. Pulcinella.

*

Cat has been unloading moans about her sixth-form 3D art project ever since the new school term began a month ago. She's caught in a dilemma, poor girl, because she can't bear to reveal any interest in things of the mind and yet she wants good grades. Cat wants to get into the architectural school and be an architect like her dad. So she knows the 3D project will have to be good. And it must have an African theme. Hermione is thinking that maybe she'll just buy a couple of books and leave them around the house for Cat to fall over. Maybe some books on those masked stilt-walkers in Mali? It's no longer possible to confront Cat about anything much these days. All it does is make her abusive. Plus, when she starts to thunder about, the floorboards always vibrate and Hermione can hear her great-grandmother's china starting to tremble and jingle in the kitchen cupboard.

*

All Hermione's three children are big, but the older two are carrying it better than Cat. Jack and Suz are imposing and efficient young Amazons; strong, coping adults, getting on with their lives. Hermione by contrast has always been exceptionally small; marked out from toddlerhood as a dainty, ballet girl. She's spent most of her adult life working as a ballet teacher. Now, at the age of forty-three, she's given it up. But she's still wearing size 8 clothes. Hermione is no longer all that comfortable about her size. Not these days. She's begun to wonder whether her couplings with Herman were perhaps injudicious all along. Maybe they were like those of that little shivery whippet she once saw getting it together with a St Bernard in the park. Is that why Herman keeps going off on trips? Has her size become repellent to him? Does Cat hate her for it? Does it compromise the family norm? In these matters, context counts for a lot. Hermione saw a photograph once, of a post-war Vietnamese classroom. Six doll-like Vietnamese eight-year-olds were sitting around a table along with one little misfit eight-year-old giant. The giant was a pale brown Afro girl, whose mother had once been intimate with a seven foot tall black GI.

*

Once Cat has taken herself off to school, Hermione drives to the shopping mall. She's been going shopping quite a lot these days. First she buys a fat shiny book on African art with lots of pictures. Then she buys a CD of Stravinsky's *Pulcinella*. After that she sits down in a cafe with a cup of coffee and she takes a look at the notes that have come with the CD. The word she's kept on hearing is not 'screw-gender', it's *struggendo*. *Mi sta struggendo*. I am consumed. With love. Then, when she gets home, she finds the letter.

Jane Stevenson

Hunger

In 1952 Edouard Wyss-Dyant, a doctor interested in climbing, coined a descriptive term, the 'Death Zone', for the region above 7,500 metres. At this height the effects of altitude on the human body are such that human life cannot be sustained. The body begins to die. Food is not digested, other physiological processes shut down, and it eats into its own muscle and bone to survive. Climbers in the Death Zone are dead men walking. The fact that they continue to put one foot in front of the other is due solely to their will to continue, while every nerve, instinct and bodily process screams its protest at this insanity. This we understand as heroism; a gauging of the individual, shrinking body against the outer limits of the possible, which has its own compelling internal logic, although, or because, the great mountaineers characteristically go on and on until some mountain kills them. We are complicit with the fact that extreme mountaineering, unlike any other sport, ultimately demands that its players should die because some hill, somewhere, will always offer an unpredictable and disastrous combination of risks. While postmodernist high culture is explicitly anti-heroic, a high cultural value is still placed on heroism, indicated by the basic yardstick of a capitalist society: it is, in one way or another, worth a lot of money. We resonate to heroism because every one of us has performed a million tiny acts of daring, going back to the first time we held onto a chair and pulled ourselves up. Heroism is common experience carried to uncommon lengths.

There is also a Death Zone in starvation. Last year in Leixlip, the little place which the Vikings called 'the salmon-leap' because of its waterfall and which is now a dormitory suburb of Dublin, four athletes of God walked into it step by step, without budging an inch from their chosen path. Josephine, or Jo, Frances,

Catherine, and Ruth-Bridget (called Breege-Ruth) Mulrooney locked themselves into a new house in a featureless executive village, and starved themselves to death. Is this, or is it not, heroism? If not, what is it? One thing it certainly is is a story of common experience carried to uncommon lengths, since we have also all committed a million tiny acts of self-denial.

If one fasts for even a day, there is a rapid progression from sharp hunger through euphoria to a sort of numb absence. After four or five days this absence becomes, somehow, congested, as if the body has become a closed system. I don't personally know what starvation feels like beyond that, since around day five I went to answer the door, fell down the stairs because my knees had given way and realized I was being an idiot. I was twenty-two years old, living alone for the first time and playing games with myself, the games of courage and self-limitation that are natural to the young. Perhaps because I was a girl I was testing my limits with respect to my own body rather than by doing something athletic and risky. Also, of course, I wanted to lose weight because everyone, including me, was agreed that being thin was beautiful, admirable, a symptom of moral worth, and would make people love me.

In fact, when I did some research, I found that my experience had taught me almost nothing about what the Mulrooneys went through. It is easy to imagine that the blockage of feeling continues, that perhaps the blurring of perception even increases during a slow, gentle slide towards death, but it does not. The thousands of people who, as you read this, are dying of starvation, are not slipping out of life in clouded, apathetic resignation. They are dying in agony, because beyond a certain point the starved body begins to turn on itself; the ravenous stomach, like a dog locked in the house with helpless owners, will turn and ravage its commensals. It begins to digest from within, eating into its own muscle and bone, which is slow, but not gentle. Not at all. As with the climber's Death Zone, the anorexic's Death Zone, once entered, is not easily left. Beyond a certain point, the individual will have permanent scars of his or her sojourn in the land of the dead. The angel of death maintains a tollbooth at the exit of the Death Zone, and the price which returnees must pay is months or years of their natural life. And, of course, those who go too far will find that it is no longer possible to come back at all.

Hunger is now for many what it has always been, a fact of life. In Munster in 1596, 'they came creeping forth upon their hands, for their legs would not bear them, out of every corner of the woods and glens. They looked anatomies of death; they spake like ghosts crying out of their graves.' This is an Irish story; and so is one of the last great avoidable famines, the Great Hunger after the ruin of successive potato harvests in the 1840s. Many people have starved, many people have frozen, in this world of unquantifiable suffering, and many still do, but that is not why mountaineers and the Mulrooneys are interesting. What distinguishes the paladins who enter one or other Death Zone is not their suffering, but their perception that to do so *voluntarily* is a triumph of the human will.

The archetypic vision of the adventurer is of the quest, the intellectual and spiritual beauty of the triumph of the will. *Excelsior*, 'ever higher'. But, quiet, strange and tenacious, there is an archetypic vision of the heroic fast, which is just as old if not older. In the Sanskrit law, codified three thousand years ago, long before Jason and his argonauts set sail on the first epic journey of the Western tradition, there was a legal sanction available to the aggrieved, called 'sitting *dharna*'. The injured person sat at the gate of his tormentor, and fasted publicly, and this ordeal by embarrassment continued until arbitrators were called and the problem settled. The whole point about *dharna* is that it depends on a shared knowledge of starvation to make the sight unbearable. If you do not know what it means to starve, then you do not, in the most literal sense, comprehend what the litigant is up to, and it is morally and socially possible to watch in incomprehension as the body withers, consumed ultimately by the fire of its own internal combustion.

The coercive fast is also a feature of native Irish law (pre- the English conquest of Ireland), where it is called *troscad* – a testimony to the impressive retentiveness of the Irish tradition, since the Hindu culture is a distant and ancient relation of our own. The archaic sense of starvation as a legal sanction underlies the very Irish weapon of the hunger strike, exemplified in the long agony of Bobby Sands and the other men who died for the right to be considered political prisoners, now part of the heroic legendry of the Irish Republican Army. But hunger strikes failed as a political weapon in the twentieth century because we have completely ceased to understand the ancient, intimate brutality of starvation. Only an absolute disjunction between our ideas of ourselves, our bodily integrity, and the threat of starvation would allow us to find beauty in the bodies of women too thin to bear children. You have to have forgotten the true nature of hunger to say that it is impossible to be too rich or too thin.

Thinness is a double-edged phenomenon in the West. On the one hand, the beautiful and glamorous are as slender as gazelles, which we see as right and good; on the other, there is an epidemic of eating disorders: young girls (mostly) get thinner and thinner, until, in some cases, they enter the Death Zone, which we perceive as tragic. With respect to extreme adventure, book after book of tight-lipped prose sets forth the basic tenets of the ultimate test of man against the elements, and represents this as a wholly sane extension of normal behaviour, though Himalayan mountaineering bears the same relationship to healthy exercise that anorexia does to healthy weight-watching. By contrast, the literature of self-starvation is cast in negative terms: 'Me and My Eating Disorder' (now a staple of celebrity journalism), recovery stories, and the positive view is unpublishable. No one would risk putting out teen-interest books on heroic fasting, but since the Net circumvents publishing as such, there is now an electronic secret literature of anorexia in which girls meet up in chatrooms to recognize, celebrate and encourage one another in feats of abstinence, suggesting that the market does exist, if anyone dared cater for it.

Anorexia is to most people 'about' beauty, 'about' body image; but if this were the whole of the story, then surely anorexics would display some sensitivity towards the fact that there is a stage beyond even extreme slenderness which is physically repulsive. For example, growing downlike hair all over the body isn't attractive, but even this symptom of extreme malnourishment doesn't act as a deterrent, which it surely would if aesthetics were central. It is also important that self-starvation can be an epic exercise of the will, which is not recognized as such because it is profoundly feminine. Certainly, women climb mountains and men fast. But all the same these are deeply gendered weapons for self-comprehension in the face of an ultimate challenge. Anorexia is pure achievement, pointless, lethal and glorious, just like mountaineering, and both are profoundly the products of a decadent society.

Mountaineering as such is no damn use to anyone, but many men have pushed themselves to the ultimate in order actually to achieve something, and many fasters have similarly gone to the limit for a reason. Even if it is no longer a recognized legal sanction, fasting beyond a certain point is profoundly coercive, as anorexics' friends and relatives rapidly discover, and political fasting is still far from obsolete as a weapon of the disempowered.

But there is yet another side to the experience of hunger which helps to explain the Mulrooneys. Fasting is also unmistakably one of the varieties of religious experience, and may be a form of prayer, as it is to this day among Jews. 'Accept my blood and fat, O Lord, as a sacrifice,' they say, in the great annual fast of Yom Kippur. There have been strands of Christian tradition which do more than offer the body's self-consumption as a sacrifice for God to accept or reject. There are Christian stories in which God is effectively coerced through the voluntary agony of his creatures, starting with Christ's forty days in the wilderness; the most remarkable is, again, Irish. In the medieval *Life of St Patrick*, the patron saint of Ireland is shown as a faster on the heroic scale in a story which sets out the authentically epic character of self-starvation. In this tale, Patrick is not trying to discipline his usual sparring partner in the *Life*, the pagan King Loegaire, he is going for the ultimate challenge, and fasting against God himself.

What the *Life of St Patrick* says is that 'he went to Cruachan on Saturday of Whitsuntide. An angel came to him, and said, God will not give you what you demand, because it seems to Him excessive and obstinate, and the requests are great.' 'Is that so?' said Patrick. 'Then I will not go from here until I am dead, or till all the requests are granted to me.' Then he stayed in Cruachan without drink and without food from Shrove Saturday to Easter Sunday – forty days and forty nights. One by one, he wrests concessions from his God. Twelve men every Saturday to be rescued from Hell. That Ireland will be submerged before the Last Judgement. That the Saxons will not dwell in Ireland, that everyone who knows Patrick's hymn – no, the last three verses, it's long – will escape from Hell, a man freed at doomsday for every hair on his chasuble... it goes on and on. According to the value system shared by St Patrick, God and the harassed angel who zips up and down between Cruachan and Heaven bearing ever more unacceptable demands, it is precisely to the extent that he has been tormented, has willingly walked in the Death Zone, that he has built up the power to coerce. His pain was comprehensible to medieval readers, so was its precise weight and significance. St Patrick has put himself to the ultimate test of fasting to the point of near death, lonely on the hill of Cruachan with nothing but the angel of the Lord to comfort him, and a diabolic swarm of black birds which swirled between him and God.

With Bobby Sands and St Patrick as guides, or perhaps, gaunt signposts, I want to look at the story of Frances, Jo, Catherine, and Breege-Ruth Mulrooney to see if there are ways of understanding it without turning it into fiction, because the crucial and shocking thing about this tale is that it actually happened. In the photographs which accompany the newspaper report here in Britain, there is a glamorous Irish pathologist who looks like Sophie Dahl playing Kay Scarpetta; her slender hands sketching eloquent arcs of incomprehension and disbelief. She might be grist to the mill of fiction, especially if what one is primarily interested in is the damage that the Mulrooneys did to their bodies. But there are also photographs of the surviving sister, in her good green coat and old lady's felt hat, a woman who looks exactly like the mother of one of my best friends, and wears the stunned expression common to those who have been crushed by bizarre and inexplicable tragedy. She was the one who got away, because she married and they closed her out, and she is a reminder that this is a story about real people.

Enter these appalling spaces. A small room; in it, four bodies, people locked in private agony, cocooned in sleeping bags, each enduring as best she might the terrible pain of her body's refusal to die. Between the bags stand brimming buckets of urine; on their forty-day fast the sisters must drink, indeed, their bodies will crave pints after pint of water, which they will piss out again in minutes, each flush of the kidneys taking with it salts and minerals which are not being replaced. We know this not merely from the pee-buckets which stood among the corpses, but simply from the timescale. Without water, they would hardly have lasted a week, and their agony prolonged itself for more than thirty-eight days. They do not talk, but for the first thirty-eight days, some of them write. They are taciturn, private women, great note and letter writers. They write letters when lesser women would scream, since they are not yet dead. 'None of us foresaw it could be this cruel and slow,' Breege-Ruth wrote to her younger sister,

> It can deteriorate worse into a slow hell for the four of us (horrible loss of sight, great pain). Please listen. I have thought long and hard about this. Let's think of exiting ourselves humanely... This is very grave. It will just get steadily worse... This is an overpowering strong feeling. I do receive correct guidance at times Jo and I have been right on several occasions in the recent past Jo...

A small tent, in it four bodies, people locked in private agony, cocooned in sleeping bags. They are probably, but not certainly, men, and they are at the last camp beneath the summit of Everest. The tent stinks of piss, because although they are profoundly dehydrated their bodies are leaking precious water, which they must get up and pass several times a night; even so, their urine is dark brown and concentrated, carrying with it a great deal which they cannot afford to lose. At any moment someone's lungs may start to fail, drowned in bubbles of bloody froth, or someone's oxygen-starved brain may try to solve its problems by sucking more and more blood into his head until he or she collapses and dies of a cerebral haemorrhage. They are not yet dead, in fact, they are not yet in the Death Zone, they are merely camped within sight of the tollbooth, but things are bad enough. Somehow, in the state they are in, they must find the energy and the will to get up, to dress, which may take an hour or more in such conditions, and to move onward and upward. One in six of the people who have gone up Everest has died there, so the statistics are against all four of them making it back to Kathmandu.

Meanwhile, what the hell is going on in Leixlip? According to an anonymous letter from a person signing as TT, Josephine Mulrooney became convinced that forty days of fasting would lead to a better life. They were hard women, the Mulrooneys. They kept themselves to themselves, neither gave nor took. Jo had as much on her conscience as any of us, perhaps. But whatever her history of the other six deadly sins, it is beyond doubt pride which sustained this enterprise; because Josephine Mulrooney decided to bypass the usual channels, the future moment at which the mountain of her mingy little sins would be raked over by angels with the expressions of public heath inspectors, the purgatorial delousing. She would demand Heaven and straight away, slapping the payment on the counter, cash down, and the question which she poses is: is mortal agony too much of a price to pay, if you think Heaven is a fact and not a metaphor? Frances, Catherine, and Breege-Ruth, two sisters and an aunt who had always been inseparably close, saw the force of this as an argument, because they went along with her. Even after thirty-six days, when Breege-Ruth writes 'our stomachs are devouring themselves', she was still also saying, 'the idea of ascending into heaven together is a good one'.

Well, then. Meanwhile in Nepal, four exhausted, sick, confused people lumber up into the Death Zone, padded almost spherical with layers of down insulation and windproofing. In Leixlip, nothing happens – within an ordinary definition of 'happen'. Nobody moves, but there is terrible evidence of the despairing revolt of the will to live. For God's sake, they write, I can see all four of us go into absolute hells of excruciating death. This is too painful, too dreadful, beyond human endurance. What is most horrible, piecing the story together, is that not one of them breaks rank. They generate a despairing fantasy about pretending that Breege-Ruth has cancer; that doctors might be persuaded to provide morphine, which they could take to disguise from themselves the fundamental fact that they are being eaten alive by their own stomachs. It is more painful than any of them could have imagined or believed, and certainly, they were weak, perhaps very weak. But no one shoved a note out through the letter box, saying 'help us', let alone broke out of the house. They held to their pristine intention.

Return now to the four rotting near-corpses at Camp Four. The choice which faces them is just as stark. If they go down, they will probably live. If they go up, they will probably die. Anyone who reaches the summit of Everest now must pass Rob Bell. One of the great climbers of the twentieth century, he came off the top in difficult conditions, having waited dangerously long for a weaker man. Four hundred feet down from the peak, he sat down and died ten feet from the lip of the South Summit: if he had got over that, the rest was downhill, and he could not do it. There is one ridge leading up to the summit, with Tibet down one sheer cliff to the east, and Nepal down another sheer cliff to the west. He will sit, the emperor of the eternal ice, till finally the wind scours him down to ground level – which it will, given time – within a few feet of where subsequent climbers must go. Rob Bell will never push up daisies, because he will not rot. The Death Zone is also the zone of eternal stasis. Those greatly favoured of God, in the Catholic tradition, are spared corruption. This is an extremely strange aspect of a religion which values the body – God incarnate, dwelling among us – as none other in the history of the world. But there is a masculine fear of corruption; of the workshop of filthy creation, the rot which generates new life, and Christianity has been overwhelmingly articulated and fleshed out by men. Rob Bell is a saint of the new masculinity, his stone-hard, incorruptible corpse, gradually being eroded, skin, muscle, bone, by the savage gales which sand the snow off the peak, stands as an icon of sacred individualism, since it will yield precisely nothing; less indeed than the climbers' faeces, which the thrifty sherpas collect from Base Camp and carry down to fertilize their fields. When this man died, his wife was seven months pregnant.

The four men (or women, or men and women) in the tent will drag themselves past Rob Bell; they will go on up. Once you have struggled as far as Camp Four, the need to go up is overwhelming. Once you have struggled to day thirty-eight of a forty-day fast, who is to say that the need to continue is any less urgent or humanly significant – but the effort of will involved represents a feminine, rather than masculine, form of askesis. Smooth as torpedoes, the Mulrooneys locked themselves into an exact, intimate archaic bargain, based on one cardinal assumption: that they and God know the value of their blood and flesh. It is possible to take the view that dying for God is simply a form of lunacy, but even in the twenty-first century this is not a universally acceptable conclusion. Fasting against God may be humanly deranged and is theologically sinful, but it is not purposeless or neurotic. Less so, perhaps, than the complete and malignant uselessness of Rob Bell's death on Everest.

Fred D'Aguiar

19 Victoria Street, Shrewsbury

For Geoff Hardy and Peter Roscoe

In this attic overlooking
March mirrored in a river,
Shrewsbury's colonial column
Almost one mile away beckons,
A spotlighted Lord Hill, hoisted
Two hundred yards nearer
Posterity among church steeples
Sprinkled by a fair spread of faithful,
Football stadium floodlights
And flocks in half a mind to migrate.
I wish a face on this Lord and less
Blood than his credentials
Advertise, I wish him back
Down to earth for history's sake.

Daylight strengthens Lord Hill's
Plinth and outline and weakens
My resolve to reform his past.
Cars gear up, a train pulls away
From Shrewsbury and more birds
Skid onto river, circle field and house
Than I can count. Blame today's
Enabling light for all this industry,
For all that is wrong with civilization!
Light shows the way for good or ill.
In this particular dawn even the gentry
Soften into a shadow of concrete,
Even water reveals its skin,
No more than a sheen wiped away

By breeze, skin that covers
Onion layers, there as hard light,
Light that paints the frosted air
Crimson. I think the river is black
Because of this skin, a black giant,
Reclined across this town. Just then
Four mallards lift off as one, push from
Water, their feathers prune the air,
They swerve up taking the river's skin
With them, peeling off skin to leave water
Raceless again, like light and mist,
So that Lord Hill towering over
Black water conquers an element
Rather than black people.

And the only race is river current
winding down to the weir,
One last bridge to limbo under,
Another town ahead for it to divide,
Pacify with kind reflections,
If only because those four mallards
Will soon rest on Lord Hill's effigy,
Make their statue-honouring bird calls
Then touch down again with those Vs –
Trails that widen on water and spread
A bird's legs to reveal, not a scar,
Opening, or any protuberance,
Just the planed, smooth face
Water turns towards light,

Soft features, wrinkled by a breeze,
Unwrinkled by calm, that contain a sky.
And such a soft touch it keeps dry
A solitary loose feather sliding on glass
Hardened in light to an iron mask,
So that everything seen in this light, all
Shrewsbury's steeples, football
Stadium, fields, satellite communication
Towers, and solitary, promoted

Aristocrat isolated on an island
In the middle of a roundabout, all
Remain captive and captivating,
Historyless as night, beautiful as black
Skin on water, true in this morning light.

*

Epigraph
Lord Hill (1772–1828) Member of Parliament for Shrewsbury in 1812, distinguished himself at the Battle of Waterloo. He became Wellington's second in command then General Commander-in-Chief of the British Army.

Jump Rope

We skipped rope we three did,
Skipped for the hell of it, no dare,
No doe ray me, nor stick and carrot.
For the jump, the landing and wait
One fraction, just a tick, weight poised
On the balls of feet, the intake of perfume
Into the perforated air intake, three kids
Free to exhale, air not ours, air
We borrowed to holler a name not
Ours, but written daily on our slate
Or else, a name that fetched what noise
We made and owned all headroom.

There to be hoorayed if a name
Could be fruit, ripe and at play
On the lowest branch, not chipped
By bird, reptile or beast. So
We hopped and dropped, our kind
In a bouncing, flouncing, trouncing game.
Three buds guided by the same
Torchlight, our lives led astray,
Astride a border of rope we skipped.
Up, down, up, down, up, and no
Down for the frame of mind
We were in, hemmed in by that frame.

Us framed, three, in a mind to be one.
Three, and a piece of string for a border.
How long I cannot tell now, removed
Now from that day to this till kingdom
Becomes Republic, gone too those two,

And that border guarded by that beast.
The border dispute turned our rope burn
Into a rope trick. Those hops in air drier
Than usual, that name, not our groove,
Played on lips free to call it to come
Out of hiding. Minds open for true
For the first time and last but not least.

Lesley Glaister

As Far as You Can Go

[novel extract]

Outback, Western Australia

They walk on. The sun creeps across the sky until it's overhead. Every now and then they stop and sip some water. Cassie squats down to pee.

Out of the corner of his eye he watches her. He wonders if it will make her dehydrate quicker. *Don't*, he wants to say, but doesn't. They don't talk much. Not a lot to say. Or not a lot there's any point in saying. His feet ache and a blister smarts on his heel. He tries to concentrate on other parts of his body instead to keep his mind off it. His stomach growls, affronted noises, not used to going without its breakfast. Not far off lunchtime now.

At last they come to an end to the blackness. Been walking hours, covered a fair few miles – must have been some conflagration. They walk across a strip of bare red. Absolutely bare and flat with creamy rocks rising from it, rounded like giant pebbles. A couple of dwarfish thorny trees. Something different to look at, at least. Sometimes a bird passes. An aeroplane high, high overhead. People sipping drinks, scoffing peanuts, watching a movie. Or maybe looking down and marvelling at the nothingness. A flock of small green parrots creak and squawk past low.

'Shall we sit down?' Cassie catches him up, points to a stone beneath which is a lip of shadow.

'Shouldn't stop.'

'Gray, I've *got* to sit down.'

They take off their shoes and sweaty socks, pour some water – just a drop – over their aching feet. They drink, scrunched into the shade of the stone. It's a strange shape, globular like a gigantic melted drip of stone. He rolls a fag, breathes in, savouring the bite of the smoke right to the bottom of his lungs.

'Remember these rocks?' she says.

'Yeah,' he lies. 'Not long now.' Truth is he remembers nothing. The truth is that with every step he takes, he gets less sure where they're heading. The track, hard to discern any more in the flat land, must be swerving round, the outlook changing till it seems they must be going back on themselves. If they only had a compass.

'Got another plaster?' he asks.

She rummages in her bag and helps stick it on the raw oval on the back of his heel where the blister has burst. They put their socks in the sun to dry and close their eyes. It would be too easy to drop off. The stone has a hot salty smell. He forces his lids up to meet the eyes of a small lizard, egg-yolk bright. Eyelids so heavy, head throbs, stomach growls. Should not have stopped. How is he ever going to start again?

He shuts his eyes, for how long he doesn't know but after a while hears Cassie moving, through his lashes sees her putting on her shoes and socks, getting up, vanishing from view.

After a few minutes she calls him from a little way away. 'Hey, come and look.'

Reluctantly he eases his feet back into sun-crisped socks and shoes, wipes his shades and puts them on – heavy and achey on his nose and ears – and stands up, steadying himself against the stone. On the the other side the bright hot sun flashes in his eyes.

'Look.' She points out a white painting, stick figures, arrows, a commotion of scratches. 'Looks like battle, doesn't it? And look – here's a funny hedgehog thing.' Despite everything, he finds a small spurt of energy for interest. They wander amongst the rocks a bit, discovering more rock painting. Like tourists, he thinks, out on a Sunday jaunt.

'Hey.' Cassie looks round nervously. 'Suppose there are aborigines about?' This might be a reservation, for all we know. We might be trespassing. They might be watching us,' she says.

'Nah,' Graham says, looking over his shoulder. 'Anyway, that would be good. They'd point us the right way.'

A beat is missed at this acknowledgement that they are lost.

She turns away from him, looks into the distance, then turns back. 'Isn't *that* amazing!' She points to a frieze of men and beasts – a desperate kind of smile on her face.

'Better get on.'

'Can't be far now,' she says. 'Here,' she says, 'have a peppermint.'

They drag on. Sweat soaks Graham's T-shirt; would take it off but then he'd fry. The sun booms, slams down, the heat actually a weight. So hot and bright, hard to look anywhere but down, but seeing the dusty blur of his moving feet makes him giddy. Walks along with closed eyes to rest them. Foot after foot after foot, throb after throb after throb of his head. His tongue feels thick and harsh in his mouth, like a doormat.

'Look!' Cassie says. He jolts himself out of some dream. '*People!*' She catches hold of his arm. He follows her finger with his eyes. And it seems there are people, a crowd of them – how distant? – spaced out and moving towards them. Small people, a scattered crowd advancing. They reach for each other's hand. *People?*

'They've stopped,' she whispers, shrinking half behind him. She's right. They are not moving. They are strange, strange figures. Not aborigines – what are they –

'Hey!' he laughs suddenly, realization hitting him. 'They're not *people*.'

'*What* – oh!'

He says, 'Remember, Mara mentioning these?' They drop hands and laughing with relief walk towards the scatter of termite mounds, which is like a field of statues. He hasn't seen them before, he's absolutely certain.

'Hope that doesn't mean we're walking back,' Cassie says.

He doesn't answer. The plaster has rubbed off his heel, skin too wet to stick, he can feel it scrunched up in his sock. His mouth is dry, head pounding with each step. A cloud of flies follows them, one buzzes against his eardrum and he thumps his face, trying to drive it off.

'But she said they were miles away,' he says. 'Remember? Don't suppose you've got any aspirin or anything?'

'Yeah. Headache? I took some a while back.' She is amazing,

burrowing her hand efficiently into her bag. She will be a brilliant mother, he can see that. She should have that. He must get her back safely so she can, one day, have that. She presses a couple of pills out of their foil and he swallows them, huge lumps scraping down his throat.

He stares round at the formations, like figures, stalactites, stumpy vegetal forms some nearly as tall as Cassie, the same burning reds and ochres as the earth, splattered whitely with streaks of bird shit. If things were different he would like to draw them. A couple of crows and a flock of black cockatoos hop about, suddenly scuttering upwards, flashing scarlet underwings. The mounds cast shadows, the sun has moved, Graham scrabbles his mind to try and work out what that means – and draws a blank. Shadows stretch towards them like a hundred fingers pointing back the way they've come. But they can't go back.

'There must be trillions of ants in these,' she says, 'or termites. Are they the same thing?'

But he has to face it sometime. He faces it with the termite mounds looming round him: they are lost. No sign of a track now for who knows how long. They might be going to die. That's what happens to stupid British people blundering about in the outback. They die.

'Come on,' Cassie says.

They walk until the termite mounds are too far behind them to see. They come to a place with withered grey bushes, thorns long as darning needles, the leaves like flecks of asbestos. There are bristly clumps of razor-sharp grass and more life, lizards, beetles, birds, a small brown snake printing S shapes in the dirt. A couple of emus stand poised against the light watching them pass and once they've passed they throw up their feathers, shriek and lollop away. What do emus eat and drink?

He doesn't look at the time. What difference does it make? The sun will go down in the end, whether he knows what hour it is or not – and then what? And so what? A couple of eagles are mauling and scrapping over a kangaroo carcass. He's never seen an eagle before, always wanted to – as a boy it was one of his ambitions. But these are not like the golden eagles of his dreams, these are thuggish things, dirty feathers billowing round their legs as their talons and beaks rip into the meat. They aren't cowed by the watching humans, carry on their dirty business unconcerned.

The light starts to deepen to mid-afternoon and a breeze springs up. They are walking straight into the sun, which must mean they're walking west – but what does that mean – the dry cogs in his head grind – is that right? Can't remember which way it was they had to go. His feet lift and fall and every time his right foot falls it's like a cheese grater against this heel and he forgets for a few steps at a time what he's walking towards or why. Cassie speaks and he's surprised, remembering she's there too.

'What do you think this is?' she says. He turns, can't see properly, the sun dazzle making after-images in his eyes. Limps back a bit, doesn't want to walk back, only forwards. She's got her hand on a post, a bit of rusty wire trailing from it. 'There's another' she points, 'we've walked past quite a few. A fence?'

A fence – and he walked straight past and didn't see. What sort of a state is that to get in? He tries to pull himself together. And now he looks there is something to the far right of them. Could have *missed* it. Distant, miles away still maybe, hard to tell, something that could be buildings, trees. Little water left in his bottle now, but he takes a sip. Maybe a station? Maybe a place of safety, water, food and bed.

'You thinking what I'm thinking?' Cassie says. Sounds like she's got a sore throat. He puts his arms round her and they hug weakly. She pulls away. 'Let's have a mint to celebrate.'

They walk towards the huddle with slightly renewed vigour. The sweet leaks sugar into Graham's blood. If only his foot didn't sting like buggery, but soon he'll be soaking it a bowl of water. A kind woman will bring him a cold beer. They can shower – or maybe there'll even be a pool. And then later food, roast meat or stew. Gallons of icy beer. A soft cool bed.

They walk side by side now, speaking little, searching as they approach. A pump comes into view beside a stand of trees. 'Gray.' Cassie stops. 'You don't think—'

'What?'

'It's not Woolagong, is it?'

'Nah.' His heart gives a sickly beat in his throat. 'Course not.'

They proceed a bit more slowly. It *can't* be Woolagong, there should be two pumps – but which direction would they be coming from? If it was, he couldn't bear the look of pure ecstatic smarm on Larry's face. *Can't* be. But at least there would be a bed to lie on, fresh water, beer and grub. He grits his teeth against the pain in his heel, scrambles his brain up trying to work something out from the sun's direction. But it's no good, that part of his head is burned out.

'What would we do?' she says.

'It's not!' he says, shaking off her arm. He can see it now, the whole layout is wrong, the whole lie of the land, type of bush, it's smaller altogether, not the same place at all, nothing like. Her hand flies to her heart. Under the sunburn and dust and crazy freckles she looks pale.

'Drink some water,' he says.

She swigs. 'Nearly gone, still it's OK now, isn't it?' She finishes it and wipes her mouth, her lips pink and wet where the dust's washed off. Looks at her watch. 'Five past four,' she says. 'Just in time for tea!'

'Come on.' He limps off towards the station. More signs of civilization – posts, a rusty bit of machinery, a broken-down shed. But no livestock in sight, cars, voices. There is movement, he sees, the pump turning. But his optimism wanes the closer they get, visions of kind women and cold beer evaporating. It is a ruin. The wreck of a station. Some trees – the most beautiful gums, startling white and green, alive with parrots, a fantastic freshness for the eyes – but otherwise no house, no people, just piles of old sun-silvered timber, corrugated iron, a couple of wrecked utes.

But there is something. As they walk amongst the wreckage they hear, smell, see it together, a splash of water – water spouting intermittently into an overflow tank open to the sky, as the breeze drives round the pump. They hurry over: the galvanized tank is deep with greenish water, floating with small dead things.

'Think it's OK to drink?' Cassie says.

'No choice.' Graham dips his finger in the tepid water and licks. 'Not salty, anyway.'

'If we catch the next gush,' she says, unscrewing her water bottle. 'That'll be OK.'

He eases the bloodstained sock off his foot, tiny fibres of cotton sticking on the raw place.

'*Ouch*,' Cassie says, wincing for him.

Graham drops his shorts, gets hold of the edge of the tank, hauls himself up and drops in. It is lukewarm, thickish and mushy at the bottom. But still the sensation of water all over his body. Just don't look too hard.

'Come on,' he says, 'it'll do you good.'

'But' – she frowns in at the bobbing mass of insects, feathers, slime and God knows what else. 'I'll just sit on the edge and wash.' Her head disappears then she pulls herself up, naked, holding a water carrier. 'To catch the gush,' she says, looking up at the rusty pump. It creaks, but doesn't quite turn. She lets her feet dangle into the water. The middle part of her is blinding white, almost blue against the tan of her legs and arms and face; her nipples a couple of soft pink flowers. She reaches down and scoops water, rubs it under her arms.

Graham dips his head under for a second to get rid of the cloud of flies, then comes up bubbling, tugs her foot and she slips in and right under, her hair streaming out, releasing a fuzz of bubbles.

'You pig!' she splutters. She grabs the side and hauls herself up. She starts to laugh then screams, looking at his arm, 'There's something on you!'

He hits at the thing. 'What the—'

'Get out,' she says more calmly. 'It's a leech.'

They scramble awkwardly out of the tank and land on the red dirt. It's clinging to his arm above the elbow. A slimy bluish sausage skin swelling as they watch. He chops at it with the side of his hand, but it just goes on getting bigger. Its mouth grips like a metal clip. He feels faint.

'Hold on—' she reaches for her bag and pulls out a box of matches, lights one but it goes out, lights another and holds it against the leech until it jerks and falls off onto the dirt releasing a bright trickle of blood.

He leans giddily against the tank a minute. Then laughs. 'Thank God for the Girl Guides.'

'What?' She looks at him crossly. 'Oh, ha ha.'

He swallows. It looks like a bloody old condom twitching in the dust.

'Get your shoes on,' Cassie says, 'ants, everywhere.' She's right. They are already swarming towards his drying blood. They pull their sweaty clothes on over damp skins. She finds him another plaster for his heel and he puts his trainers on, undone, minus the socks. They wait beside the tank for ten minutes or so till there's a gust of breeze strong enough to turn the pump and gush maybe a pint of clean water into the bottle. They take a swig each. It is warm but clean, tastes of clay.

'At least we won't dehydrate,' she says.

He looks at her and shakes his head. 'How did you know what to do about the leech?' he asks.

'Obvious, isn't it?' she says.

'No.'

She slathers suncream on her arms. 'I do feel a bit cleaner,' she says.

A big white cockatoo lands on the edge of the water tank. Stiff white quiff like a frosted Elvis.

'Hello,' Cassie says in a stupid voice.

'*Cockie, cockie,*' it replies, in a creaking voice. '*Good boy, Cockie.*'

She laughs. 'Cockie?'

'*Cockie, cockie.*'

'Poor thing. Must have belonged to whoever—'

'But this place must have been derelict for *years*.'

'Maybe things rot quicker in this climate. Anyway, parrots live ages.' She slaps her calf to get rid of the ants climbing her leg. 'Let's get away from here.'

They go across to a pile of sun-bleached, splintery timber and sit down. Flies settle on their faces, crawling at the corners of their lips so they have to keep their mouths tight shut. The late afternoon light is shading to a syrupy gold. No proper breakfast, no lunch and soon no supper. Graham manages between the awkward planks, to wangle himself a place to stretch out. He has a smoke, a fly crawling on his fingers, the fag, the corner of his mouth. Above him the sky is still blue though the quality of the light is changing. The breeze rustling the leaves of the trees sounds like the sea. Imagine the cold North Sea. His stomach moans.

'Yeah,' Cassie agrees, batting a fly away from her eyes. 'If we only had some food we'd be fine.'

He shuts his eyes. Obviously they'll stay here tonight. And then? Shuts his mind to the question. Too tired, too hungry. The wood is warm to lie on. He's starting to melt towards sleep when Cassie says:

'Get up!'

The tone of her voice makes him obey and it is not until he is standing on the ground that he sees the snake, a skinny, black and red thing, deadly looking, rearing up, flickering its tongue. They back away. The snake holds its pose for a moment and then flows away under the woodpile.

'*Exactly* the sort of place for snakes and all sorts,' she says. 'We should have thought.'

'Yeah.' He looks forlornly at the comfortable plank.

'Let's scout around for something to eat,' she says. 'There must be something.'

They find a patch of melons the size of tennis balls. He splits one open but it is dry inside, thready and bitter. Inedible.

'We could dig up grubs,' Graham says, 'they're meant to be nutritious.' He means it as a tease, but Cassie looks at him quite seriously.

'Only if the worst comes to the worst,' she says.

'Or I could *kill* something,' he suggests, looking at the white cockatoo which is getting on his tits, hopping round with them, congratulating itself. '*Good boy, Cockie.*'

'Not *him*!' she laughs. 'Anyway, it won't hurt us not to eat for one day,' she says. 'Think of it as a detox. We've still got a couple of mints. Want yours now or save it?'

Graham holds his hand out. Puts the sweet in his mouth and tries not to crunch. His jaw is aching to chew something. What about tomorrow? But can't face the question now. If he can't eat, he must at least get horizontal. But where? The place is heaving with bugs, snakes, there's a great tough spider's web stretched between two bushes, thick as fuse wire. Imagine the bugger that spun that.

'If you could have anything to eat, anything in the world, what would you have?' Cassie says. He looks at her in disbelief. She closes her eyes and smiles. 'I'd have a glass of lemonade – with ice – and a huge slice of Victoria sponge. With strawberry jam and fresh cream. Thick, cool, white—'

'*Shut up.*'

'Don't – ' she begins, then stops. 'Hey?' She holds up her hand, 'Hey, *listen.*'

'What?' The breeze flutters the leaves, the pump creaks, a splash of missed fresh water. Should have rigged something up to catch it –

'*Listen –* '

He strains his ears. She's right, there is something. An engine sound. He shuts his eyes to listen better. The noise quickly gets louder. A plane! It is a plane! They go out into the open, search the sky till it appears, a small plane, flying low enough, surely, to spot them.

Graham takes off his T-shirt waves it, Cassie waves her hat, jumping as the plane comes low. '*Here, here, here,*' she shrieks. The plane dips a wing and circles low and then away again.

'It must have seen us,' she wails.

He waits, watches. 'It's coming back.'

'Oh thank God, thank you God. Oh no—'

It seems to be leaving, but it is only banking into a turn.

'Working out where to land,' Graham says. The blood roars in his ears, feels he might pass right out with the relief. He pulls his T-shirt back on. '*Oh, thank you,*' he looks back at the sky, at whatever, '*thank you.*' He pulls Cassie towards him holding her tightly, she is alive, he is alive, it is all OK. They stand waiting. Holding hands like a couple of kids until the plane finally does touch down and bumps towards them sending up a storm of dust. The cockatoo croaks and flies away.

They grin at each other, walk towards the plane and – at the same instant – stop.

Bill Broady

In a Mist

Once upon a time they had lived in fine confusion. Where were they? Who was this person next to them? What had happened last night? Every morning they'd had to piece it all together... Then, slowly, everything regularized. Now weekdays were work, evenings reading; Saturday was shopping, movie, meal; Sunday was newspapers, and – if it wasn't raining – walking.

And so that midsummer morning they were toiling up the slopes of Ilkley Moor. Clouds of flies, ignoring his whirling arms, settled on his face and neck: bristled legs slipped into his open pores, tiny kissing mouths drank his sweat. She wondered why they ignored her, recalling her old headmistress's words, 'Horses sweat, gentlemen perspire, but young ladies merely glow.' She felt obliged to mimic his distress and so, long after the flies had vanished, beyond the bracken line, she still wanly flapped her scarf.

Regular steps were cut into the cliff, as if to lead to the front door of the ogre Rombald, after whom the moor was properly named. She rolled her fleece jacket under the rucksack's loops and then knotted the scarf to the webbing. Their dog, a fat pale Alsatian cross that had never grown into its donkey ears, kept looking back at them with an annoyingly patient, Christ-like expression. A sudden breeze shifted the fur along its back: her scarf flickered like a prayer flag.

To the south, windsurfers' sails were becalmed on Weecher Reservoir and caravans clung like lice to the side of Baildon Moor. Behind them cairns nippled the horizon beyond the enormous white domes, unmarked on the maps, of the radar station above Blubberhouses.

'I thought they'd have closed that down by now,' she said. 'It

wasn't put there for the Russians,' he said. 'It's there to watch – '
he lowered his voice – 'US!!'

The tops were crowded: mountain-bikers, their wheels deep-rutting the path; an OAP walking party, split into male and female halves twenty yards apart; hearty couples in fluorescent leisurewear, trailing their gloomy, gothic kids. And they all trilled 'Good morning!' although it was well past midday. At the Twelve Apostles' stone circle a child stood on each menhir, singing 'Happy Birthday' to a little girl sobbing in the middle. 'She's six today,' said a woman with a Camcorder. It was their next-door neighbour. They'd come to get away from everyone, only to find that everyone was already there, getting away from them.

She walked the rutted path with certainty and grace: he stumped along as if in suction boots. Her feet were clean, while he was muddied above the gaiters. A succession of threatening shapes breasted the heather, but it was always the dog, somehow ranging from side to side without being seen to cross their path.

They had coffee at Horncliffe Well in the ruins of what had been a Poor School. He told her how Teacher Briggs had doubled as a besom maker, his pupils chanting Pope's *Homer* while gathering the ling. Young John Nicholson, the wool-sorter poet, had walked the eight miles there and back in all weathers: his own students struggled to make the two flights up from the bar. He didn't blame them: they'd sussed that college existed solely to keep them off the streets ... As he talked, her thoughts drifted to next day's case conference. She hated meetings: when everyone looked at her it felt as if her eyes were being sucked from their sockets. Would they finally eject Tracey from the hostel? She reminded herself yet again not to think of 'they' but 'we'.

Beyond the grouse butts they passed a series of carved rocks. The cup and ring symbol – sun? moon? eye? omphalos? – formed the basic unit for a whirl of designs. What was life like five thousand years ago? Numbingly empty or teeming unimaginably? Perhaps nothing ever really changed. The same boredoms, irritations, awkward silences. You breathed in, breathed out, and felt the sun on your neck. Still, as usual, he touched one for luck, while the dog, following, gravely pissed on them. She eyed the stones with distaste: obscene graffiti, she suspected, or some stupid game. Across the valley, the listening domes appeared to have shifted position, as if tapped around by a giant croquet mallet.

On the descent clouds of flies again attended him – so fiercely that he ran the last quarter-mile, beating wildly at his own head. Her mind elsewhere – what if Tracey's drunken mother turned up? What if she didn't? – she thought he'd gone mad. When she reached the car he was still swatting around inside.

Even as she removed her rucksack she knew something was wrong. The scarf had gone. She emptied it, then put everything back, then did it again. When she retraced the path a little way the flies attacked: so they hadn't disliked her, just preferred him. She tried to recall a moment when the pack had felt suddenly lighter or she had heard a faint sound, above the soughing heather, as the scarf fell behind her. Hopeless: they gave it up for lost.

Driving back, he picked out an unlabelled tape: that weird jaunty-sad piano piece by Bix Beiderbecke, 'In a Mist' – inappropriate because, even through shades, the glare still dazzled. Her fingers were working knots on the dog's lead: without the scarf her blue-veined neck looked long and vulnerable. When they reached home she'd convinced herself that she hadn't been wearing it at all and ran upstairs to search. Spooning out the dog's mephitic meat, he heard the footsteps padding to and fro, a crescendo of slammed drawers and cupboards, then silence.

That evening he marked the essays on *King Lear*: 'Shakespeare might have been whatever you like but he was not an artist': surprising that this conclusion had been independently reached by Dean Quigley and Count Leo Tolstoy – he'd credited Dean with more sense. She reread Tracey's key worker's reports: 'Tracey took Nicki's boots ... Given final warning ... Tracey threatening and abusive ... Given final warning ... Tracey bit Cathy ... *absolutely* final warning ... we can't work with her.' On the contrary, she thought, they'd worked a miracle ... from mouse to monster in eleven weeks of 'CARE' – they – we – should be proud.

Sometimes they glanced at each other, but their eyes never met. Social worker and teacher: who would ever have thought it? They still pretended to believe that their humiliation was provisional, but what else was there for them to be? The silence remained unbroken. He marked the last few essays unread: B minus.

They slept badly. She lay on her back, as if pinned, a milky-metallic taste in her mouth. She'd acquired that scarf in her first week at college: it was just there when she emptied the spin dryer. She'd worn it constantly since: the colours matched almost everything. It had been bandanna, snood, kerchief; worn through coat epaulettes or tied round a bare midriff; as towel or, in her anorexic phase, as halter top; she'd recently even used it to staunch a client's slashed arm – the blood had all washed out. She recalled its feel – surprisingly heavy with a mesh-like cling, rough as a cat's tongue – but what was the pattern? Butterflies or flowers? It was blue – but light or dark? It was *too* familiar, taken for granted. If it came to that, what colour was her own hair? Her own eyes? She lay in the darkness trying to picture her own face.

His dreams reran the day in slow motion. A sharp image of her tying the scarf recurred: it was as if the very care she took somehow provoked its loss. She'd been wearing it when they first met: that it had gone felt as unnatural as a rip in the sky.

They were up well before the alarm. She made coffee while he read the last five essays, carefully erasing the minus signs from two of them. They watched the weather forecast: black cloud shapes had driven away the smily yellow suns.

'Let's go back and get your scarf,' he said.

'But what about work?'

'We'll ring in sick.'

He was the only person in the department who never took time off; she was covering for two and a half colleagues' nervous breakdowns.

Why did they have to be the only healthy ones? His students could stay in the bar and Tracey could be given another final warning. For the first time in an age they felt the rush of irresponsibility.

It was grey and damp, twenty degrees colder. They carried the dog, grumbling and half-asleep, to the car: maybe if they said 'seek' it might do something useful. Leeds was gridlocked and they hit fog along the Wharfe. A black dormobile, half-eaten by rust, overtook them on a bend. The worse the visibility the faster people drove: was it a death wish or the feeling that in such dream landscapes the worst that could happen would be to wake up? Stopping at a phone box they rang in for each other: for some reason he simulated a menacing bass while she pitched her voice quavery and high.

Again they followed the White Wells path. Where did flies go in the rain? Had the spiders eaten them overnight? He kicked the cobwebbed bracken: with a rattling cry a grouse flew at his face. He saw the red tongue vibrating in the back of its throat: as he warded it off it felt disgusting, not quite alive, like a thrown cabbage.

There were no views from the top: they could hardly see each other.

'What's the difference between fog and mist?' she asked.

'Fog's denser, I think.'

'I thought fog was yellow and mist was grey.'

It took him ten minutes to find the trig point, only regaining the path by following the sound of her voice. They crossed Backstone Beck, yesterday a trickle but now in spate. Landmarks seemed to have vanished and shifted: a wayside boulder like a hang-nailed thumb kept replicating itself, giving the impression that they were going in circles. The dog stayed close, tail down, pressing its trembling flank against her.

The duckboards over the peat hags were now covered with emerald slime. He followed Wainwright's dictum: 'Watch where you put your feet and you will never fall' – but all that happened was that he saw exactly where he was going to slip. He skidded a few yards on one leg, until it shot up to join the other, leaving him hanging in mid-air for long enough to notice the d-rings missed by his laces, before he returned to earth, left forearm breaking his fall. She toppled sideways like a felled tree, landing on top of him. All that trionic technology couldn't even keep them on their feet in summer, on level ground. They clutched each other and, as an unsteady quadruped, inched to the end of the boards, sweating so much under their Gore-tex that they'd have been better off without, soaked by fresh rain rather than their own grease.

Mud gave way to sand: the remains of the gritstone's cap, the strand leading to the Twelve Apostles. The standing stones, no longer white but eau-de-nil, flowered with lichen, looked closer together and larger, as if they had ingested the children of the previous day. One of them – a thirteenth! – seemed to sway slightly, then broke ranks and moved towards them. It was a large human figure, in army surplus drab: it threw back its parka hood, revealing a bristled, flaring face under a mass of back-combed lemonish hair. Tucked under its arm was a tripod, without theodolyte or camera. The dog growled but stopped as the man growled more convincingly back.

'Old,' said the man. 'Very old. These stones.'

'Bronze Age, aren't they?'

'Older. Been here f-f-f – ' he stuttered ' – for ever. Before the earth. Stones hanging in space.'

'I heard that these are replacements: that the original Apostles disappeared long ago.'

'Not Apostles. Nowt to do with them c-c-c – ' more stuttering – 'cowards. Thrice lost. Thrice brought back by m-m-m-m-m-magicks.'

The split toes of his baseball boots flapped as he hopped from foot to foot. She noticed a hospital tag on his wrist – probably from one of the Victorian asylums in the valley. From beneath overhanging eyebrows his red eyes groped at her body. There'd been plenty like him on her caseloads, but out here, in the middle of nowhere, it was a different matter.

'If you're not f-f-f-for them, you're against them.' The man leaned against the nearest stone and then whipped his hand away as if burned. 'The old ones.' He pistoned his arms wildly. 'The young ones. Their times are coming again.'

He repelled her. Steam was rolling off him, as if from internal stews of sickness and loneliness. What if he attacked them? – Two and a dog against one. Her hands balled into fists: she wasn't afraid.

'Actually, we're looking for my wife's scarf.' He wasn't afraid of the man either: he knew that real danger always wore a suit or appeared silently, without announcements –

'We lost it yesterday. Have you seen it?'

'A sccccc – ' the word stuck like a fishbone in his throat – 'ccc-cc-cc carf. Up here. You're fuck-uck-uck-uck-uck – ' his head was trying to rip itself off his neck – 'uck-uck-uck-uck-uck-uck-ing mad!' He wiped his lips and sighed. 'If it's lost, it's gone. Summat's taken it – ' his hands fluttered around his face like playful small birds – 'for summat.'

As they searched, he wrestled with the tripod's collapsing legs, repeating 'fucking mad' like a be-bopper deconstructing a riff. As they moved off again into the mist there sounded a last 'fuck-uck-uck-uck-uck-uck-uck-uck' – a perfect simulation of the alarmed grouse's cry.

The sheep were out: grey and striated among the rocks, perfectly camouflaged against long-extinct predators. A cropping gimmer had petrified when they reached it, while a millstone grit boulder abruptly trotted away. The wind pitched them forward, then with a counter-gust returned them to the vertical, so that they progressed in a series of jerks. Searching was pointless: they could hardly see their own feet.

At last they hit the cold black stone of the spinal wall and followed it west to Horncliffe. Again they ate and drank in the ruins, listening to the traffic below moving invisibly from nowhere to nowhere. Again he imagined the Briggs children, coming through the mist, their eyes dazzled by the pitiless sun over the plains of Ilium. Dean Quigley once asked him who won the Trojan War and he'd replied that although the Greeks took the city the Trojans hadn't lost. 'Why?' – Because they were beaten by a trick, because Hector had been history's one flawless hero, because a righteous cause can never be finally defeated. 'Nice guys finish last,' replied Dean.

'I never thought we'd find it,' she said, 'I just wanted to show that it mattered.'

'We're only halfway. And when this lifts we could start again.'

'Or come back tomorrow.'

They looked into each other's eyes and smiled.

'I like it better like this,' he said, 'wet, freezing, dangerous. More atmosphere.'

*

They somehow missed the great stone-capped barrow, but on Green Crag Slack the fog thinned and they could search again. Under the topstones of successive cairns they found a holed blue glove and a wooden toy engine but no scarf. The rain had filled the cup-and-ring grooves, sharply outlining their patterns – hooks, ladders, swastikas, roses. 'More stones hanging in space,' he said. She knelt next to him and ran her hands over the rocks' stubbled surface. An upward airflow, as if from a puncture, seemed to emanate from a deep central cup. She clapped her hand over it, the span exactly fitting the radius of the ring. The dog kept raising its leg, but was too wretched to produce even a drop.

Suddenly she felt faint. There was a roaring in her ears and her eyes unfocused. Her skin prickled, as when the madman had ogled her. She tried to withdraw her hand but it was held fast, as if by suction. Everything went black, then she glimpsed a strobing landscape under a nauseous acid green sky. The roaring swelled, a guttural shouting of warning or welcome in a language she couldn't quite recognize. Then the stone released her and she fell backwards. She watched numbly as the red circle in the centre of her palm slowly faded.

The fog closed in again but they descended safely, although they'd passed their car before the dog's barking drew them back to it. Not until they were belted up did they notice, across the windscreen, an unfamiliar motionless shape like a long, dark, red-headed snake. Only when they got out did they recognize the scarf, elongated by furling and folding, plaited with moor grass, dusted with sandgrains, slimed as if by the tracks of snails.

She shook it, brushed off the dirt, wrung it, then stared hard as if memorizing it lest it should vanish again. It was navy, fading to lilac, with a yellow and red border frieze of flowers and leaves, broken by a motif of three long-beaked birds, one flying left, one right, the third straight towards her. At its centre was the profile of a woman wearing a similar headscarf on which she was herself depicted and so on to infinity or until it blurred at the fourth recession. He saw the weave's silver threads glitter as she swung it with a wet slap back over her shoulders.

They sat in silence. There was nothing to say. She locked the door then unlocked it. He started the engine, then turned it off again... After a while he began singing 'On Ilkla Moor Baht 'At' – she joined in, but they could only remember the chorus and something about being eaten by worms. He put on a tape ironically labelled 'Nostalgia' and they shouted along with those old Punk numbers – Clash, Pistols, Damned – which suddenly sounded potent and menacing again.

Now he was driving flat out, overtaking everything. He could have done it with his eyes shut: a sixth sense had taken over, leaving the other five free to concentrate on her. Although the sound rippling up her slender throat was atrocious, her face was glowing, transfigured. He pressed her hand to his lips, turned off the headlights and put his foot right down. The rusty van from that morning loomed ahead. As they passed, its driver – the stutterer from the moor – gave them a regal wave.

They didn't go into work on Tuesday or the rest of the week – and, on Saturday morning, when they again went shopping, they bought different things.

Tamar Yoseloff

Weekend

You wanted to stand on the edge of England.
Land's End so close – no bus until spring.
We found a room with an ocean view
just visible over the roof of the nursing home.

The tinkly ice-cream van rattled against the wind.
We struggled along the front, our light city clothes
clinging to our skin, the amusement arcade
shrinking behind us, a town in a glass ball.

We passed a man walking a tiny dog.
He tipped his hat and smiled. I wanted him
to tell us of shipwrecks and squalls,
anything to take up our silence.

The sea swelled almost to our feet. You guided me,
your hand never forceful or demanding.
I wondered then if you would ever see
Land's End, if some woman would make it

her business to take you. Back in the warmth
of our little room, after we shook off our wet things,
I crawled into the smell of your skin
and breathed you in, before we called it a day.

Christmas in London

The skaters glide across the ice like songs
like the skaters who sliced the frozen Thames.

The bus stutters across the bridge; the red
lights of OXO, the cranes dressed in lights,

the restless Eye lit blue, its tourists
lifted above the skyline, above the tower blocks

above the wedding spire of St Bride's
above the fat dome of St Paul's,

shivering allotments, the ragged greens
the greens where houses stood, where houses stand

no more. The alleys wet with condensation,
the darkened streets, the rivers running

just below the ground, the Wandle, the Walbrook,
the Tyburn, the Fleet. The silent churchyards

with their crooked stones, each stone
a marker for a man.

Wayne Burrows

The Archway Altarpiece

All is vanity and vexation of spirit

– Ecclesiastes: 2:17

Shit happens, he shrugs, then turns from his mate
to head for wherever he's going next,
draws thin denim round his shoulderblades
then shouts from the backboard as the bus pulls
    out,
forget it, y'hear me? There's nowt y'can do...
His voice fades fifty feet away to a trail of words
only the conductor and the angels hear
though he stands, his hand on the silver bar
till he's out of sight. *Still*, says the one he's left
    behind
to himself and the world, *still and all*,
kicking his heels as he lopes uphill with all the time
on the clock to spare. They're both sixteen.
I lean over railings, half a cigarette burning down
to the knuckle of my one free hand;
braced in the other between palm and thumb
is a yellow hardback *Satyricon*.
At my back, the dark, exhaust-stained stone
of *The Archway Clinic of Sexual Health*
extends asylum behind electric doors
to every conceivable shade of love.
In the subway, scrawled on a convex mirror,
Sexi Girls floats over pregnant steps,
Jason is Gay × 500 Times and *Im The KING*

like the outstretched arms of a crucifix
tagged in marker on either side.
I am waiting, expecting nothing in exchange for
    my time
but a smoke, Trimalchio, and the test's return.

A Game of Pool

'I'm on the level,' says the man in black, waving his hand
through cigarette smoke, the air at the bar
chilled to a hum of air-conditioning: *'It ain't exactly a secret now*
that your guy Newton was kinda limited . . .'
'Whatever,' you tell him, picking up the accent and the attitude,
roll the foil from your Marlboro pack to a golden ball
then sling it down on the wooden floor, *'can we just shoot pool?'*
You rack the balls while he gets the beers, lay two coins
on the metal tongue of the tabletop, lift an empty pyramid,
set the white on its faded spot. You chalk a cue,
draw its length along your knuckles' back to test its weight.
He pots a red from the opening break, necks the bottle
and looks across at you. *'It was the German guys – Planck and Heisenberg –*
changed the way things seemed, "the act of observing . . ."
and all that jazz . . .' He tries for a rebound on the second shot,
just clicks the edge as the white slows down
and breathes relief: *'Course this game's Newton's even now . . .'*
You lean to the baize, lower your sight to an easy mark
then whack it down. Then the next, and another,
take a pause for beer, show off on the fourth with a cushion shot,
watch the white roll in between the yellow and black
like the cream squeezed into a chocolate eclair.
You stand back, smiling, saying: *'Newton, one . . .'*
'That,' he answers, *'is a bastard trick,'* forfeits the shot and
    doesn't leave much.
But now the green is only a processed light,
the colours moons adrift round the black.

The speed and hurtling crack of the game is water rushing,
an electron gale, your presence only a one-course meal
served in bone china on the deck of a yacht
at the height of a storm. *'This,'* you are thinking, *'is all there is.'*
   In the sight line you're holding on the final shot
your beer and the coins you're about to make
sit like placebos on the edge of the world, already yours.
You feel your arm flow forward, the spheres break loose,
think of *Mappamundi, Schrodinger's Cat*. Then close your eyes.

Underground

The Tube is hurtling through the dark, windows lacquered
    like a Chinese box
where faces, pale as petals from an orchid, gaze through
    themselves
at the line of ghosts in a parallel train, nothing there but
    the heat and noise
of fetid tunnels veiled in black, the clatter of wheels on
    burnished rails,
thin pages turning as someone leaves through a sheaf
    of notes.
A woman who boarded two stops back is mumbling
    apocalypse from an open book,
whispering hymns that barely shape her breath as she stares
    at her shoes;
*All worldly things shall return to dust, and we shall rise
    up to be judged –*
*We shall be clothed in naught but sin, and His wrath shall
    pour like rain . . .*
A man who clutches a child to his breast, its small mouth
    staining an aureole
in the powder-blue fleece of his tracksuit top, glances
    uneasily right and left.
Yet we flow through the earth like words in a wire, the
    blood in a vein,
will rise among gleaming escalators into the sunlight of
    the ticket halls.
We shall flood junctions, stations, buildings, streets, like
    a surge of power in a circuit board

before a system crash. This is only a moment, a single
   forward step in time
that might have ended up anywhere, but seems to end
   right here.

Matthew Davey

Waving at Trains

The day my father died was a huge relief. He'd been back home for a week or so. They'd delivered him to us in an ambulance. Two burly orderlies lifting him out of the back and wheeling him in his chair down the garden path to our front door. He was wrapped in a red shawl and his shrunken, idiotic face beamed at the flowers that overflowed from the bordering beds. As he reached the door, his brow wrinkled as he gazed at us with confused grey eyes. My mother hugged him and the orderlies carried him upstairs. My brother and I made way, watching with blank expressions.

Ed was two years older than I. We didn't fight much. He didn't really need to bully me. He knew he was going to be the man of the house before too long. 'Restraint is a virtue,' my father often said. He'd had vague ideas about creating leaders of men. Ed was his first shot.

We lived in the country and it was my father's habit to take long walks in the lanes, Ed and myself in tow. Exercise, he said, was a necessity and, besides, he enjoyed bird watching. Ed and I were hardly concerned with ornithology, but the walks themselves were the central axis to family existence. Mother usually stayed at home, but Ed, Father and I, wellington- and anorak-clad, would stroll out whatever the weather. Father would carry binoculars around his neck. His camera was entrusted to Ed, who would hand it over whenever required. Although jealous of this responsibility, I noticed how the huge leather case bounced around, oversized on Ed's chest, as he hurried to keep up with Father. He'd march on regardless of our pace, discoursing to the wind on a myriad of subjects too lofty for our years. Now and then, he'd lower his head to us and, with kindly, crafty eyes, inform us of something or solicit our opinion.

One stretch of lane ran alongside the railway. We'd hear the trains in the distance, their throbbing sound growing until they came into sight and hurtled past in a blast of diesel engine and rattling carriages. We'd try to guess what type of locomotive it was before we saw it. The class 50 had the sound of tribal drums, the 125 high-speed trains screamed. The 125 had two power cars, one at each end. I'd watch the first go by, hands over my ears, and then, taking them away and turning to watch the carriages disappear, be jumped by the second scream as it crept up from the rear.

The trackside was a haven for wildlife, our father informed us, as were motorway embankments. They were protected by the National Trust. No one could disturb them, not that they'd want to, but that was the case. Although they were noisy and dirty, rare plants and animals thrived. There were no boots trampling all over them. A good place to find nature he'd tell us, leaning over the fence with its 'No Trespassing Maximum Fine £200. British Rail' sign, and point out a cluster of yellow flowers or a scurrying shrew.

America, he informed us, had no railways and the motorways weren't fenced off. Therefore there were no rare species on the entire North American continent. 'Arse,' we'd shout at him. He'd regularly test us with ridiculous information that we were to spot and dispute. 'Arse' was the word he told us to shout at such trials. He wanted us to develop enquiring and critical minds. The passive mind is no mind at all, he said. Whoever shouted 'Arse' first was awarded ten pence, should they correctly identify any nonsense. Should we call him incorrectly, however, he'd appear hurt and demand ten pence from the offender. Ed, for example, disputed his claim that scorpion colonies lived between the railway tracks in certain parts of southern England.

A little further on the lane swung away from the railway, which then disappeared into a tunnel. We'd stop at a five-bar gate and rest a while, my father scanning the countryside through his binoculars, Ed and I throwing stones into the fields or teasing one another. We were twenty feet or so from the tracks. When we heard the growl of an approaching train, all three of us would climb up and, leaning forwards, stand on the third bar of the gate. As the train rounded the bend, we'd all raise our arms and wave, Dad on the left, Ed in the middle and me on the end. We called it the 'Stairs Wave', reckoning that it would be more noticeable and thus more likely to elicit a response. We often got reciprocal waves, people in their seats, others out of open door windows. Every so often the driver would let off his horn and we'd cheer. It wasn't often, but sometimes no one waved back at us. The buffet sandwiches were probably particularly bad that day, our father would opine. We only ever waved once. Father said it was bad luck to do more. I once 'Arsed' him on this issue and he agreed to test the fact. We waited five minutes and waved at the next train. Although someone responded, my father took ten pence to prove his rule.

We'd walk on and away from the tracks until we came to a decrepit nineteenth-century farmhouse. A small annexe that opened onto the road housed a mangy old donkey. He was always there, leaning over the wooden half-door that separated him from the road. His eyes were stupid and gentle, black orbs that blinked at us with all the interest he could summon. Father said his owner was an old man, too wicked and lazy to let him out into the fields. He'd produce a plastic bag filled with oats and we'd take it in turns to feed him handfuls. He'd pull his ugly lips back and nibble at the oats, careful and ticklish, never once nipping. We called him Donk. It was Ed's idea.

One day he came home from school and announced, 'The donkey's fuckin' dead.'

'Arse,' replied my father from his armchair. My mother slapped Ed and screamed at my father. My father had to give Ed ten pence. The donkey had, indeed, died. Boredom and neglect had finally done him in.

After that we'd walk past the same old farmhouse, only both half-doors were closed. We never said anything more about it as far as I can remember. We'd walk on, either side of the endless stripe of shit and straw that divided the road, dry and crusty in summer, wet and sloppy in winter.

My father was an architect. A successful architect and so we had a big house. It was a cottage, but a big one, large garden, green lawns, and flowerbeds, an apple tree in the corner at the back that gave us delicious worm-ridden Coxes. Being in the country, we lived a long way from anywhere of importance. My father worked at home. He never had friends over, none that I can recall. My mother worked in the social services department in the nearest big town. She'd drive off to work every day in her battered green Renault Five. She never had friends over either. Mother and Father were self-sufficient. They had each other. That was all that was required.

It wasn't as if they laughed, kissed, or even talked much. They knew the other was there and that sufficed. It was love, of that I'm certain. An ancient hermaphroditic love, impenetrable. Mother was a woman of very few words. She worked, cooked, sewed and read historical fiction. Father smoked a pipe and chuckled to himself. Ed and I roamed the gardens, bedrooms and attic, slaughtering Germans and Japanese, subduing the noble American savage. Quietly.

The first time Father became ill, Mother became pale and permanently clenched her jaw. She spoke even less than usual and would pace the house tidying, never sitting down for longer than ten minutes at a time. Father would stop her with both hands and then hug her with a slightly patronizing smile. We knew that something was wrong.

Ed and I were sent to live with an uncle while Father was in hospital. We visited him once. He was bald, save for scattered wisps, and his face was parched and tired. Mother took us in and he gave us a brief, clinical account of his situation before proceeding to ask us about our new daily routines. Mother sat expressionless with his hand in hers. After about fifteen minutes we were led outside. Mother stroked our hair and told us to be brave, before kissing us back into the custody of our uncle.

Father survived the chemotherapy and returned home. After a month's convalescence, we too rejoined the house. Father resumed his work and we continued our walks. Mother and Father became a little more tactile but, other than that, all was as before. Six months later Father's cancer returned.

He went back into hospital, but this time Ed and I stayed at home. We learnt how to cook. Mother continued working, but when she wasn't at the hospital she stayed in her bedroom, or sat in the lounge, or at the kitchen table. With unfocused eyes, she would stare into nothing. Ed and I began taking walks alone together. At the five-bar gate, we'd wait and wave. If someone waved back or the driver tooted, we'd talk on the way back. If they didn't, we wouldn't. The uncle and his wife called round a couple of times, bringing food and hopeful sentiments. We'd nod earnestly, my mother included, and wait for them to leave. At no time did Ed or I visit the hospital.

He decided to give up and come back home. Mother informed us, 'Boys, your father has decided that his medicine is too horrible to take any more, so he's coming back to be with us for a little while.' Ed and I just nodded. I'm not sure how much we understood of the situation. Ed may have grasped it better than I. We didn't talk about it.

And so he came wheeling down the garden path. An oblivious fool with a flat cap to cover his head. The doctor explained his medication to Mother, while the orderlies carried him up to the bedroom. After they had all gone, Mother gave us a weak smile, went upstairs and shut the door. Ed and I watched television, sat close to the screen with the sound down low.

Mother kept us away from Father. She said he needed rest. She began to cook our meals for us again, as she was always so busy anyway. Up and down the stairs she'd go, fetching food and medication, carrying away dirty plates and bedpans. She asked nothing of us but our silence. We willingly complied. Books, board games, quiet TV. We went walking, but avoided the railway. We didn't talk much.

After a week, Mother told us to go upstairs to Father. He had summoned us. Mother was giving him large doses of morphine to contain the pain. His bed sheets were tight, clean and white. He looked like the ghost of a Dales' shepherd, emaciated with a flat cap. His watery eyes bulged at us in excitement.

'Boys,' he said, gathering us close. 'I have visitors here, here in this room. Little flying saucers, spacemen. They take me away in their ships and they show me heaven. The colours, boys, you should see the colours.'

I could feel Mother's presence behind us.

'Arse,' I said.

She slapped me so hard that my ear rang.

Two days later my father died.

We went to stay with my uncle while the funeral was arranged. It was my first funeral. Closed casket. I wasn't impressed. There weren't many people there; a number of relatives I'd met a couple of times, some of Father's colleagues, the uncle and his wife. Afterwards, there was a small wake at our cottage. Mother seemed very tired, but smiled a lot. She seemed relieved. She stroked our heads and smiled down sadly. It was the only time during the whole business that I nearly cried.

We moved back in after that. Mother went back to work and we helped her with the cooking and housework. She was quiet, as she always was, but I felt that she knew we were there. It was winter, so it was dark when we got home from school. On the weekends, we went to stay with the uncle.

One morning, around a month after the funeral, Mother didn't come down for breakfast. Ed went up to check on her. He came down a couple of minutes later. I was still eating my cornflakes.

'She's dead.'

'Dead?'

'Yes. Dead.'

'How do you know?'

'She's not breathing. She's got puke all over the sheets. I took her pulse. She's cold, too.'

'Oh.'

I finished my cornflakes and then we put on our coats and wellington boots. For the first time, we did our walk backwards. We passed the locked donkey door and came to the five-bar gate. We stood on the third rung and waited. A scream approached and we waved furiously at the passing 125. Nobody waved back. We didn't say anything, just climbed down. Neither of us knew what to do, so we stood there looking into the distance or at the ground. A drumming diesel sound came to us. We climbed back onto the gate and, as the train appeared, began waving. Someone waved back.

Amanda Smyth

Look at You

Someone must have told her and maybe, because she didn't like housework and the kids were gone all day at school, Sandra started going too. She said it was another world altogether and everyone should try it, especially religious and political leaders. Come, she said. See for yourself. My mother wasn't so sure. But then, in those days, she wasn't sure about a lot of things.

Soon Sandra was going more often; sometimes two or three times a week. She kept saying how good she felt, and maybe what Shipper said was true: you must sort out your soul before it's too late; if you don't get it right this time around, you have to keep coming back until you do. Shipper could see auras and angels, Sandra said. He knew if you'd been a slave, an artist or a high priestess. There was a light brotherhood and a dark brotherhood, and you'd better watch out or you might fall into the wrong one. Sandra said there were all kinds of people working for the dark, especially famous people. Sometimes, if her husband was at home taking care of the children, Sandra stayed late talking about Shipper.

I don't know if it was the idea of reincarnation, or if it was Sandra's growing reverence for a spiritual life that caught hold of my mother, but it was the second week into the new course when she said, Shall we go, tonight? I said, Why not? There's nothing on the television. Apart from anything else, I didn't want her to go alone. She had spent most of that day in the back room, where I thought she was writing letters. But when I went in to say lunch is ready and do you want to eat outside, I found her lying under the mosquito net, her eyes open and staring; for a moment, I thought she was dead. My grandmother said she couldn't understand why my mother wanted to go. What's the point, she said: God is right here and God is all there is.

The meditation classes were held in a school on the outskirts of the city. It didn't take long to get there and, for once, the cooler was working in the car. We parked and followed the signs to the reception area, then up the stairs to the classroom. The wooden chairs were placed in a half circle and there was a separate chair at the front; desks were piled up in a corner. On a small table there were flowers in a vase. I thought they looked fake, but then tropical flowers often look that way. Like the pink lilies under the trees at the back of the house, or the orange flowers you see in a forest, or the red ones hanging on the mountains you drive through to get to the beach. They are thick and hard, and often full of tiny, biting black ants.

There was a ceiling fan, but it wasn't working. Someone said, Let's get some air in here, and a woman with her hair in a turban, like my mother's when she's just washed and wrapped it up, only this turban was fitted and coloured with a green design, started opening the louvres. There were only two men and they didn't look very comfortable. One reminded me of my brother, the other was older and looked worried. But then no one was talking and no one looked particularly happy, and I thought it was like in school when you start a new class and you want it to be over.

Sandra had said the woman running the class was more English than the English. So I imagined she would look like one of my mother's friends in England. Like Jan, who lived up by the village church and wore stretchy jeans and sweatshirts. Or Ann, who ran the boutique, drove a silver car and looked glamorous all the time, even if you stopped by on a Sunday morning. But when Shipper's wife walked in, she didn't look like someone my mother would know. She wore a full-length flowery dress. It had a high collar and long sleeves, and a frilly hem. Her fair hair was pinned at the back and free strands fell about her face. Her skin was pale and freckled, as though it had never seen the sun. Like sand on snow, I thought. Get a bit of sand, throw it in the snow and there she is. She was wearing tan sandals; they reminded me of sandals I used to wear in first grade.

'Good evening,' she said in a small, clipped voice. Then she went around the group, looking at each person for a long time. She kept her arms by her side, while her eyes, clear and cold and grey, shifted from one person to the next. When she came to me, I looked away at the wall where there was a picture of Jesus. I noticed it was crooked. When I looked back she was still staring. Then, at last, she sat down and closed her eyes.

Sandra said it was a shame we got her and not him. Shipper didn't just sit there with his eyes closed; he talked about awareness and attention, and how to keep your mind clear so you don't get confused. That way, if you want something really bad, then you can get it.

'The key to your happiness lies within; let go and let peace in,' said Sandra. We were standing in the driveway leaning against the car, but when Sandra said this she stood away from the car and looked up at the sky. For a moment, I thought, What is she looking at? Then I asked if Shipper was handsome and she flashed me a different look. 'Well?' I said, easing myself onto the slippery bonnet.

'Kind of.' She was smiling now in a typical Sandra way, showing her bright white teeth. Then she fished in her shoulder bag and took things out: a comb, keys, pieces of paper, her wallet, a tiny torch, and put them on top of the car. The photograph was yellow around the edges. When I said, Not my type, she said, 'Look, silly, it's an old photo. Don't you know you can't always tell by looking at a picture?'

*

So we started going once a week. And every week we saw the same people, apart from one or two, like the men, who didn't come back. And every week the woman with the turban, whose name I could never remember, opened the louvres, and when Sheila came in we all sat down and looked at her in that same way that she looked at us. And after a while, although they seemed cold, I didn't mind looking into her eyes because it was part of being detached. When you're detached, Sandra said, you can be more compassionate. There's no point getting sentimental.

Mostly we meditated for twenty minutes and then we talked about what had happened. Some people saw light or felt themselves drifting into other realms of consciousness. Others started to cry when they talked about someone who had died, or they saw themselves as a child. Put your arms around your inner child, Sheila would say. And if I opened my eyes, I sometimes saw the blonde woman, rocking back and forth; I wondered what had happened to her.

I knew I wasn't doing it right because I never felt peaceful. When you meditate, Sheila said, you're meant to close your eyes and empty your mind. But when I tried to do this it was almost impossible. I remembered a movie I wanted to see, or someone's telephone number went round and round. I tried to let my thoughts go like Sheila said: let them go like leaves in the wind. But then I started thinking about leaves and where they might blow, and I'd find myself in a wood. I didn't want to think about the wood, so I'd get back to the room as quickly as I could, and look at the wall, at the crooked picture of Jesus. Whatever happened, I always ended up in the same place. Once, when Sheila asked me what I had seen during the meditation, I didn't know what to say, so I said I saw Jesus. Everyone thought that was very special.

Sandra said that maybe my mother could bake a cake for the end-of-term party at Shipper and Sheila's house. All three groups were going to be there: the beginner's, intermediate and advanced. Everyone had to bring something. Sheila was making vegetarian burgers to be cooked outside on the open fire. The party would start in the afternoon and go on into the evening, at the end of which there would be a group meditation.

My mother didn't know what to wear, so she asked my grandmother to make her a plain dress. I decided to wear shorts and a blouse and sandals.

*

There were cars parked along the road and some were in the driveway. The house was white and small, with a sloping silver roof, and burglar proofing over the windows. A mango tree made the front yard dark, and though the grass was short, the bushes with blue flowers were high and wild. The garage was full of boxes, and furniture covered with white sheets.

In the kitchen, where food was arranged on wooden trays, Sheila was stirring a large pot. She looked hot and tired. But when she saw my mother and I, she smiled in a cheerful way and said hello. Then she took the cake and told us to go into the yard, where Shipper was lighting a fire. There were drinks out there in a cooler. 'Please ignore the house,' she said, 'we still haven't unpacked.'

Apart from the boxes stacked along the passageway, the house was almost bare. In the living room there was a sofa and an American recliner chair. The tiles on the floor were grey and peeling, and the thin curtains were also grey. I thought how dismal it was, and even if we didn't have much, how bright my mother and I had made our simple home. But then, I thought, our house was like this too when we first moved in.

Outside, the woman with the turban was unfolding a chair. She was listening to someone I couldn't see. Then she was laughing, and I realized I had never seen her laugh before. My mother said, Come on, dreamer girl.

*

Shipper was shorter than I had imagined and his dark hair, neatly cropped in the photograph, was almost long enough to make a ponytail. He saw my mother, and then he saw me and came across the grass towards us. He was wearing blue trousers and a yellow T-shirt. His feet were bare. 'You must be Angela,' he said, taking my mother's hand. My mother said yes, and that she had heard so much about him from Sandra. 'And you saw Jesus in a meditation,' he said, turning to me. His eyes were lively; they reminded me of a movie star, but I couldn't remember who.

Most of the afternoon was spent sitting in the shade. Some people were talking in the kitchen, others were on the veranda, where there was a table laid with plates and salads and fruit. When Sheila wasn't serving drinks or carrying dishes to and from the table, she was hovering around the guests, making sure they were all right. Her long white dress made her look like an apparition. This heat is too much, she said, fanning herself with a straw heart-shaped fan. I remember thinking how odd she looked, and what it would be like if we suddenly swapped clothes.

My mother chatted with the blonde woman, who, it turned out, had lived in England for a while. She talked about English department stores and how she missed being able to go in and find what you want in ten minutes, not like here, where you have to drive all over the island to find a pair of shoes. When she said she must go, Shipper said he wished she wouldn't miss the meditation. Then the doorbell rang and Sandra was suddenly there, holding a watermelon. I thought how pretty she looked in her pale lilac dress; I had never seen her wearing a dress before. She was wearing lipstick too, a light glossy lipstick. 'Tell her to stay,' Shipper said to Sandra, his hand on the blonde woman's shoulder.

'My husband's the same,' said Sandra, nodding slowly. 'He's not sure about meditation.'

I wanted to say, He calls it mumbo-jumbo.

I was surprised to find Shipper looking at me. His eyes seemed smaller and less friendly than before, and for a moment I felt afraid and looked around for my mother, who, like everyone else in the group, was sitting with her eyes closed and breathing deeply. But then he smiled, and I felt a strange heat rise inside, like when you see someone you know and you're glad to see them. And his face looked almost holy. And I thought about old religious paintings of saints and apostles and wondered if he could be an apostle, one that came back to put things right. And then I thought, Be careful – you'll go mad as a hatter.

*

Looking back, I wonder if Sandra would ever have told me if Shipper hadn't met my mother in the store. Sandra has all the details, he said. Ask your daughter to give me a call. It's only for the summer vacation. When I saw Sandra, she said she didn't tell me right away because the kids were on holiday and there wasn't a spare minute. Also, she didn't think I would be interested; it was probably dirty work, particularly in the mornings when I'd be helping Sheila. There were boxes to unpack, rooms to clean, and walls to paint. In the afternoons, I would work in the small office; follow up any interest from potential investors with phone calls or typed letters. She said Saturdays were never a good time to call people at home because they had things to do. She had tried telling Shipper, but he wouldn't listen. The idea was to get them to know about the meditation programme; not an easy task. She would do the job herself, at least the sales part, only weekends were impossible. Of course, I would have to find a way to get there too.

When my mother heard Sandra's voice she came outside. She leaned against the wall and asked me what I thought, and when I told her it sounded just fine, she said it was up to me; if I wanted to go, she would drop me there and pick me up at the end of the day.

Sheila was at the store and Shipper was working with a client when I started on the books. They were unusual books with unusual titles, like *Metaphysics in the New Age* and *Jesus in the New World* and *Mind, Magic and Mysteries*. There were diagrams in some, with rainbow colours to illustrate different bands of energy and how they flow around the body. There were photographs of men floating in the air and a child with long hair who bled from her wrists. There were exercises in how to locate your higher power, how to find your destiny. There was a drawing of a palm with each line marked and labelled. I couldn't find my headline and my destiny line was broken into dashes. But according to the diagram I was going to have three male children and hardship in my middle years. By the time Sheila came home I hadn't done very much. She said it was OK and would I help her in the kitchen.

*

Sheila came from a middle-class family in Wales. She had met Shipper on a retreat just after she finished university. She knew he was special the moment she met him; there was something both ancient and modern about him, she said. When a mystical teacher told Shipper he was here to do important work, he decided to forget about his law degree and start training in particular metaphysical practices. They were married in a field of blue flowers. After the ceremony someone sang 'Stairway to Heaven', and they jumped over a stick like pagan people. One day, if they were to separate, the stick would be broken in two. It was that simple. The stick was in the bedroom. I didn't expect it to be so long.

*

For three weeks, while Sheila was at the store and Shipper was working, I unpacked boxes. When Sheila came home, she would tell me what to put where and sometimes, when she was unsure, she'd say quietly, 'Oh, don't worry about that,' and put it to one side. Now and then Shipper came into the room and looked around. If Sheila wasn't there, he sat on the American recliner chair and asked questions: about my mother, or England, or what I wanted to be when I grew up. Not that you are a little girl, he once said. Sixteen is pretty grown up. A hundred years ago you might have had a kid or two already. I liked it when he talked to me in this way; it made me forget about certain things – school, my mother, my grandmother, the house where I lived. I often wanted to tell him about that time last year when I had lost my virginity to an older boy, who, afterwards pretended that he didn't know me. But I thought he might think badly of me, so I didn't. After a while, Shipper would get up and go back to work.

Eventually, the books were on the shelves, the record player was working and all the albums were stacked, cushions and pillows unwrapped, ornaments and vases dusted and wiped, pots and pans and special cutlery put away, photograph albums placed in drawers, sheets and towels in the laundry cupboard, more pictures were on the walls (but only for a while because the walls had to be painted), and the tools were out in the shed. Sheila helped me put the empty boxes by the gate. When Shipper saw them, he said I was a star.

*

I thought the walls in the living room should be painted yellow. My room is yellow, I said, and when the sun comes in it is lovely and gold. Sheila said it must be pale, like a daffodil yellow, nothing too heavy. Shipper said, Let her decide, and tousled my hair as though I was a small child. 'Don't you think so, Sheila?' Sheila didn't say anything. But when she left for the store the car made a screeching sound. I must have looked worried because Shipper said, The gears are giving trouble. Then he sat me down on the recliner chair, and told me about the snake sleeping at the bottom of my spine.

Shipper said everyone has a snake there. The snake needed to wake up, and when it was awake everything would change. It would start to uncoil and rise through my body, making its upward journey through the different energy centres located at specific points. The aspects of the centres would be opened and rediscovered. The journey might take months or years, but each stage was marked by distinct changes in consciousness associated with particular psychic powers. My energy was blocked, Shipper said. But he could help me release it. Then he looked at a place below my stomach and put his hand there. 'Breathe,' he said. 'Breathe.' So I did.

*

Sometimes we waited until Sheila was at the store. As soon as the car pulled away from the drive, Shipper would come into the kitchen, where I was usually washing or cleaning or putting away dishes. He led me to the recliner chair, where I lay down and closed my eyes and tried to stop my heart from racing. Then he played music with chimes and bells, and spoke in a calm, slow way. He told me to imagine the snake waking up, uncoiling, rising through my spine, pushing through the centre and bursting out of the top of my head. If I opened my eyes, he smiled and covered my lids with his warm hands.

Sometimes, to wake the snake up, I opened my legs and he put his hand inside. At first I was uncomfortable and a little self-conscious, but after a while I didn't feel so uncomfortable. I knew, more than anything, that Shipper wanted to accelerate my spiritual growth. Now and again he blew healing white light into the place where the snake slept. Or I took off my vest, and he put one hand on my bare back and the other on my heart. 'Breathe in the white light,' he'd say. 'Breathe.' Sometimes I worked the light with my fingers; that way Shipper could make sure the energy was moving upwards. 'Like this,' he would say breathing deeply, 'in and out, like this.'

When he was inside me, Shipper said I became other women; women with different eyes and different skin. At first I was alarmed, but then I wanted to know who they were, these other women. He said I was a geisha and an African slave. I was a maiden from Denmark, a Spanish gypsy. I had had lifetimes in Egypt and Japan. He'd say, 'Look at you, like a maiden.' Or, 'Look at you, like a gypsy.' And sometimes he became someone else too: a young boy, or a pharaoh, or a soldier from the war. I'd want to say, Look at you, like a boy. Or Look at you, like a prince. But usually, I didn't say anything, apart from near the end when I'd tell him not to get it on my clothes. The first time it seemed to be everywhere, like thick glue: on my mouth, in my hair, on the front of my blouse.

When Sheila was at home, she was usually in the yard watering the young trees or cutting the grass or the hedge, so we went into the office, where there was a lock on the door. That summer, I took to wearing dresses so I only had to remove my underwear. We lay on the floor, or perched on the desk, or balanced on a chair. I knew she couldn't see what we were doing because the curtains were closed. But when I heard the hose, or the clipping of the shears, I suddenly felt uncomfortable. Shipper said I mustn't feel that way or think about all that. Sheila had her own karma to work out. At some level she knew what was happening, and at some level she was in agreement with our relationship. Otherwise how could it happen?

If Sheila knew there was something going on, she never let me know. Only once, in the bathroom, when I saw her in the mirror while I combed my tangled hair. I said, 'Hey, Sheila.' But she didn't say anything. She walked away down the corridor like someone in a dream.

*

That night Sandra dropped by. We took our cold beers onto the veranda. Although I didn't feel like talking, in a way I was glad to see her. She said she couldn't stay long because her husband was still complaining about the time she had spent away from home. He said Shipper was bad news, that she ought to get her priorities right. It was one thing to go on a spiritual quest when you're young and free; it was another thing when you have a family. Sandra seemed angry and sad at the same time. She had lost weight, her dress looked loose. These days she always wore dresses. 'If I don't go out, I go mad,' she said.

When she asked about my job, I said it was fine and not dirty work at all. I wanted to say, Thank Christ for you, Sandra, it's you I have to thank. But instead I talked about the organic store that had recently opened in the city. Then I talked about October, just around the corner. And how, in this hot place, you might never know it was coming. I talked about the new term, starting soon, and how I hoped to skip intermediate and go straight into the advanced course; how my mother wasn't sure about going back to classes because there were too many things to do around the house.

Then Sandra told me about her idea. She wanted to organize a trip. We could hire a house by the sea, and a whole group of us could stay there for the weekend. She would tell her husband it was the last group gathering and he had to let her go. I said it sounded great and maybe I could ring around.

*

The boat was leaving at seven. By the time my mother dropped me at the docks, there were crowds making their way along the platform to the lower deck; from below, each level of the boat appeared full. I wondered how I would find the others. My bag was heavy with vegetables and fruit. I had a pineapple too, long and sweet, with its top cut off so it wouldn't tear my clothes. I was suddenly glad my mother had decided not to come. At first I thought she might, but then she had said no, that she really must start looking for a part-time job next week. She had said Sandra would look out for me. And my grandmother was just down the road if it all got too much. I wanted to say, You don't have to worry about me, Shipper will be there.

The group was gathered on the top deck. Sheila was sitting on a bench surrounded by bags and boxes. The blonde woman was leaning against the rail and watching the passengers below. She was wearing a bright orange dress and her hair looked like it had been set in curlers. 'Hello,' I said in a cheerful way and put down my bag. Then I said, 'That's a nice lipstick.' She said thanks and smiled.

The woman with the turban was transferring something from one bag to another and complaining about the heat. There were a couple of people I hadn't seen before. Away from the group, Sandra was talking intensely to Shipper, who was looking up at the clear night sky. I wondered what she was talking about. The sea was huge and black, except where the thin moon tossed a silver glow. There was a strong, salty breeze.

*

I didn't notice the man at first. Not until Sandra pointed him out. He was wearing ordinary clothes: trousers and a shirt and sandals. His hair was greased and slicked back from his fine-boned face. He didn't seem to be bothering anyone, but then Sandra had said from the moment he came upstairs he was looking at Sheila in a strange way. In fact, she said, he was staring at each member of the group, but he was looking at her more than anyone else.

Then Sheila started feeling hot and peculiar. I thought she looked very pale, more pale than usual. I looked around for Shipper, but couldn't see him. The woman with the turban said he had gone downstairs to get something to drink. 'But why would he buy a drink,' I said, 'when we have a whole cooler of sodas, right here?' The woman shook her head, and glanced over at Sheila, now leaning against a large box. 'I'm going to find him,' I said.

The lower deck was overcrowded. People were sitting against the walls of the boat and some were lying on mats. It was hot, though the air conditioner was supposed to be working. Some were smoking and some were drinking rum or Scotch. Bottles rolled about the floor and I thought, Christ, if I fall over, I might never get up.

The bathrooms were marked, but as I got closer the smell was so strong I couldn't go inside. A lady said, 'Don't bother with that, miss. Find a corner somewhere. It's dark, no one will know.'

I was about to go upstairs when, through a window overlooking the deck, I saw a woman's fair hair blowing out like a bright flag. She had a foreign look: German or Swedish. It looked like Shipper was standing beside her, but I wasn't quite sure. Then I realized I couldn't see Shipper properly because his mouth was fastened on her neck. I pressed my face against the glass, blocking out the light behind me. Shipper's hand was crawling up her thigh; the other was on her back. When I banged on the window – my fists struck so hard that if it hadn't been made of special glass, the plastic kind they use on boats, I would have broken through the window at once – Shipper and the foreign woman looked up at me as though I was a lunatic. Her tilted, startled face appeared unreal, like somebody in a cartoon. Then, I don't know why, but in a high voice I yelled, Sheila! Sheila!

Sheila was sitting with her back pressed against the side of the boat. She put her head between her knees and tried to breathe under Sandra's instruction. Her forehead was wet and her hair was sticking about her face. When Shipper helped her up so she could see the glittering lights of the approaching bay, she looked so weak I thought the wind might throw her down. Shipper wanted to know where the man had gone. 'He could be anywhere,' Sandra said angrily. 'He could be anywhere.'

While Shipper went to find a taxi, Sandra held Sheila's arm and supported her back; I tried to fan her face with a magazine. 'We will have to find a priest,' Sandra said. 'A priest?' I suddenly felt very afraid. 'This happens sometimes. Someone comes along and they are full of dark energy. Then they try and take you over. It's a kind of possession. That man transferred something onto her.'

Sheila started to groan and her head flopped forward like a puppet's. Sandra tilted it back and together we propped her up against the nearby wall just as Shipper reappeared. We have to take two cars, he said, looking at the others gathered near an enormous tree. Then he said, Who is going with who? I said, Isn't it bloody obvious?

By the time we reached the villa, Sheila was shaking and white; her eyes were glassy and she was speaking in a garbled way. Saliva was running in a line towards her chin, leaving a trail like a small slug. Shipper carried her inside and laid her down on the sofa while everyone stood around and watched. Someone gave him a blanket. I didn't know what to do, so I sat by the door and looked out. I thought, If I can think about the flowers on that vine, if I can think about the Lady of the Night, then everything might be OK. But suddenly Sheila started singing a hymn in a high voice, and she was up, and standing with her arms outstretched, and Shipper was trying to push her down. 'Breathe in the light, Sheila, breathe in the light.' Shipper sounded unsure and he looked afraid. Sheila began to sing louder, so the tune became distorted, and if I hadn't remembered the words, I would never have known it was 'All things bright and beautiful'.

'Sheila, Sheila. It's going to be OK,' said the blonde woman, holding onto Shipper's arm like it was a rail. But Sheila looked at her as though she was a demon and the woman ran outside. Then Sheila pointed at Sandra and her eyes went into dark slits. I thought, Oh God she's going to rush at Sandra. But she didn't. Instead, she turned to me and shook her head like a horse shaking off heat or flies. Then Sheila fell on her knees and began to cry.

From the end of the road I thought she sounded like an animal. I could still hear her crying from my grandmother's house.

Helon Habila

Harmattan

[novel extract]

1

The scream wakes him up with a start. It is a woman's voice, high-pitched and visceral, song-like, and from the sound there is no mistaking the cause, someone is dead. Mela turns his face to the window and watches the weak sunrays streaming in through a crack. Death, and so early in the morning. He wonders who it might be. Someone young, no doubt – the screams are not so soul-raking if it is an old person – someone in his prime, gone in mid-stride, forever blind to this sun streaming in through the crack in the window. The scream tears through the morning landscape like a sickle, a question mark, scything through the branches of the mahogany trees that line the streets like reception committees, over the thatched roofs to the outlying hillocks that flank the village in a horseshoe to the west. What was quick and possible now lies cold and limited; dust has returned to dust.

Gradually, one by one, other screamers are joining the scream. Bent on their knees before the triangular stone hearth, the kerosene poured, the match about to be struck, they hear the scream and abandon everything to answer its summons. Here in Keti death takes precedence over every other thing: religion, birth, marriage, work. For the next week all activities, except the most basic, will be suspended, people will readjust their schedules to fit in with death's schedules, they will change the way they talk, walk, recompose their countenance to look sad as they troop to the house of mourning to pay their last respects to the dead. Being simple and not very eloquent, they will express sympathy merely by their presence. The men will sit outside the compound on straw mats beneath nim trees, shifting the mat whenever the shadow shifts, playing cards, exchanging small talk, easing the passage of the grim, painful hours. Within the compound the women will roll on the ground and scream and knock their heads against the earth, trying to exorcise the monster of heartbreak, till they are exhausted – but with each newcomer the ritual will start all over again, on and on till the tears gradually bleach the pain and memory and make them lose their sharp sting, till they are nothing but a dull murmur in the secret recesses of the mind.

One week for death, then life, like a river that has been dammed, will be allowed to resume its course.

Mela forces himself out of bed. He feels weak. Death always has that effect on him. His almost forty years on earth have been marked at every turn by death, and when he looks back he sees the headstones lining the passage of years like milestones: uncles, aunts, father, mother, brother – his very first day on earth was tainted by death, his mother's, barely an hour after she had given birth to him and his twin brother, Mol-Mela. And as a sickler,* he has lived all his life literally under the shadow of death.

Footsteps from the direction of the living room come to a stop outside his door. Aunty Kale. She knocks and calls out, 'Are you awake, Mela?'

He is standing by the window, the light in his face, staring at his eyes in the mirror, seeking for telltale signs of death; one can always tell if one knows what to look for, if one is as well-read as Mela in things of death. Mela saw it on his brother's face on the day he died, a shadow, like an eclipse, around the brows, a certain lack of focus in the eyes – as if they are gazing at something far away, something beyond life itself.

*

'I am up,' he says, putting down the mirror. His face is normal, but death is a sly customer, it takes you from behind when you least expect it. He puts on a sweater and old khaki trousers and opens the door. She is dressed in a grey blouse with matching wrapper; a narrower wrapper is thrown round her shoulders,

---

* Person suffering from sickle cell anaemia

shielding her neck and chin from the savage cold. Already her face has assumed an appropriate gravitas.

'I have to go out, there has been a death. One of Salomi's children,' she says. Her arms are crossed over her bosom. Mela's tall, round-shouldered figure towers over her as he steps into the narrow passage outside the door. She is short and stout, not up to five feet five inches, the top of her head barely reaches to his chin level. But whereas her squat peasant figure radiates good health, his thin frame, his sunken eyes, his effete limbs, give him the appearance of a person just emerging from a sick bed. She turns and follows him as he passes her into the living room. She has kept a flask of tea on the table for him. The cold wind whooshes in through the half-open door, sharp, skin numbing. He pours out the tea into a plastic cup and holds the cup in both hands, enjoying the warmth; he raises it to his face, inhaling the warmth and the aroma, something only the living can do. He sits down and sips the tea. He wonders what killed the man; he asks her.

'I don't know. Poor woman, with her husband dead not too long ago, and now this. Poor woman. I have to go now.' She starts for the door then stops, one hand on the door handle. 'You will come and pay your respects, won't you?'

'I will see if I can.'

She turns round and takes a step into the room. The carefully arranged mournful look gives way to a frown; now she looks exactly like her brother, his late father: the knotted forehead, the arched eyebrows, the eyes like needle points, the lips just a line across the lower face.

'What do you mean, "I will see"? What does that mean? Salomi is your kin, have you forgotten that? She is your mother's cousin.'

'But my mother is dead,' he wants to tell her. 'I never knew my mother.'

But he knows that his mother's kinship with Salomi is not the real issue here. The real issue is that he has not stepped outside the house since his brother's death three months ago. He has sat out the days in the living room, wilting before her eyes, browsing desultorily through books, staring for hours into space, and quickly retiring as soon as it gets dark. With the coming of harmattan his maudlin mood has deepened. Some days he never bothers to step outside his room at all. Although she is used to his silence and odd ways, she knows that the present interiority is different, malignant, and like physicians who use a mild strain of a disease to cure its more virulent manifestation, she wants to use this death to coax him out of his depression.

He blocks his ears to her long litany about relations and their importance to a man. He sips his tea, slouched in the old and broken cushion chair, trying to keep warm, his expression far away.

'. . . so, will you come?' she says, at last pausing.

'I will see if I can come,' he repeats.

After a long, glare-filled silence in which he refuses to raise his head to look at her, she adjusts the cloth round her neck, throwing it over her shoulder with an angry gesture, and walks out, leaving the door wide open behind her. Poor Aunty Kale, she is the only one who hasn't given up on him, even though it is causing her days and nights of anxiety and frustration, wearing her out. Most of his friends stopped coming to see him after the first month, more loyal ones dragged on into the second month, but even the hardiest gave up in the third month, when they waited for hours in the living room and Mela would be in the bedroom, or when he came out and sat with them for hours, not saying a word to their forced, over-optimistic chatter.

Through the open door he watches Aunty Kale head for the gate; she is not yet sixty, but already her walk has taken on a stilted, geriatric shamble. Here in Keti women age in fast-forward, worn out by worrying over all those things that their men folks simply won't worry about. The women throw away every attempt at physical self-preservation as soon as they are married, as if marriage is the sole purpose of their lives; and to them perhaps it is, for what else is there for a woman after marriage in a small, cloistered village like Keti but the rearing of children, slow decomposition from myriad minor anxieties, and finally death? He watches her shamble past the acacia tree in the middle of the courtyard, turn to the right and pass the ghost room, past the nim tree by the barn from which Mol-Mela fell and broke his arm on their tenth birthday, till she finally disappears at the gate. She shuts the rickety iron gate firmly behind her. Over the wall, faraway in the hills, the harmattan clouds rise and swirl like sheets of smoke, covering the stunted, leaning trees on the hillside.

*

He shuts the door and brings a blanket from the bedroom; he swaddles himself in it and lies on the couch and sips his tea, a book of verse in his hand and he thinks: this is how I spend my days, drinking tea, reading verse, and trying to keep warm – but life gets colder each day in spite of my efforts. This is how death might find me one day, drinking tea, reading verse and trying to keep warm. And waiting.

Often his mind drifts from the page before him to float aimlessly like a dry leaf in the wind. Now it drifts to the somnolent village outside: in such a village what could be more remarkable than death? And what death in the village has been more remarkable than his brother's, who was chased all day by the police – through the compounds, through the fields of unripe millet on the outskirts of the village, finally to die with a bullet in his guts, mourned as a hero by the whole village? Or his uncle Haruna's, who hanged himself when he tired of chasing the ghosts of his fallen comrades two years after the civil war? Aunty Kale found him early in the morning on her way to the outhouse, dangling from the nim tree behind his room; she cut him down and dragged him to his room and laid him on the bed, as if he merely slept, before she called Mela's father. Mela wonders what it would be like to have that courage, to wake up one day and say: end it all. But is it courage, or desperation? It is certainly not cowardice. So many times he has found his mind veering dangerously towards that brink, but purely as a speculative possibility. Now all he does is wait, as if for some god from a machine, he waits... he knows not for what, but he has grown quite adept at it. The silence, the inertia, have taught him patience. He can sit for hours in his seat, not moving a muscle, a part of the fittings. Once he gave Aunty Kale a fright when she woke up in the middle of the night to go to the kitchen. He was in his tableau mode in the living room, alone in the moonless, shroudy darkness of the rainy season, staring at a single pinprick of light on the window. He had been there for hours.

'What in God's name are you doing here in the dark, all alone?' she exclaimed when she turned on the light.

'Waiting,' he replied without turning.

'Waiting for what?' came the perplexed reply.

'Just waiting.'

He could have added that he was waiting for his life to begin or to end, he wasn't sure which. But at thirty-eight, he knows that he is too old to be playing at waiting; yet the life he waits for has still not arrived, or it might have come and gone and he did not recognize it.

2

Aunty Kale returns earlier than Mela expected. Her entry wakes him up from the light slumber into which he has drifted. The time is only two o'clock; usually the women stay all day at the house of mourning to keen until their eyes get all puffy and half-blind from the salty tears.

'You are back early.'

The day is getting dark because of the harmattan haze outside; it is going to be a terrible one this year, it is only November, the beginning of the harmattan season, but already it has gone two days without the sun showing its face.

'Yes, I brought someone to see you,' she says with a smile. Ah, he thinks with relief, we are friends again. A shadowy form hovers behind her by the door, a woman, blinking, trying to adjust her sight to the poor light in the room. He frees his legs from the blanket and stands up and turns on the light.

'Sit down, my dear, sit,' Aunty Kale says, bustling about, straightening up the cushions. She sounds excited. It is not every day that they have visitors. He hides his curiosity, taking his time to carefully fold the blanket and put it in the seat beside him before turning to the woman; she is already seated, looking at his gaunt face with a half-smile on her lips. Aunty Kale cuts off his view as she goes to the table and picks up the empty cup and flask.

'Tea, tea, he has nothing but tea all day. I wonder how he doesn't have an ulcer by now,' she says to the visitor. 'Let me get some for you.'

'Thank you.' The visitor speaks Hausa with a thick Yoruba accent. A stranger, it is easy to tell from her dress: a black knee-length skirt, a white blouse beneath a grey cardigan and medium-high heels. The village women at her age – Mela puts her age somewhere below thirty – go about in long wrappers and bubas, with a child, inevitably, dangling from their backs.

'You are welcome,' he says to her in English. She is seated directly opposite him, her handbag clutched in her lap, her legs crossed, the half-smile still on her face.

'You will excuse me,' he continues in English, standing up and slipping his feet into a pair of plastic slippers, 'I have been sleeping all morning. Let me pour some water on my face.'

Outside, the cold is fierce. Sudden frolicsome gusts drive up the dust in tiny wind devils, covering the nostrils with fine, silt-like sand, turning the hair white, parching the lips till they crack. Mela feels unaccountably sad all of a sudden, and nostalgic. It must be the desolate weather. There's always something about the grey horizon, the dry variegated leaves on the ground, the cold howling wind, that pulls at his heart. But it might not be the weather at all; nowadays youth and beauty, like the one inside, make him feel old and sad and nostalgic. He reminds himself that he is only thirty-eight, but the feeling persists.

Aunty Kale is in the smoky, thatch-roofed kitchen, pouring steaming water into the flask.

'Who is she?'

'She has a letter for you, from Mol-Mela's wife!' she whispers, her eyes shining. He feels his heart lurch.

'Mol-Mela's wife? But how, where...'

'She came with the boy's widow. They brought the corpse from Lagos, all the way, just two of them...'

'What boy?'

'Salomi's son. He lived in Lagos. His wife is Yoruba...'

'The letter, what did she say about it?' He has also fallen to whispering. They are like conspirators in the tiny, smoky kitchen, whispering, their eyes turning to the half-open front door, where the stranger waits.

'But isn't Mol-Mela's wife in Sierra Leone?' he says, sounding as excited as his aunt.

'Well, she is in Lagos now and she has sent you a letter,' Aunty Kale whispers, pushing him towards the door. 'Go, go to her, she has the letter.'

Without washing his face he returns to the living room. He finds the woman standing before his oversized bookstand. The stand is old and broken, it leans precariously against the wall facing the door, most of the books have fallen out of the shelves to the floor and are dust covered. For the first time Mela notices how shabby the room is. The seats are broken, with their cushions falling out of the wooden frames; cobwebs hang from the ceiling and in corners. The table by the window overflows with books and papers. The carpet has holes and stains in it.

'You have so many books,' she says. She is holding one in her hand, shaking it to remove the dust.

'Yes,' he says. He inherited most of them from his father. 'I am a teacher. I used to be, that is.'

'I am a teacher too,' she says with a laugh, returning to her seat. Her laughter is short, tiny, as if she has buck teeth and is careful not to open her mouth too wide.

'What a coincidence,' he says, restraining himself from asking for the letter. 'What do you teach? I used to teach history.'

'I teach chemistry.'

'The sciences,' he says, nodding his head. 'That's good.'

A long silence ensues. Small talk is not one of his strong points, but she does not seem bothered by the silence, she is looking at the back of the book, her head down.

'So, you came yesterday?'

When she raises her head, he sees that she is not as pretty as he thought at first. Her skin is bleached unnaturally yellow, with ugly black patches on the backs of her hands, like the fallen leaves outside. She has a coquettish way of avoiding his eyes, lowering hers a split second after meeting his. She keeps opening and closing the book in her lap. Her voice is hoarse, raspy, as if she suffers from a cold. The widow is her sister. In her raspy, lisping voice, she tells him about their trip from Lagos, interspersing her English with pidgin.

'She don promise her husband say she go bury am for this village. He was sick for over a month before his death. It took us two days to get here. E no easy at all. None of us been come north before, we lost for road, at Lokoja, and we had to spend a night there. We kept the corpse at the hospital mortuary and collected it the next day. E don begin to smell by then.' She gives her tiny laugh as she recollects, covering her mouth girlishly.

'That's very courageous of you,' he says.

'E no easy at all, at all. We had to get another car to bring us here from Lokoja, our first driver deserted us there, wicked man. He said na bad luck to carry dead body about.'

Aunty Kale comes in. 'Here's your tea,' she announces.

As she pours out the tea she keeps looking into Mela's face, trying to determine if he has already seen the letter. After pouring out the tea she hovers behind his seat, listening, though not understanding a word of the English the visitor is uttering.

'Shola, soon we have to go to the graveside for the burial,' Aunty Kale tells the visitor in Hausa when she has finally decided that the letter has not yet been given, glancing at Mela meaningfully.

'Yes, ma,' Shola replies.

Unable to restrain himself any longer, Mela leans forward in his seat, puts his cup on the table and unconsciously tapping the table with his long, tapering fingers, asks, 'So, how did you meet my brother's wife?'

'My sister's husband . . .' she begins and then, remembering that she is supposed to be in mourning, corrects herself solemnly,' . . . late husband, used to work for Oga Matthew, your cousin. Your late brother's wife has been staying with Matthew since she came from Sierra Leone, she is not feeling too well. She is pregnant. Na Oga Matthew bring the letter himself when we de come, he tell us to bring it to you.' She rummages in her bag as she talks, and finally brings out the letter. Matthew is Mela's distant cousin, he lives in Lagos; they have met only once as kids.

Seeing the letter, Aunty Kale comes round and sits down. She looks keenly at the letter, which is now in Mela's hand, as if hoping to pierce the plain brown envelope and reveal its content by the sheer power of her gaze. Mela turns the envelope in his hand and looks at the neat, feminine handwriting on the front: *To Mr Mela Lamang, Keti.*

As if to stop the urge to rip open the letter immediately, he keeps it on the table; he turns to Aunty Kale and, switching to Hausa, asks, 'Can you hear the mourners passing?'

It is true: a dull murmur, as from a swarm of migrating bees, can be heard coming from the path that passes in front of the compound. The coffin, which everyone has been waiting for, has finally arrived and the burial procession is on its way to the cemetery. Aunty Kale jumps to her feet and begins to adjust her wrapper.

'Let's join them,' she says to Shola. The visitor stands up, smoothing her skirt. Mela also stands up. Aunty Kale looks at him questioningly. There's something light and gay in his eyes, an animation she has not seen there in a long time.

'I think I will come too,' he announces.

A winding path that rises in easy stages from the tree-hedged, untarred road leads to the cemetery at the foot of the hills. For as far back as the oldest man in Keti can remember, this has been the village burial ground, saturated with bones. About the size of five football pitches joined together, it is a bald, unpicturesque piece of land, interspersed with huge baobab trees, which stand like thick-trunked, grotesque giants over the headstones. The hills form a looming, almost menacing backdrop, adding to the picture of desolation. Most of the graves are indistinct, the headstones sunk into the red, coarse soil, the mounds flattened by rain and wind – as a result the grave-diggers often progress by means of trial and error, refilling a hole when they encounter bones, and sometimes, when in haste, pushing aside ancient bones to re-inter them later with fresh ones.

Mela is by the graveside shaking hands. He catches people's surprise on seeing him. He nods and smiles, exchanging words of condolence. The grave has been dug in the shadow of a baobab tree, beneath which the men are standing, their hands in their pockets, their heads bent against the cold wind. The grave-diggers, youths from the deceased's family, are sitting to one side, shirtless, their legs and arms covered in red earth, their implements lying at their feet. The pastor, in his dog collar, stands alone, bible in hand, a solemn expression on his face, once in a while lifting his face to glance at the group of women, who are standing far away from the men. They have formed a circle round the widow, some holding her hands, some whispering words of encouragement in her ears.

A loud wail goes up when the pick-up truck bearing the coffin arrives. The people draw closer to the grave. Mela watches without moving, so that now he stands alone where formerly he was in a crowd. His limbs feel leaden, he hears the words of the pastor as if coming from afar, indistinct. The sound of the first shovelful of earth on the coffin sends a light tremor through his body. He is the first to leave the burial ground, and despite the cold there is a fine sheen of sweat on his forehead.

Back in his living room, he grabs the letter and tears it open. It is a short letter, saying no more than it is supposed to say, for although the writer is his sister-in-law, they are perfect strangers. They have never met, she is a white woman whom his brother had met and married in Liberia. Now the brother is dead, and the wife is in the country, and, according to the letter, in a week's time will arrive in Keti. Aunty Kale returns not long after him, breathless, her chest heaving, as if she has run all the way.

'Well, what does the letter say?'

He translates for her:

Dear Mela,
    I write to inform you that I arrived safely three weeks ago from Sierra Leone, only to be met with the news of my husband's death.
    I am presently in Lagos, staying with your cousin Matthew, who has been so kind as to have me here. I however think it is better for me to come to Keti, to see my husband's grave, and to discuss some important issues with you.
    I am presently not feeling too well because of my pregnancy. I propose however to set out in a week's time.
    I look forward to meeting you.
      Jane

'She comes in a week's time,' he adds unnecessarily, after reading the letter.

'A week,' Aunty Kale echoes. She sounds collected, almost thoughtful. 'Well, we have to get the place ready, then,' she adds and leaves for the kitchen.

Matthew Sweeney

Hair

Imagine a rain of hair
from all the barber shops in China
falling on the world.
Imagine the first clumps dropping
softly on your face.
Reach up and rub some
between your fingers.
But soon the ground is covered
and hair keeps falling –
and among the loose hair
pigtails, ponytails, wigs.
And now blond northern hair
has joined the black and brown.
Dog hair, too, wool even,
and you're brushing it into piles
but burnt, it stinks to heaven.
Buried, it comes back out
or that's what it looks like
when more covers the graves.
And now you're swallowing some
and it's snarling your guts,
and your eyes are stinging
and it's filling up your nose,
so grab a few handfuls,
better still, cut your own off,
braid it into a rope and strangle
yourself. Then lie there
till the hair dissolves your corpse.

Emma Brockes

Visiting Time

I had it all worked out. I'll tell you the truth, I've never been a liar. I'm six-foot six on the left. On the right I'm six-foot four. Broke my leg in a motorbike accident in the sixties, riding pillion. I walk on the slant but I have the advantage of height, which is handy when you're planning on killing a man.

As I saw it, if I went into that prison and I knew roughly how tall it was, and if I could get my hands in the correct position, get my thumbs fast enough under its chin, I could break its neck. I'd worked out where I'd have to stand and how fast I'd have to do it, how long before the screws came in. I never told my wife. I try to keep her in the dark, like if there's a programme on TV about murder, I'll tear the page from the *Radio Times*. We don't discuss it. We haven't referred to it since the day of the sentencing. Therapy whatnot, we don't need reminding. It's how we get along.

Before I entered the prison, I went to a church across the road and said a small prayer. Then I walked into the governor's office. I'd seen the murderer standing roughly where that chair is there and I walked over and the governor was there and I asked to use the toilet and I went in and was saying the prayer again and running cold water on my wrists. I was thinking, if you harm it, it's more aggro for the wife. She'll have the police at the door again, don't know if she can take it. But simultaneous I'm thinking, I want it dead. So I come out of the toilet, walk straight towards it and everyone's looking at me thinking this is it, which way am I going to go?

There's things flashing through my brain, all the traumas, like how when I was a kid my best mate was killed by a lion. It sounds funny, but it ain't so funny. The teachers said we could venture off round the zoo, so we went to the lion enclosure. We came up the wooden steps and the chicken wire that keeps kids away was all open. Alan, John and Tony got through the wire, but I couldn't get through, I was too big, so they told me to sit there and look after the luggage. I sat on the school bags and watched them through the fence. The boys swung on the ropes that lifted the weights that opened a sheet of metal into the lion's den. Tony crawled through. I'll never forget. He died in hospital. We were ten years old. There's one loss.

The brain can only take so much and then it goes crash. All the teachers told us, honesty is the best policy, crime don't pay, and all this about the coming of the second prophet. They was all lies; I wish I could sue 'em. If I'd brought up my kids the way the Krays brought up theirs, perhaps we'd be rich. Instead of that, you remain nobody and John ends up getting murdered and John's nothing, but the murderer's likely to come out and be found a respectable job and everything that goes with it.

After school, I got a job in St Thomas's hospital: maintenance, pushing trolleys. I met the wife and got on a building site as a labourer, then with a stone masonry firm and that's where I was working right up to when we lost Johnny. My epilepsy was just another hurdle; so what, tell me about it, I couldn't care less.

John had gone to Waltham Abbey that day to pay for his holiday. His friend had died in April from a brain tumour and, come September, John and his friend booked a holiday to get over the loss of the boy, Richard. So they went to pay for this holiday, which was to be in Norfolk and they came out and were standing at a bus stop. John told us, 'If I miss the last bus home, I'll stay with Jimmy.' So when he didn't come home we didn't get bothered. Then the police came. Valerie collapsed in the kitchen, chipped two tiles. She's got asthma and they had to call an ambulance. Jane our daughter started screaming and ran upstairs. Our son Peter, who's eight years old, was asleep. I had to go and wake him up. I didn't know what to say to him. I half lied. I said would he go to the hospital with his mum. I said John was there and he was unwell.

They were standing, the five boys, at the bus stop. Just up the road was a pub called the Queen's Head. These twelve adults had been drinking and came out of the pub and headed to the bus stop to start trouble. This 21-year-old, who had thirty-six previous convictions, stabbed and wounded Jimmy in the stomach. Jimmy got away, into a woman's house nearby, and she phoned for an ambulance. While this was going on, our son tried to defend his friends. He stepped forward and was stabbed directly in the heart. And he staggered over to a lady who was sitting in a car waiting for a friend and asked her to help me, please help me and told her he'd been stabbed and fell to the ground. She read all this out in court and the murderer's solicitor asked her a question with a big grin on his face and she was in tears. When he asked her a second time, I jumped up in the court and done me nut, I said, 'Well she ought to remember because the last time you asked her you had a fucking big grin on your face.' I was chucked out of court for that. I apologized and they let me back in.

Eventually, it testified and it did everything it could to sound like a bleeding little poor type of character. Bad childhood, bad home. The confidence it had was ridiculous. I have to fight to bring words back now because there's something in the brain that tries to block it all off.

Me and the brother-in-law went to the trial on our own, that way none of my family knows what the murderer looks like. So they could pass it in the street and they'd never know the difference. See what I mean? And that's how it should be, surely.

Every neighbour will tell you their hearts were broken, they miss John. This particular morning, as he run out of the house, there's an old lady coming out with two bags of shopping and John stops and says, 'You don't carry that, I'll carry that.' He would cut sandwiches in the kitchen and take them to the church and give them to men who'd dropped out of society. That's something we live by: do as you're told and stick by the rules. So, all right, we stuck by the rules and look where it got us.

We got John a decent funeral. About five hundred came, we had the wake at the fire station and there was the chief there, Doug, he died from a brain tumour at a later date, his son and John were friends.

I decided to go to prison and talk to the boys who were in on minor charges, who hadn't been done for the full violent murder but were heading that way. I set it all up, they was brought into a room with two coffee pots and as many fags as they wanted and they could eff and blind and walk out of the room feeling OK. I was told that when a policeman or a judge comes in, they play them up cos they think they're do-gooders. So it was a case of: how are they going to react to me?

We sat there and after they'd given me all their who they ares, I eventually told them who I am. I told them how I wake up in the morning and I think, first of all, where's John? Then I think, it wasn't a dream, it was true, so that means every day we're one day further from John, but that's one day closer to him getting out. The coffee pot didn't get touched; the fags didn't get touched. They just sort of shut up and listened.

The following month, I'm down there again and I'm in the governor's office and a man comes rushing in, a boy rather, and he's wearing this chef's uniform and he's wiping his hands and he says, 'Bill, I can't stop, but what you said last time is right.' He said, 'I've got a five-year-old daughter and a wife and I'm not coming back in any of these places,' and he thanked me for doing him a favour.

Eventually I decided, I wanna meet it direct, John's murderer. Now if I wait until its parole, they'll give it a different name and I'll probably never see it again. I want it now. So I start the ball rolling, push push, five years that went on for, to get the right contacts, MPs, the House of Lords. It was 1986 when it was imprisoned, and it was '91 that I was given the go-ahead to visit it. Restorative justice they call it now. Back then, though, it hadn't never happened before. Letting the families meet the murderer.

Arrangements were made for me to see it in prison. First, I had to talk to these two probation officers, to make sure I was of what they called sound mind and pure intention. There was one there, his name was Brian, and he came up with some right insulting-type questions, but I knew why he was doing it – he thought if he could wind me up and suddenly I blew it, he wouldn't let me anywhere near the murderer. Because if I'm in there with the murderer and the murderer's only got to say the wrong thing and I'm up in arms and they've got trouble on their hands. But, of course, I had it worked out different.

I don't know where it comes from, but there is such a thing as a guardian angel. I had one there and it was holding me down.

It just would not happen. I was managing to find the right answers and this Brian said, I don't get it, every time I get through to you a brick wall pops up. He said, I tear it down and you put up another one. So I said, Don't have a word with me, I'm only the labourer, have a word with the bricklayer. Those sorts of arguments and they're taking notes. Eventually they decided that the best thing in the world to happen is for me to go in and see it for myself.

I had it all worked out. I'm six-foot six on the left, on the right I'm six-foot four. It was smaller by four inches. I could knock it out in a matter of minutes. There's two pressure points in your throat that if you have a go at with enough force you can kill a man before there's time to pull you off, or at least do it brain damage. When I entered the governor's office, the murderer sat back, mister clever and it looked pretty smart, scrubbed shirt and navy blue jumper and short-cut hair and I tell you on the quick who it looked like, you ever seen that O'Sullivan, the very fast snooker player? It looked close to him – and his father was a murderer too, funny enough.

See what I mean, all the stupidity of life? The things you think of. I can be sitting there talking and my wife will say, Do you want a tea or coffee, simple as that. And I have to say, Hang on hang on hang on, what was that again? And she says it three or four times and I'm trying to sort the words out, because inside I'm thinking, 'John is dead.'

I blinked. The light was one of them bright ones, fluorescent, which cut shadows in its face. It was pushed back in its chair, one leg on its knee, small and cocky like. It's not much to look at, narrow shouldered and smirking while it waits for me to say something. I don't say nothing. Its neck's where I'm looking. I'm looking so hard I think I can see its pulse. There's a thud in my wrists and this beat in its neck and I'm still undecided, which way to go? It stops smirking. It shifts in its chair. Suddenly I see my calculations are wrong, I could do its windpipe in half the time or hammer its head on the wall, which is pale and glossy green, like was used in the hospitals. I feel enormous, like a giant, and the bigger I feel, the smaller it looks until I see that it's nothing really, nothing at all, just a badly sewn boy of no fixed identity. I can feel its heart fluttering, its breath sucking in and out and I think, Yeah: at the end of the day that's all it comes down to, the blood going round. I see that it doesn't take much to kill a man. This much we both know.

I put out my hand. 'Luke Slater,' I say. He stands up and shakes it.

No I'm sorry, no I forgive you, no call for the priest either way. I feel a huge weight lift off me, like I've jumped ten feet in the air or won a race. 'I've come to let you know we exist, Valerie and me,' I say, soaring. He does a shrug. 'Mr Garrison,' he says, 'you don't understand, I've had it hard too.' He fiddles with the hem of his shirt. 'My life wasn't easy neither.' I let that one settle, then I tell him how I sometimes imagine John is in Australia, how every year I sign his name on a Christmas card and give it to my wife and each thing I say pushes him back in his chair. I'm landing them on him one after another. He says feebly, 'It ain't over for me either, like how am I going to find a job when I get out?' He shifts and his eyes flit about. He tries to get one over by saying about some bloodstains the police never found. I said, You've killed my son and I've shaken your hand. I said, Do you really think there's anything else you can do to see me blow my lid? After that we sit in silence. Then he pushes his chin out and says, 'I'm sorry, Mr Garrison,' like he's wheedling to his father. I say, 'It's too late for that.' When I shake his hand at the end of the visit I feel the small bones of his fingers chafe against each other. His eyes are round and frightened.

At a later date, the probation officer told me that ten days after the visit he still hadn't come out of his cell. He was pacing up and down, punching the bed, saying, 'How can a man come in here and do what he did after what I did to his son?' I never laid a finger, but in a way my hand's still round his throat. I went in there to kill a man, and to my way of thinking that's just what I did. He won't rest in peace. If that's been done properly, telling him how it's been for Valerie and me, then he's gonna wake up in a bit of a sweat now and then, and turn to find me lying there beside him.

Nicolette Hardee

Wordperfect

'This may be serious,' he said.

I have always put my faith in words, the reassembling of chaos into manageable phrases. Serious was a word that I would have used without hesitation. An OK word. Serious music, serious literature, serious money. I found that I did not like it applied to my state of health. I went off serious.

'If we operate there is a good chance of success.'

Chance had always seemed an open sort of word. A sky-blue conjunction of possibility. Now chance became a chink of grey light seen through a closing door. Chance became dicey.

During the months which followed I found out other things. I found that I would have liked a different family. Parents who had left me a second home in the country. At least three dependable brothers, and enough sisters to like at least one. Rich indulgent uncles and a rota of indomitable aunts.

'Never say die,' they would have said, as their knitting needles clicked and the hairs on their chins bristled. 'Where there's life there's hope,' and they would have undone their corsets the more comfortably to fix death with a stern eye. And I would have been able to say gratefully that blood was thicker than water.

For this was another thing that I learnt about words. A cliché is a wonderful artefact hacked from the mountain of the past, a sort of relay baton to keep you going to the finishing line. It fits so neatly in your hand once you've grasped it, you'd be surprised.

I would like to have had other friends. Fat jolly ones, quiet listening ones, one who made cakes. A gynaecologist, a solicitor, a Radio 4 producer to put on decent plays in those long afternoons and longer nights. God.

But it was like a Scrabble game with only the consonants left in the tray. Nobody could put together a word that would score.

So by the time the serious had been dealt with and the chance had turned blue again, I was not the same person. Previously I had been Jennifer. Not a bad name, but stale with the smell of hospitals and waiting rooms and bulging cardboard files. Jennifer was electronically tagged. A few clicks on the keyboard and her most intimate secrets could be scrolled down the screen. I bought a book for naming babies and ran my finger down the lists, waiting to be reborn.

I didn't have to pack much. Survival was obviously not dependent on hand-decorated spongeware teacups or a set of matching polyester-cotton pillowcases. Captive so long to the voice of the radio, I was now liberated. I pushed its antenna down and pulled out the plug.

I took the tube to Victoria and the train to Dover. It was the beginning of autumn and getting chilly, but I had a warm coat, warm shoes, an optional scarf, some soft leather gloves. I had chosen all these items carefully in a sort of muddy beige. 'Discreetly fashionable,' I might have said, when I was still choosing my words like sweeties. 'Tasteful.' But now I was what I was, a woman wrapped up warmly in a sensible colour for travelling, standing on a boat between an island and a continental land mass. I stood on deck until we set sail, then I went downstairs and had fish and chips and two cups of tea. I read the *Daily Mirror* and *The Times*, and when I'd finished I put them both in the rubbish bin.

The light was fading as the boat docked, for we had lost an hour at sea. Ah, lucky sea, the recipient of so many unspent hours. A superfluity of hours, or something along those lines, I would have said once, but I am finished with wordplay, so I watched the men on the quay struggling with the great rope that was going to tether us to the land. They shouted things to each other that I could not understand. Inside I felt a cord loosen.

I am good at French, but it has to be written down. That is the way my generation learnt it. Written down. If the inhabitants had captions coming out of their mouths I could tell you what they are saying, otherwise not. That is the way I wanted it – not. I was cutting adrift from words. I had come to the land of hand signals and facial disdain. The shrugged shoulder, the curled lip, the nasal expletive.

I walked to the high-speed train and stepped inside. Three hours later, emerging from the metro, I consulted the map pinned beneath the wrought iron. A red circle around my feet, a red arrow confirming my position at a junction of streets in a foreign city. 'Vous êtes ici,' said the sign – and indeed, I couldn't argue with that. Against all those dicey odds, I was.

In the hotel room I laid out the map on the dressing table between two high windows. I opened the shutters and sat on a brocade chair with curly gold feet, looking out over the low railings. French windows.

During the serious, my life had rolled before me just like it's supposed to. Not all at once in my case, for I was only metaphorically drowning, and therefore had more time to look about me on the way down, but slowly, over the months, and every so often a scene would shoulder its way to the front, reconstructing itself from all those dead brain cells, grainy but determined.

'Remember me?' it would say.

And one scene kept replaying on the old newsreel. A long busy road, an old apartment building, a neglected garden, the smell of dust and drains and diesel. And I saw Annie as clearly as if she had been the nurse who put the needle in my arm every evening. I thought I would remember the nurse for ever, the unkind one, but my brain is closed for imprints. Annie was there though, clear in every detail after thirty years.

'Je m'appelle Annie.'

I found it easily on the map. It was not far away, on the southern outskirts of Paris. There was a confusion of new roads, a motorway, an outer ring road, lines of blue and red that crossed and recrossed the writing, making it slightly indistinct. I folded the maps, put on my coat and went down to the street. In the bar on the corner I ordered an omelette, a salad, a carafe of wine. Once I was frightened of waiters. What a waste of time.

In the morning I took the metro to the Gare de Lyon and went to consult the timetables. My heart jolted when I saw it printed there, as if it was the name of an old flame. To me it was a lost domain, beyond the realm of timetables, but SNCF had known about it all the time.

'J'habite une petite ville à vingt kilometres de Paris.'

It was midday when the train stopped at the station. I set off, walking south. I saw the ribbon of road ahead and then, in the distance, the long climbing hill and knew I was in the right place. Then lorries had thundered through the town, swaying dangerously close to the narrow pavement. 'Prenez garde, mes enfants, prenez garde.' Now the road was quiet. The motorway had taken the traffic.

Her picture had arrived in an envelope with spidery writing and the number of the house at the wrong end of the line. Inside, her face stared out from a crinkly edged photo, a half smile, slightly raised eyebrows.

'C'est moi,' she had written on the back, 'Annie. Est-ce que tu veux me visiter en France?'

I went in July. That first summer we did not stray far from the building. There were four flats, but no one came into the garden. We lay in the itchy grass and giggled and looked at pictures in flimsy, shiny magazines. Brigitte Bardot, Sylvie Vartan, Johnny Hallyday, Jean-Paul Belmondo.

'Je ne l'aime pas,' I said. 'Il n'est pas beau.'

In the magazines, boys lounged on motorbikes in black leather jackets, heavy lidded, their cheeks sucked back to their contemptuous bones. On fly-blown cinema posters, blue-shadowed brown skin and electric black hair lurked in half-painted shadows. In the town, men with hollowed faces leaned against walls, wreathed in pungent smoke and garlicky menace.

'Les hommes sont differents ici,' I said.

'Hn?'

'Est-ce que tu as un ami?'

'Un ami? Phw!'

I had an orange cardigan.

'A French girl would never wear so much a colour,' said Annie, curling her lip. I put it on and went into town. Everyone stared.

At Easter she came to England. For three weeks my world

slewed out of focus beneath the faint upward curve of her eyebrows.

'Funny men,' she said, but any noun would have done.

'What's yours like?' my friends asked. 'She doesn't say much, does she?'

The second summer her brother Gérard was home from national service. He had a friend called Daniel. There was nothing like them where I came from. They both had scooters. I had got rid of my orange cardigan, but I was still too obvious. I was just there. You could see me all at once. I needed some blue shadows, a bit of contempt in my bones, less skin. I needed to acquire some inner shrug.

Occasionally, when they had nothing better to do, they would take us out on the scooters. I rode behind Gérard, pressed up against his French jacket, looking at the back of his French haircut, breathing in his French sweat and cigarettes while the engine throbbed beneath us. It was the first time that anything in my life had approximated to art. If you were making it up, this is what it would be like.

'Qu'est-ce que tu veux faire quand tu seras grande?' I asked.

'Oh,' said Annie, 'phw!'

I went home. I spent the winter on a pillion seat, my cheek turned sideways, shoulder blades arched outwards, hair swept up and falling down, staring wide-eyed over the curve of a non-existent collar.

The next year exams intervened.

'So shall we be clever?' wrote Annie. 'It is so boring, no?'

But I was not bored. This was the bit I could do.

'I wish that I could have seen you this summer,' I wrote back.

I had mastered the subjunctive, but it seemed unnecessary. In England we mostly didn't bother with it any more. The future no longer seemed so conditional. There were boys with button-down collars and suede boots and increasingly interesting hair, with whom communication was not dependent on a small blue dictionary.

'Have you heard of the Beatles?' I asked.

'It is necessary that I decide what to be,' wrote Annie. 'You too? Are you still wearing the orange?'

But calculating the time it would take to acquire hidden depths, pragmatism had prevailed and I had taken a short cut. I had painted my eyes into smudged charcoal shadows, grown my hair across my face and taken to wearing black. Sometimes, when I sucked in my cheeks, I could have been a picture in a shiny magazine.

'Come here,' I wrote, 'come and see me.'

I sent a photo, a three-quarter-profile pout through spiky lashes against a pleated curtain. It had a murky, mysterious quality. The film was under-exposed.

'Donnes mes regards à Gérard,' I wrote on the back, and imagined the photo placed in the inside pocket of his leather jacket, gradually acquiring the smell of Gauloises.

'I think it is best you come here,' she wrote the next year. 'I am not so much free now. I have to work.'

She had grown her hair, dyed it blonde. She worked in an office near the station.

'So boring. Always everything the same. You don't think so?'

Gérard had gone to work in Lyon. I had no idea where this was, and as I sat on a chair in the garden above the itchy grass, reading Sartre, I imagined him at the counter of a large Gallic teashop, forever serving coffee and baked beans on toast to men with berets, and women with narrow ankles and facial hair.

'Let us go away,' said Annie on the Friday.

'For the weekend?' I asked.

'No, for a long time.'

'Why?' I said.

'To see what there is.'

'But I have exams,' I said.

'Phw. Always exams, always clever. Everything in books.'

But I still had great hopes of books. All those words must mean something. If I kept putting the right ingredients in, surely I would soon come out fully baked.

'I'll come away afterwards,' I said.

'I think I will need to go before you are finished. You are taking such a long time.'

'But where will you go?'

'Phw. Anywhere. Just to see.'

I saw her picking her way through the world, shoulders and eyebrows flexed, distilling it all into three lines on a postcard.

'Don't forget me,' I said. 'After next summer I will be free.'

I forgot to ask her what she thought about the Beatles. I don't think she would have liked their suits, but she might have liked Paul's lids and John's mastery of the curled lip as a total lifestyle. You can never tell with the French. If they came from further away, they would seem less strange.

'I am going away,' she wrote, 'but I remember what you said, and one day I will come back and tell you what there is, and you will tell me how good is clever. I hope you have what you want. Adieu. Annie.'

I knew it would not be next year.

I saw us, indistinct older beings, sitting in the long grass with floppy hats on, the other side of whatever it was we were this side of now. The air around this picture was calm, there was no sound. The antennae were down and the energy had gone.

Sometimes postcards came. St Tropez, Morocco, Greece.

A picture of a bust of Socrates. 'Funny men everywhere,' it said on the back.

A gap of five years and a postcard from Mexico. 'A lot of orange here. You would like it.'

Then, three years ago, just after Christmas, a card with a Paris postmark. An art nouveau painting of a woman watering a garden. She wore a long petrol blue dress with a flowing scarf. Behind her, large poppies and sunflowers and a tree, and beyond them, enclosing the whole, a small trellised fence. A strange New Year card. Written diagonally across the inside were the words, 'Not far after all.' I turned it over to see the title of the picture. 'Juillet,' it said.

It sat on my mantelpiece through the sleepy beginnings of January. A trip to Paris seemed a small thing to fit into all those new days. In February I took it down and placed it in my writing case. But she had come back into focus. I liked to think of her just over there, as she used to be. A small hard receptacle of our former selves.

'Annie. Je suis ici.'

Sometimes, searching for stamps or the right-sized envelope,

I would catch sight of the picture of the woman in the garden. I thought of framing it, but I didn't want to put her behind glass.

Of course I still planned to travel. I saw myself at some indeterminate future date, generously accoutred with all the many things I had never had a go on, pale beige leather suitcases, rooms in hotels with vine-covered balconies, the right table in the right restaurant by the window overlooking the bay. These things happened to a calm and thinner me who had all the right clothes.

I still thought I could put it all together. Like a child's puzzle of silver balls rolling towards elusive holes in a small box, I was sure it could be done: it just needed concentration and a steady hand. But one ball kept rolling free as another one fell into place and the puzzle was never complete.

'You are taking such a long time.'

Then six months ago the balls had rolled free for ever.

So now I had come back to find her. To hear about what there was, and to tell her the end of the clever story and the failure of words, and then to sit with my antennae down, in the long grass, in the silence.

In my head I can already see her. Her shoulders will rise and curve forward, her lips will push out, and a single sound will escape, expressing so eloquently, everything that no one has ever been able to say.

Sasha Dugdale

The Film Director Explains His Concept

'I would film it as a zoom in from the sky –
A helicopter pirouetting over respectable Surrey
And remaining humming-bird high over gardens
Of roses, cultivated, grafted, each telling a tale
Of intense undying love, a gardener's devotion to their flesh.
The camera would enter via a window, mock leaden panes
Thrown open so the sheets might air that day, waxy floors
Shining in the afternoon sun. For it is afternoon, make a note.
A woman sits in the chair, soft, slim, scented
And shiny-haired like Lauren Bacall, with those exquisite waves –
Which draw the bees from the flowers, and the butterflies.
She is eating a Bath bun, hungry with the terrifying boredom of life.
Maybe a slow motion here, as the sultanas, crumbs fall on the paper bag
Opened on the table like a plate, with a cut to the dresser filled with Crown Derby.
In her mouth the most charming of pearly teeth are ripping the soft entrails.
The house is perfect to the last degree, if you checked under the sofa
The floor would stretch away as pure as still water, the lampshade is dustless
And the table reflects it as an endless oxblood mirage.

'In the next shot she is hurrying up the road. No one around.
She is muffled in a coat and scarf and she is walking towards
   the station.
I'll give you some background: she's waiting for the husband
To return from work – he's in a bowler hat and starched shirt.
She goes up there early each day, before twilight and smokes
   on the platform.
We're making this one about exiles – not the groundbreakers,
Trailblazers, dissidents, poets and bards. This is for the women
Whose brief lives and contexts are plucked and placed in bowls,
The ones you'd never pity, and probably hate,
Their reluctance to age, their prettily spoken husbands' views,
Their pettiness and disapproval. Let me tell you that underneath
They are all wound, all loss, raped of reality, eaten out.
They have nothing left but fags and Bath buns, starvation,
Two fingers in the throat after tea parties, or milk with pepper.
Fuck it, men, we're talking about women. This is one for them.'

Faking It

Behind the window there is an exercise class
In full swing. The ladies are kneeing – left, right
Like it was their husband's groin they focused on
And the pistons working in their thighs
Were fuelled by some mysterious hate: calories
Men, toddlers, parking spaces. This is their space
For purity of the flesh. Air-con, fluorescence, lino-ed
They burn the fat like souls in hell, they sweat
    and taste
Fresh water from a baby's bottle. And one . . .
    and one . . .
They pelvic-thrust and curve like cats, and hop
    and clap
And jump and tap like figure-conscious dervishes.
And the woman at the front, whose model moves
    and model size,
Inspire, exhales, screams thirty-something years
    with him,
And let me tell you one thing, girls – if you fake it,
    it's no sin.

Jill Dawson

Flat Earth

I love my job. It's a lovely job, when you think about it, isn't it? Helping people. I've always wanted to do it, and Father knew that. He took no notice of other people when he passed the business on to me, a slip of a girl at barely twenty, but I think he must have known, heard the nicknames, the cat-calls. Spook. The Ghoul. That kind of thing. It never bothered me. I had a young woman in here a couple of days ago, from Ely Community College, doing an interview she said, for their magazine. Unusual jobs. What's unusual about my job? I asked her. Well, she said, all those dead bodies. Don't you find it creepy? Nothing creepy about it. Perfectly ordinary, when you work with them, every day.

Young people, they never get it, do they? They sit there and look at you and to them you're just those age-spots freckling your hands, you're a stone heavier than they are and you wear the same kind of shoes as their mother. She asked me the cheekiest thing, then. Quite took me aback. Did working in here mean I had thought about my own funeral? Did it make it easier for me to 'confront the reality' – I'm not joking, those were her exact words! – *confront the reality* of my own eventual death? I'm only forty-five for God's sake, was what I said. Only I said it politely, with a laugh, to show I wasn't offended.

I've never seen a dead body, the girl said, looking straight at me. Smiling. As if that explained everything. She had a clipboard on her knee, and balanced on that a mobile phone covered with some kind of bright-pink fluffy cover. I've never seen one of those, I told her, meaning the phone cover. But now I have. So what? She left then. I think she found me . . . a tad bolshy. Or maybe insensitive. But I'm bursting with sensitivity. I have to be, don't I, doing what I do, dealing with the *bereaved* all day long, I have to be Sensitivity Itself and mostly, most of the time, I think it's safe to say I manage it.

Not today, though. Nothing could have prepared me for today. Twenty-five years in the business could not have prepared me for today.

I'd come to work in my usual good mood. The drive from Littleport across the fens to Ely does it for me every time; I try to leave after nine-thirty a.m. so I can have the road to myself, like cars in the ads. There's so much sky here, and this morning, although it's only just September, there was a mist covering the stand of poplars in the distance and the sky just one big blank sheet. Driving towards it was like pointing the nose of the car into the middle of nothing. I sometimes think about those Flat Earth Types, you know the ones who still refuse to believe the world is round, no matter how everyone else tells them it is. You have some sympathy for them when you live out here: and especially if you take that particular drive. The yellow and black lines of the fields slide into wide stripes on either side of you and your car seems to cleave the world in two. You would drop right off the end. Into what, I don't know. Nothing, I suppose. Nothing, whatever that is. Or more big sky. I haven't thought that far.

And are you religious? that skinny college girl asked. Cheeky little madam! Do you believe in an afterlife?

I spend a lot of time with clients, listening to them murmur, 'He's at peace now,' and I've heard plenty who say, 'If he's watching, he'd be having a good laugh at that.' You nod and smile, you have to. You don't start attacking their beliefs, or questioning things you know nothing about. Things too big for you to answer, in any case.

I like to put some Country music on, when I'm driving. Not the old-fashioned stuff, something modern like ... who's that young woman singer? Trisha something or other. *I'll buy you boots down in Texas, A hat from New Orleans/ And in the morning you can tell me your dreams.* I can sing along then, get myself into a really good mood, all set up for the tragedies of the day. I haven't been to America, but from what I've seen on TV some of it's quite like the fens. All horizontal lines and long views, nothing in them except road. Houses dotted here and there and people who keep horses and guns, people who nail handwritten 'Keep Out' signs on their trees and cultivate rusty old cars covered in grass as if they were prize beans. We've plenty of them. Old fen types. Those and gypsies.

We get a lot of gypsies. They always want the caskets. Fancy, you know. All the trimmings, horses, that kind of thing. You'd think they wouldn't be able to afford it, but you'd be surprised. It matters to them. I show them the pictures and they always choose the same one. The hinged casket. I've often wondered about that. Is it the workmanship, the decoration, that they appreciate? Or is it some part of their beliefs, that there has to be a hinge, that the box has to be able to open? I never ask. They're a bit touchy these days. I've told Ed not to call them pikies, that it's as bad as saying Nigger, but he never remembers. Me, I'm always trying to steer them towards economy. I tell them the truth about the costs. Fifteen hundred quid, an average funeral, these days.

It wasn't a gypsy who was waiting for me outside the office when I arrived. You can always tell by the cars. Hers was something decent, a Ford Mondeo, I think. She was sitting inside it, waiting for me, dabbing at her eyes with a proper handkerchief. I just saw greying hair; salt and pepper, glasses. I didn't recognize her at first. But as she climbed out, as she stood up, the two things came together. The name she gave on the phone yesterday and the face. Alison Wilde. It could mean only one thing. My legs started trembling, but I held out my hand in a professional way and walked carefully across the gravel to her. Stones crunched under the soft soles of my shoes and, for the first time ever, I noticed each one.

Do forgive me, I said, thinking quickly. A bit of a hold-up at Queen Adelaide, a train stopped on the tracks. I mean, there aren't many reasons to be late. You couldn't claim traffic, not in a place like this.

It was her, all right. Jack's wife.

She said nothing. Well, that's normal too, for the bereaved. They're kind of on automatic. They do what's required, they answer your questions, but all the time, right through the funeral, they're hardly there. That's why we offer the after-care service.

Sending them a list of who attended. So they can thank that long-distant cousin they hadn't seen in years, the one they managed to completely blank at the do itself.

Usually they bring someone with them, an eldest son, a friend, that kind of thing. I particularly wished Alison Wilde had.

I showed her into the office, unlocking the front door myself. I don't know if she noticed that my hand shook and how I struggled with the key. From the look she gave me, that bare look, the look of someone who no longer knew or cared that others were looking at *her*, I knew she didn't recognize me. Her and Jack moved to Downham Market in any case, quite a few years ago. It's possible she had no idea who I was.

When we got inside the cleaner had been and that syrupy smell of coconut was overpowering, almost disgusting. It smelled like a teenager's hair or a cheap cocktail. I took one deep breath by mistake and almost threw up. I'll have to have a word with her. June. The cleaner, I mean.

Now, Mrs Wilde, can I take your coat?

She offered it up. Marks & Spencer. I might have scoffed at that a few years back. But things change. My own tastes are a lot more sober these days. Dark jackets. Blouses, for God's sake. I have to look smart and sort of discreet and much as I might like to wear my cowboy boots and a long fringed-skirt I know it wouldn't be considered... what's that dreadful word? Appropriate. It wouldn't be appropriate. We used to say, right and proper.

She's a funny-looking woman and always was. Tall, big eyes. Monkey, her nickname was at school, on account of her walk, her long arms. She was a year older than me. Good at netball, I remember that much. Those arms made it easier for her to reach the net. But when Jack married her I was surprised. I thought she was a bit sexless. One of those wholesome types who made sex seem as healthy and natural as milking a cow, but to my mind that wasn't what a man wanted. I didn't think it was what Jack wanted, I believed he was *on the rebound*. A phrase we used a lot then. You don't hear it much these days. Perhaps people don't marry on the rebound any longer.

She must be here about him. Could it be anyone else? One of

their children, perhaps? I heard they had four. The roof of my mouth felt dry, my tongue glued itself to it and my opening lines didn't come out well. In fact, I broke my own rule, the one Father taught me. Never utter those two words, he said. They'll crumble every time. They'll dissolve and that's just what you don't want. You have to get through your list of questions, keep things on a firm footing.

But I didn't. I was thinking of Jack and watching her face for signs and so I forgot myself and they slipped out: I'm *sorry*. I'm *so sorry* to hear about your – husband?

Father was right. As I spoke, her head seemed to sink of its own will, to slip from her neck and into the hands she held out for it, just like ripe fruit falling from a branch. It was true then. Jack must be dead.

*

Jack Wilde at twenty-five is a sight to behold. Imagine, if you can, Jack Wilde without his shirt on: a few light blond hairs curling on a sunburnt chest, his slight frame, his defined muscles, a body that just oozes light and health and goodness. It's 1977 and this sexy magazine has started up, I think it's aimed at women, but probably it's gay men who buy it. Anyway, I saw a copy once and although I laughed myself silly the image stuck. Ever after, I like to picture Jack naked, except for his workman's boots, and standing amongst the haystacks, carrying a pitchfork. Sunlight glowing behind him. Curves along his forearms as smooth as waves in the sea. Actually he works on a building site, which is where he gets his tan and his muscles. I could have pictured him naked except for a hod and a van to lean on, but that didn't do it for me. I preferred the haystacks.

It wasn't just all the golden haystack goodness that appealed, it was his sadness of course. People I meet are always sad. I was just the junior then, the boss's daughter. I made the tea and listened. Father allowed me to stand beside him in the embalming room, handing him whatever he asked for, and one day soon I was about to take my embalming diploma at Cambridge; qualify to work here all alone.

You know when that college girl asked me about dead bodies,

I didn't tell her, but the first one I saw, I was younger than she is now. I was fifteen, working in the summer for my uncle, another funeral director, over in Chatteris. I mostly did the paperwork, the admin, like I do now, but one hot afternoon I took Uncle Bob a cup of tea into what we called the Cold Room, the mortuary, where he was working and he said, Hey Martha – are you ready for this? and whipped back the sheet.

I wasn't quite ready, but there wasn't much to see. An old man, must have been ninety, on his back, in his blue striped pyjamas. He looked a bit waxy. His eyebrows needed sorting, tidying up. Apart from that, I didn't think much of it. Uncle Bob was disappointed, of course, that I didn't run out or scream or faint or throw up. Any kind of reaction, probably. I was a puzzle to him, with my practical nature. He said I didn't have a romantic bone in my body. He was a bit of a funny one, Uncle Bob, always taking hold of my hand and gazing too long into my eyes when he gave me the money to buy the Paris buns and lemonade at elevenses. But I'm not the hysterical sort. It took more than an old man's dead body to scare me. I've been the same ever since. I saw at once there was nothing to be scared of.

It's the living you have to worry about. Jack Wilde for one. The man might have been handsome, glowing with the kind of sadness that draws women like flies, and eyes like a golden, warm, light oak veneer (force of habit, any kind of brown has to be described in terms of wood) but boy, did he know it. He'd come with his father and his two elder brothers to arrange his mother's funeral. He was forever in here, all that week and the weeks afterwards, settling up the bill, bringing a card to thank Father for all his kindness in their 'time of need' (I didn't need to read it to know it said that. They all said that. There are so few phrases to choose from); hanging around the desk to talk to me, to ask me all sorts of nonsense about my own plans and why I did such work and did I like dancing and whatever else, I can't remember.

It was true that Father did a good job with Jack's mother. Father always took pride and did his best. He drained the fluids and added new, chemical ones; a bright pink preservative injected behind the ears. The face would plump up and the features fill out and it was true that occasionally, if he did an exceptional job, some aspect of the dead person might return fleetingly.

We'll make him a better man than he ever was, Dad would say, stitching ears which had always protruded like jug handles, back towards the head. We'll make you a sight for sore eyes, he told Jack Wilde's mother, but by the time he'd finished she was only the fat, short, mousy dinner lady she had always been. No more, no less. I was not romantic like Father, but I was impressed somehow at Jack's ability to stare at his mother, quite tearless. He told me later that the mother he loved was lively, she was always yelling at him, and waving her cigarette around and flapping the tea-towel at his legs and calling him a *Great Wazzak*. She was not that silent, still, coiffed-haired doll-like thing, lying in her pink-frilled coffin. Although he was quick to reassure me that Father had done a good job. I liked that about Jack. He spoke as he found, as I do, but he cared about people.

I was six years younger than him at nineteen and my body was having what I think now was a kind of hormonal delirium. I don't know what it was. My body just hummed with sex all day long, like something simmering on the hob. Every minute of every day. I mean, I've been married to Ed now for nearly twenty-five years and I don't think I've once felt like that. I used to come into work and see a note from Jack Wilde on my desk, glance at his sweeping black handwriting and just that glimpse would make my tongue dry and a jolt would go in my belly, as if there was a baby there, kicking. Not that I know, of course. How that feels. We were never blessed, me and Ed. We've got used to it, but sometimes – well, it's too late now. Sometimes, though, I wonder if it's some sort of sign. Incompatibility, you know. Ed says that's a load of old bollocks, and although he would have made a lovely father, he's not bitter. He accepts things. He's not one to stir up a hornet's nest or open a can of worms. That's my department.

The odd thing is that now I try to think of it, I don't know why I broke up with Jack. I can remember every detail of lying beside him in that Ford Transit he used to have, him with just his white pants on, and sunlight sneaking in through those grimy windows, with the message Clean Me/Fuck Off scrawled in smeary finger-writing on the outside; and his blond chest-hairs would be lit up, and he'd be smoking and blowing smoke up towards the ceiling, and narrowing his eyes and pushing out his bottom lip and, well, you can imagine. The belter of a kick inside me. I wanted to fuck his boots off, if you'll pardon my French, every minute of every damn hour. I was always a plain-speaking girl, as well as one who prided herself on being able to look things in the face. I told him what I thought and he laughed and no doubt he rolled me again onto that filthy bit of carpet he'd put down and never mind that he was due back at work half an hour ago and all his mates would tease him, asking if he enjoyed his lunch break of 'leg-over and chips'.

I used to think my insides were breaking up, dissolving like sugar in hot tea. Then I would remember the Cold Room and the latest body lying there, and what I knew to be true of a person's insides. I'd tell myself not to be ridiculous.

Perhaps I thought I was too young for him. Maybe it scared me, just a little, the effect he had on me, Jack Wilde. I don't know why, I don't even remember the conversation, when I told him. I've thought and thought about this, all today, struggling to remember. I can picture myself with my hair that used to be much curlier, and down to my waist and the freckles I had across the bridge of my nose in summer and Jack touching them and grinning and how he was always lit up, it seemed: it was fen light, you know, extra powerful and clean, dishing things up fiercer and brighter, too vivid really, the way I think it must be if you take drugs. I mean that's what I've heard. LSD or something. Of course, not that I've ever taken anything like that. Never even a cigarette, me. No, mine's been a quiet life. Apart from Jack Wilde. Apart from that brief period. I remember how I felt when he married the gangly Alison Meadows barely six months later. That was sharp. That knocked the breath from me.

In my head, I made excuses for him. He was lost and couldn't say so. His mother had just died, remember. And I was . . . dull, dazed. In the dark. All lightness, all spark had left me. He had poured light into me, under my skin, the way Father poured the preservative into those dead bodies and plumped them up and filled them and made them seem alive, more alive than they'd ever been, and now it had gone out.

I think I kept expecting us to talk about it. That there would be time, some future date and it would all be put right. Yes, that's it. That's why my hands are shaking and my stomach sinking, *plummeting*, sitting here, talking to Alison Wilde about the arrangements for her husband's funeral. We're talking about my Jack and in my head, all these years, it has always been there. The thing, and the phrase. *All the time in the world.*

He used to whistle a lot. He had a beautiful way of whistling, Jack. It wasn't cheery, like the milkman – it was like a kind of instrument. I can see now just the way his mouth looked and that hollow sound, papery. The notes, floating across my skin, when he laid beside me, whistling.

I hope he didn't – suffer? I ask her, which is an unprofessional question. You never ask for details, unless they're volunteered. She says right away that it was a heart attack and as I calculate it, she adds: he was only fifty-one.

Heart attack.

A moment of silence then. Confusion. The flowers on the carpet levitate up towards my eyes, blurring. Pink and red together, one big bloody mess. It's a horrible choice, this carpet. I'll have to have a word with Ed. Get around to changing it.

And do you have your green form, Mrs Wilde, as I can't go forward without that?

(I don't call it the death certificate. There's no need to call it that.)

And have we decided? I lean forward, showing her the catalogue again. Is it the Etheldreda we're going for, or the Cromwell? The Cromwell, remember, is a tad more expensive, but you know, he was a big man – you say – and I think he'd be more comfortable in here.

I once suggested to Father that we call one of the coffins the Adventurer. After the Fen Adventurers. He said it was in poor taste. I was shirty, then. Do you think anyone knows who Etheldreda is? I asked him. If it's good enough for Ely Cathedral, it's good enough for us, he said.

Jack's wife nods her decisions: the Cromwell, she says, bleary and glazed, but she looks up then and stares at me.

A big man. Jack. Yes, I suppose he was.

What does she mean? What's she saying to me, and why is she smiling like that? It might almost be a joke, an acknowledgement of something. Only I couldn't believe it of her, not here. Not under the circumstances.

She is standing up. I hold out her coat for her.

Everything will be taken care of Mrs Wilde. Don't worry about a thing.

Thank you, she says, in the voice they always use. The bereaved. A meaningless voice. They mean nothing by it. They don't even know you exist. You're nothing to them, no more than furniture. I didn't need to worry. It's only years later that she might think of me. Think of the irony, if she figures it out.

That it was me, the last person to touch his body. That I dressed him, tenderly, lifting his feather-weight limbs. That I planted a kiss on his cold, bloodless mouth. That I, Martha, who have worked here every day for more than twenty-five years, could still be shocked, still realize she knows nothing, nothing at all. That I drove home across the fens and put my foot down and drove right into that great white space of sky, felt the fields smudge into lines on either side of me, but could never make it happen again, never again believe it possible to drive right over the edge, over the plate of the flat earth.

Royston Swarbrooke

The Last Dodo

[novel extract]

The History – When Capstan Met Alec

It was the summer of 1995 and for a micro-second everything seemed possible. Fresh from the provinces and eager to achieve the impossible, Capstan and Alec were two unemployed actors whose only seriously paid job, apart from the odd role as 'Background Artists' and minor roles in profit-share fringe theatre, was on the South Bank.

The South Bank is a phrase that, if used by an actor, can mean only the National Theatre. When asked at parties what they did for a living and where they worked, Capstan and Alex would reply, 'We are actors on the South Bank.' Instantly the other person would think, 'Ah, you are gentlemen who tread the boards at the Olivier or the Lyttelton, and think of modern interpretations of Ibsen by David Hare, with Juliet Stevenson in black, prop handlers flying ducks south across the stage to Moscow, Michael Sheen pacing, Ian McKellen holding master classes in Shakespeare, Alan Bennett directing, and Hopkins, Sher, Dench, et al, stalking the dressing rooms before retiring to Hampstead for left-wing intellectual debate and fine wine. Even if you were just a spear carrier or messenger it didn't matter, as long as it was at the National Theatre. More often than not it would lead to sexual intercourse and invitations to further parties, where the words 'actors on the South Bank' would steal the show.

What many people didn't know was that, apart from the National Theatre, there was another place where actors could be employed on the South Bank. True, you didn't get many trained at RADA, Lamda, Bristol Old Vic or Glasgow working there. At

£140 a week it wasn't even a basic Equity contract. And the parts on offer weren't Caliban, Lear, Hamlet, George III or Toad of Toad Hall. But it was acting, sort of, and you breathed the same rarefied air, shopped at the same book market and shared the same Tube station. The Museum of the Moving Image, hidden under an arch of Waterloo bridge and part of the National Film Theatre, was where the history of television and film was brought to life via exhibits – and where actors dressed in period costume interacted, often precariously, with the public. The parts available were Victorian Magic Lantern Operator, Russian Train Propagandist, 1940s Odeon Cinema Usherette and 1920s Hollywood Director.

Each year three companies of eighteen were put together for a five-month contract, recruited by adverts in the back of *The Stage* (in between the ones looking for glamour models, and the ones needing people to hand out leaflets in shopping malls dressed up as a large cartoon animal, and the ones that read 'Resting? Why not earn some extra money with Telephone Sales? Time off for auditions, guaranteed.') It was on this not-so-hallowed soil that Capstan and Alec met.

Capstan lived at the time in a splendid toilet in New Cross, while Alec resided up the road in Camberwell; part gentrified, part grim reality trap, with the gulf of Peckham sprawling in between. One night while drunk and in need of another ale, they decided to chance New Cross's premier (and only) night club, imaginatively named the Venue – a meat market and zoo of illicit sex, where cheap Es were downed like aircraft in the Bermuda Triangle. Apart from drugs, sex, alcopops and the co-operative time-share of one brain cell by ten bouncers, it specialized in putting on tribute bands. It seemed at that particular time in the nation's backward-turning evolutionary loop, that every band that had ever been had a tribute band. The early instigators were obvious, acts like the Bootleg Beatles, Bjorn Again doing Abba and the Australian Pink Floyd. Now, though, it wasn't just bands which no longer existed that you were able to witness in an intimate setting. It was possible to experience any number of past and present bands live and in the look- and sound-alike flesh. The situation had become so bizarre that an Oasis tribute band

No Waysis had managed to secure a record deal on the strength that they performed songs which Oasis had in their turn ripped off. It was post-modernism run riot and Capstan, who deeply hated contemporary music, embraced it as a sign that music as an artform was now redundant.

What both Alec and Capstan loved about tribute bands was that the experience was infallible; you couldn't have a bad night or lose out with them. If you were really drunk or on drugs, it felt like seeing your favourite band in a small, personal venue. If they were chronically awful, it was just hilarious, especially if they took themselves seriously. Alec's favourite band was The Still Ills, a Smiths' tribute, because they were appalling, with the lead singer undertaking his Morrissey impression in a righteous and earnest manner, obviously believing that he was the Chosen One, while the rest of the group looked and acted like Motorhead roadies on a night out with Girlschool, each with his own crate of lager by his feet, each intent on trying to pull female members of the audience and each refusing to acknowledge the Morrissey clone's existence. The best gig was their final one when, during the song 'There is a light and it never goes out', the bass guitarist kicked the fey, shrub-pocketed singer into the drum riser and then stamped on his spectacles. Capstan's personal favourite was Nylon Overground, a Japanese girl band who played Velvet Underground songs. The four girls were all from Tokyo and were studying at the London College of Printing. He became such a fan that one night, drunk and in love with the drummer, he approached them after the gig at the bar to ask if he could manage them. It was the most constructive act he had undertaken since applying for a passport. He was told in polite Japanese fashion that they managed themselves.

It was Alec who one morning put the question to Capstan, while stuck in traffic on the number 12 bus, halfway up the Walworth Road: 'If you were to form a tribute band, what band would you choose to pay homage to and what would your name be?' His reply was instant. 'It would be a tribute to the work of the Dead Kennedys and the name would be "Mount Rushmore". And yours?' Alec thought hard in silence, as the bus filtered past the Elephant and Castle's neon pink shopping centre towards

Westminster Bridge. From this starting point – as they made their way along the side of the Thames to the Museum of the Moving Image for their final day of employment, on a gusty early October day - the idea of the Dodo Anthology evolved. By lunchtime the inspiration had solidified into the idea of a band dedicated to playing the most distressed and dark songs of all time, or songs by artists who had died in tragic circumstances; the ultimate being miserable artists who had died miserable deaths. With unemployment looming fast and only jobs as height-challenged elves in department store plastic grottoes to look forward to, they began to make plans. Alec spent his final wages at Argos on a Casio keyboard and Capstan dug out his Jaguar guitar from his parents' attic. They chose ten songs to learn and camped out in Alec's flat for a month of practising.

The month in SE5 went through four important stages. The first: a sincere endeavour to do the songs justice, which lasted three days. The second: the realization that they were pitiful musicians with severely restricted abilities and limited instruments; this they became aware of on the fourth day. The third: depression – the subject-matter of the songs got them down and they saw buried parallel connections with their own lives (Capstan's Nan had owned a dog named Shep); this lasted two weeks and three days. The fourth, final and most decisive stage: they began finding the songs hilarious and broke into hysterical fits of giggles followed by catatonic stupor. Quickly they jettisoned any attempts to emulate the core of the songs' meaning in favour of taking the piss. Though they would never admit it to each other, both men felt a twinge of sorrow that they no longer related to the angst and melancholy of most of the songs' contents. Once they had listened to these outpourings of sonic grief wide-eyed, innocent and in awe. Now, as they choked back fits of laughter, it felt as though they had lost part of their youth.

Age. A touchy subject. Capstan, who rarely sat, but perched on the edge of his seat like an expectant budgerigar awaiting its owner's return from the shops, was obsessed by age – and hexed by the possibility that he was a failure.

At his most desolate he would launch a conversation with, 'So-and-so was twenty-four when such and such happened to him. When I was twenty-four I was temping in an office as a junior. A junior at twenty-four! I've fucked up, Alec. I've fucked up!' All the people he compared himself with had one thing in common: they were famous. Age was Capstan's Achilles heel, and as he moved beyond thirty it was spreading to his ankles and lower abdomen.

Alec remembered the day that he became aware of this flaw in Capstan's make-up; it was one morning two months into the MOMI contract. Waking up inside a large cushion in Capstan's New Cross toilet, after a quick after-work drink became a full night's work, he heard Capstan returning from the shop. The door shut and Capstan roared, 'Yes, yes it's OK! It's a beautiful day and it's going to be OK. There is an order to life! Coffee?' He beamed as he gave Alec a gentle wake-up kick. 'Water,' gasped Alec, attempting to swallow the rotting fishing net of dead-dog fur in his mouth. 'Just water in large amounts, please'. Capstan rarely got hung over: 'London water's been recycled seven times,' he said, passing Alec a pint of water, 'which in laymen's terms means that seven other people have already drunk that one glass and then a few hours later pissed it down a toilet's U-bend, probably as part of a shitting ritual.'

'Thanks for pointing that out,' replied Alec, taking the glass.

'You're much better off with bottled, though you can never find bottled around here.'

'Water?'

'Coke,' said Capstan, swigging from a can.

'Are we late for work?'

'No,' said Capstan, lighting the first of the day's numerous cigarettes.

'So, what's going to be OK?'

Capstan pointed at a page in the morning's newspaper. 'My position in the great scheme of things is going to be OK.'

'Is it a job advert?'

'A job advert! Fuck no. I don't look for jobs, work comes to me, or will. It's a parallel destiny. A sign that I am unconsciously following in preordained footsteps.'

Capstan had been reading an article on his way back from the newsagent's, about a well-known and respected male actor who hadn't got started in his extremely successful career until he was thirty-one. 'There's hope, Alec. Our days of pissing about in the outskirts of tacksville dramarama land are numbered. This bloke was thirty-one and doing deader than dead-end jobs until it finally clicked and he was on his way.' Alec was too busy contemplating whether it was the mother ship of a doner kebab he rounded the evening off with, or the final tequila shot, or the seven-times-purified pint of water, or the dry blue smoke from Capstan's cigarette that was going to cause him to throw up.

'That's, reassuring, excuse me. I . . . ugh.' Alec's palm shot over his mouth and he sprinted to the kitchen, barking up the sick onto the cooker's hob, as the sink proved to be a bridge too far.

'I told you that water was rough stuff.'

The age question had progressed and become more pronounced after that, slowly revealing itself as one of Capstan's major preoccupations. Not so much a bone of contention as a whole skeleton's worth. His hero was Tom Baker. This was because, before he found a purpose in life as Dr Who when he was thirty-six, Baker had decided to kill himself. After fruitlessly toiling on a building site and giving away an item of furniture each week, he'd been left with just an antique chaise longue, on which he was going to lie down and die. Capstan loved the idea that it was only a call from the BBC casting department that saved Baker. He took strength from this and believed that his own life was going to run along the same lines.

One day, in an effort to add a little reality to the hypothesis, Alec made the fatal mistake of challenging Capstan about this. He'd read the same biography, on Capstan's insistence, and over a drink observed, 'It's all very well thinking that Tom Baker was a 36-year-old failure. But he didn't just spring from nowhere to the BBC's attention. I mean, he was a trainee priest, was working in theatre in his twenties, got married, had a child, was in a few films and even worked with Pasolini. He was just having some kind of breakdown, that's all.'

Capstan sat in mute silence.

Alec carried on. 'I just think that you have to find your own way and not compare yourself with anyone else. We're all different. You've got to stop being so fatalistic and hard on yourself.'

Capstan was mortified. 'Why do you have to undermine me? Tom Baker was a no-hoper dipstick in ghastly circumstances up to and until the age of thirty-six. Just like me and, even though you won't face up to it, you!'

'Actually, I don't think that I am a no-hoper dipstick in dire circumstances and nor would you, if you stopped taking such an unhealthy interest in other people's lives. You're obsessed with celebrities. It's a vapid and pointless endeavour that will lead you nowhere. Be yourself before it's too late.'

With his body visibly shuddering, his mouth looking as if he was chewing on an onion and trying to pass it off as an apple, and his eyes frantically blinking like a strobe light flashing at 450 bpm, Capstan stood up and pronounced, 'I am working class. You are middle class. So don't preach to me!' With that he wobbled off. 'I am working class' was a phrase that Capstan brought up on average once a month. 'I am working class,' Alec realized, was a full stop, a debate killer and a signal that Capstan was about to blow a gasket.

In an effort to save their friendship they therefore reached an agreement. Alec promised never to discuss Tom Baker or any other famous people in Capstan's company and Capstan promised to refrain from passing on date lines of the rich and famous. With that oath they sealed their not-so-beautiful friendship.

Patrick Neate

Good TV

'*Gringo!* You liking suck my dick?'

Olly said nothing. He didn't cry, whimper or even flinch, but just stared at the Paisley swirls that circled before his blindfolded eyes. It wasn't that he was brave; he simply had a very limited imagination (two characteristics often confused). And, besides, the pulsing pain of his headache seemed to grant his cerebrum a purity of process that allowed only one thought – whether abstract or applied – at a time. And, at the moment, these were building in numbered order rather like a shopping list or bullet-pointed memo to self.

First, Olly noticed that his headache seemed to have short-circuited his brain into an aural spate of spoonerisms so that, while he knew exactly what *o Dono* had *said*, he'd actually heard, 'You liking duck my sick.' Second, he couldn't but find it ironic that, for all *o Dono*'s repartee, he'd have gladly given him a quick gobble to get out of this alive. Third, he was surprised by *o Dono*'s overt and apparently relaxed connection between his weapon (actual) and his weapon (figurative). After all, none – or, rather, neither – of the Porsche drivers he'd met had ever been prepared to admit as much. Fourth, Olly was intrigued to discover that the metallic taste of the gun barrel reminded him of the day he sucked a twopence piece as a kid. And fifth . . .

'You liking duck my sick?' *o Dono* said again.

Olly had assumed this was a rhetorical question, but now he realized he was expected to reply. This was tricky. Partly because he wasn't sure of the right answer and partly because he had a mouthful of gun. In the end, he settled for 'nice' accompanied by a little shrug of the shoulders, because that seemed suitably non-committal in a vaguely positive sort of way. From around the barrel it came out as 'aith', but it seemed to satisfy his captor nonetheless.

'I bet you wonder, "*Babalosha*! How I ending up in Commando Verde shit hole giving gun blow job," eh?'

'Well,' Olly thought, 'at least we're on the same wavelength.'

Because, allowing for peculiarities of tongue, grammar, syntax and spoonerism, this was exactly what he'd been wondering. In fact, it was the fifth of his five points.

*

Olly had been in the country four days, but he still had no idea where it was. Somewhere in South America; Central America perhaps. It was one of those places you only ever heard of every decade or so; when some fashionista discovered its cows offered especially fine-quality leather, say, or the Americans decided to oust or impose a dictator, or Trivial Pursuit® threw up a tricky question about a dam. Because, for all the WTO's talk of a global village with a one-way system, this place was still well outside the ring road. Look at it this way: even Sting, who'd made a panpipe album in the rainforests to the north, would have struggled to find it on a map.

It was hardly Olly's fault. Less than a week ago he'd been called into his bosses' office at Panther Television on Charlotte Street in London, to find the pair of them, Harry and Trevor, head to head over a computer. 'Take a seat, Oliver,' Harry had said.

Panther was their baby; a medium-sized production company, growing all the time on the back of Harry's connections and Trevor's hard-headed nous.

To say that Harry and Trevor were television stereotypes doesn't even begin to cover it. In Olly's eyes, they were more like Platonic forms of the opposite ends of the TV spectrum. Harry was a lord by birth, a queen by inclination and a coke addict by mistake. Most importantly (for him and Panther) he was a regular face everywhere from the *Sun*'s 'Bizarre' column to *Tatler*'s 'Party Scene'. Trevor, on the other hand, was a professional Scouser whose twenty years in London had only strengthened his accent. Trevor didn't speak, he insulted. And his favourite insults invariably included one of 'middle class', 'southern' and 'poof' (often all three). He had a house in Dulwich, another just outside Carcassonne and his third wife had briefly presented aerobics on GMTV.

As for Olly? He'd been at Panther almost four months as a junior researcher. Joining the company because of its reputation for quality documentaries, his arrival had unfortunately coincided with the success of Panther's *Sex Planet* and subsequent shift in emphasis ('dumbing up', Trevor called it). So far Olly had worked on three shows – *Fat Brother*, *Top Ten Serial Killers*, and *Ecstasy Unwrapped*; all a good deal more fatuous than factual.

Consequently, that day, when Harry told him they were thinking about a 'serious investigation' of Commando Verde, Olly jumped at the opportunity.

'Commando Verde? The drug faction? You've heard of them, I take it,' Harry said suspiciously.

'Sure.'

'A poof like you?' Trevor added.

'Coke dealers.' Olly nodded. He just had to keep it brief because he knew this was a game of bluff. 'Read something in *The Economist*. Networks all over the continent.'

Harry studied him closely. 'Drug trafficking. Human interest. We're looking to lay bare the inside story. Tragic.'

'Tragic.' Olly nodded.

That evening he caught the Gatwick Express with a DVC in his hand luggage. Preliminary research, they'd said.

*

Fourteen hours later Olly was in a city whose name he'd forgotten in a country of unspecified location. Even the language offered few clues since it was a bizarre Creole of Portuguese, Spanish, Lucumí and Carson Daly. He did know the name of his hotel, however. It was called *O Waldorf*. He knew this because it said so on the room key and he chose to believe that rather than his sheets (which claimed to belong to Hilton Hotels Inc.), his bathrobe (Holiday Inn Tucson) or his individual sachet of shampoo (Radisson Worldwide). After all, the key had opened the door, right? And so, clearly, had the man who was sitting on his bed examining his passport when Olly emerged from the shower wrapped in a towel (Sacramento District Hospital).

This guy was squat and solid-looking, hair tied back in a ponytail, a pair of sunglasses resting high on his forehead. He was wearing a baggy fluorescent-pink vest, a pair of yellow shorts and Gucci loafers. When he looked up and saw the half-naked Olly, he immediately pulled an enormous gun from the waistband of his shorts.

'Who are you?' he asked.

'Olly,' Olly said and lifted one hand in a 'hands up' kind of way; the other still clutching the towel. The guy flipped to Olly's passport photo and compared the snapshot with the real thing with undisguised suspicion. 'It's not a great photo,' Olly said.

The man beamed a smile and tucked away his gun. 'All *gringos* looking same anyway,' he said. 'You wanna sell passport? Good price US dollar?'

'No thanks. Umm . . . who are *you*?'

'João,' João said. 'Your guide.'

'My guide? Harry never said.' João shrugged. 'Look. I'm not being funny. But don't you think you should have knocked.'

'You in the shower, man.'

'But you could have been anybody; a thief, a gangster . . .'

'I got a gun. Full clip.'

'Right but . . .'

'Sure,' João said. 'No problem. Put your pants on, man. Let's get outta here.'

On the way down to the lobby, Olly thought it best to explain the requirements of his research. It didn't take long. He said, 'Look, João. I need to see Commando Verde strongholds, see the dealing, the sort of firepower they're using, that kind of thing.'

João stared at him. 'OK, *gringo*. Let's go the beach.'

*

João parked his little Fiat on the promenade, which overlooked a long stretch of white sand, and spread out a tourist map on its bonnet. According to João, if you wanted to understand the city, this was where you had to be; partly because from here you could look back on the whole place and partly because the whole place decamped here every day anyway.

João explained it like this. 'This city, man? Nothing like what you see. Is divided in two. There is *asfalto* (meaning, like, main city, OK?) and there is *desperdiçado*. *Desperdiçado* is how you call shanty town. *Asfalto* controlled by city council, *desperdiçado* controlled by *soldados* of Commando Verde drug faction, OK? Nobody from *asfalto* go *desperdiçado* unless they rich kid wanna buy drugs. Nobody from *desperdiçado* go *asfalto* unless they *soldado* wanna buy trainers or DVD. Is cocaine and marijuana go one way, Nike and Michael Jackson go other way.

'In sixties council find shanty town kinda – what you say? – *humiliating* when Kissinger visit from US talking about how to rinse Allende. Then Mayor Costa having brilliant idea. He say, "Just ignore them." So is what he did.'

João pointed along the beach to the cliffs at the far end, where an expansive, dilapidated slum climbed the jagged rock; its ramshackle buildings looking like they might drop into the sea at any moment. 'You see that, *gringo*? City of Angels. Is my *desperdiçado* and home of *Commando Verde*.' Now he marked the corresponding point on the map with his finger. 'And you see it there? No? Is not on map, man! Council have no *desperdiçado* on map in case they scare tourist or aid agency. Is better pretend they no exist. Is what I say, man. This city nothing like what you see.'

Olly leant on the railings that overlooked the sand.

Coming from a city like London, where thighs are pink and dimpled, he found the view almost pornographic, an orgy of exposed, bronzed flesh. It was as if, that morning, someone had stolen all the city's clothes and left an enormous ball of string in payment. Barrel-chested men with short legs were playing keepy uppy with a football, their ill-concealed stubby cocks jitterbugging with every jump and stretch. There were androgynous girls, feminized by vast womanly arses, playing limp-wristed beach tennis in the surf and gorgeous Amazonian chicks with magnificent breasts, who took turns to rub oil over each other. There were also a few raw-fleshed *gringos*, who studded the sand like pimples. 'Your people, eh?' João said, shaking his head. 'Is coming here work for aid agency. Giving us jack. We giving them skin cancer.'

João followed Olly's goggle-gaze to a particularly eye-catching pair of boobs that jiggled beneath cascading blonde hair. 'You like our women?' he said.

'Sure.'

'So you know is a man, right? A word of advice: you see breast like that? Is always *maricones de playa, siliconada*, chicks with dicks. Okay?'

'OK.' Olly swallowed. 'I knew that.'

Suddenly, at that moment, there was a small, chocolate-skinned kid sprinting towards them along the sidewalk pursued by a pasty, bespectacled *gringo* yelling, 'Thief!' at the top of his voice. The pedestrians parted to let them by, but João blocked the boy's path, pulled his gun and trained it on his head. '*Policias*!' João announced and the child skidded to a halt. There was a brief exchange of looks, matter of fact on João's part, resentful on the boy's. Then the boy shrugged and handed over the wallet. João cuffed him around the head and he ran off without another word.

By the time the *gringo* caught up, João was already emptying the wallet of its cash, which he stuffed into the pocket of his shorts. 'Police,' João said, smiling broadly as he returned the wallet to its owner. It seemed like the man was about to speak, but João made an airy gesture with his gun as if to say *de nada* and the man turned on his heels.

'I didn't know you were a cop,' Olly exclaimed.

João tutted: 'What I tell you, man? Nothing like what you see.'

*

Olly spent the next three days in the City of Angels. It seemed João was a connected guy and he'd secured permission with *o Dono*, the boss of Commando Verde, for Olly to film in the *desperdiçado*.

Walking into this shanty town was like walking into another world; a world of permanent impermanence, where smells were shapes and life was shadows. Lookouts from the faction, positioned on every roof, let off firecrackers when they entered so that everyone knew a *gringo* had arrived. When the smoke cleared, the crystal sun revealed shades of people moving through medieval-narrow streets of open sewers and open cooking pots where the stench of shit and food was glutinous and overpowering. Tin shacks fought for position with precarious brick constructions, cripples cowered in low doorways, broken men smoked thin cigars and competed for shrinking splashes of shade, weather-beaten old women sold odds and ends on straw mats: a broken pair of sunglasses, two batteries, a creased postcard of Tupac Shakur.

Olly kept saying, 'I don't believe this place. Why doesn't someone do something?' until João became irritable.

'Who? I told you, man. Is no exist for no government.'

'What about charities then?'

'Aid agency no get in without word of *o Dono* and they say they no dealing with no gangster. So they no get in.'

'So what do they do?'

'They go beach, man.'

Barefoot kids played World Cup games with footballs made of envelopes and masking tape while their older brothers, in their early teens, played war games with AK47s and AR-15s. These were the dealers and *soldados*. You could tell by their flip-flops and Bermuda shorts (by Hilfiger and Adidas), their coke-dilated pupils . . . and their guns, of course.

João introduced him to several of these child soldiers and they were suspicious but friendly enough. They all had absurdly elongated nicknames that João translated and wouldn't, Olly figured, have been much use in a shootout. ('Hey little-negro-with-big-heart! Tell blonde-kid-who-[to-the-eternal-pain-of-his-mother-and-the-Blessed-Virgin and-Oluwo-lord-of-Awos]-still-lives-in-this-shithole to watch the door!') But Olly's problem was that they refused to be filmed with their guns and, every time he raised the camera, the weapons vanished to be replaced by cherubic smiles.

'I need to film some gangsters!' Olly complained.

João shrugged. 'What you figure? They no be filmed with no gun unless *o Dono* say so.'

João suggested that they follow the sounds of firecrackers which, as well as the arrival of a *gringo*, marked an incursion by a rival faction. They might get lucky and catch a gunfight. Unfortunately it turned out that the firecrackers were also set off to signify a goal for the local football team, Rosa Santos-Baptista's ninety-fifth birthday and the fact that one of *o Dono*'s right-hand men (scary-guy-with-coffee-skin-and-coffee-breath) had just taken delivery of a Zanussi microwave and was handing out free popcorn.

On the third night Olly took a call from his bosses on speakerphone while João rifled through his suitcase looking for stuff to buy, barter or thieve. Olly ignored him. He was getting used to this.

Harry did most of the talking. He was over-excited, probably high. 'So how's it going over in . . . there?'

'Fine,' Olly said. 'Great in fact. Brilliant.'

'Because we need some good footage. Guns. Maybe a corpse or two.'

'Right. No problem.'

'Because you know what I've done? Shall I tell you what I've done? Shall I tell you what I've only gone and done?'

'Sure.'

'I've only gone and got this show commissioned so you'd best get back here with some top-notch material.'

'Great.'

'One-hour special. Channel 4. Friday night. The pub slot. Only the pub slot! Called, wait for it, *When Gangsters Go Crazy*.'

'Sorry?'

'*When Gangsters Go Crazy*. Think *Ibiza Uncovered* meets *When Animals Attack*. It's brilliant!'

'*When Gangsters Go Crazy*?'

Trevor spoke up for the first time. 'You got a problem with that, you little southern poof?'

'No,' Olly said. 'No problem at all.'

On putting the phone down, Olly turned immediately to João, who was playing, curiously, with his tube of Mostly Men moisturizing milk.

'Is for what?' João asked.

'Moisturizer. Look . . .'

'What for?'

'I dunno. Look. I have to speak to *o Dono*.'

'Why?'

'That was my boss on the phone. I have to film *soldados* with their guns so I have to speak to *o Dono*.'

'Why?'

'Why what?'

'Why *o Dono* gonna say yes?'

'Because!' Olly exclaimed, as though explanations were all too obvious. But then he realized he couldn't actually think of any. 'Because it's good publicity,' he tried.

'Publicity? *O Dono* is gangster not Coca-Cola, man.'

'But it'll put this city on the map.'

'Is already on map! *Desperdiçados* not on map, but I no think TV gonna make no difference.'

Olly sighed. 'Look. I have to film *soldados* or I'm stuffed. I have to have something dramatic to show, y'know? Something, like, dangerous. It will be good for the *desperdiçados*. Show their plight to the world, how they live in poverty under the . . . the . . . shackles of politicians and gangsters. Don't you want the UK to know how your people suffer? It'll be an audience of millions.'

'*Gringo*.' João shrugged. 'You think *o Dono* give a shit about TV? When we first get rap videos in this country? Suddenly all *soldados* think they black *americanos*, man.' He made a gun from his fingers. 'Everybody, like, "Word up dog! I'm OG." Pow! Pow! Like that. Is what you want? You want kids in UK to wear flip-flop and say, "Hey, *gringo*! I'm *soldado* for *Commando Verde*?" Pow! Pow!'

'I don't think . . .'

'No. *O Dono* no stupid. Is about money. Man get big titties become *siliconada*? Money. Kid get Uzi become *soldado*? Money. You make TV? Money. So where the money for *o Dono*?'

'Well,' Olly mumbled, 'it's a big budget production. I'm sure . . .'

'Is all I need to know, man,' João interrupted. 'I'll arrange meeting for tomorrow, OK? What your show called?'

Olly swallowed and then blurted it out. 'It's called *When Gangsters Go Crazy.*'

João stared at him for a moment unblinking, his brow furrowed. 'Once I see show on satellite called *When Animals Attack*,' he said. 'You make that?'

'No. This will be much more . . .'

'I love that show. *When Animals Attack*? Animals is *loco*, man. *Loco*.'

*

'I bet you wonder, "*Babalosha!* How I ending up in Commando Verde shithole giving gun blow job," eh?'

They'd arrived in the City of God early and met up with a young *soldado* called bollocks-like-coconuts-and-big-*ishu*-too (João didn't know the English for *ishu*).

'You want to see *o Dono*?' the *soldado* asked.

Olly had to agree to wear a blindfold and to João not going with him. 'OK,' Olly said.

As soon as the blindfold was in place, the *soldado* raised his gun and smacked Olly across the back of the head. He hit the ground like dropped shopping. The *soldado* looked at João and shrugged. '*Gringo* got soft head, man.'

When Olly came to, he was on his knees with his hands tied behind his back and a gun in his mouth.

Now, as the drumming pain of Olly's headache began to recede, so his thoughts started to coalesce and multiply and, for all his lack of imagination, he realized he was well and truly screwed. 'All for the sake of the subplot,' he thought. He was even thinking in spoonerisms.

O Dono seemed to have lost his cool and he was now barking angry: 'So you come see *o Dono* to be on TV show, eh? You think he just some Third World *aberinkulá* who confuse *pau* and *ishu*? You wanna see what happen when he go crazy? He gonna pull this trigger and the last thing you thinking, "*Yeye!* Is one crazy gucking fangster, man."'

That was it. *O Dono* pushed the gun deeper into Olly's mouth and the combination of concussion, fear and the barrel against his soft palate propelled him over the edge and he gagged and vomited, sending sour bile streaming from his nose and spraying from his mouth.

He heard hoots of laughter as *o Dono* pulled the gun away with a curse. Now who was 'ducking sick'?

Olly screwed up his face, anticipating the gunshot, but it never came. After a moment he felt hands loosening the binding at his wrists and, when his blindfold was removed, he found himself looking up at João ruefully shaking puke off his gun. To his left, bollocks-like-coconuts-and-big-*ishu*-too was still filming on Olly's DVC.

'You get that?' João asked.

'*Si Dono. Tudo*,' the *soldado* replied.

João turned to Olly, frowning, and offered him a hand up. 'You OK, man?'

Olly tried to get to his feet, but then he retched again. 'I thought you were a bloody cop!' he spat.

João shrugged. 'Police? Gangster? Nothing like what you see, *gringo*. But is good TV, eh?'

Sarah Maguire

The Foot Tunnel

for Andrew

The dream always dreamt just before dawn:
walking the cool white tunnel to its end,
pace echoing pace,

the chill white tiles streaming with breath,
with rumours of the Thames
(its brown tons of water and cargoes,

its river creatures, silt) dragging above us,
pointing the walls with a century of damp.
We pass through a ghost-mist, drawn on

by a row of dim lamps pinned to the ceiling
pulling us downwards through walled-up clay
deep underneath the cold throat of the river.

Spilt out of the wood-panelled, rickety lift
we are shocked by air, by seagulls soaring and diving,
by the world swivelled round, clouds, the sudden

smell of the sea. We have walked under
water, to be drenched to the bone
by a joyful June downpour, punched from the skies.

Maria McCann

Minimal

'Total chaos,' Ellie says. 'Slippers under the sink, fuse wire in the bathroom cabinet. God knows how she found anything.'

'Old people don't mind,' says Mack. 'They're not in a hurry.'

'It was always like that, even when Nan was in her fifties.'

Mack knows all about Nan. He takes the big two-handled wok and pours soup into the bowls. They eat in silence, facing one another. Mack likes to concentrate on his food and Ellie, buffeted all week by office chatter, appreciates quiet intimacy. The soup is clear and spicy, studded with prawns.

'Delicious,' Ellie says, finishing up the last spoonful. How lucky to be chosen, to live with Mack, whose cookery is not, like some men's, an occasional self-indulgent performance. Mack devotes to their food his serious, inclusive attention. Now he nods, weighing the compliment, and glances at the rota taped to the fridge door:

> *Sunday – steamed chicken. Stock to fridge. Kedgeree*
> *Monday – cold chicken. Bean soup, chicken stock*
> *Tuesday*

Mack frowns. He has evolved a system of radiant simplicity, each meal setting up the next with no junk food or waste, but so far he has not abolished mid-week shopping. There are externals, as he calls them: bread, Cheddar. He has suggested to Ellie that they cut out dairy products. Lots of people do.

*

A month ago Mack and Ellie declared a house detox. It started when Ellie complained that the landlord had filled the cupboards with rusty spoons and bent corkscrews.

'Throw 'em out,' Mack suggested. 'He'll never notice.'

They eyed one another. Ellie giggled.

'Well, are you up for it?' Mack's eyes were brilliant, as they were sometimes during a prolonged bout of sex. In answer, Ellie threw her arms round him. They ran out to the supermarket in the rain and staggered back under heaps of cardboard boxes. They gutted the kitchen, piling up the boxes with trash: novelty bottle openers, the blunt knife Mack had always hated, twee eggcups, worn and superfluous melamine chopping boards. There were shocks: one drawer contained the corpse of a large spider which Mack had to take out in a tissue because Ellie can't bear to see, let alone handle, any spider living or dead. They sat back a while, brewed coffee, and considered what they should offload next. Of course, that thinly enamelled bottle-green saucepan, further uglified by flakes of rust. And then the cracked, orphaned plates, fit only for smashing against the walls.

'I wonder who bought these?' Ellie said. 'I feel sad just looking at them.'

It was Mack's great moment. 'You know,' he said, 'Chinese people cook everything in a wok. I mean *everything*.'

Ellie wasn't sure. She had nothing against Chinese food, but every day? You have to *be* Chinese, know the cuisine, have access to authentic ingredients.

'That's not the idea,' Mack reassured her. 'I mean, you can cook anything in it. Cakes even. *A wok is all you need*.'

Ellie considered. No more greasy pots. It was mad and magnificent.

'Chuck that horrible old cooker,' wheedled Mack. 'Get a gas ring, have it on the table, even.'

'I can't cook with just a wok!'

'Let me, then. I'll do it.' Mack left his chair and came over to Ellie. He kissed her neck, then her ear.

Two days later the council scrap lorry loaded up the stove.

*

Mack plans and shops and cooks and serves. Ellie scalds the wok and seals it with oil. Rubbing it down with a paper towel, she considers Mack: his sweet order and clarity, his compact body. In her teens Ellie's sexual fantasies thudded with tall muscular men. But the reality proved uncomfortable: her neck ached from constantly looking up to them, and in bed they crushed her. 'Well, you go on top then,' they would say with a sporting touch of resentment. In fact Ellie prefers lying underneath. She is not a very active lover and is prone to sciatica. Mack is light, he is gentle, he is clean, his hands and feet are as shapely as the rest of him and he always seems content.

Since they began living together he has spawned many schemes for simplifying life. Tireless Mack, hatching successive refinements. If they visit a new place he takes notes; she sees him doing this at friends' houses, though the friends, mercifully, seem not to notice. Any DIY bore intent on inflicting a tour of his garage conversion finds Mack able and willing. Ellie teases him, but she admits the house is improved. Nor does Mack confine himself to men's work. Why should underwear and linen tumble in unregenerate squalor, sheets lurking between towels, knickers entangled with socks? Is anything worse, he asks, than an overstuffed wardrobe? He has given it thought, he has given everything thought, and as a result they have drawer dividers made of cardboard, and interchangeable unisex fleeces, and forty pairs of one-size black socks that always match, and a kitchen table, made by Mack himself, which attaches directly to the wall, making it easy to clean the floor beneath.

After the prawn soup Ellie and Mack lie on the sofa watching a black-and-white movie, snuggling in the way that is their familiar prelude to an early night and sex. What is better than lying in your lover's arms? And yet –

'I'll get the paper tomorrow,' Mack says. 'Go through the jobs pages.'

Ellie rumples his hair. 'A part-time one.'

They are agreed that, unless you're rich, you need some kind of employment. You can become what the papers call a 'dole scrounger', but it's harder than people imagine, harried by the training agencies and by snoopers eager to examine your sleeping arrangements. Mack's job was in the council offices, handling complaints, until he was made redundant; Ellie's is full-time, but she plans to change that. Why work so much when you need so little?

'A DIY store,' says Mack dreamily. 'I'd get discounts.'

Ellie kisses his forehead. 'How about a delicatessen?'

'No . . . a wholefood shop.' He curls his arms and legs round her. Of course, thinks Ellie, odd slices of pâté and cheesecake would only throw the food system out of kilter. Oh, *bless* him, was there ever a man so earnest?

'Bedtime,' she says. They move to the bedroom, where they make easy, familiar love, rolling apart afterwards like two halves of a cleft apple.

*

Ellie's sleep is troubled. Usually it is nothingness, a soundless ooze of treacle in the brain, but tonight she dreams she is back in her old room, in Nan's house. A stiff quilt perches on top of her, too small to tuck round and so heavy it cramps her feet. She feels it slithering off the bed and reaches out to stop it. An ornament falls on the lino and breaks. Then Nan is in the room, shouting, smacking.

*

Friday – beansprouts, green bean and mushroom stir-fry. Scrambled eggs with smoked slalom

'You've put *slalom* for salmon,' Ellie points out over breakfast.

'I'll change that,' Mack says. 'Later, when I do the emails.'

He sits down before the computer at eight-thirty every evening. Otherwise, he tells Ellie, you can become obsessed and their watchword is simplicity, isn't that right? Ellie agrees, up to a point. When they first went online she would check the mail several times a day, disappointing herself. Her friends couldn't write often enough. Still, isn't flexibility the best thing about email? Look at it just once a day and you might as well be dependent on the postie, who arrives each morning at seven and sometimes pushes their mail through next door's letterbox.

'I'm not sure I want slalom anyway,' Ellie adds.

'Not want—?' He tenses, relaxes again. 'OK, you just have eggs.'

'No.' Ellie twists her hands together. 'It's lovely, you do it beautifully, but I feel like, well, you know. A bit of a change?'

'But it was you who chose scrambled eggs,' Mack says. 'You love them.'

I *did* love them, Ellie retorts silently. Aloud she says, 'It's too much, Mack. I can't go on eating the same stuff over and over. It's a great idea, but in practice it's not so, so . . .'

'You just need a bit longer, to get into the habit.'

'Mack! Watch my lips. I don't want salmon and eggs, I can't stand salmon and eggs, if you give me salmon and eggs I'll throw up.'

'All right.' His voice is surprised and hurt. 'I thought seven days was enough. Shall I move on to tomorrow's menu?'

'*I'll* do dinner. Roast lamb – ' She remembers they have only a wok. 'No, pilaff.'

Mack rises and puts the smoked salmon back in the ice compartment of the fridge. 'If we had a freezer,' he says, 'I could cook multiple meals.'

'Get a job and we'll get a freezer.' Ellie pushes away her breakfast bowl and takes a last mouthful of tea. In the hallway, putting on her raincoat, she is sorry. 'Mack?' she says, coming back into the kitchen. 'It's just a bit soon for me.' She kisses his stubbly cheek. 'Why don't you work out a two-week rota, give us more variety?'

'Could do,' says Mack, brightening.

*

At work Ellie is tormented by nausea, her innards clogged by the threat of eggs and fish. All morning she suppresses painful, swamp-gas belches. Fortunately, her colleagues are unlikely to hear them. Everyone is answering phone queries about credit-card accounts: the office chimes with soothing female voices overlaid by electronic boops and bips. For seventeen minutes Ellie reasons with a woman who claims that she has no obligation to pay a bill addressed to Mrs Calamint when her name is Mrs Calarmine. Trying not to burp into the receiver, Ellie promises to correct the records. Mrs Calarmine repeats, and repeats, that she was promised this would be sorted out the *last* time she telephoned. Would Mrs Calarmine like to speak to a supervisor? Yes, she would, the incompetence of Ellie's organization is staggering, if this is the way they run their affairs then she's not sure she wants to do business with them. Ellie passes her over to Miss Rumm.

The telephone room is crowded, falsely patient, a parody of the calm she enjoys with Mack. Some callers are courteous; others bark orders, or won't wait for her to get the information onscreen. Having offloaded Mrs Calamint/Calarmine, she speaks to an agitated woman whose husband has run up unexplained expenses while on business in Birmingham. 'Probably a restaurant,' Ellie says cheerfully. 'All that networking they do.' And that is exactly what it will look like, she thinks: escort agencies hide behind innocuous trading names like Hamilton's or Da Capo. The woman decides to ring back later.

On her way to the lavatory, Ellie wonders if anyone could calculate how much misery floods the banks of telephones each day. Pointless, self-inflicted pain. One woman, a non-payer forever insisting they must have lost her cheque, has run up an overdraft of £500 on a single pair of shoes.

In the washroom Ellie examines herself in the mirror. Her cheeks are flushed and patchy. Glancing beneath the doors of the cubicles, she sees that they are all empty, and at last allows herself a deep, sulphurous belch.

At breaktime comes one of the predictable surprises of office life: birthday cakes. Barbara, an older woman, invites her: 'Go on, Ell. Live dangerously.'

Ellie picks a chocolate eclair. Shreds of icing peel away as she prises it from its plastic cradle. She plunges her tongue into the crease, gouging out cream.

At noon Ellie walks through fitful rain along Cotterston Place. She is lunching at home. When she opens her front door the hallway smells of stir-fry.

'You're late,' Mack says as she seats herself at the table.

'I did some shopping.'

Mack juggles vegetables and noodles onto her plate. 'Enjoy.'

It's certainly wholesome. And artistic: the green beans are cut on the slant, the sliced mushrooms paper thin. Ellie wouldn't have the patience.

'What did you get for tonight?' he asks.

'Shall we eat first?'

'OK.' He twirls noodles round his fork. 'I've been thinking.'

'Mmm?'

'Do we still need two wardrobes? We could use some space in the bedroom.'

He has a point. Since they weeded the rails and introduced the sock-and-fleece system, the wardrobes are half empty. Take one out, and the room will be less cramped. It makes perfect sense, except that Ellie doesn't want her clothes finally absorbed into Mack's, or Mack checking she's put things away. She says in a strained voice, 'I don't know.'

Mack rubs the back of his neck as if tired.

'I'm sorry,' Ellie finds herself saying, though she isn't.

'I thought you didn't want to be like your nan. That's the sort of thing she'd have, two wardrobes. I thought we'd agreed to simplify—'

'We have! We've done loads already. But you can't simplify down to *nothing*, you have to find what suits—'

'This isn't down to nothing, Ell.'

'I'm sorry,' Ellie repeats. She rises and goes over to the Doan's carrier bag. Normally she would lift out the individual items but now she makes room for the entire carrier inside the fridge.

Mack notices. 'So what did you get?'

'Hamburgers. They'll fry in the wok – '

'Not very healthy.'

' – and coffee cake.'

Her lover begins to stack plates, clashing them together.

'It's only the once, Mack.'

'Oh, go back to work,' he says.

Passing Doan's, Ellie stops and buys a large bar of Cadbury's Dairy Milk. That afternoon, between calls, she breaks off two or three squares at a time. She wonders who first swathed the chocolate in metallic paper; who chose that lurid, whorish purple.

That night they make love. Mack is different, rougher perhaps, though you could never call him *rough*. He grunts.

*

Monday – chicken pittas (Ellie), chicken salad (Mack). Potato and leek soup

Every Monday Ellie takes a short lunch break so that she can leave half an hour early the following Friday. Flexible working is encouraged. Her lover makes her up a packed lunch, a portable version of what he will eat at home. This Monday, opening the box, she finds wholemeal pittas with vegetables and chicken. Mack has added a handful of raisins, 'Because you need your energy,' as he murmured before pushing his tongue into her ear at breakfast. Sex has been lively lately. Ellie, catching sight of a glistening slice of chicken, remembers.

Mack has resigned himself to the second wardrobe and forgiven the hamburgers, though she knows this forgiveness is conditional: there must be no more lapses or the results will be extravagance and pimples. His regime now operates on a two-week timetable. Salmon scrambled eggs come round every second Thursday and she almost enjoys them.

Last night, however, Mack returned to the question of furniture. Surely they don't need two armchairs as well as a sofa? Ellie dislikes the shit-coloured, scratchy armchairs, but she reminded Mack that sometimes they have company.

'Cushions,' Mack said. 'You stack them and they don't take so much space.'

'We can't have guests sitting on cushions if we're on the sofa. Or the other way round. It's embarrassing.'

'Only if you define yourself by your possessions,' Mack said.

Ellie chews over this discussion along with her pittas. Perhaps he won't be satisfied until the house is empty. Why bother with cushions, even? She's surprised the TV has lasted so long. Probably he watches cookery programmes, boning up on technique. She doesn't worry about the computer. He spends too much time on it. It will be the last thing to go.

Has *she* changed? Clearing the kitchen, binning the rubbishy past, was exhilarating. True, she suffered qualms about the wok, but most of what they threw away she has never missed. And yet... since then each new idea has touched her with unease.

Foolish Ellie. She always said she wanted someone original, unconventional. How fortunate, then, to have found him!

Ellie lays down her headset at five o'clock, logs off and walks home grateful. She has a man who cares for her, a lover whose interests are both creative and erotic. She finds Mack, handsome and somehow shy-looking, as if he's not sure whether she likes him, cooking over the gas ring. Oh, lucky woman. She hugs him from behind, puts her hand up his T-shirt and pinches a nipple as he stirs the potato and leek soup.

'I'm just your kitchen boy,' he says, stretching his arms over his head.

That does it. Got to have him now.

'I want you, kitchen boy.' Ellie pinches again and slides her other hand down his jeans.

He hesitates. 'It's nearly ready.'

'Oh Mack, come *on*!'

He lays the spoon on the table. She notices the care with which he does this, placing it parallel to the table edge, and laughs at him, with him, because he's so particular and she's about to turn his neatness all tangled and sweaty. They go upstairs giggling to the strange new bedroom, where Ellie looks around at the newness and strangeness, trying to understand it, and sees that her wardrobe has gone.

*

She can't taste the soup. It's the result of crying for so long: her nose and mouth feel glazed.

'You'll spoil the flavour,' says Mack as she adds salt and pepper.

'Shut up.' What has happened to all that sex, surging up so fizzily until she saw the dirt marks on the wall? Perhaps she has sobbed it out.

'You always get like this,' he says.

'Oh, right,' Ellie says. 'I'm not angry because you went behind my back, it's just PMT. That must be a comfort to you.'

'It was for the best, Ell!'

'Best for who?' He must have advertised, got them to ring

while she was at work. He has even arranged her bras and knickers.

'You're tired. Why don't you leave the house stuff to me?'

'Why don't *you* get a job?' She is horrified, hearing herself say this. At the same time she wants to roll about on the floor, pulling out tufts of his hair.

'You're saying I'm lazy.'

'I'm saying you lied to me!' Ellie whams down the spoon into her left-over soup. It fails to break the bowl.

*

Friday – raw beansprouts, rice, ice

Ellie is on her way to work. When she looks down, she sees the pavement through her shins and realizes her legs have turned to glass noodles. Alone at her desk she unlocks the drawer and takes out a sheeny, voluptuous slab of chocolate. She slides three chunks on top of her tongue. Dissolve, mmm, you just let it melt until *mmm* –

'Ellie?' It's Mack, coming upstairs. She didn't hear his key in the door. Lying on her bed in the office, she tries to pull the sheets over her.

'What're you doing!' Mack screams. He flings himself on the bed and twists the chocolate out of her hand. 'It's poison!' There is chocolate in her hair, down her skirt, between her legs. He smacks her, his face huge and distorted; he's wearing Nan's lilac cardigan. 'You naughty girl, you naughty, dirty girl!'

She wakes, incredulous but still frightened; Mack, his face defenceless, is clinging to her forearm. *Where* was she? Already the dream is fading. Is it really rice and raw beansprouts today? The meals he's been preparing lately are so simple you might as well drink a glass of water. Mack's thriving on it: last night they made love five times.

Breakfast is muesli moistened with orange juice, and organic coffee drunk with soya milk. Ellie refuses to give up coffee. It may have too much caffeine, as Mack keeps telling her, but the stagnant stench of his camomile tea reminds Ellie of childhood visits to her parents' grave and the green slime in the cemetery vases.

'Don't you think this room is nicer now?' he asks, admiring the bare walls.

'Like a medieval peasant's hut,' she answers from the cushion, where she sits cross-legged, the muesli bowl on her lap. Mack smiles. Clever Ellie, to hit on such a good answer.

'They had simpler meals, of course,' he says thoughtfully. 'Porridge would be the modern version.'

'Like in prison?'

She wonders what will depart from the house today. She is used now to finding things missing; she remains calm while questioning him: Where's the bread bin? Mack, what happened to the toaster? Such detachment has not come easily. She was so beaten, so broken, when the armchairs went, that she confided in Barbara.

'If you want me to tell you straight – ' Barbara said, pausing for emphasis – 'I'd go, love. Before the landlord comes looking for his stuff.'

'It was only old furniture,' Ellie pleaded.

Barbara shook her head. 'You get out.'

Finishing up the muesli, Ellie rises and takes her jacket. The vegan lunch is already packed and Mack fetches it from the fridge: beansprouts, chickpeas and carrot, not the meal of her nightmare but she feels distaste anyway. Anger, or incipient indigestion, rises in her.

'Mack, aren't you looking for a job any more?'

'We agreed I wouldn't bother,' Mack says. Ellie is so astonished that she comes close and examines him as if he were a waxwork, noting his curling eyelashes, the open pores on the sides of his nose. His gaze is level and sincere. She realizes that he believes what he has just said. She tries to keep her voice light, non-accusing: 'When? When did we agree that?'

'Oh, I don't know . . .' he wrinkles his forehead, dredging up the memory. 'We were in here.'

'And what did we say about *my* work? Because I'm fed up with the call centre.'

Mack considers. 'We said we'd get everything perfect here first.'

'So when do you think it'll be perfect?' And then Ellie hears herself, playing along, *talking like a shrink*. Her chest is ripped by a pain so bad she knows it's a heart attack. A minute later she knows it isn't, but she has lost whatever Mack said. He's smiling at her. Reassuring.

'I'd better get to work,' she says.

Her eyes brim over as she crosses Cotterston Place. It's embarrassing when your eyes fill in public. She resists the temptation to go into Doan's, in case the man behind the counter asks what's the matter. In work she settles to the usual round of calls, the querulous, the bossy, the confused. At breaktime she joins the rest for coffee, with real milk.

'You all right?' Barbara says, coming up to her. Ellie nods. Another woman, passing by, smiles kindly and Ellie knows that her story has gone the rounds of the office. She feels no resentment. She wants to run after the unknown woman and weep on her shoulder, the way she'd once sob out her little problems in Nan's arms.

*

By the time Ellie walks home she is more cheerful. She treats herself to a chocolate bar. It's a soft, bright evening; in the past, she and Mack would stroll for miles in weather like this. So much beauty for free: blossoming trees, birdsong, cloud shapes, kisses, the aimless happiness of love. It was love, oh yes it was. You know when you've had it.

She will ask him to come out with her. Perhaps, away from the familiar obsessions, she will get through to the old Mack. She will put questions to him, arouse his sleeping reasonableness. He was always reasonable.

Taking a deep breath, she turns the key in the lock. 'Mack! It's me!' There is no answer, and no smell of cookery. For a moment she thinks he has removed himself, along with everything else, but going into the kitchen she finds a bowl of grated raw spinach and onion. She pushes open the living room door. Mack, holding a saw, is sitting cross-legged on the carpet, surrounded by slivers of wood which he appears to have hacked from a ragged log in the corner.

He is naked.

'Mack – ?' Her presence of mind has been stripped away with his clothes. She sees an axe lying along the skirting board. At the thought of him using the axe and saw, naked, her entire body shrivels.

'You can make a stool from a single piece of wood,' Mack says. 'All in one, no fitting together.'

'We had stools,' Ellie says. 'You threw them out.'

'Yeah, but this'll be more solid, see, it'll last for ever.'

He grins at her. She doesn't know if a stool can be made in this way, it's hardly the point. 'I thought you didn't want anything but cushions?' she asks.

'It was a surprise for *you*.'

Any minute now Ellie will throw back her head and howl. She forces herself to take deep breaths.

'I'm doing the whole thing naked,' he goes on proudly. 'It's a form of simplicity. When it rains, we put clothes on, and they get all wet, but Japanese fishermen, they take their clothes off and put them on again when their skin's dry.'

'I see,' says Ellie.

She wants to shout, as people shout at foolish children, bullying them into safety: *You'll cut your prick off.* Instead, she says, 'Shall we have our meal soon?' and walks upstairs, away from the sight of him, so that she can think. How long has he been wandering round the house like that? He's left the curtains open. The neighbours will have seen him already.

She opens the wardrobe, taking stock. Thanks to Mack's system, she can pack a bag in ten minutes. Mack will miss her. He's so defenceless, sometimes; like when he's on the brink of orgasm and he moans *Oh, oh, oh,* like a woman. She lists the essentials: toothbrush, money, knickers.

'Ellie!' Mack calls.

She goes to the top of the stairs and looks down at him. He is dressed now. From the corner of her eye she sees that the ottoman from the landing has disappeared.

'Come on,' Mack says. 'It's full of vitamins and minerals.'

'Mack, where's the ottoman? Did you take our blankets out?'
'What blankets?'

Downstairs the dish of spinach and onion is on the table. Each place is set with a smaller bowl and a fork. There is no oil, salt or pepper. Ellie sits opposite Mack and watches him divide the salad between them.

'We could eat out of one bowl,' she says experimentally.

'And share a fork, take turns at using it.' He is excited. 'I never thought of that.'

Ellie forces down raw spinach and onion. She pictures the madness proliferating like yeast inside his skull: one fork, one spoon, one coat, one shoe.

After the meal Mack goes upstairs. Ellie checks the phone book and writes a number on the back of her hand. Soon, anorexic music threads its way down the stairwell: the computer. She steps outside, closing the front door behind her.

At the Double Happiness Chinese Take-Away she orders curried chips. There is a payphone on the wall.

'Is this working?' Ellie says.

The young woman behind the counter nods. Ellie picks up the receiver, puts it down.

'Works,' the woman encourages her.

The curried chips arrive in a foil tray. Ellie rips off the lid and plunges her hand into them. She squeezes, extruding violent yellow mash from her fist, then crams the mess into her mouth. The woman opens the door leading to the kitchen, says something in Cantonese.

Ellie thrusts her chin into the tray and uses the little plastic fork to shovel chips onto her tongue. Potato and sauce drop down her dress. Still holding onto the tray, she dials the number scrawled on the back of her hand.

'I'm sorry, you have to,' she mumbles into the smeared receiver. 'No, he won't. Yes . . . yes, I know. Oh, thank you, thank you. Yes. I'm going there now.' She hangs up and dumps her half-eaten chips on the counter. The Chinese woman moves away from her.

She's in the street. It's happening here, *here*, leaning against a parked car, chocolate and coffee and spinach and onion and curry jerking in spasms from her straining belly. She stays bent over the gutter, wiping strings of vomit onto her sleeve.

Someone has to be there with Mack when the doctor arrives. Nevertheless she stays crouched against the car. It feels reliable. She thinks it may continue to support her weight, continue solid and real, until she can stand upright and begin the walk back to the house.

Sukhdev Sandhu

'One-ah, Two-ah'

How do we remember the past? For some of us it's a smell – that broth, full of cabbages and stuff, whose recipe was known only to our mothers, whom we begged to stay in the kitchen for decades on end so that they'd magic up bowl after bowl of steaming liquid joy. Or maybe there are particular colours that rekindle the past most potently – that gauzy, membrane-thin yellow we saw as we gazed out at the sun slinking away at the end of long days messing about with the ginger-ale bottles and trolleys discarded at the back of the local allotments.

For me the past – who I am, where I come from, who I will forever be, whether I like it or not – is embodied by a tuft of hair. The hair belongs to Dickie Davies. Long retired, Dickie is best known as the presenter of *World of Sport*, a Saturday afternoon sports show broadcast on ITV for much of the 1970s and 1980s. It was meant to be a rival to the BBC's longer-established *Grandstand*, but whereas that programme featured classy fare such as Division One football, showjumping from Hickstead, the Oxford and Cambridge Boat Race, *World of Sport* was cheaper and more downmarket. It had to make do with speedway and American competitive lumberjacking.

Dickie himself was quite a figure. He looked like a cross between a travelling salesman and an adult-video company director. In my mind's eye he always seemed to be wearing double-breasted sports jackets, action slacks, tan slip-on shoes – very possibly with tassels. He lived in motels, was the celebrity member of the judging panel for Miss Dudley 1975. He probably drank Campari.

As a child I considered Dickie to be the last word in slightly raffish sophistication. Part of this was down to his scrupulously groomed moustache, which was quite unlike the proletarian green stubble of my father and his workmates, the only men I knew. Part of it, too, was his sly, slight grin, which exuded a 'Why don't you come back to my apartment?' Lothario quality. What was most captivating about him, though, was his hair. He had what Catherine Cookson called 'the Mallen streak': a prematurely grey ziggurat that shot across his brown mane. It was transfixing. It was unusual. That grey shiver seemed to promise, though I'm sure I couldn't have put it into words at the time, a break from normalcy, some kind of *sturm und drang* alterity, that a change was gonna come.

For less than an hour each week it did. Dickie became a conduit, a gateway to more thrilling times. At around four o'clock each Saturday afternoon millions of men and women would rush home from their weekly shopping, quickly rustle together some tea, and then gather round the television set with their children to see Dickie ooze his smile and hear him say 'NOW' (my mother would start clapping excitedly), 'it's time to hand over to Kent Walton, your commentator for this week's wrestling.' 'Hello again, grapple fans,' Kent would greet us in his Canadian accent both honey-smooth and authoritative. For the next forty to fifty minutes half of the country would be bouncing about on their living-room sofas, transfixed, whimpering with joy and horror.

Whenever Frank Sinatra came to England to perform during the 1970s he would make a point of watching ITV wrestling in whichever swish hotel he was staying. The Queen was meant to have been a fan too. But its real audience – its heartland – was far from London or any of the big cities. Just as the bouts took place, not in aircraft-hangar-sized arenas or glossy exhibition centres, but in local town halls and leisure centres, wrestling was a provincial sport. All that sweat and blood, those unremunerative bruisings: metropolitan people the world over have always shied away from such reality.

Wrestling was often entertaining, but it was not Entertainment. There'd be no flash ceremonies. No 'Eye of the Tiger' or Tina Turner bawling 'Simply the Best'. No flying carpets. No razzmatazz. But sometimes – if, for instance, there was a national championship title being contested – the sense of occasion was palpable even to those watching at home. The promoter and MC would beseech the audience: 'Ladies and gentlemen, I do ask you to show your deference to Her Majesty the Queen by being upstanding while the national anthem is playing.' And so they would – dutifully, happily. Within seconds of the bouts getting started, though, the crowd would begin to rev up. 'Where'd yer get yer hair from then?' they would heckle the ageing referee, Max Ward.

I used to be fascinated by how many women went to watch the wrestling. It was the only sport they had any time for. They sat in the front rows looking a bit sour-pussish initially, their arms folded or placed primly on their laps. Many of them smoked like chimneys, sparking up with clockwork regularity. During the earlier, less eventful parts of each bout, you could see them rummaging in their handbags for the pastilles they used to bribe their kids to stop twittering and fidgeting. On a good week you might even spot them slapping the kids because they kept chewing their own bogeys. Suddenly a bone-crunching fall would grab their attention, the fight would heat up, and they'd start yelping like crazy – 'Go on – smash his face in!' 'Give him a warning!' 'Bloody cheat!' 'Give it 'im!'

In the rings stood the wrestlers, huffing and growling at each other. Most of them had bashed-in noses, cauliflower ears, necks the thickness of Michelin tyres. They had big, immersion-tank bellies that teetered over their skimpy red trunks and hairy thighs. They had hairy backs too. And hairy bodies. They were hard men. They were also an ugly bunch of bleeders. Unsurprisingly so, for week after week, year after punishing year, they spent their Saturday afternoons with twenty-stone man-mountains sitting on their heads. As they lay on the ring floor, pile-driven and pulverized, the referee would bend down beside them and start counting to see if a fall had been scored: 'One-ah, Two-ah'. The ref's vowels were stretched out and pained. They seemed to be taunting the agonized fighter pinned down before him. And pitying him too.

These men may have been wrestlers, but they weren't so very different from the blokes in the part of Gloucester where I grew up. Blokes who had never got even close to finishing a book; blokes who lugged machinery all their lives; blokes who didn't believe in personal grooming. They weren't buffed and oiled gymnasts like the American World Wrestling Federation wrestlers who succeeded them on British screens. In fact, they weren't telegenic at all. The wrestling on *World of Sport* had its roots in a pre-TV age. It harked back to music hall and old empire shows and fairground boxing booths. It was entertainment – sometimes fake, sometimes choreographed – but it was nowhere near as slick or stylishly packaged as what followed it. It held onto a sense of municipality, of makeshift locality that disappeared in the transition to the now globally dominant WWF. Its intimate, winning amateurism is exemplified by a hall official's slightly nasal voice that came through on the tannoy system one week, right in the middle of a bout at Aylesbury Civic Centre: 'Ladies and gentlemen, I do have an announcement to make. Would the owner of the Ford Granada parked adjacent to the LWT outside broadcast van kindly remove it as it is obstructing traffic.'

Most of the wrestlers *on World of Sport* were, fairly predictably, from the white working classes. Some exceptions: Rollerball Rocco, the moustachioed American, was a lively baddie; fake Orientals such as Kendo Nagasaki, the masked man who hid his real identity from the public, and who was later immortalized by pop artist Peter Blake. There was the odd black fighter too – Johnny Kwango, or Honeyboy Zimba from Sierra Leone. Some people swore that Zimba was actually a Mancunian. I heard him complain to the ref about something once and his accent was 100 per cent Cheadle Hulme.

Winters used to be cold in England. We, my parents especially, spent them watching the wrestling. The wrestling they watched on their black-and-white television sets on Saturday afternoons represented a brief intrusion of life and colour in their otherwise monochrome lives. Their work overalls were faded, the sofa cover – unchanged for years – was faded, their memories of the people they had been before coming to England were fading too. My parents, their whole generation, treadmilled away the best years of their lives toiling in factories for shoddy paypackets. A life of drudgery, of deformed spines, of chronic arthritis, of severed hands. They bit their lips and put up with the pain. They had no option but to. In their minds they tried to switch off – to ignore the slights of co-workers, not to bridle against the glib cackling of foremen, and, in the case of Indian women, not to fret when they were slapped about by their husbands. Put up with the pain, they told themselves, deal with the pain – the shooting pains up the arms, the corroded hip joints, the back seizures from leaning over sewing machines for too many years, the callused knuckles from handwashing clothes, the rheumy knees from scrubbing the kitchen floor with their husbands' used underpants.

When my parents sat down to watch the wrestling on Saturday afternoons, milky cardamon tea in hand, they wanted to be entertained, they wanted a laugh. But they also wanted the good guy, just for once, to triumph over the bad guy. They wanted the swaggering, braying bully to get his come-uppance. They prayed for the nice guy, lying there on the canvas, trapped in a double-finger interlock or clutching his kidneys in agony, not to submit. If only he could hold out just a bit longer, bear the pain, last the course. If only he did these things, chances were, wrestling being what it was, that he would triumph. It was only a qualified victory, however. You'd see the winner, exhausted, barely able to wave to the crowd. The triumph was mainly one of survival.

As time went by, though, I started to weary of the groans and keening of the fighters. Their victories began to mean less and less to me. What, I used to think to myself, was the big deal about survival? I had an inkling that wrestling, and those who watched it, were a bit vulgar. I was an adolescent now. My levels of pretension were burgeoning. I told my mother and father that wrestling was stupid and boring (my vocabulary had yet to catch up with my newly perfumed ways) and that they should switch over to BBC2 instead to watch whichever old black-and-white film was being screened there.

I was after something different, but exactly what I wasn't sure. Like my parents, I struggled to imagine what tomorrow would be like. Pretty much the same as yesterday, probably. Going to university? Getting a flash job? We knew no one who had done either. Nobody in our area had that breezy, can-do sense of ease and entitlement that the middle classes have always had. We weren't used to choice, to experimentation. Year after year my family wore the same clothes and ate the same food. We never went abroad or to places in England other than Southall, where, every other year, we would spend a week at my cousin's two-bedroomed terraced house. This was as much exoticism as my parents desired. They didn't see the point of abroad – abroad was pricy, the people there uninteresting, the food and the customs needlessly different. Abroad threw up problems that challenged the routines and self-sufficiency they, and many Asian immigrants like them, had built up over the decades. Years before, quite soon after they lugged their luggage off the carousels at Heathrow, they came to understand that they weren't especially wanted in this country, that no one was going to give them anything. So be it, they thought. They quickly got used to hoarding, to making do, to hunkering down for the long journey ahead. They developed their ways and they stuck to them.

Eager to try and assert my independence, I used to think I was very different from them. But I wasn't. Perhaps that's why of all the old black-and-white films on BBC2 that I exhorted my parents to watch instead of the wrestling, the one over which I swooned the most, the one that affected me most grievously, was *Brief Encounter*. That 1945 film, an adaptation by David Lean of a Noël Coward play written before the Second World War, has been parodied a lot over the years. For some it's the ultimate expression of old-fashioned stiff-upper-lip values, a dismal and joyless account of all that was, and perhaps still is, bad about repressed England. That may be so; yet few films spoke more directly about my life and those of the people – Asian, Caribbean and even English – around whom I grew up in Gloucester. The dinginess, the murkiness of those tea rooms at Milford, the platform waiting rooms – they had the colour and texture of those old photos of my grandparents which, crinkled and foxed, we had on our front-room mantelpiece.

What struck me most forcefully was how circumscribed Laura Jesson's world is: 'We're a happily married couple and we must never forget that. This is my whole world and it's enough.' Her week is spent almost exclusively on grocery shopping, tea drinking and sock darning. Pleasure, as she has been brought up to see it, is borrowing a new title from Boots Lending Library or going to a matinée show at the Palladium. Marriage and family are at the centre of everything. As for her husband Fred, the only thing about which he gets passionate is his crossword. 'Hurry up with all this beautifying. I want my dinner,' he says at one point. He could have been every Asian man of a certain age. And when Dolly Messiter cries triumphantly, 'Wild horses wouldn't drag me away from England and home and all the things I'm used to. I mean, one has one's roots, after all, hasn't one?' – well, that could easily have been my mother speaking.

My Asian parents, like immigrants from time immemorial, craved continuity, cultural reproduction. Their world was governed by shame, guilt, fear. They handed down those values to me, so that, though I did not realize it at the time, even in the act of disavowing them I was acknowledging their hold on me. Laura Jesson, giddily intoxicated by the new man she's met, Dr Alex Harvey, says she feels it's shameful to feel so gay, so happy and released. See sense, be sensible – those injunctions have dogged me and second-generation Asians who grew up before the 1990s to a greater or lesser extent all our lives. Life, we were told, is not about pleasure. We have no right to happiness. We do not have rights full stop. We have traditions. We have habits and duties.

If this seems a lesser form of existence, a life more ordinary – perhaps it was. I remember gasping the first time I heard Alex Harvey tell Laura that he specializes in breathing difficulties, in dealing with fibrosis of the lung. Because, at times, chiefly when I was in my more self-consciously operatic and teenage moods, and for the first few years after I left home, it seemed to me that it was our immigrant world that was asphyxiating, that was clogging my lungs and stopping me from inhaling freedom. To which both my father and Laura's husband would no doubt say, 'Pull yourself together.'

I learned from *Brief Encounter* that the life I lived was not so very different in texture and feeling from those lived out by many white English people. Laura imagines that romance is almost impossible in England: abroad is where she dreams of, that's where passion happens – in Paris she and Alex will go to the opera, in Venice they'll be serenaded by gondoliers, on tropical beaches they'll gaze at the midnight moon. If abroad is champagne, then England is a chipped mug of lukewarm tea. Most of the white people in Gloucester, though not as posh as the characters in the film, would have agreed. Most of the time this wasn't a source of especial tragedy; things were what they were. Most of the time we didn't even think about these things. We just got on with stuff.

It's possible to see all this in melancholic terms. Maybe what I've been trying to describe sounds too much like a slow-burning existence, a life on half-simmer. A world of austerity and rationing. Yet it was enough for most of the time and for most of my parents' generation. There was a quiet dignity to it. It was certainly no more constraining than the lives they would have lived out had they stayed in the Punjab. My parents always felt, rightly I think, that they had more in common with white working-class people than with the Indian middle classes with their fancy rugs and their Moghul miniatures and their drinks cabinets and their interest in classical dance. Some people on our street may have gossiped about us or preferred us to be white. Others seemed to like us, even though they'd be kept awake at night by my father shouting at my mother. They exchanged Christmas cards with my parents, talked over the fence once in a while, bought tuppenny ice lollies for me and my sister. Slowly, gradually, they learned to live alongside each other.

My parents will never go back to live in the Punjab. They used to say they would. Now they don't even bother to try and kid themselves. But then, in their hearts, they never really left their home villages in the first place. I love it when I watch them scoffing samosas and reminiscing with their relatives or in-laws. They'll talk about things that happened – games that they played, dogs that they drowned – many years ago. Their voices will rise, they'll remember odd details ('The dog had half a tongue!'), there'll be oohs and ahhs and mad cackling. Sometimes, when I walk in on my mother boiling spinach in the kitchen, I'll find her singing along to the same Hindi love songs on Sunrise FM that she first heard on a big radio in Jagraon forty years ago. She was a young girl then. She wasn't even married. And now, for two or three minutes, before the DJ starts puffing up some Bollywood

PR bonanza in Wembley, she's a young girl again. As Cornershop sang, 'Some sounds some burdens can release.'

Just as my parents never entirely left their old village behind, I'll never leave Gloucester behind – the weeded pavements, the soda siphons, the porcelain firemen displayed in the front window. That whole attitude to life – 'Mustn't grumble. Probably will' – has shaped my slightly lugubrious bent. And it's made me realize that class and place are at least as important as nationality in helping to define people's sense of who they are. I asked my mother recently if, after thirty-five years in this country, she still felt she was Indian. She replied that she'd never been Indian – that we, not she, were Sikhs of a certain caste, from villages in a certain neck of the woods, that her father was a good man, and that please would I not walk around the house in my pyjamas, it had gone past midday and what would *gumandi* (the next-door neighbours) be saying?

She thinks about England even less than I do. She's got more important things on her mind. The bad weather we've had over the winter means this year's rhubarb is not going to be up to much. The daughter of the lady who runs the cornershop where she works part-time needs a kidney transplant urgently. A sister-in-law in Hounslow has gone doolally: the other week she got laid off from the pickle factory where she's worked for fifteen years and is now refusing to eat anything at all. These things aren't small or trivial. They're about money and family and health. No question is of more urgency to my mother – and certainly not that concerning the need to reformulate national identity in devolutionary, transnational times – than when her two eldest sons are going to get married.

She has never felt especially excluded. And neither have I. I would never call myself British because the term is too legalistic, like something from a bullet-pointed job seeker's allowance form. It evokes statistics and pie charts, a piece of number-crunchery. I believe that soil and land and territory affect one's sense of belonging. And the soil I know best belongs to the old PE teacher into whose back garden my friends and I used to clamber at lunchtime so that we could uproot his flowerbeds, or that at the back of the local garage, where we would sit after school staring at dirty magazines with sadness and wonder.

These are meant to be critical times. It's often said that there is a crisis of representation, of definition. Many historians and cultural critics want us to think about Who We Are. Some, apparently speaking on behalf of those few millions of Britons who aren't white, feel they have the answer. Most famously, *The Parekh Report on the Future of Multi-Ethnic Britain* offered a series of binarisms that counterpointed old, monocultural, white Britain to breezy, young and multiracial Britain. It states, 'The futures facing Britain may be summarised as static/dynamic; intolerant/cosmopolitan; fearful/generous; insular/internationalist; authoritarian/democratic; introspective/outward-looking; punitive/inclusive; myopic/far-sighted.'

Funny, really. I tend to think that the negative part of these binarisms – fearful, insular, punitive, authoritarian – are characteristics which are as much, if not more, the preserve of migrant communities (especially Asian ones) than they are of white England. And, though it made – and makes – life a little rough, it was these characteristics that helped Asian people to get where they are today. Without parading them as a kind of model minority or ignoring the levels of poverty that pock some groups – especially Bangladeshi, and also those living in the north of England – Asians are doing remarkably well, getting along with things. And the main reason for this is that clenched and embattled curmudgeonliness of spirit that pervaded most waking moments during our youths.

Things have changed over the years. The world I have been trying to describe has long been on the wane. When I go back to the area where I grew up the kids – white and black and brown – puff and shuffle and show out in a would-be Wu-Tangery style that makes me giggle. The roads bear the marks where telecom companies have been laying cable lines so that they can be connected to the wider world from which my mother and father sought to shield me. Class has been supplanted by consumer niches. And the ancient ethnic certainties have changed too. My parents and their friends are older, weaker. Exhausted, some of them have taken early retirement; they springclean their houses less often; the chapattis they make get thicker and thicker; large parts of the day are devoted to tut-tutting over *kumleh* (idiotic) talk shows. They often remark that their kids are so very plucky, so very demanding. It's true: second-generation Asians want – and expect – to have embellished lives. We aspire towards a glossy world, and live in one in which black and brown have become styles rather than colours, sartorial fashions rather than psychologies.

Yet pluck us away from our internet consultancies, the account-handling departments and the corporate law offices where we earn more money in a year than our parents did in a decade; get us together – at a fancy wine bar, in a corner of a flash East Midlands hotel where a cousin of ours is getting married – and you'll hear us getting increasingly sentimental for the old, blinkered ways. There'll be a sense of gratitude for the privations our parents went through, and an appreciation of their dictatorial, joyless ways. And what we'll say, mystified and whispering perhaps, is that though we didn't always believe it, there's actually more to life than pleasure. Having described the routes by which we got from a shabby terraced home in Walsall to a five-bedroomed ranch in Buckinghamshire as a journey towards liberation and autonomy, a journey from constraint to freedom, we now find ourselves gingerly speaking up for constraint, duty, timidity.

This second generation isn't that young any more. Our dancing days are nearly over. Many of us got married long ago. We've got kids too, whom we lavish with the sweets and toys denied to us by our own penny-pinching parents. But there's a price to be paid for the lack of privations, and it concerns the loss of memory. As second-generation parents, men and women to whom the idea of struggle was second nature, we're starting to worry that our children may be too innocent, too complacent. We want our kids to understand that life is not solely about entertainment or instant fun. We want them to appreciate the meaning of those terms that were central to our own parents and which are so unfashionable today – duty, sacrifice, responsibility, restraint, slowness. We want to revive the idea of burden. Toil and struggle were essential to our parents' lives, and the moment we forget that – or fail to feel it viscerally, as a physical sensation – is the moment we are orphaned from history.

A couple of years ago I went to visit an uncle in Hounslow. His wife had died a few months before. Both his son and daughter had managerial jobs in the City and were married. They would come round whenever they could, but that wasn't too often. He was sixty-seven at the time and had lived in Hounslow for nearly forty years – starting off in the local Nestlé factory and ending up loading luggage at Heathrow. It was a good job. The mortgage had been paid off. But his ankles hurt and he couldn't get around as easily as he once had. The house was wearing a bit, more shabby and less genteel each year. The area was changing too. Lots of new people. Things weren't quite what they used to be. I said to him, 'Uncle, if you could have anything in the world, one wish come true, what would you like best?' 'Feltham,' he replied, 'I would like to move to Feltham.' A small town, just five miles up the road. It seemed to me then to be a laughably small ambition.

Not now, though. Before, all I wanted in life was pleasure, delirious satiation; to ditch the past, to escape everything that seemed local, downbeat, specific (I even elevated such goals into a kind of political creed.) Now it seems like my knees are always playing up and, when I trip and fall, the scabs don't come off as quickly as they used to. I no longer look at the world through Dickie Davies's eyes, but through the lens of the wrestlers he introduced. I see that fighting to survive is no easy thing. It's the biggest, most compelling drama there is. Dickie, always sporting that sophisticate's smile, may not have known that. My parents certainly did. And me? I still have a long way to go, but I'm going, I'm going.

Biographical Notes

Diran Adebayo is the author of two acclaimed novels: *Some Kind of Black* (Virago, 1996), which won the Saga Prize, a Betty Trask Award, the Authors' Club's Best First Novel Award, and the Writers Guild's New Writer of the Year Award for 1996, and *My Once Upon a Time* (Abacus, 2000), 200. He has also written stories for radio and television, and is a frequent cultural commentator in the British Press. His third novel, *The Ballad of Dizzy and Miss P*, comes out in 2004.

Patience Agbabi is a British-born Nigerian poet, who has performed her work all over the world. Her publications are *R.A.W.* (Gecko Press, 1995) and *Transformatrix* (Payback Press, 2000). She lectures in creative writing at the University of Greenwich and the University of Cardiff. She is currently working on her third collection, *Body Language*.

Rajeev Balasubramanyam was born in Lancaster in 1974. His first novel, *In Beautiful Disguises* (Bloomsbury, 2000), was a winner of a Betty Trask Award in 1999, and was nominated for the Guardian First Fiction Prize 2000. His short story, 'The Dreamer', won an Ian St James Award in 2001. His short story, 'A Man of Soul', was first written for the Scrittore Giovani project for the Festivaletteratura in Mantua, the Guardian Hay Festival and the Berlin Internationales Literaturfestival in 2002, to address the theme 'Things Change'. He is currently working on his second novel, *The Dreamer*.

Nick Barlay is the author of three acclaimed novels, *Curvy Lovebox* (20/20, 1997), *Crumple Zone* (Hodder & Stoughton, 2000) and *Hooky Gear*, (Hodder & Stoughton, 2001) which map out the underbelly of contemporary London. He has written award-winning radio plays, works as a freelance journalist and is currently writing his next novel. He was born in London to Hungarian refugee parents.

Hilda Bernstein was born in London. She moved to South Africa at a young age, where she became very active politically in the struggle against apartheid, about which she wrote extensively. Eventually she was forced to resettle in England, where she now works as an artist and journalist. She has published several books about South Africa, including a novel.

Bill Broady was educated in York and London. He has worked as a croupier, cartographer and caretaker. He is associate editor of Red Beck Press and the author of *Swimmer* (Flamingo, 2000) and *In This Block There Lives a Slag...* (Flamingo, 2001), which was winner of the 2002 Macmillan Silver Pen Award. Bill is currently working on a novel, *Eternity Is Temporary* and researching a biography of the actor Peter Lorre.

Emma Brockes was born in 1975. After studying English at Oxford she joined the *Scotsman* as a feature writer and moved to the *Guardian* at the age of twenty-two. She was named Young Journalist of the Year at the British Press Awards in 2001 and Feature Writer of the Year in 2002.

Julia Brosnan worked as a BBC Radio 4 producer and as a print journalist before – still in search of a free lunch – moving into PR. She has published a range of poetry and short fiction. Her first novel, *Fat Life*, won the North West Arts Best Novel in Progress Award, but remains strangely unpublished. *Left* is her second novel.

Wayne Burrows published a collection of poems, *Marginalia*, with Peterloo Poets in 2001.

Alex Clark is a freelance journalist and broadcaster. She specializes in contemporary fiction and has recently helped to select Granta's *Best of Young British Novelists*. She is currently writing a book about only children.

Fred D'Aguiar's latest novel, *Bethany Bettany*, is his fourth novel, published by Chatto & Windus (2003). A collection of selected and new poems, *An English Sampler* (Chatto & Windus), which draws from four previous poetry collections, appeared in 2001 and a verse novel, *Bloodlines* (Chatto & Windus), in 2000. Born in 1960 in London of Guyanese parents, D'Aguiar grew up in Guyana and returned to London for his secondary and tertiary education. He left England to teach creative writing in the United States.

Matthew Davey was born in 1973 in Thornbury, south Gloucestershire. He has lived in Manchester, Prague, London and Osaka, and now lives in Bristol. His poetry is regularly published in the small presses. Matthew has no hobbies. His short story, 'Waving at Trains', won the *Observer* Short Story Competition in 2002.

Jill Dawson was born in England. Her best-selling third novel, *Fred & Edie* (Sceptre, 2000) was translated into a dozen languages. It was shortlisted for the Orange Prize and for the Whitbread Novel of the Year Award. She lives in Cambridgeshire with her partner and two sons and teaches at the University of East Anglia. Her latest novel is called *Wild Boy*.

Sasha Dugdale is a poet and translator. Her poems are published in *Oxford Poets 2002* (Carcanet, 2002) and her first collection will appear in 2003, published by Oxford Poets / Carcanet. She translates plays and poetry from Russian and is consultant to the Royal Court on a programme of new Russian writing. She is the winner of the Gregory Award, 2003).

Vicki Feaver was born in Nottingham in 1943. She has published two collections of poetry, *Close Relatives* (Secker, 1981) and *The Handless Maiden* (Cape, 1994), which was awarded a Heinemann Prize and shortlisted for the Forward Prize. A selection of her work is also included in the Penguin Modern Poets series. She lives on the edge of the Pentland Hills near Edinburgh.

Adèle Geras has published more than eighty books for children of all ages. Her first adult novel, *Facing the Light* (Orion), was published in March 2003. She has won several prizes for her poems, and a collection, *Voices From the Dolls' House* (Rockingham), appeared in 1994. She has lived in Manchester since 1967. www.adelegeras.com

Lesley Glaister is the author of nine novels, the latest of which was called *Now You See Me* (Bloomsbury, 2001). She also writes short stories and radio dramas. She has three sons, lives in Sheffield and Orkney and teaches novel writing on Sheffield Hallam University's MA course in creative writing.

Julian Gough grew up in London, Tipperary and Galway. His first novel, *Juno & Juliet* (Flamingo, 2001), is beautiful, realistic and narrated by an intelligent eighteen-year-old girl. His second novel is the opposite. 'The Great Hargeisa Goat Bubble' is taken from the second novel, which is not yet published.

Helon Habila read literature at the University of Jos, Nigeria. He was the literary editor of Vanguard newspapers in Lagos before his move to Britain to be a Writing Fellow at the University of East Anglia. His first novel, *Waiting for an Angel*, was published in 2002 by Hamish Hamilton.

Gideon Haigh is a London-born, Melbourne-bred journalist, with abiding interests in sport and business, who has written a dozen books about one, the other or both.

Nicolette Hardee was born in north London and attended Hornsey College of Art and Essex University. She has worked, researched books, and written articles and stories, whilst bringing up her two children. She lives in London with her family and spends a lot of time in Barcelona. She is currently working on her second novel.

Alan Jenkins was born in 1955, and was educated in London and at the University of Sussex. He has worked at the *Times Literary Supplement* since 1981, first as poetry and fiction editor and, for the past ten years, as deputy editor. He has been poetry critic on the *Observer* and *Independent on Sunday*, and has taught creative writing in England, France and the United States. His books of poetry include *In the Hot-House* (Chatto & Windus,

1988), *Greenheart* (Chatto & Windus, 1990), *Harm* (Chatto & Windus, 1994), which won the Forward Prize for Best Collection that year, *The Drift* (Chatto & Windus, 2000), which was a Choice of the Poetry Book Society, and *The Little Black Book* (Cargo, 2001). *A Short History of Snakes*, selected poems, was published in 2002 by Grove Press, New York.

Tim Liardet was born in London and has published four collections of poetry. He is associate lecturer in creative writing at Bath Spa University College and has recently been awarded a Hawthornden Fellowship. His third collection *Competing with the Piano Tuner* (Seren, 1998), was a Poetry Book Society Special Commendation and his fourth, *To the God of Rain*, is a Poetry Book Society Recommendation for spring 2003.

Maria McCann is a novelist and lecturer. Her first book, *As Meat Loves Salt* (Flamingo, 2001), was the story of a violent, self-destructive man on the run in Civil War England. She is currently working on a novel set in the period before and during the Second World War.

Sarah Maguire's most recent book is *The Florist's at Midnight* (Cape, 2001). The first writer sent to Palestine and Yemen by the British Council, Sarah is translating the poems of Mahmoud Darwish. Her selected poems, translated by Saadi Yusef, will be published in 2004 in Damascus. She teaches at SOAS.

David Morley is a scientist, of Roman extraction, who directs the writing programme at the University of Warwick, where he develops and teaches new practices in scientific as well as imaginative writing. He recently edited *The Gift: New Writings for the NHS* (Stride, 2002), which was given free to over 30,000 medical workers.

Patrick Neate's work includes *Musungu Jim* (Penguin, 2000), which won a Betty Trask Award, and *Twelve Bar Blues* (Penguin, 2001) which won the Whitbread Novel Prize. Spring 2003 saw the publication of both his latest novel, *The London Pigeon Wars* (Penguin) and *Where You're at* (Bloomsbury), an exploration of global hip hop. He divides his time between London and Lusaka.

Maggie O'Farrell was born in Northern Ireland, and grew up in Wales and Scotland. She has worked as a waitress, chambermaid, cycle courier, teacher, arts administrator and journalist. She is the author of two novels, *After You'd Gone* (Review, 2000) and *My Lover's Lover* (Review, 2002).

Alice Oswald is married with two children. She lives in Devon and has published two books: *The Thing in the Gap-Stone Stile* (O.U.P., 1996) and *Dart* (Faber, 2001).

Glenn Patterson lives in Belfast, where he teaches on the MA course in creative writing at Queen's University. His novels are *Burning Your Own* (Chatto & Windus, 1988), *Fat Lad* (Chatto & Windus, 1992), *Black Night at Big Thunder Mountain* (Chatto & Windus, 1995), *The International* (Anchor, 1999) and *Number 5* (Hamish Hamilton, 2003). *Punishments* will be published in 2004.

Sukhdev Sandhu has taught English literature at New York University. *London Calling: How Black and Asian Writers Imagined a City* will be published by HarperCollins in July 2003. He is currently chief film critic for the *Daily Telegraph* and lives in Whitechapel.

Ian Sansom lives in Northern Ireland. His book *The Truth about Babies* (2002) is published by Granta. He is currently writing a novel.

Amanda Smyth, born in 1967, is Irish/Trinidadian and was brought up in England. After completing an MA in creative writing at UEA, she finished her first collection of short stories, *Little Fishes*. She lives in London.

Jane Stevenson was born in 1959 and brought up in London, Beijing and Bonn. She is a professional academic who teaches at the University of Aberdeen, and is currently working on a study of women who wrote poetry in Latin. In 1999, she embarked on a second career writing fiction. Her fifth novel, *The Empress of the Last Days*, is due out in the summer of 2003.

Royston Swarbrooke was raised in the county of Salop. There he fronted the Geekais, perhaps the definitive sound of Shrewsbury, (second only to T'Pau), whose seminal six-track LP, *Nincompoop*, sold forty-three copies. He has since spent quality time in Manchester, London and Munich. At present he works with young people on the Oxmoor Estate in Huntingdon.

Matthew Sweeney was born in Co Donegal, in 1952. He lived in London for many years. His books include *Selected Poems* (Cape, 2002) and, for children, *Up on the Roof: New & Selected Poems* (Faber, 2001). He has also written a novel, *Fox* (Bloomsbury, 2002). He was the co-author, with John Hartley Williams, of *Writing Poetry*, and a new collection, *Sanctuary*, is forthcoming from Cape in 2004.

Barbara Trapido is the author of six novels – *Brother of the More Famous Jack*, winner of a 1982 Whitbread Special Prize for Fiction (Gollancz), *Noah's Ark* (Gollancz, 1984), *Temples of Delight*, shortlisted for the 1990 Sunday Express Book of the Year Award (Michael Joseph), *Juggling* (Hamish Hamilton, 1994), *The Travelling Horn Player*, shortlisted for the 1998 Whitbread Novel Award (Hamish Hamilton) and *Frankie and Stankie* (Bloomsbury, 2003).

Binyavanga Wainaina lived in South Africa for ten years. He moved back to Kenya in 2000 and began to write seriously. In 2002 he won the Caine Prize for African Writing with a story he had published on the internet. Recently he has been involved in setting up *Kwani*, Kenya's only literary journal. Binyavanga is also working on two novels and a non-fiction book about Kenya.

Gerard Woodward was born in London in 1961. He studied painting at Falmouth School of Art and anthropology at the LSE. He has published three collections of poetry with Chatto & Windus – *Householder* (1991), *After the Deafening* (1994) and *Island to Island* (1999). *Householder* won the Somerset Maugham Award and the two others have been Poetry Book Society Choices. His first novel, *August* (Chatto & Windus,

2001), was shortlisted for the Whitbread First Novel Award. He now lives in Manchester.

Sophie Woolley is a writer and actress from London. She wrote the infamous D.J. Bird diaries in *SleazeNation* and has written for the *Shoreditch Twat*. She performs satirical character monologues in galleries, bars and nightclubs. One day she will leave Hackney and live somewhere else instead.

Tamar Yoseloff's first collection, *Sweetheart* (Slow Dancer, 1998) was a Poetry Book Society Special commendation and winner of the Aldeburgh Festival Prize. She is co-ordinator and tutor for the Poetry School. In 2001 she received a bursary from London Arts for her second collection, *Barnard's Star*. She is currently working towards an MPhil in writing at the University of Glamorgan.

Copyright information

Introduction copyright © 2003 Jane Rogers, Blake Morrison and Diran Adebayo; 'That Which Was' copyright © Glenn Patterson 2003; 'The Gun', 'The Borrowed Dog' and 'Gorilla' copyright © Vicki Feaver 2003; 'Talking About Love' copyright © Nick Barlay 2003; 'The Great Hargeisa Goat Bubble' copyright © Julian Gough 2003; 'Seeing Red', 'Celtic' and 'Man and Boy' © Patience Agbabi 2003; 'Where Do We Live?' copyright © Ian Sansom 2003; 'Come back, we'll do some calculus'- copyright © Diran Adebayo 2003; 'the square' copyright © Adèle Geras 2003; 'Room 226' copyright © Hilda Bernstein 2003; 'Milk' copyright © Gerard Woodward 2003; 'Ludus Coventriae' and 'Patrin' copyright © David Morley 2003; 'The Distance Between Us' copyright © Maggie O'Farrell 2003; 'Epic Slinky' copyright © Sophie Woolley 2003; 'The Wait', 'Tidal' and 'Wildlife' copyright © Alan Jenkins 2003; 'Only' copyright © Alex Clark 2003; 'According to Mwangi' copyright © Binyavanga Wainaina 2003; 'Give Him My Love' copyright © Julia Brosnan 2003; 'Madame Sasoo Goes Bathing' and 'Chickens in Chinatown' copyright © Tim Liardet 2003; 'C. L. R James' copyright © Gideon Haigh 2003; 'The Stone Skimmer', 'River Psalm' and 'Time Poem' copyright © Alice Oswald 2003; 'A Man of Soul' copyright © Rajeev Balasubramanyam 2003; 'Letters' copyright © Barbara Trapido 2003; 'Hunger' copyright © Jane Stevenson 2003; '19 Victoria Street, Shewsbury' and 'Jump Rope' copyright © Fred D'Aguiar 2003; 'As Far as You Can Go' copyright © Lesley Glaister 2003; 'In a Mist' copyright © Bill Broady 2003; 'Weekend' and 'Christmas in London' copyright © Tamar Yoseloff 2003; 'The Archway Altarpiece', 'A Game of Pool' and 'Underground' copyright © Wayne Burrows 2003; 'Waving at Trains' copyright © Matthew Davey 2003; 'Look at You' copyright © Amanda Smyth 2003; 'Harmattan' copyright © Helon Habila 2003; 'Hair' copyright © Matthew Sweeney 2003; 'Visiting Time' copyright © Emma Brockes 2003; 'Wordperfect' copyright © Nicolette Hardee 2003; 'The Film Director Explains his Concept' and 'Faking It' copyright © Sasha Dugdale 2003; 'Flat Earth' copyright © Jill Dawson 2003; 'The Last Dodo' copyright © Royston Swarbrooke 2003; 'Good TV' copyright © Patrick Neate 2003; 'The Foot Tunnel' copyright © Sarah Maguire 2003; 'Minimal' copyright © Maria McCann 2003; 'One-ah.Two-ah' copyright © Sukhdev Sandhu 2003.